TRADED TO THE SHEIKH

TRADED TO THE SHEIKH

BY

EMMA DARCY

First published in Great Britain 2005
Large Print edition 2006
Harlequin Mills & Boon Limited,
Eton House, 18-24 Paradise Road,
Richmond, Surrey TW9 1SR

ISBN 0 263 18976 7

Set in Times Roman 17¾ on 21 pt.
16-0606-43612

Printed and bound in Great Britain
by Antony Rowe Ltd, Chippenham, Wiltshire

CHAPTER ONE

SHEIKH ZAGEO bin Sultan Al Farrahn was not amused. Not only had there been criminal trespassing in the walled grounds of this family property—his mother's pleasure palace on the legendary spice island of Zanzibar—but also criminal use of the private harbour by a drug-running French yachtsman who was actually offering him a woman to warm his bed in exchange for letting him go.

Did the sleazy low-life think he was speaking to the kind of man who'd indulge in indiscriminate sex?

'She's very special,' the drug-dealer pleaded with all the oiliness of a practised pimp. 'A genuine strawberry-blonde. Hair like rippling silk, falling to the pit of her back.

Beautiful, bright, blue eyes. Lush breasts…' His hands shaped an hourglass figure. 'Fantastic legs, long and…'

'A virgin, as well?' Zageo cut in mockingly, despising the man for thinking he could trade his whore for his own freedom, for thinking the trade could even be an acceptable possibility.

'Completely untouched,' Jacques Arnault instantly replied, a consummate liar, not so much as a flicker of an eyelash nor the twitch of a facial muscle to betray any unease with the question, despite the impossibility of there being anything virginal about a woman who had to be his partner in crime.

'And where is this precious pearl?' Zageo drawled, barely holding back his contempt for a man who was prepared to sell flesh to save his own skin.

'On my yacht. If you get your security people—' he glanced nervously at the guards who'd caught him '—to take me out to it, they can fetch her back to you.'

While he silently sailed away in one hell of a hurry!

Zageo gave him a blast of scepticism. 'On your yacht? You've managed to sail from the Red Sea, down half the east coast of Africa to this island, without being tempted to touch this fabulous jewel of femininity?'

The Frenchman shrugged. 'Stupid to spoil top merchandise.'

'And where did you get this *top merchandise*?'

'Picked her up from one of the resorts where she was working with a dive team. She agreed to help crew the yacht for free passage to Zanzibar.' His mouth curved into a cynical smile. 'A drifting traveller who could go missing indefinitely.'

'A fool to trust you with her life.'

'Women are fools. Particularly those with an innocent turn of mind.'

Zageo arched a challenging eyebrow. 'You take me for a fool, as well?'

'I'm being completely straight with you,'

came the swift and strongly assertive assurance. 'You can have her. No problems.' His gaze flicked around the lavishly rich and exotic Versace furnishings in the huge central atrium which had always served as the most public reception area. 'With all you have to offer, I doubt you'd even have to force her. Unless you enjoy force, of course,' he quickly added on second thoughts.

Anger burned. 'You are breaking another law, monsieur. The slave trade was abolished in Zanzibar over a century ago.'

'But a man of your standing and influence…who's to question what you do with a woman no one knows? Even if she runs away from you…'

'Enough!' Zageo gestured to his security guards. 'Put him in a holding room. Have his yacht searched for a woman. If there is one onboard, bring her to me.'

Arnault looked alarmed as two of the guards flanked him to escort him elsewhere. He spoke quickly in anxious protest. 'You'll see. She's everything I said she is. Once you're satisfied…'

'Oh, I will be satisfied, monsieur, one way or another,' Zageo silkily assured him, waving his men to proceed with the execution of his orders.

Zageo doubted the woman existed, certainly not with all the attributes ascribed to her by Jacques Arnault. He suspected the Frenchman had been dangling what he thought would be a tempting sexual fantasy in the hope of getting back to his yacht and somehow ditching the men escorting him. Even though the security guards carried guns, a surprise attack might have won him time to escape.

However, if there was a female accomplice, she had to be brought in and handed over to the appropriate authorities. While she might not have been actively involved in drug-dealing, there was no way she couldn't know about it and would surely be able to supply useful information.

He relaxed back on the thronelike sofa, reached over the elaborately rolled armrest to pick up the mango cocktail he'd previously set down on the entwined monkeys table, and sipped the refreshing drink slowly as the anger stirred by the Frenchman's attempt to use sexual currency turned onto Veronique, who had declined the invitation to accompany him on this trip.

'Your mind will be on business, *cheri*,' she had prettily complained. 'It will not be fun.'

Was the amount of *fun* to be had the measure of their relationship? His three-month tour of checking the hotel chain he'd established throughout Africa could not be called a hardship on anyone's agenda—luxurious resorts in exotic locations. How much *fun* did she need to feel happy and satisfied?

He understood that for the much-in-demand French-Morrocan model, pleasure was inextricably linked with exciting leisure and being taken shopping. He understood that what he provided in this context was the trade-off for having her as his mistress. He had not understood that Veronique was only prepared to give him her company on her own totally self-indulgent terms.

Intolerable!

He had indulged her far too much. It wasn't enough recompense that the sex was good. It wasn't enough that Veronique was invariably a splendid ornament on his arm, superbly dressed to complement her dark-skinned exotic beauty. He found it deeply insulting that she had so little respect for *his* wishes.

His father was right. It was time he ended this too long fascination with women of different cultures and found one of his own kind to marry. He was thirty-five years old and should be thinking of settling down, having a family. He would cut his connection with Veronique and start considering more suitable candidates for a lifelong commitment—well-educated women from other powerful families in Dubai, women whose background ensured they would share his life, not just his bed and his spending power.

None of them would have strawberry-blond hair, blue eyes and fair skin, but such factors were hardly prime requirements for marriage. They weren't even factors to inspire a lustful dalliance. Right now the idea of trading in sex was particularly abhorrent, and Zageo found himself actually relishing the opportunity to hammer this home to Jacques Arnault's female yachting companion.

He hoped she did exist.

He hoped his men would find her on board the illicit yacht in the private harbour that served this private palace.

He hoped she actually measured up to the Frenchman's selling spiel.

It would give him considerable satisfaction to demonstrate that regardless of how attractive her physical assets were, they were worth nothing to him.

Absolutely nothing!

CHAPTER TWO

'I WILL get out of this! I will!' Emily Ross kept reciting as she struggled through the mangrove swamp.

These mutterings of fierce determination were interspersed with bursts of self-castigation. 'What a fool I've been! A gullible idiot to be taken in by Jacques. I should have just paid the money to fly here. No hassle about arriving in time. All safe and sound...'

Talking blocked out the fear of having made another wrong step, of putting her life in hopeless hazard this time. Yet reason insisted that the Frenchman could not have been trusted to keep his word about anything. The only sure way of staying in Zanzibar and getting to Stone Town to meet Hannah was to jump ship while Jacques was still off in his dinghy doing his drug-running.

So, okay…she'd done the swim from the yacht to shore, dragging all her essentials in a waterproof bag behind her. No shark or fish had attacked. Her feet had not been cut to ribbons by shells or coral or sharp rocks. Now she just had to find her way out of the mangrove swamp that seemed to cover the peninsula she'd swum to.

'It's not going to beat me. I *will* get out of it.'

And she did, finally emerging from the mud and tangled tree roots onto a wide mound of firmer ground which turned out to be an embankment above a small creek. More water! But beyond it was definitely proof of civilisation—what looked like the well kept grounds of some big property. No more swamp. The worst was over.

Emily's legs shook from sheer exhaustion. Now, with the fear of being swallowed up by the swamp receding and much easier travelling in sight, she felt like collapsing on the bank and weeping with relief at having made it this far. Nevertheless, the need to cling to some self-control persisted. She might be out of the woods but this was still far from the end of her journey.

She sat herself down on the bank and did some deep breathing, hoping to lessen the load of stress—the huge mental, emotional and physical stress attached to her decision not to cling to the relative safety of Jacques Arnault's yacht, not to remain captive to any further devious plan he might make.

Free…

The thought gathered its own momentum, finding a burst of positive achievement.

Free of him. Free of the swamp. Free to go where I want in my own time.

It helped calm her enough to get on with assessing her current position. A high stone wall ran back into distant darkness on the other side of the creek. It gave rise to the hope it might lead to a public road.

'If nothing else, it should give me cover until I'm right away from Jacques and his dirty business,' she muttered, trying to whip up the energy to move again.

Through sheer force of will, Emily drove her mind into forward planning as she heaved herself onto her feet and trudged along the bank of the creek until the stone wall was directly opposite her. Once across this last body of water, she could clean herself up and dress respectably in the skirt and T-shirt she'd placed at the top of the waterproof bag. Wearing a bikini at this time of night was hardly appropriate for meeting local people and sooner or later she had to confront someone in order to ask directions to Stone Town.

Waist-deep in water and hating every second of wading through it, Emily was concentrating on her footing when a commanding voice rang out.

'Arretez!'

The French verb to stop certainly stopped her!

She almost tripped in sheer shock.

Her heart jerked into a fearful hammering as her gaze whipped up to fix on two men pointing highly menacing rifles at her. They wore white shirts and trousers with black gun-belts, giving them more the appearance of official policemen than drug-running gangsters, but Emily wasn't sure if this was a good thing or a bad thing. If they'd caught Jacques and were connecting her to his criminal activities—which the use of French language suggested—she might end up in prison.

One of the men clapped a small mobile telephone to his ear and spoke at speed in what sounded like Arabic. The other motioned her to continue moving to their side of the creek bank. Having a rifle waved at her did not incline Emily towards disobedience. She could only hope these people were representatives of the law on this island and that the law would be reasonable in listening to her.

A giant fig tree on her left had obviously provided an effective hiding place for them to watch for her emergence from the mangroves. She wondered if other patrols were out looking for her. Certainly her appearance was being reported to someone. As she scrambled up their side of the creek bank, one of the men came forward and snatched the waterproof bag out of her grasp.

'Now hold on a moment! I've got my life in there!' Emily cried in panicky protest.

Having her passport, money and clothes taken from her was a very scary situation. Thinking the men might believe the bag contained contraband, she tried persuading them to check its contents.

'Look for yourself.' Her hands flew out in a gesture of open-palmed innocence. 'It's just personal stuff.'

No response. The men completely ignored her frantic attempt to communicate with them both in English and in her very limited tourist French. She was grabbed at the elbows and briskly marched across quite an expanse of mown grass to a path which eventually led to a massive three-storey white building.

At least it didn't look like a prison, Emily thought, desperately trying to calm her wildly leaping apprehension. The many columned verandahs on each level, with their elaborate wrought-iron lace balustrades, gave the impression of British colonial architecture serving some important government purpose.

Maybe a courthouse?

But why on earth would Jacques do his drug-running right under the nose of legal officialdom?

Could it be terribly corrupt officialdom?

This thought frayed her strung-out nerves even further. She was a lone foreign woman, scantily dressed, and her only tool of protection was her passport which she no longer had in her possession. It took all her willpower not to give way to absolute panic when she was escorted up the steps to the front verandah and was faced with horribly intimidating entrance doors.

These were about four metres high, ominously black, intricately carved around the edges, and featuring rows of big pointed brass studs. They were definitely the kind of doors that would deter anyone from gatecrashing a party. As they were slowly swung open Emily instinctively decided that a bowed head and downcast eyes might get her into less trouble in this place.

The first sight she had of the huge foyer was of a gorgeous *Tree of Life* Persian rug dominating a dark wooden floor. As she was forced forward onto this carpet her side vision picked up the kind of splendid urns one might see in an art museum, which suggested this could be a *safe* environment.

A burst of hope prodded her into lifting her gaze to check out where she was being taken. Her mind absolutely boggled at the scene rolling out in vivid Technicolor right in front of her. She was being led straight towards a huge central atrium, richly and exotically furnished in the style of a palatial reception area.

A walkway to the rest of the rooms on the ground floor surrounded the two-steps-down sunken floor of this incredible area, which was also overlooked by the balconies which ran around the second and third floors. Above it was a domed roof and from the circumference of the dome hung fantastic chandeliers of multicoloured glass that cascaded down in wonderful shapes and sizes.

As amazing as all this was, Emily's gaze almost instantly zeroed in on the man who was certainly the focal centrepiece of this totally decadent and fabulous luxury. He rose with majestic dignity from a thronelike sofa which was upholstered in red and gold. His clothes—a long white undertunic and a sleeveless over-robe in royal purple edged in gold braid—seemed to embrace Arabian culture but he didn't look like an Arab, more aristocratic Spanish. What wasn't in any doubt was that Emily was faced with the most stunningly beautiful man she had ever seen in her life.

Beautiful…

Strange word to apply to a man yet handsome somehow wasn't enough. The cast of his features was perfectly boned and balanced as though he was the creation of a master sculptor. A thick mane of straight black hair was swept back from his forehead, falling in shaggy layers to below his ears but not to shoulder-length. It was a bold and dramatic frame for a face that comprised brows which kicked up at a wicked angle, lending an emphatic effect to riveting dark eyes; a classically straight nose ending in a flare of nostrils that suggested a passionate temperament; a mouth whose upper lip was rather thin and sharply delineated while the lower lip was full and sensual.

The man fascinated, mesmerised, and although she thought of him as beautiful, there was an innate arrogant *maleness* to him that kicked a stream of primal fear through her highly agitated bloodstream. He was fabulous but also very foreign, and he was unmistakably assessing her female assets as he strolled forward, apparently for a closer examination.

Because he was at a lower floor level, Emily had the weird sense of catapulting back in time to the days when Zanzibar was the largest slave trading centre of the world, with herself being held captive on a platform for the buyers' appraisal.

He lifted a hand to seemingly flick a hair back from his forehead as he spoke in Arabic to one of the guards holding her. The scarf she'd tied around her head was suddenly snatched away, the rough movement dislodging the pins which had kept her hair in a twisted coil around her crown. The sheer weight of the untethered mass brought it tumbling down, spilling over her shoulders and down her back.

'Hey!' Emily cried in frightened protest,

her imagination rioting towards being stripped of her bikini, as well. She was suddenly feeling extremely vulnerable, terrified of what his next command might be.

A burst of fluent French came from the Spaniard/Arab. It was accompanied by a cynical flash of his eyes and finished with a sardonic curl of his mouth. While Emily had picked up a smattering of quite a few languages on her travels, she was not up to comprehending this rush of foreign words and she didn't care for the expression that went with them, either.

'Look, I'm not French. Okay?' she pleaded. 'Any chance you speak English?'

'So—' one black eyebrow lifted in sceptical challenge '—you are English?'

'Well, no actually. I'm Australian. My name is Emily Ross.' She nodded to the waterproof bag still being held by one of her guards. 'My passport will prove…'

'Nothing of pertinent interest, madamoiselle,' he cut in drily.

Emily took a deep breath, pulling her wits together enough to address the *real* situation here. 'Then may I ask what *is* of pertinent interest to you, monsieur?'

He made an oddly graceful gesture suggesting a rather careless bit of interest he was just as happy to dismiss. 'Jacques Arnault gave a description of you which I find surprisingly accurate.' He spoke in a slow drawl, laced with irony, his eyes definitely mocking as he added, 'This has piqued my curiosity enough to inquire if he spoke more truth than I anticipated.'

'What did he claim?' Emily asked, her teeth clenching as she anticipated hearing a string of lies.

'That you are a virgin.'

A virgin!

Emily shut her eyes as her mind exploded with the shocking implications behind *her promised virginity*.

It could mean only one thing.

Jacques Arnault...who couldn't lie straight

in bed at night even if he tried, the consummate con artist who'd tricked her into crewing on his yacht, the sneaky drug-runner who had no conscience about anything, whose mind was completely bent on doing whatever served his best interests…had obviously come up with a deal to save his own skin.

She was to be traded off as a sex slave!

'No!' she almost spat in fierce indignation, her eyes flying open to glare at the prospective buyer. 'Absolutely not!'

'I did not believe it,' he said with a dismissive shrug, the tone of his voice a very cold contrast to her heat. 'Since the evidence points to your being a professional belly-dancer, I'm sure you've had many patrons.'

'A professional belly-dancer?' Emily's voice climbed incredulously at this further off-the-wall claim.

He gave her an impatient look. 'Your costumes were found onboard Arnault's yacht, along with the other luggage you abandoned in fleeing from being associated with the

Frenchman's criminal activities. Avoiding capture.'

Capture!

So Jacques had definitely been nabbed doing his drug-dealing, and his yacht subsequently searched, leading this man to think she'd twigged that the game was up and had taken to the water to escape being caught up in the mess.

'I was not fleeing from capture tonight, monsieur. I was fleeing from being a captive on that boat since it set sail from the Red Sea.'

'Jacques Arnault was holding you against your will?'

'Yes. And any belly-dancing costumes your search turned up do not belong to me, I assure you,' she stated heatedly, resenting the implied tag of being a professional whore, as well.

The heat in her voice slid right down her entire body as he observed in mocking detail every curve of her femininity; the voluptuous fullness of her breasts, the smallness of her waist, the broad sweep of her hips, the smooth flow and shape of her thighs, calves, ankles…

'Your physique suggests otherwise, Miss Ross,' he commented very dryly.

Emily burned. Her arms, released by the guards who were still flanking her, flew up to fold themselves protectively across her chest. Her chin lifted in belligerent pride as she stated, 'I'm a professional diving instructor. I have a certificate to prove it amongst my papers in the bag your men took from me.'

Her inquisitor smiled, showing a flash of very white teeth, but something about that smile told Emily he was relishing the prospect of tearing her into tasty morsels and chewing on them. 'It's my experience that people can be many things,' he remarked with taunting ease.

'Yes. Well, you're not wrong about that,' she snapped. 'Jacques Arnault is a prime example. And I think it's time you told me who you are and what right you have to detain me like this.'

Emily was steaming with the need to challenge him, having been put so much on the spot herself. The idea of bowed head and downcast eyes was long gone. She kept a very direct gaze on his, refusing to back down from her demands.

'You were caught trespassing on property that belongs to my family and you are closely linked to a man who was engaged in criminal activity on this same property,' he clipped out as though her complaint was completely untenable—a total waste of time and breath.

'You have no evidence that *I* was engaged in criminal activity,' Emily swiftly defended.

He rolled his eyes derisively.

'I swear to you I wasn't,' she insisted. 'In fact, the costumes you found probably belong to the woman who posed as Jacques Arnault's wife when I was tricked into becoming the only crew member on his yacht.'

'Tricked, Miss Ross?'

'I needed to get to Zanzibar. Jacques said he was sailing for Madagascar and would drop me off here if I helped...'

'With his drug-running?'

'No. With sailing the yacht,' she cried in exasperation. 'I didn't know about the drug angle until after I woke up onboard and at sea, having been drugged myself.'

'So...' He paused, his expression one of weighing up her account of the situation. He lifted a hand to stroke his chin as though in thoughtful consideration. But there was something simmering in his eyes that sent a warning tingle through Emily's taut nerves as he concluded, '...you claim to be an innocent victim.'

'I *am* an innocent victim,' Emily pounced, swiftly asserting, 'The deal was for me to be company for his wife as well as being another crew-member for the duration of the trip.'

One wickedly derisive eyebrow arched. 'Where is the wife?'

Emily heaved a fretful sigh. Probably her story did sound unbelievable but it was the truth. She had nothing else to offer. 'I don't know. She was gone when I woke up the morning after I'd gone onboard.'

'Gone,' he repeated, as though underlining how convenient that was. 'Without taking her belly-dancing costumes with her?' he added pointedly.

Emily frantically cast around for a reason that might be credible. 'Maybe she had to abandon them to get away from Jacques. I left quite a lot of my things behind on the yacht…'

'In *your* bid to escape.'

'Yes.'

'To escape what, Miss Ross?' he asked silkily. 'You must admit Arnault has kept to the bargain you made with him, bringing you to Zanzibar, as agreed.'

'Not to the public harbour at Stone Town, monsieur.'

'This private harbour is along the way. He was on course to Stone Town.'

'I couldn't trust him to take me there. After doing his business at this location, he might have set sail for Madagascar, keeping me on as his crew.'

'So you chose to commit yourself to a formidable swim in unknown waters, then brave facing a mangrove swamp in the darkness. This is the act of a desperate person, Miss Ross.'

'A determined person,' she corrected, though she was beginning to feel deeply desperate in the face of this prolonged cross-examination.

'The kind of desperate person who will do anything to avoid facing prison,' he went on with an air of ruthless logic. 'A guilty person…'

'I haven't done anything wrong!' she yelled, cracking under the pressure of his disbelief in her testimony. 'I promised my sister I'd be in Stone Town for her and I wasn't sure Jacques would take me there.'

'Your sister. Who is your sister?'

'Who are *you*?' she whipped back, so frustrated by his incessant questioning of *her* position, the urge to attack *his* completely dismissed caution. 'My sister and I have important private business. I'm not going to tell a stranger what it is.'

Her defiant stance earned a glance that told her she was being utterly ridiculous in his opinion, but Emily didn't care. She wanted some answers, too.

'You are addressing Sheikh Zageo bin Sultan Al Farrahn,' he stated loftily.

A sheikh! Or was it a Sultan? He'd spoken both titles and either one made instant sense of this amazing place. But did he have any jurisdiction here?

'I thought Sultan rule was long gone from

Zanzibar and the island is now under the government of Tanzania,' she threw back at him.

'While it has become part of Tanzania, Zanzibar maintains its own government,' he sharply corrected her. 'And I command considerable respect and influence here. Instead of fighting me, Miss Ross, you would do well in these circumstances to seek my favour.'

'And what does seeking your favour entail?'

Fiery contempt blazed from her eyes. Her nerves were wound up so tightly, she felt like a compressed spring about to explode from its compression. If he dared suggest a *sexual* favour…if he dared even lower his gaze to survey her curves again…Emily knew she'd completely lose it and start fighting like a feral cat.

Fortunately she was not dealing with a stupid man. 'Perhaps you need time to consider your position, Miss Ross,' he said in a reasoning tone. 'Time to appreciate the importance of giving appropriate information so you can be helped.'

Emily's mind slid from attack mode and groped towards wondering if she'd taken a self-defeating angle throughout this interview.

Her questioner lifted his arms into a wide, open-handed gesture. 'Let us continue this conversation when you are feeling more comfortable. A warm bath, a change of clothes, some refreshment…'

She almost sagged at the heavenly thought.

'I'll have my men escort you to the women's quarters.'

Right at this moment, Emily didn't care if the women's quarters was a harem full of wives and concubines. It would be good to be amongst *females* again, great to sink into a warm bath and get cleaned up, and a huge relief to be dressed in clothes that provided some sense of protection from the far too *male* gaze of Sheikh Zageo bin Sultan Al Farrahn.

CHAPTER THREE

ZAGEO glanced over the contents of the waterproof bag, now emptied onto a side table in his private sitting room and divided into categories for his perusal. He picked up the passport. If it was a genuine document, Emily Ross was an Australian citizen, born in Cairns. Her date of birth placed her as currently twenty-eight years old.

'You have looked up this place...Cairns?' he asked his highly reliable aide-de-camp, Abdul Haji.

'A city on the east coast of far north Queensland, which is the second largest state in Australia,' Abdul informed, once again proving his efficiency in supplying whatever Zageo did or might require. 'The paper certifying Miss Ross as a diving instructor,' he went on, gesturing to a sheaf of documents on the table, 'is attached to various references by employers who have apparently used her services, catering for tourists at The Great Barrier Reef. They are not immediately checkable because of the different time zone, but in a few hours…'

Zageo picked up the papers. The certificate was dated six years ago so Emily Ross had apparently been plying this profession since she was twenty-two. 'The resort on the Red Sea where Arnault supposedly picked up this woman…'

'Is renowned for its diving around magnificent coral reefs,' Abdul instantly slid in. 'However, it also employs belly-dancers for nightly entertainment.'

Zageo flashed him a sardonic smile. 'We will soon see if that picture fits.' He waved to the meagre bundle of clothes. 'This appears to be survival kit only.'

'One can easily replenish lost clothes by

purchasing them very cheaply at the markets.'

Zageo picked up a small bundle of American dollars and flicked through them to check their value. 'There's not much cash money here.'

'True. No doubt Miss Ross was counting on using her credit card.'

Which was also laid out on the table—a Visa card, acceptable currency in most hotels. All the same, transactions and movements could be traced from a credit card, which didn't exactly tally with criminal activities.

'Surely there should be more ready cash if she is involved in the drug-running,' Zageo observed.

Abdul shrugged. 'We have no direct evidence of her complicity. I am inclined to believe she did make a deal with Arnault—free passage to wherever she wanted to go in return for crewing on his yacht…'

'And sharing his bunk.'

The cyncical deduction evoked a frown that weighed other factors. 'Curiously the search of Arnault's yacht indicated separate sleeping quarters.'

'Perhaps the man snores.'

'There does not appear to be any love lost between them,' Abdul pointed out. 'Arnault is eager to trade Miss Ross for his freedom and…'

'She jumps overboard rather than be caught with him. As you say, no love lost between them but sex can certainly be used as a currency by both parties.'

'Then why would Miss Ross not use her very blatant sex appeal to win your favour?'

It was a good question.

In fact, she should have done. It was what Zageo was used to from the women he'd met in western society. For Emily Ross to be an exception to the rule made no sense whatsoever. It was a totally perverse situation for her to look furious at his taking note of her feminine attributes, and to try blocking his appreciation of the perfectly proportioned curves by folding her arms. Women who wanted to win his interest invariably flaunted every charming asset they had. It was the oldest currency in the world for getting where they wanted to be. So why was Emily Ross denying it?

By her own admission she was not an innocent virgin.

Nor was she too young to know the score when it came to dealings between men and women.

Many things about this woman did not add up to a logical answer. The way she had spoken to him—actually daring to challenge him—had verged on disrespect, yet there had been a quick and lively intelligence behind everything she'd said. Those amazingly vivid blue eyes could have played flirtatious games with him, but no, they had burned with the strongly defiant sense of her own individuality, denying *him* any power over her, showing contempt for his authority.

'That woman needs to be put in her place,' Zageo muttered, determined to do it before the night was very much older.

Abdul's brow furrowed into another frown of uncertainty. He started stroking his beard, a sure sign of some perturbation of mind. 'If she *is* Australian…'

'Yes?' Zageo prompted impatiently.

'Perhaps it is because they are from a country which is detached from everywhere else…I have found Australians to be strangely independent in how they think and act. They are not from an authoritarian society and they think they have the right to question anything. In fact, those who have been in our employ at Dubai have bluntly stated we will get a better result if we let them perform in their own way.'

Zageo waved dismissively. 'You are talking of men. Men who have gained some eminence in their fields.'

'Yes, but I'm thinking this may be an endemic attitude amongst both men and women from Australia.'

'You are advising me that this woman may not be in the habit of bowing to any authority?'

Abdul grimaced an apologetic appeal to soften any offence as he explained, 'I'm saying Miss Ross may not have the mindset to bend to your will. It is merely something to be considered when taking in the whole.'

'Thank you, Abdul. I will give more thought to the problem of Miss Ross. However, until such time as you have checked the references from her previous employers, we will pursue the course I have laid down. Please ensure that my instructions are followed.'

Abdul bowed his way out.

His aide always understood authority.

To Zageo's mind it was utterly intolerable for Emily Ross not to bend to his will. At the very least the woman was guilty of trespassing. It was unreasonable of her to keep defying all he stood for.

She had to bend.

He would make her bend!

Emily's bikini had been taken away while she was relaxing in a luxurious spa bath, enjoying the warm bursts of water on tired, stiff muscles and the aromatic mixture of lavender and sandalwood oils rising out of the bubbles. She'd been invited to wear a wraparound silk robe during the subsequent pampering—a manicure and pedicure while her hair was shampooed and blow-dried. Five star service in these women's quarters, Emily thought, until it came time to discard the robe and dress for her next meeting with the sheikh.

She was ushered into a sumptuous bedroom where there was only one outfit on offer. It had not come from her waterproof bag. It had not come from the luggage she'd chosen to leave behind on the yacht. It did not belong to her but Emily knew instantly what it represented. Sheikh Zageo bin Sultan Al Farrahn wanted to see how well she fitted the contentious belly-dancing role. Without a doubt this was one of the costumes he'd accused her of owning.

The skirt seemed to be a concoction of chiffon scarves with colours ranging from deep violet, through many shades of blue to turquoise. These layers were attached to a wide hip band encrusted with royal-blue and gold and silver sequins with a border of dangling gold medallions. Violet lycra hipster panties came with the skirt. The cups and straps of the accompanying turquoise bra were also exotically patterned with sequins and beads.

Clearly this was not a cheap dress-up outfit.

It was an intricably fashioned professional costume.

Emily felt a twinge of concern for the woman to whom it did belong. What had happened to her? What was the story behind the storage of these specialty clothes on the yacht?

'I can't wear that,' she protested to Heba, the oldest of the attendants who'd been looking after her. 'It's not mine,' she insisted.

'I have been instructed it is for you,' came the inarguable reply. 'His Excellency, the sheikh, has commanded that you wear it. There is no other choice.'

Emily gritted her teeth. Clearly His Excellency's word was law in this household. He'd allowed her the leeway of cleaning up and feeling more comfortable, although most probably this indulgence was a premeditated softening up process and Emily was highly suspicious of the motive behind it.

Was the sexual trade-off still being considered?

Had she just been prepared for the sheikh's bed?

It had been so easy to accept all the pampering but now came the crunch!

She could either dig in her heels and remain

naked under the flimsy and all too revealing silk robe—not a good option—or don the belly-dancing costume which was probably less sexually provocative and would definitely leave her less physically accessible.

Given there would be no avoiding facing the sheikh again tonight—he'd have her hauled into his presence if she tried disobeying his instructions—Heba was right. No choice. It had to be the belly-dancing costume.

Emily quelled a flood of futile rebellion and grudgingly accepted the inevitable, thinking that with any luck, these blatantly sexy clothes wouldn't fit and *that* would show him she'd been telling the truth.

Naturally the lycra panties proved nothing, stretching to accommodate her derriere. No problem. Annoyingly the skirt sat snugly on the curve of her hips—not too loose, not too tight. Emily eyed the bra balefully as she discarded the silk robe. It looked about right, but hopefully it wouldn't comfortably reach around her back.

To her intense frustration, the straps were perfectly positioned for her shape, the hooks and eyes met with no trouble at all, and the wired cups designed to uplift breasts and emphasise cleavage made her look so voluptuous it was positively embarrassing. Okay, her breasts were not small, but they weren't this *prominent*.

The belly-dancing costume actually made her feel more self-conscious of her body than the swamp-soiled bikini which had been whisked away the moment she'd discarded it to step into the spa bath. The skimpy two-piece had been a far more natural thing for her to wear. It hadn't been exotic and erotic, aimed at titillating a man's mind. It had simply been an off-the-peg garment for swimming.

However, there was no point in asking for it back.

Heba had her orders and clearly disobeying the sheikh was unthinkable.

Emily argued to herself that although she might *feel* caught up in a scene from *The Arabian Nights*, it couldn't be true, not in today's world. Even Heba was now using a very modern slimline mobile phone, undoubtedly reporting the state of play.

This forcing her to wear the belly-dancing costume had to be a pressure tactic, wanting her to feel more exposed, more vulnerable in the next interview about her activities. It couldn't have anything to do with a sexual trade-off. Not really.

Two security guards and a bearded man whom they clearly regarded as a higher authority arrived to escort her elsewhere. The women's quarters were on the second floor. Emily expected to be taken all the way down to the opulent atrium but she was led to a door on the first floor, which instantly evoked a wild wave of apprehension. At least the hugely open atrium had been like a public arena, overlooked by anyone on the ground or upper floors. She hoped, quite desperately, that some kind of official office was behind this door.

It wasn't.

The bearded man ushered her into what was undoubtedly a private sitting room, richly furnished and sensually seductive with its many cushioned couches surrounding a low circular table which held a tempting display of food and drink. It was occupied by only one person who instantly proceeded to dismiss her usher.

'Thank you, Abdul.'

The bearded man backed out of the room and closed the door, leaving Emily absolutely alone with a sheikh who apparently believed the only law that had to be respected was his own!

He strolled forward, intent on gaining an unencumbered view of her from head to foot—front view, side view and back view—in the costume he'd chosen for her to wear.

Emily gritted her teeth and stood as still as a statue, determined not to betray her inner quaking and hoping that with her head held high, she looked as though she disdained any interpretation he took from how well the skirt and bra fitted her.

He moved behind her. Her spine crawled with an awareness of how close he was. Within an arm's reach. And he did not move on. His out-of-sight stillness played havoc with her pulse, making her temples throb with acute anxiety. What was he doing? What was he thinking? Was she imagining it or had he touched her hair, sliding fingers around a tress, lifting it away from the rest?

'You must fetch a very high price…as a dancer.'

The comment was spoken slowly, consideringly, his voice thick with a sensuality that raised goose-bumps all over her skin.

Emily swallowed hard to work some moisture into a very dry mouth. Her inner agitation had bolted beyond any control.

Remaining still was beyond her. She swung around, catching sight of a swathe of her hair sliding out between the thumb and fingers of a hand that had been raised to his mouth. Or nose. The idea of him taking the intimate liberty of tasting it, smelling it, created total havoc in Emily's mind.

'You're making a big mistake about me,' she cried, struggling to find some defence to how he was making her feel.

'That was meant as a compliment, Miss Ross,' he answered, his mouth still curved in a look of sensual pleasure. 'There is no need for you to bristle.'

He didn't have the right to touch her without her permission. Emily wanted to say so but she sensed he would only laugh at the objection. Right now he had the power to do anything he wanted with her. All she could do was try to change his view of who and what she was.

'It sounded as though you thought I was a…a call-girl,' she protested.

His smile tilted with irony. ‘I think it more a case of your choosing whom you’ll take as a lover…as it suits you.’

Emily wasn’t sure she liked the sound of that, either. She had the weird sensation of being silently enticed to choose *him* as her next lover. Or was he setting a test—a trap—for her?

‘Come—’ he waved her forward to one of the couches close to the circular table ‘—you must be hungry after the rigours of your escape from Jacques Arnault.’

Her stomach was empty—so empty it kept convulsing with nervous energy. ‘Does this mean you believe I was escaping from him and not involved in the drug-running?’ she asked, not yet ready to take a step in any direction.

He swept her an open-handed, graceful gesture. ‘Until we reach a time and place of complete enlightenment, I would prefer you to consider yourself more my guest than my prisoner.’

'You mean you *are* actually checking me out,' Emily pursued the point, hoping for some sense of relief from his false assumptions about her.

'Different time zones do not permit that process at the moment but rest assured nothing will be taken for granted. In the meantime…'

'I am hungry,' she admitted, thinking she'd feel safer sitting down, safer keeping her mouth busy with eating if she could make her stomach cooperate with an intake of food.

Again he waved her forward. 'Please…seat yourself comfortably, relax, and help yourself to whatever you'd like.'

No way in the world could she ever relax in this man's company, but putting a table between them seemed like a good defensive move. 'Thank you,' she said, forcing her feet to walk slowly, waiting for him to indicate where he would sit so she could settle as far away from him as possible.

Apparently he wanted to be face-to-face

with her so she didn't have to manoeuvre for a position opposite to his. He took it himself. Nevertheless, there was still a disturbing sense of intimacy, just in their being seated at the same table. The couches around it were curved, linking with each other so there was no real sense of separation.

'What would you like to drink?' he asked, as though she truly were a guest. 'You have a choice of mango, pineapple and hibiscus juices, coconut milk…'

'Hibiscus juice?' She'd heard of the flower but hadn't known a drink could be made from it.

'Sweet, light and refreshing.' He reached for a jug of hand-painted pottery depicting a red hibiscus. 'Want to try it?'

'No, thanks. I've always loved mango.' Which she was long familiar with since it was such a prolific fruit tree around her home city of Cairns.

His dark eyes danced with mocking amusement over her suspicious refusal of the hibiscus jug. 'Where has your adventurous spirit gone, Miss Ross?'

The light taunt goaded her into shooting some straight truth right back at him. 'I feel like having some familiar comfort right now, Your Excellency.'

He picked up another pottery jug and poured mango juice into a beautiful crystal goblet. 'The familiar is safe,' he observed, a glittering challenge in his eyes as he replaced the jug and watched her pick up the goblet. 'A woman who plays safe would never have boarded Arnault's yacht. She would have taken a far more conventional, more protected route to Zanzibar.'

Emily fervently wished she had. Never more so than now. Dealing with this sheikh and his attitude towards her was undermining her self-confidence. She didn't know how to even set about *getting out of this*. Telling the truth didn't seem to be winning her anything, but what else could she do?

'I've crewed on yachts many times around

the Australian coast. I was looking for a way to save the cost of plane fares.'

'You took a risk with a stranger.'

'I thought I could handle it.'

'And when you woke up and found there was no wife…how did you handle it then, Miss Ross?'

'Oh, then it came down to the rules of survival at sea. We needed each other to sail the yacht so agreements had to be reached and kept. Jacques only tried to cross the line once.' Her eyes hardened with the contempt she felt for the Frenchman. 'I think he found it too painful to repeat that particular error in judgment.'

The sheikh's mouth twitched into a sardonic little smile. 'Perhaps this contributed to Arnault's belief you were a virgin, Miss Ross, fighting for your virtue.'

She rolled her eyes. 'One doesn't have to be a virgin to not want a scumbag sharing your bed.'

'A scumbag…'

'The lowest of the low,' she drily explained.

'Ah!' One eyebrow arched in wicked challenge. 'And what of the highest of the high, Miss Ross? Where does your measure start for a man to be accepted into your bed?'

The highest of the high...

Emily's heart catapulted around her chest.

He was speaking of himself. Had to be. Which made this question far too dangerous to answer. If he actually did want to be accepted into her bed...the speculative look in his eyes was making her toes curl.

Emily quickly reached out to pick up some tasty tidbit from the table to stuff in her mouth.

Eating was safe.

Speaking was dangerous.

She was suddenly heart-thumpingly sure that a desire for sexual satisfaction was more on Sheikh Zageo bin Sultan Al Farrahn's mind than a desire for truth, and what he wanted from her was capitulation, vindicating everything he thought about her.

No way.

Never, she thought fiercely.

But what if he kept her here until she did give him the satisfaction he expected from her? She might never get to Stone Town for the meeting with her sister!

CHAPTER FOUR

ZAGEO watched Emily Ross eat. The consumption of an array of finger food was done with such single-minded focus, she could well have been absolutely alone in the room. *He* rated no visible attention whatsoever.

In any other woman's company he would find this behaviour unforgivably rude. In fact, he couldn't recall such a situation ever happening before. Emily Ross was proving to be an intriguing enigma on many levels, and perversely enough, her constantly challenging attitude was exciting more than just an intellectual interest in her. Mind-games with a woman were always sexy.

He suspected if he made some comment about her concentration on the food, she would lift those incredibly vivid blue eyes and state very reasonably, 'You invited me to help myself. Do you now have some problem with me doing it?'

What reply could he make to that without sounding *un*reasonable?

The plain truth was he felt peeved by her refusal to show more awareness of him. It pricked his male ego. But he could wait. Time was on his side. Let her satisfy this hunger. If she was using it as an evasive tactic, it would come to an end soon enough and she'd be forced to acknowledge him again.

Besides, the Frenchman had not been wrong in his assessment of this woman's physical attractions. She was intensely watchable. Her hair alone was a visual delight—not just one block of colour but an intriguing meld of many variations in shades of blond and copper. The description of 'strawberry-blonde' had suggested red hair and pale skin, but there was more of an overall warm glow in Emily Ross's colouring. Her skin did not have the fairness that freckled. It was lightly tanned to a golden-honey shade.

Copper and gold, he thought. A woman of the sun with eyes the colour of a clear, sun-kissed sky. But her body belonged to Mother Earth, the fullness of her breasts and the width of her hips promising an easy fertility and a natural ability to nurture that Zageo was finding extremely appealing.

Perhaps it was the contrast to Veronique's chic model thinness that had him so…fascinated…by this woman's more opulent femininity. The lavish untamed hair denied any skilful styling by a fashionable hairdresser. The lavish flesh of her body—not fat, just well covered, superbly covered—allowed no bones to protrude anywhere, and would undoubtedly provide a soft cushioning for anyone lying with her—man or child.

She was a creature of nature, not the creation of diet and designer wear, and Zageo found himself wanting to lie with her, wanting to sink into her softness and wanting to feel her heat envelop him and suck him in to the deepest part of her where secrets melted and intimacy reigned. That was when she would surrender to him. Utterly and completely.

Zageo relished the thought of Emily Ross's ultimate submission as he watched her eat. He was inclined to believe the Frenchman had not managed to get that satisfaction from her. Arnault's sexual frustration would have primed his readiness to try selling her on, demonstrating a total lack of perception about Zageo's character and the woman's. Emily Ross was of the mettle to play her own game by her own rules.

Nevertheless, Zageo had no doubt she could be bought, just like everyone else.

It was always a matter of striking the right trade.

The challenge was in finding out what buttons to press for the door of opportunity to open.

'Where were you aiming to meet your sister in Stone Town?' he asked.

Important private business—if Emily Ross had spoken the truth about her motive for coming to Zanzibar—invariably provided leverage.

Emily chewed over that question as she finished a tasty egg and asparagus tartlet and sipped some more mango juice. She didn't like the past tense he'd used, suggesting she wasn't going to be allowed to keep her appointment with Hannah.

Her gaze targeted his, projecting very direct intent. 'I still aim to meet her. She's counting on my meeting her. I left the yacht and swam for it because I didn't want to let my sister down.'

'Is she in trouble?'

The quick injection of concern almost tripped Emily into spilling her own worries about Hannah's situation. Caution clamped onto her tongue before it ran loose with information that was better kept private. Being an Australian, she was in the habit of assuming the world around her was safe unless it was proved otherwise. She had just been learning—the hard way—that she trusted too easily. Blithely believing that most people were of goodwill could land her in very nasty places.

'It's just a family meeting. I said I'd come. She'll be expecting me,' Emily stated, trying to sound matter-of-fact rather than anxious.

'Miss Ross, if I am to believe you were not in league with Arnault and his drug-running…' He paused to give emphasis to his line of argument. 'If I am to believe in your determination to meet your sister in Stone Town…there must be a designated place—be it hotel, shop, or private residence—and a name that can be checked there, giving credence to your story.'

Okay, she could see there was a credibility gap here that had to be crossed or her guest/prisoner status would remain as long as the sheikh cared to keep it in place. On the other hand, from the way he'd been eyeing her over, Emily had the distinctly uneasy feeling that not even credibility would earn her release from his custody. Still, she had to offer some proof that she was on a completely separate mission to Jacques Arnault's.

'The Salamander Inn. I don't know if Hannah has booked ahead. Unlikely, I'd think, since she was unsure of when she'd make it to Zanzibar. But that's our meeting place.'

'The Salamander Inn is a boutique hotel. It offers the best and coincidentally the most expensive accommodation of all the hotels on this island. I know this.' He smiled with an arrogance that somehow implied she'd just been very stupid. 'I own it.'

Oh, great! The chance of escaping from this man anywhere on Zanzibar looked increasingly dim!

'Fine!' she said on an exasperated sigh. 'Then you can easily check if Hannah has arrived or not.'

'Her full name?'

'Hannah Coleman.'

'Not Ross?'

'Coleman is her married name.'

'So your sister is not likely to book under the family name of Ross?'

'Hardly. Ross is *my* married name.'

That information ripped him out of his languid pose against the heaps of satin cushions on his couch. His body jerked forward, his loose robes suddenly pasted to a tautly muscled physique that seemed to bristle with assault readiness. Yet he spoke with a soft silky contempt which crawled straight under Emily's skin, priming her into retaliation mode.

'Where is your husband, Madame Ross?'

'His ashes were thrown to a breeze out at sea…as he'd once said he'd prefer to being buried,' Emily grated out, hanging firmly to being matter-of-fact so that she wasn't embarrassed by one of the waves of grief which could still sweep up and overwhelm her when she thought of Brian's death.

They'd been school sweethearts, rarely parted during all the years they'd spent sharing almost everything in each other's company. Then to have him taken from her so abruptly…being left behind…alone…cheated of a future together… *No, no, no, don't go there, Emily!*

She concentrated on watching her antagonist digest the news of her widowhood, the withdrawal of all expression from his face, the slow emergence of more sympathetic inquiry in his dynamic dark eyes.

'How long ago?' he asked quietly.

'About two years.'

'He was young?'

'Two years older than me.'

'How did he die?'

'Brian was with a rescue team during a cyclone.' She grimaced. 'He died trying to save an old lady's pet dog. A panel of flying roof hit him.'

'A brave man then,' came the thoughtful observation.

She managed an ironic smile. 'I don't think fear ever had any influence on Brian's actions. He just did whatever he set out to do. We used to go adventuring a lot, working our way around Australia.'

'You do not have children?'

She shook her head. 'We weren't ready to settle down with a family. In fact, we were getting ready to set off on a world trip…'

'When the cyclone happened,' he finished for her.

'Yes,' she muttered, frowning at the realisation that she'd spoken more of Brian in the past two minutes than in the entire two years since her departure from Australia.

You have to move on, she'd told herself, and move on she had, a long slow trip across Asia, more or less going wherever the wind blew her on her travels, not wanting to face making any long-term decisions about her life—a life without the man who'd always coloured it.

She'd attached herself to other groups of

people from time to time, working with them, listening to their experiences, soaking up interesting pieces of information, but what was highly personal and private to her had remained in her own head and heart.

So why had she opened up to this man?

Her mind zapped back the answer in no time flat.

Because *he* was getting to her in a highly primitive male/female way and she'd instinctively brought up the one man she'd loved as a shield against these unwelcome feelings. Her marriage to Brian was a defence against other things, as well, like the idea she was a belly-dancer with indulgent sugar-daddies on the side.

She was, in fact, a perfectly respectable widow who hadn't even been tempted into a sexual dalliance by the many gorgeous eye-candy guys who'd offered to share their beds and bodies while they were ships passing on their separate journeys. Sex without emotional involvement hadn't appealed, and it didn't appeal now, either, she fiercely told herself, willing her body to stop responding in this embarrassingly *animal* fashion to a very foreign sheikh who wanted to treat her as a whore.

Having worked up a head of defensive steam, Emily lifted her gaze to the man in the ruling seat and noted that his disturbingly handsome head was cocked to one side as though viewing her from an angle he hadn't considered before, and the heart-thumping power of those brilliant dark eyes was thankfully narrowed into thoughtful slits.

'So what is *your* marital status?' she bluntly demanded.

His head snapped upright, eyes opening wide with a flash of astonishment at her temerity. 'I beg your pardon?'

'Fair's fair!' Emily argued. 'If you have the right to ask about mine, I have just as much right to ask about yours.'

If he had a string of wives and a bevy of

concubines, perhaps he would cease to be so attractive!

His face clearly said she was being incredibly impertinent but Emily didn't care. 'After all, what do I know about you?' she pointed out. 'I'll accept you're Sheikh Zageo…whatever…whatever…and you own this place as well as The Salamander Inn, which obviously means you're terribly wealthy and probably influential, but—'

'Zageo bin Sultan Al Farrahn,' he broke in haughtily, supplying all the names she'd forgotten in her current fraught state.

'Right! Quite a mouthful to remember,' she excused. 'Though if it's a big issue to you, I'll try to hold it in my mind.'

'Rather than test your mind too far,' he drawled in a mocking tone that once more raised Emily's hackles. 'You may call me Zageo in my private rooms.'

'Well, thank you very much. It was really sticking in my craw, having to address you as Your Excellency,' she tossed at him. 'I mean honestly...how do you keep a straight face when people call you that? Though I suppose if you actually believe it fits you...' She paused to look at him in arch inquiry, then testingly ask, 'Do you consider yourself totally excellent?'

His jawline tightened. Emily sensed that pride was warring with his own intelligence which had to concede the presence of a few little flaws. No man—nor woman—was perfect.

'It is simply the customary form of address to any sheikh in my culture,' he stated tersely. 'I doubt Her Majesty, the queen of England, considers herself majestic. Nor think herself the highest of the high when addressed as Your Highness.'

'Okay. Point made,' Emily granted, smiling to show she hadn't meant to give any offence, though secretly she felt very pleased at levelling the playing field, if only a little bit. 'If I'm allowed to call you Zageo, you needn't keep on with Miss Ross. Emily will do just fine. It's actually what I'm more used to. We're not big on titles back home in Australia.'

And he needn't think she was overly impressed by his!

'Thank you, Emily.'

He smiled, instantly driving her mind into a jangling loop that screamed *Danger! Danger! Danger!* He'd just made her name sound like an intimate caress, sending a sensual little shiver down her spine. As for his smile…it was definitely projecting a pleasurable triumph in having won this concession from her, interpreting it as a dropping of hostility and bringing a much closer meeting ground between them.

She had a mental image of him storming the ramparts of her castle and it seemed like a good idea to pull up the drawbridge and shut the gate. 'So let's get back to *your* marital status,' she said, needing back-up support to hold the barriers in place.

'I have not yet taken a wife,' Zageo answered, undermining Emily's defensive plan.

Feeling decidedly miffed by this, she remarked, 'I thought sheikhs could take as many wives as they liked. You're a late starter aren't you?'

'I believe the right choice of wife in any culture deserves deep and serious consideration, given the intention of a lifelong commitment and the resulting alliance with another family.'

'Nothing to do with love, of course,' she tossed off flippantly.

'On the contrary, I have observed that compatibility tends to breed a more lasting love than the rather fickle chemistry of *being in love*.'

She pounced on what seemed like a beacon of relief from any sexual pressure from him. 'So you don't think giving in to chemistry is a good idea.'

'It is not something I would base a marriage on, Emily, but for a time of pure pleasure—' his eyes positively glittered with white-hot sexual invitation '—I think giving in to chemistry is a very sweet and satisfying self-indulgence, to be treasured as something uniquely special to the man and woman involved.'

Emily had to suck in a quick breath to stop an imminent meltdown in her bones, brain and other body parts she didn't want to think about. 'I take it you're not a virgin then,' she shot at him, mocking the value that had apparently been put on *her* virginity.

At least it temporarily interrupted the bolt of heat from his eyes, making him blink, then triggering a rippling peal of laughter, lessening the scary tension in the room and leaving Emily feeling slightly safer.

'I have not foresworn the pleasures of the flesh…no,' he eventually drawled, his eyes dancing an all too overt anticipation of pleasures *she* might provide, which did away with any sense of relaxation.

Emily drew in a deep breath and expelled

it in a long, slow sigh, desperate to reduce the seesawing inner apprehension which made thinking nimbly very difficult. She felt stripped of any clothing armour and he'd just ripped off the mental armour she'd tried to put in place. Somehow she had to keep her mind at battle readiness because the fight for freedom would probably be lost if she let herself be distracted by this man's insidious promise of pleasures, which his eyes said were hers for the taking if she co-operated with what he wanted.

The big problem was he was the kind of man who'd tempt any woman into wondering how it might be with him…if, indeed, he would deliver amazing pleasure. Probably it was *The Arabian Nights* thing again, messing with her mind, making her think of Omar Khayyam's poetry expressing regret for the fleeting sweetness of life and love, which, in turn, tapped into the lingering emptiness of missing Brian, all contributing to her feeling of *why not experience this man*?

A harsh strain of common sense insisted it would compromise her whole situation if she did. 'I have to be here for Hannah,' she muttered, savagely reminding herself of her prime motivation.

'There cannot be any urgency about this meeting with your sister or you would not have chosen to come by yacht,' Zageo pointed out.

'Even by sailing, I figured I'd make it here by about the same time as Hannah. And I preferred to save my money.'

His mouth curled into a mocking little smile. 'Staying at The Salamander Inn does not equate with *saving money*, Emily.'

He was still doubting her story.

'I didn't say *I* was going to stay there,' she reminded him.

'Where did you plan to stay?'

'If Hannah wasn't here already, I intended to find a place that suited my budget while I waited for her.'

'Then you should have no problem with

accepting my hospitality while you wait for your sister's arrival in Zanzibar,' he said silkily. 'That would undoubtedly suit your budget best. No cost whatsoever.'

'Oh, right!' Emily mocked back before she could stop her tongue from cutting loose on him. 'And I suppose you'll expect me to belly-dance for you every night!'

His elegant hands performed their graceful invitational gesture. 'If you feel you should recompense me in some way, by all means…'

'What if Hannah is at the inn already?' Emily cut in, hating the sense of being helplessly cornered, and feeling that Sheikh Zageo bin Sultan Al Farrahn was enjoying himself far too much at her expense!

'That can be checked immediately.'

He leaned forward and picked up a mobile telephone from the table. The modern means of communication again struck Emily as odd in this setting but the evidence of its use all around the palace assured her that life in the twenty-first century was not excluded here. Unfortunately most of the one-sided conversation she subsequently listened to was not in English. Of all the words spoken, only the name, Hannah Coleman, was recognisable.

Emily literally sat on the edge of her seat as she waited, hoping for news that would validate her story, as well as assure her of Hannah's safe arrival. 'Well?' she prompted anxiously, once the call connection had been ended.

The dark eyes targeted hers with riveting intensity. 'Your sister is not at the inn. Nor has there been a booking in her name.'

Disappointment warred with doubt as to the truth of what she was being told. 'How do I know you're not lying?' burst from her tongue.

His face tightened forbiddingly. 'Why would I lie?'

Even to her overstrained mind, *to get me into your bed* sounded absurd, given his extraordinary good looks and incredibly wealthy resources.

Zageo's dark eyes blazed with angry suspicion as he pointed out, 'It is you, Emily Ross, who has cause to concoct many lies in order to paint yourself as an innocent victim.'

'I swear to you on any amount of bibles or Korans or whatever carries weight in both our worlds, I've told you nothing but the truth.'

One black eyebrow arched in sceptical challenge. 'Where is your sister coming from?'

'Zimbabwe.' Realising she now had to explain more, Emily offered, 'You must know about the political problems in that country. It's world news. Everyone knows. Hannah's husband is trying to hang onto his farm, but he wants her and the children out while he…'

'Children?'

'They have two young daughters. The plan was for Hannah to bring them by road into Botswana when they thought it was safe enough for her to do so, then…' A helpful link suddenly leapt into Emily's mind. 'Hannah and her husband, Malcolm, spent a vacation at The Salamander Inn five years ago. That's why she picked it as a meeting place. She knew it and thought it was somewhere safe for both of us to get to. Since you own the inn, surely you can have a check run on the records…'

'Not at this time of night.'

'Then first thing tomorrow morning.' Emily jumped to her feet, seeing a chance to end this highly unsettling encounter with him. 'In fact, by tomorrow morning I'm sure you have the power and facilities to have lots of things about me checked, so talking any more right now is really inefficient, isn't it? I'm terribly tired and if you'd just have me taken back to the women's quarters, I'm very happy to accept your hospitality for the night and…'

He rose from his couch, choking off Emily's speech with the formidable force of energy that rose with him. For several fraught moments, his gaze locked onto hers, telegraphing a strong and ruthless promise that if she was playing him for a fool she would pay for it.

Dearly.

But he did dismiss her from his presence.

'Until tomorrow morning,' he said in sardonic agreement with her timeline.

Pretend as she might about accepting an offer of hospitality for tonight, Emily found nothing remotely hospitable about the security guards who escorted her back to the women's quarters.

She was not Sheikh Zageo bin Sultan Al Farrahn's guest.

She was his prisoner.

CHAPTER FIVE

ZAGEO paced around his sitting room, incensed by the outrageous impertinence of Emily Ross, taking her leave of him as though she had every right to do as she pleased. This woman, who had to know she was a trespasser on his goodwill, had treated him in the same intolerable manner as Veronique. Which reminded him…

With a heightened sense of deadly purpose he moved to pick up the telephone and call the Paris apartment. He had bought it to accommodate the relationship with Veronique and she had recently taken to using it as her main residence. Zageo decided it would be a suitable parting gift as he waited impatiently for her to come on line.

'Ah, *cheri*! What a lovely surprise,' she responded with a gush of pleasure when he announced himself. 'Are you missing me?'

If she wanted some proof of her pulling power she was testing the wrong man. 'Veronique, we are at an end, you and I,' he stated matter-of-factly.

'What?' Shock. Then anxiety. 'What do you mean, Zageo?'

'I mean our relationship has run its course. You were happy to remain in Paris…and I now find myself attracted to another woman.'

'You are leaving *me* for another woman?' she screeched into his ear.

A sobering lesson for taking him for granted.

'I will sign over the apartment to you—a memento of our time together and one I'm sure you'll appreciate.'

'I don't want the apartment without you in it,' she cried wildly. 'I want you, Zageo.'

A claim that left him completely cold. If she wanted him so much, she would be with him. Clearly Veronique had thought she could have her cake without supplying the ingredients that made it desirable for him, too. A deal was a deal and as far as Zageo was concerned, she hadn't lived up to her end of it. Nevertheless, he was prepared to be generous.

'Please have the grace to accept it's over, Veronique. There is nothing more to be gained by carrying on. It cannot serve any good purpose. I promise you will have the apartment. I'll put the legalities in train tomorrow.'

'You've found another woman?' Her voice shook with hysterical incredulity.

An unforgiveable wound to her pride?

'I'm sure you'll find another man,' he drawled, aware there were many ready to slide into the place he'd just vacated.

'You can't do this to me. I won't let you—'

'Move on, Veronique,' Zageo cut in ruthlessly. 'I have. Let us meet in future as old friends who still hold some affection for each other. As always, I wish you well.'

He ended the connection before she could pour out any further futile protests. It was far better to part with a sense of mutual respect than with a tirade of mutual grievances. He hoped Veronique would be pragmatic enough to accept what would not be changed and count herself fortunate to have profited so handsomely from their relationship. The gifted apartment in Paris would undoubtedly provide balm to wounded pride.

The burning question now was…how to deal with Emily Ross?

She was showing no signs whatsoever of bending to his will. Quite the contrary. Despite the fact she had to realise her immediate fate was in his hands and it would serve her well to win his favour, she was flouting his authority at every turn.

If Abdul was right about this kind of attitude being common amongst Australians, perhaps it was not meant to be so offensive.

On the other hand, Zageo did not care to accept it from a woman. Of course, he could turn her in to the local authorities, move her straight out of his life, and that was certainly the most sensible path to take, given that he'd decided to find himself a suitable wife.

Emily Ross was a distraction from what he should be doing. On the other hand, for the duration of this business trip through Africa, he would very much enjoy having her in his bed and teaching her who was master of the situation.

Tomorrow he would know more about her.

Knowledge was power, especially when it came to dealing with people.

However, when tomorrow came, enlightenment did not come with it.

'Government offices are not open in Australia on Saturdays and Sundays,' Abdul reported. 'We cannot check a marriage certificate or a death certificate until Monday.'

More frustration!

Having finished eating his breakfast, Zageo took a long deliberate moment to savour the aroma of his Kenyan coffee, wanting at least one of his senses satisfied. Then he once again considered the challenging and highly vexing enigma of Emily Ross. Investigating her was like chasing evaporating smoke—no substance to be found anywhere.

Abdul had already informed him that the Australian employers who had written her references were no longer at the same place of business. Reef Wonderland Tours had changed management eighteen months ago and Whitsundays Diving Specialists was now a defunct company. As for the Red Sea resort where she had supposedly been working with a dive team, no-one admitted to knowing anything about her, which raised questions about what profession she had plied there since her name was not on any record books.

Had she spun a complete tissue of lies last night?

Was anything about her self-presentation genuine?

'The belly-dancing costume fitted her perfectly,' he remarked drily.

'Indeed, it did, Your Excellency,' Abdul agreed.

Zageo frowned over the form of address all his staff customarily used with him. Normally he just took *Your Excellency* for granted, barely hearing it, but in real terms the title *was* ridiculous, as that highly perverse and provocative creature had pointed out.

'The authorities have come from Stone Town to take Jacques Arnault and his Zanzibar connections into custody,' Abdul ran on when no further comment came from Zageo. 'A decision should be made whether or not to include Miss Ross in this criminal group.'

'Not.' The answer was swift and emphatic. He would feel…*defeated*…by Emily Ross if he washed his hands of her before coming to grips with who and what she really was. 'We have no absolute proof of involvement,' he added. 'I'm inclined to allow her the benefit of the doubt, given how very difficult it is to undo an injustice once it has been committed.'

'Do you wish to keep her here or set her free to go about her own business?'

'Since Miss Ross has no prearranged accommodation, I shall hold her here as my guest. At least until Monday.' He gave Abdul a look that conveyed his determination to pursue more background information. 'As to her business, clearly it is not urgent since a Hannah Coleman has not, as yet, booked into The Salamander Inn. If, indeed, there is a sister to be met.'

'A search of the five-year-old records at the inn did turn up a Mr and Mrs M. Coleman.'

Zageo shrugged, unconvinced by a name that could belong to any number of people. 'One wonders if that is confirmation of my new guest's story or mere coincidence,' he drawled derisively. 'I think I shall amuse myself by doing a little more testing today, Abdul.'

His chief advisor and confidante took several moments to absorb and interpret this comment. He then cleared his throat and tentatively inquired, 'Has the…uh…affair with Veronique run its course, Your Excellency? Are there some…arrangements…you'd like me to make?'

'No. It's done. I made the call and the arrangements last night. The decision had nothing whatsoever to do with Miss Ross, Abdul. It was made beforehand.'

Although Emily Ross featured highly as a replacement for Veronique in his life, having completely obliterated his former mistress from his mind.

'I've given her the Paris apartment,' he went on. 'Ownership will need to be transferred into her name. You'll see to it?'

Abdul nodded. 'Speaking of names, the Coleman name *was* attached to an address in

Zimbabwe. Do you wish me to make inquiries in that direction?'

'It could be fruitful. One might well ask why hasn't the sister turned up? Yes…' Zageo smiled to himself. 'Pursuing this question presents a nice little demonstration of concern for those whom Miss Ross apparently holds dear to her heart.'

A weapon in the war, he thought, feeling an extraordinary zing of anticipation in the plan he would soon put into operation.

CHAPTER SIX

EMILY had to concede that being a prisoner in this astounding place was not hard to take. Her physical needs were wonderfully pampered. She'd slept in a heavenly bed. Of course, after the bunk on the yacht, almost any normal bed would have been heavenly but the lovely soft mattress and pillows and the amazing curtain of mosquito netting that had been pulled all around the bed to protect her from any possible bites had definitely made her feel as though she was sleeping on clouds.

Then to wake up and find her own clothes restored to her—even those she'd had to leave behind on Jacques's yacht—all washed, ironed, and either hanging up or set on shelves in the dressing room adjoining the bedroom…well, surely this was evidence that her real life had been verified and everything was moving back to normal. The fears generated by the grotesque situation last night seemed rather incredible this morning.

She'd happily dressed in a favourite skirt made of a pink, blue and green floral fabric that swirled freely around her legs—lovely and cool for what was shaping up to be a hot day on the island. A blue top with little sleeves and a scooped neckline completed what she considered a fairly modest outfit, definitely not overtly sexy, just…pretty…and feminine. If there was to be another face-to-face encounter with the sheikh, hopefully he wouldn't have any grounds for viewing her in a morally questionable light again.

Breakfast on the verandah outside her suite in the women's quarters became quite a social affair. As well as Heba serving her a very tasty array of fruit and croissants, her two other attendants from last night's grooming session, Jasmine and Soleila, fluttered around, eager to please Emily in any way they could.

A selection of magazines were brought for her to flick through as she finished the meal with absolutely divine coffee. Heba, herself, opened a copy of *Vogue* to show photographs of celebrities at some big premiere in Paris.

'See?' she pointed out proudly. 'Here he is with Veronique!'

Emily felt a weird catch in her heart as she stared at the stunningly beautiful Sheikh Zageo bin Sultan Al Farrahn in a formal black dinner suit, accompanied by the stunningly beautiful world-famous model, the highly unique Veronique, who was wearing a fabulous evening gown of floating ostrich feathers that only she could have carried off so magnificently.

This photograph was not a slice of fantasy out of *The Arabian Nights*. It was real life on the international scene, the jet-setting, ultra-wealthy beautiful people doing what they do, connecting with each other for fabulous affairs—social and personal.

Feeling considerably flattened, Emily realised that her imagination must have been in an extremely feverish state last night, running hot with the idea of being seen as a desirable woman to this man. Why on earth would he want her when such an exotic and classy model was available to him?

'Have they been a couple of long standing?' she asked Heba.

A shrug. 'Almost two years.'

Two years comprised a fairly solid attachment. Emily now felt thoroughly confused over why the sheikh was bothering with her when she could have been simply passed along to the local authorities for them to sort out her association with Jacques Arnault. Why had he taken such a *sexual* interest in her? Was it only a titillated interest because the Frenchman had tried to trade her for his freedom?

'But Heba, Veronique did not come with

him this time,' Jasmine pointed out, giving Emily an archly knowing look as though it was obvious to her who was being singled out to fill the sheikh's empty bed.

'Perhaps her professional commitments didn't allow it,' Emily reasoned, unable to feel the least bit flattered by the idea of being *taken* as a temporary replacement. Totally repulsed by it, in fact.

'This could be so,' Heba agreed. 'The sheikh will be travelling through Africa for some months. Veronique may join him somewhere else on his tour of the Al Farrahn hotels.'

The Salamander Inn was obviously one of many such places, Emily thought, more proof of fabulous family wealth. Not that she needed it. What she did need was to plant her feet firmly on the ground and find a way to walk out of the hothouse atmosphere of this palace and get back to normal life, no matter how difficult her normal life could be at times. At least it was real, she told herself, and she knew how to deal with it, more or less.

'Am I allowed to leave?' she asked Heba. 'I need to get to Stone Town.'

'You must wait for a summons from His Excellency,' came the firm reply.

There was no budging the women from that position and without inside help, any chance of just walking out of the palace was zero. The only way down to the ground floor was by the balconies overlooking the central atrium and security guards were posted at the foot of each staircase. It was impossible, wearing her own clothes, to get past them without being seen and apprehended.

No doubt about it.

She was stuck in this gilded prison until Sheikh Zageo etc etc decided to release her from it.

As the morning wore on, Emily felt more and more on edge about being kept here at his leisure. What was happening? Why couldn't he make up his mind about her innocence in regard to Jacques's activities? When the summons finally came, she was bursting with impatience to be led to the man who ruled her current fate, her mind fizzing with persuasive arguments to win her freedom.

It wasn't acceptable to be either his prisoner or his guest. Now that she knew about his relationship with Veronique, any further offer of hospitality from him would have to be viewed as highly dubious. Besides, it was better all around to put this whole stressful episode behind her as fast as possible.

She did not expect to be escorted right out of the palace, transported to the harbour she had swum out of last night, and ferried to another boat!

Jacques's yacht was gone.

This was a sleek and very expensive looking motor cruiser.

Emily did not want to get out of the small outboard motorboat and climb up the ladder to the deck of a cruiser that was capable of whisking her right away from Zanzibar. Rebellion surged through her veins. She looked at the water. Was swimming away an option this time?

'It would be wasted effort, Emily,' came the sardonic remark from above.

Her stomach contracted at the sound of that voice. Her heart fluttered in a panicky fashion. All the prepared arguments in her mind started crumbling as they were hit by a sudden sense of futility. She knew with instinctive certainty that until this sheikh willed an end to the *hospitality* he was extending to her, there would be no end.

All the same, her natural independence would not roll over into abject submission. Her chin tilted defiantly as her gaze lifted to his. 'Why am I here?' she demanded. 'I thought you were going to have me checked out.'

'Unfortunately the weekend is not a good time for reaching sources of information.'

'When will be a good time?' she challenged, though mentally conceding that what he said was probably true.

He shrugged. ‘Perhaps Monday.’

Monday. Two more days of living under a cloud and forced to endure the sheikh’s company whenever he commanded it.

‘Be my guest, come onboard,’ he urged.

They were orders, not invitations. Emily heaved a fretful sigh as she rose to her feet and stepped up to the ladder. ‘Some guest,’ she darkly muttered. ‘A considerate host would care about where I want to be and it’s not on another boat.’

‘But this is a pleasure boat which is fully crewed. No work at all for you,’ he assured her in the silky tone that made her skin prickle with an acute sense of danger lurking.

‘It’s still on the water,’ she grumbled.

‘What a strange complaint from someone who is supposed to be a professional dive specialist!’

‘Diving is something else,’ she insisted.

‘We shall see.’

There was something ominous in those words but Emily was hopelessly distracted from pursuing that thought. He offered his hand to help steady her as she stepped down onto the deck and it was so startling to find him very informally clothed, wearing only a white T-shirt and casual shorts, she accepted it, and the strong fingers suddenly encompassing hers gave her a further jolt of physical awareness.

She tried not to look down at his bare legs, specifically his thighs, a glimpse of which had felt far too erotic for comfort. On a powerful male scale, they added immeasurably to his sex appeal, as did his taut cheeky butt when he turned to give instructions to a crew member.

In an instinctive need to get a grip on herself, Emily wriggled her hand out of his grasp and folded her arms across her rib cage. Then she ended up flushing horribly when he swung back to her and observed that her block-out body language had inadvertently pushed up her breasts.

'Relax, Emily,' he advised with a quirky little smile and wickedly challenging eyes. 'We're simply going for a ride to Pemba Island where the water is crystal clear and the coral reef provides superb diving.'

'How far away is it?' she asked sharply.

'Not far. People travel to it by ferry from Zanzibar.'

Ferry! Well, if she got marooned there, Emily reasoned, at least there was some form of public transport to get her back to Stone Town.

'Come.' He urged her towards the door leading to the cabin. 'We will sit in the saloon for the crossing.'

The saloon on this boat was a far cry from the cramped cabin on Jaques's yacht. Not only did it contain an elegant dining table that could seat ten people, the lounging area was also sumptuous; cream leather couches running along underneath the windows, plus a cosier conversational area with a grouping of chairs and sofas around a low table to allow the serving of light refreshments.

Emily chose to sit by the windows, her arm resting along the padded backrest of the couch as she looked out at the harbour Jacques had sailed into last night. She felt the vibration of the cruiser's big engines being revved up and knew they were about to power this motorboat out to sea.

Her *host* moved past her, seating himself on the same couch about a metre away but turned towards her, his arm hooking over the backrest, his hand dangling within easy reach of hers. Although she was acutely aware of his close presence, Emily resolutely ignored it, watching the mangrove swamp being left behind as the boat carved through the water towards the exit from the harbour.

'Do not be disturbed. We shall return,' Zageo assured her, apparently not insensitive to her inner tension.

'Why are you taking me with you to Pemba

Island?' she asked, still not looking at him, afraid of revealing just how vulnerable he made her feel.

'The reefs around it are largely in a pristine condition, unspoilt coral gardens supporting a vast array of marine life,' he informed her. 'As a professional diver yourself, you may well have heard that this area is an underwater naturalist's dream.'

'No. I hadn't heard.'

'I am surprised,' he drawled. 'Pemba is now listed as one of the top dive spots in the world.'

The taunt over her ignorance of this fact goaded Emily into locking eyes with him. 'I didn't come to Zanzibar for diving,' she stated belligerently, resenting his forceful interruption of her personal mission. 'Why don't you just let me go to get about my own business?'

'What is there for you to do?' he retorted reasonably. 'Your sister has not yet checked in at The Salamander Inn. I have instructed the management there to notify me the moment Hannah Coleman arrives and identifies herself. In the meantime, what better way for you to spend today than taking up a superb diving opportunity?'

His logic was difficult to fault, yet undermining it was the undeniable fact she had been given no choice. 'You don't believe me, do you? You still think I'm a drug-running belly-dancer. And this—' she waved an arm at her luxurious surroundings '—is just another gilded prison.'

The hand lying close to hers on the backrest of the couch moved in a lazy dismissive gesture. 'I believe that most things reveal themselves, given enough time, Emily.' His eyes glinted a very direct challenge. 'If you are a professional diver, for example, I should have no doubt whatsoever about it after our visit to Pemba.'

'You want me to prove myself to you?'

His smile was slow in forming and caused her pulse to quicken. 'Perhaps I simply want to share a pleasure with you,' he suggested seductively, stirring a whole hornets's nest of hormones that buzzed their insistent message that he wanted more than an *underwater* pleasure with her.

Emily jumped to her feet, too agitated to remain seated beside him. 'Why are you doing this?' Her hands flapped in wild incomprehension of his motivation as she directly confronted him. 'I'm nobody to you. Just a passing blip on your radar screen. Totally insignificant. Why put your personal time into…?'

He surged to his feet, seeming to tower over her, causing her throat to close up, cutting off her ability to communicate by speech. He took her waving hands and planted them palm flat against his chest, holding them still with his, forcing them to feel the heat of his body through the thin cotton of his T-shirt, feel the strong beat of his heart, feel the rise and fall of his breathing, which all made her feel a terribly, terribly intimate connection with this man.

'An accident of fate?' he finished for her, though it wasn't what she'd meant to say.

Emily couldn't remember what she'd meant to say. She found herself staring at his mouth as it shaped more words—soft, silky words that slid into her ears and infiltrated her mind, somehow deactivating her own thought processes.

'Sometimes things happen for a reason—a time, a place, a meeting which no one can foresee—and it is a huge mistake to deny it any significance. It may not be random factors driving the seemingly accidental collision, but forces of nature which we would do well to ride, Emily, because they were meant to be…meant to gain a result that would not be achieved otherwise.'

What result?

How could anything significant come from this…this mad attraction?

He slid her hands up to his shoulders and

even though he released them, did she pluck them away from the tensile strength of the muscles supporting the breadth of those extremely masculine shoulders? No, she didn't! Her hands were stuck in self-indulgent mode, wanting to feel what he'd silently commanded her to feel.

And the mouth she was staring at was coming closer, still shaping words but she no longer heard them. Her heart was thundering in her ears. A wild wantonness gripped her mind and rippled through her entire body, urging an eagerness to experience whatever was about to come her way.

His lips brushed hers, the softest possible contact yet it started an electric tingling that begged for a continuation of the exciting sensation. Emily didn't move away from it. She closed her eyes and concentrated on her response to what was barely a kiss, yet it was sparking some volatile chemistry which was surprising, stunning, mesmerising.

Another brushing.

A slow glide of the tip of his tongue, sensually persuasive in parting her lips, caressing the soft inner tissues.

She felt him move, stepping closer to her, hands sliding around her waist, arms drawing her into a full body contact embrace. One part of her mind warned that she shouldn't be allowing this, but the clamouring need to feel and know the full extent of her response to him overrode any niggling sense of caution.

All her nerve ends seemed to be humming in vibrant anticipation of more and more stimulation. To deny the desire he stirred was impossible and she couldn't find a strong enough reason to fight it. The sheer, dizzying maleness of him called to her female instincts to revel in his strength, exult in his desire for her, savour the potency of the sexual chemistry that obliterated the differences between them—the differences that should keep them apart.

His mouth took possession of hers, no longer seductively intent, but ruthlessly confident of kissing her in whatever way he willed, smashing any inhibitions Emily might have, arousing mind-blowing excitement, inciting highly erotic passion that shot quivers of need through her entire body—a thrilling need, an aching need, a rampant all-consuming need.

She felt his fingers entangling themselves in her hair, tugging her head in whatever direction his mouth wanted to take in kissing her, felt his other hand tracing the curve of her back, reaching the pit of it, applying the pressure to mould the softness of her stomach around the hard thrust of his erection.

His sexual domination of her was so strong, Emily barely registered that she was perilously close to letting the situation reach a point of no return. She forced her mind out of its whirl of sensation long enough to consider what the outcome might be from having sex with this man.

She didn't know.

Couldn't even begin to guess.

And the sense of losing all control of her life was suddenly very frightening.

CHAPTER SEVEN

ZAGEO was so acutely attuned to the flow of mutual sexual desire between them, he instantly felt the sudden jolt of resistance that spelled imminent change. Emily's pliant body started to stiffen, muscles tightening up, shrinking from contact with him. She jerked her head back from his, shock on her face, panic in her eyes. Fight would come next, he realised, if he didn't act to soothe the fear and calm her agitation.

'Enough?' he asked, forcing his mouth into a whimsical little smile, even as his gut twisted painfully at the necessity to reclaim control of the extremely basic need she'd ignited in him.

Her lovely long throat moved convulsively

as she struggled to get her thoughts in order and make a sensible reply. The vivid blue circles of her irises were diminished by huge black pupils, yet to return to normal size. She licked her lips, as though desperate to wipe the taste of his from them. But there could be no denial of her complicity in what they'd just shared. He had given her time enough to reject a kiss. She had not rejected it. Nor any other move he'd made on her up until now.

'This is not a good idea!' she pushed out emphatically, then scooped in a deep breath to deliver more oxygen to a brain which was probably feeling even more heated than his.

'On the contrary, the most beneficial existence comes from having one's mind in harmony with one's body. Mentally fighting what comes naturally is the bad idea, Emily,' he asserted.

'Right!' Another deep breath as she collected her wits, belatedly plucking her hands off his shoulders and spreading out her palms in an appeal for understanding. 'Well, just so you know, Zageo, my mind was off in la-la land and my body took a turn all on its own, which doesn't come under the heading of *harmony*!'

'And if your mind had not been in la-la land, what might it have thought?' he swiftly challenged, needing an insight into what drove her behaviour.

She eased her lower body back from his and he dropped his hands from her waist, letting her move to whatever she considered a *safe* distance.

'I'm sure you're well aware of being attractive to the opposite sex,' came the quick chiding, her eyes already deriding any protest on that score.

'You are not without attractions yourself,' he pointed out.

A tide of hot embarrassment swept up her throat and into her cheeks. 'Sometimes it's definitely better to ignore all that stuff because it's a distraction from really important things,' she argued. 'Getting personally involved with you…'

'May well be the best way of resolving the important things you speak about,' he suggested.

'No-o-o…' She shook her head vehemently as her feet backed further away. 'That's not how I conduct my life. I don't go in for using people.'

'There is nothing wrong with fair trading. If each person gives and receives something equitable…if mutual pleasure is reached…'

'I don't believe in poaching on other people's territory!' she hurled at him, fiercely defensive, her eyes flaring an accusation of unfair play.

Zageo frowned, puzzled by the offence she clearly felt. 'You gave me to understand that no man had any current claim on you,' he reminded her. 'Naturally I would have respected…'

Anger erupted. 'What about respecting the relationship you have with Veronique?'

Enlightenment dawned.

Gossip in the women's quarters.

Emily forgot about retreating further and took a belligerent stance, hands planted on her hips as she delivered a blast of scorn. 'Just because she couldn't come with you doesn't give you the right to play fast and loose with any woman who crosses your path.'

'Veronique is in Paris because being there is more attractive to her than being with me,' he drily informed. 'Our relationship has come to an end. So I am completely free, Emily, to be with any woman I choose.'

He could see her mentally floundering over the news that he had no moral obligation to Veronique. Having a strong defensive line demolished at one stroke was not easy to absorb. He wondered if her sense of morality was as sharp as she'd just indicated or had she snatched at Veronique as an excuse to evade the truth of her own desire for him?

But why did she *wish* to evade it?

'*You* choose,' she repeated, picking up the words with the air of grabbing new weapons for a further fight between them. She flung her hands up in the air. 'All the choice is yours. *I'm* not getting any choice in what's going on here. You have me kept in the women's quarters of your family palace, brought out to this boat…'

'I did not imagine your willingness to be in my embrace, Emily,' he cut in with unshakeable authority. 'As to the rest, is it not better to be under my personal protection than to be locked up in a public prison while the local authorities sort out the situation that has evolved from *your* choices?'

'At least it would have been in the process of being sorted,' she threw at him, apparently undeterred by the prospect of being forced into the company of more criminals.

'Believe me, Emily, it is best left to me to do the sorting as I have a personal interest in getting answers. However, since a choice means so much to you, I offer you one. You can come with me to Pemba Island and demonstrate how proficient you are at diving or I can instruct the captain of this vessel to take us directly to Stone Town where you can be taken into custody by local officials and rot in jail while *they* get around to checking your story in their own good time, dependent on how much paperwork is already on their desks.'

'You could just let me go,' she pressed, her whole body taut with exasperation at the limitations he was imposing on her.

'That is not an option,' Zageo answered, ruthlessly intent on keeping her with him.

'Why not?'

'I would not be doing my civic duty to release a potentially dangerous drug-runner into the community.'

'But you don't mind kissing a potentially dangerous drug-runner,' she mocked.

'It was not doing any public harm and I was prepared to take the personal risk,' he mocked straight back.

'You're not risking anything.'

'Do not speak for me, Emily. Speak for yourself. Make your choice. Do you wish me to call the captain and change our destination or do you wish to dive with me at Pemba Island? I might add that your professional referees are out of contact so there is no quick way of checking your story today. That has already been tried.'

Her long lashes dropped but not before he glimpsed a look of helpless confusion in her eyes. She heaved a long ragged sigh. 'Okay,' she finally said in a tone of reluctant resignation. 'I'll need a wetsuit. And I'll want to check the diving equipment.'

'There is a Diving Centre at Fundu Lagoon where we will drop anchor. I have directed that a diving specialist be on hand to outfit us correctly and guide us to the best viewing places around the reef.'

She nodded distractedly, her gaze flitting around the saloon and fastening on the staircase. 'Does that lead down to a…a powder room?'

'To the staterooms, each of which has an ensuite bathroom.' Aware that she was emitting frantic vibrations in a pressing need to escape him, he waved her off on her own. 'Just go down and open the first door you come to, Emily.'

'Thank you.'

She shot him a look of almost anguished relief which Zageo pondered as she hurried to the staircase and disappeared below deck.

Was it a desperate call of nature that had to be answered or a desperate need to get away by herself to reassess her position?

Zageo had to concede feeling a considerable amount of confusion himself. He'd kissed and been kissed by many women in his time. None had ever transmitted the sense of being inexperienced, innocent, virginal. It had been strangely fascinating to feel Emily Ross focusing an intense awareness on the touch and taste of his mouth, as though she'd never been kissed before, or it had been so long since she'd had the experience, she'd forgotten what it was like.

Needing to clear his own head of that tantalising impression, Zageo left the saloon and moved out to the rear deck where he could feel the sea breeze in his hair and the light spray from the boat's wake on his face. It was good to cool off. He hadn't anticipated the swift fuelling of his own desire for her. Giving in to temptation often proved a disappointment—the experience not living up to the promise. But Emily Ross…the way she'd responded…it had been *without any artfulness*!

Unless she was an unbelievably good actress, so steeped in deception it came naturally to her, Zageo could not see her fitting the frame of a belly-dancer with patrons on the side. It was far more likely that she had only known one lover—a young husband who had not been well skilled in the erotic arts. How else could those quite electric moments of stillness from her be explained? Stillness followed by a flood of chaotic excitement. It was definitely not a *knowing* response to him, more instinctive, primal, and so strong it frightened her.

It made her even more attractive.

More desirable.

Zageo decided he would pursue a relationship with her, regardless of whether it was an appropriate move for him or not. It had been a long time since he felt so vibrantly *alive* with a woman.

CHAPTER EIGHT

EMILY clasped her cheeks, willing the heat in them to recede. She'd splashed cold water on her face over and over again, but still it burned, her blood temperature at an all-time high from a chaotic mix of anger and fear.

She was furious with herself for succumbing to the stupid urge to discover what it might be like to be kissed by such a total foreigner, who just happened to be powerfully charged with sex appeal. Now he'd think she *was* a belly-dancing bedhopper. Besides which, it hadn't just been a kiss!

That man had to have the most wickedly exciting tongue in the world, not to mention knowing how to incite such a flood of passionate need, her breasts were still aching from it, her thighs felt like jelly, and the moist heat still lingering at their apex demonstrated an appalling carnal desire for a more intimate connection with him. She'd never felt like this with Brian!

And that thought made her feel even more uncomfortable. Disloyal. Brian had been her mate in every sense. She'd loved him. There'd never been anyone else. She'd never wanted anyone else. The sex they'd had together had seemed natural, good, answering their emotional needs at the time. It felt wrong to look back now and think it hadn't really been a potent force between them, not a nerve-shaking, mind-bending, stomach-twisting, overwhelmingly dominant force!

Though exploring these feelings further with a man who was forcibly holding her *under his protection* went totally against her grain. It was all very well for him to claim he was saving her from a nasty situation by not handing her over to local authorities. She still had no real freedom of movement. No free choices, either. And knowing herself innocent of any wrong-doing, she hated being a victim of circumstances.

It wasn't fair.

Being hugely attracted to a man who was so completely outside her possible relationship zone wasn't fair, either.

So what was she to do now?

Emily doused her face in cold water once again, wiped it dry, took several deep breaths, rolled her shoulders, then concentrated her mind on making a plan.

Until more checks into her background yielded the information which would be consistent with her account of herself, she might as well resign herself to being Zageo's *guest*, so why not pretend to be one? A guest would be sociable. A guest would show pleasurable anticipation in the exploration of the pristine coral reef around Pemba Island. More importantly, a guest's wishes should be taken into consideration and she could certainly challenge Zageo on that point.

Emily mentally girded her *guest* loins and set off to not only face the devil and the deep blue sea, but smile at both of them!

Amazingly, once she had accepted the idea of being taken on a delightful adventure, she really did enjoy herself. Fundu Lagoon looked like a great holiday retreat with its beach lodge and bungalows built from mangrove poles and palm thatch, giving the place a sense of fitting perfectly into the beautiful island environment, while still providing every modern convenience and equipment for all watersports.

The reefs around the island were fantastic; great, plunging walls of coral with all the colourful Indian Ocean marine life swimming and hunting in the wondrous playground. Distractions were plentiful, making Emily less conscious of how Zageo looked in a sleek black wetsuit and less sensitive about how she herself looked in the second-skin garment.

The sexual tension which she'd found so

difficult to set aside while still on the boat, dissipated while they were underwater, sharing the pleasure of what they found and watched. It also helped that she had plenty to chat about after the dive, recalling what they'd seen, comparing it to experiences in other places.

They lunched at the beach lodge, sitting on a balcony overlooking the turquoise waters of the bay, hungrily demolishing servings of superb grilled fish, several different tasty salads and a platter of freshly sliced fruit. Emily was thinking that now was the perfect time for a siesta when Zageo spoke, shattering any sense of safety her *guest* role had given her.

'We could retire to one of the bungalows.'

'What?' Her whole body jerked in shock at the suggestion which immediately conjured up images of sex in the afternoon.

'You looked sleepy,' he observed, watching her through his own lazily lowered lashes.

'Just feeling replete after such a lovely

meal,' she quickly trotted out. 'Are we going to dive again this afternoon?'

'Do you want to?'

'I guess the question is…are you satisfied?'

He cocked one eyebrow as though considering which area of satisfaction she was referring to, and the sensual little curl of his lips was very suggestive of much more satisfaction being desired on many levels.

Emily's heart skipped a beat then rushed into beating so fast she suffered a dizzying rush of blood to the head. Words spilled into erratic speech. 'I meant your test. About me being a professional diver. You wanted to know if it was true. That's why we came here, wasn't it? For me to prove I wasn't lying?'

'It was one of the reasons.' The glimmer in his eyes suggested others were of more interest to him. 'I no longer have any doubt that you are comfortable with being underwater. But as to satisfaction…'

He *was* talking sex. She could hear it in the

sensual purr of his voice, feel it in the prickling wash of it over her skin. Her stomach contracted with anxiety. It was difficult to fight her own ambivalent feelings. With Zageo feeding the tempting desire to simply give in and tangle intimately with him, she could barely remember why it would be stupid to do it.

Hannah…

Real life…

Shedding complications and getting directly to where she should be…

'Stone Town,' she said emphatically, cutting off whatever else Zageo might have put to her because all her instincts were quivering with the very real possibility of her becoming enmeshed in something she might never escape from. She pasted a brightly appealing smile on her face. 'Could we go to Stone Town now?'

He viewed her quizzically. 'You sister is not there, Emily.'

'You just spoke of satisfaction, Zageo,' she

picked up pointedly. 'I've been aiming to get to Stone Town ever since I stepped foot on Jacques Arnault's yacht. That trip carried a load of unexpected stress and last night's swim and trek through the mangrove swamp wasn't a picnic, either. Now here I am, close to where I started out to be, and feeling really frustrated that you're holding me back from it.'

She heaved a feeling sigh and poured what she hoped was an eloquent plea into her eyes. 'If I could just have the satisfaction of going to The Salamander Inn myself…'

His mouth quirked into a sardonic smile. 'You don't believe me, Emily?'

'No more than you believe me, Zageo,' she shot back at him.

He shrugged, his dark eyes dancing with amusement. 'What reason would I have to lie?'

'I think you find me a novelty and since you have the power to play with me, that's what you're doing,' she stated unequivocally.

'A novelty...' He mused over the word, nodding as he spoke his thoughts. 'Something new...or is it something as old as time? Certainly you are not like other women I've known. Which I find intriguing. But *playing* with you...'

His eyes narrowed to glittering slits as though harnessing their penetrating power into intensely probing beams. Emily felt as though she was pinned inside his mental force-field and her heart was under attack. She couldn't think, couldn't move. She had to wait for him to release her from this eerily hypnotic connection.

'This is not a game, Emily,' he said quietly. 'It is a journey where the signposts are not clear, where the turnings are yet to be decided, where the destination is still obscure, yet...I will take it. And you will take it with me.'

Emily was swamped with a sense of inevitability. Her mind thumped with the certainty that whatever he willed was going to happen. She fought to assert her own individuality, to gain at least one foothold on the life she'd had before meeting *him*.

'Well, one signpost is very clear to me and that's Stone Town,' she insisted wildly. 'So why don't we go there right now before our journey takes us somewhere else?'

He laughed, tipping his head back in sheer uninhibited joy in the moment, making her pulse dance in a weird mixture of relief in the normality of laughter and a bubbling happiness at his pleasure in her.

'Are you sure you would not prefer to idle some time away in one of these bungalows first?' he teased, his eyes flirting with the promise of more physical pleasures. 'Indulge ourselves with some rest and relaxation under the cooling whirl of a fan…'

'With the air-conditioning in the saloon, we'll be cooler on the boat,' she quickly argued.

One black eyebrow arched wickedly. 'You do not wish to enjoy some heat?'

'It will still be hot in Zanzibar when we return there.'

'Why choose one satisfaction over another when you could have both?'

'It's as you said, Zageo. I don't have a clear signpost on anything but Stone Town.'

'Then we shall get Stone Town out of the way so we can progress beyond it.'

He rose purposefully to his feet and rounded the table to hold back her chair as she stood up, ready to leave. The zing of triumph at having won this concession from him was short-lived. He took firm possession of her hand for the walk through the beach lodge to the wharf which led back to the boat, and when she wriggled her fingers in a bid for freedom, his interlocked with hers, strengthening the hold.

Still a captive to his will, Emily thought, though he had ceded to her wishes on the destination issue. It was probably an indulgence he could well afford, letting her see the meeting place nominated by her sister. An unimportant sidetrack. The journey he wanted them to take revolved around physical contact and the insidiously distracting heat his hand generated was already beginning to erode her sense of purpose.

What was she going to achieve in Stone Town?

'How old were you when you met Brian, Emily?' Zageo asked as they reached the wharf and began the long stroll to the end of it where an outboard motorboat was waiting to transport them back to the cruiser.

Her mind gratefully seized on the reference to the man who had been the love of her life, hauling out the memory of their first meeting and blowing it up to blot out her current confusion. 'I was fourteen. His parents had just moved up to Cairns from the central coast of New South Wales and he came to my school that year.'

'School? How old was *he*?'

She smiled at the surprise in Zageo's voice.

'Sixteen. Tall and blond and very hunky. All the girls instantly developed crushes on him.'

'Did he play the field before choosing you?'

'No. Brian played it very cool, not linking up with anyone, just chatting around, but every so often I'd catch him watching me and I knew I was the one he liked.'

'The one he *wanted*,' came the sardonic correction.

Emily bridled at Zageo's personal slant on something he knew absolutely nothing about. 'It wasn't just the sex thing,' she flashed at him resentfully. 'Brian *liked* lots of things about me.'

'What's not to like?'

The slightly derisive retort was accompanied by a long sideways head to foot appraisal that shot Emily's temperature sky-high.

'I'm talking about the person I am inside,' she declared fiercely. 'Brian took the time to get to know me. He didn't take one look and decide what I was, as you've done!'

The accusation raised one mocking black eyebrow. 'On the contrary, despite what I'd call damning circumstances, I have continued to look at you, Emily, many times. And I am still gathering evidence as to your character.'

'But you don't care about it. You don't really care,' she hotly countered. 'You would have taken me to bed in one of those bungalows back there if I'd said yes.'

'You are not sixteen anymore, and sexual attraction does not wait upon niceties.'

'But I do have a choice over whether to give into it or not.'

The look he gave her ruthlessly blasted any hope she might be nursing about holding out on that score. Emily shrivelled inside herself, wishing she hadn't challenged him on it since they were on their way back to where a number of staterooms were readily available for intimate privacy. Not that he would stoop to raping her. He would disdain using force with a woman. But if he somehow trapped her into another kiss…

Extremely conscious of her vulnerability to his sexual magnetism, Emily kept her mouth firmly shut and her gaze averted from his as they rode in the outboard motorboat the island wharf to the air-conditioned cruiser. Zageo also remained silent but it was not a restful silence. The sense of purposeful power emanating from him had her nerves jangling and her mind skittering along wildly defensive lines.

At least he had agreed to take her to Stone Town.

Maybe Hannah would arrive any minute now.

Some action was needed to save her from this man and the sooner it came, the better.

CHAPTER NINE

ZAGEO maintained his darkly brooding silence until after they were served coffee in the saloon. Anxious to separate herself from any physical connection to the man who was now dominating her consciousness, Emily had seated herself in an armchair on one side of the low coffee table, but he sat opposite her, granting the relief of distance although there was no relief from the direct focus of his attention.

She listened to the powerful motors taking them back to Zanzibar, mentally urging them to make the trip as fast as possible. She was so wound up in willing the cruiser to speed them over the water, it came as a jolt when Zageo spoke.

'So...tell me the history of your relationship with the man you married,' he tersely invited.

The edge to his voice sounded suspiciously like jealousy, though Emily reasoned he simply didn't like coming off poorly in any comparison. Regardless of his motivation for seeking more knowledge of Brian, she was only too eager to fill this dangerous time talking about her one and only love, recalling shared experiences which had nothing to do with *sex*.

Words tumbled out, describing how from being school sweethearts, she'd followed Brian into a career in the tourist industry which was a huge part of the economy in far north Queensland. They'd worked on dive boats, been proficient in all water sports, crewed on cruise ships that worked the coastline around the top end of Australia, sailed yachts from one place to another for the convenience of owners to walk onto at any given time.

'When did you marry?' Zageo asked somewhat critically, as though the timing of the wedding had some relevance to him.

'When I was twenty-one and Brian twenty-three.'

'A very young man,' he muttered deprecatingly.

'It was right for us!' she insisted.

'Marriage is about acquiring and sharing property, having children. What do you have to show for the five years you had together?'

'Marriage is also about commitment to each other. We had a life of adventure…'

'And that's what you're left with? Adventure? Falling into the company of a man like Jacques Arnault?' Zageo remarked contemptuously. 'Your husband made no provision for your future, no—'

'He didn't know he was going to die!' she cut in, hating the criticism. 'The plan was to wait until we were in our thirties before starting a family. After we'd been everywhere we wanted to go.'

'Did it occur to you there is always another horizon?'

'What do you mean?'

He shrugged. 'Your Brian acted like a grown-up boy, still playing boys' games with the convenience of a committed companion. What if it was not in his psyche to ever settle down and provide a family home?'

'It's people who make a family, not a place,' she argued.

'You would have dragged your children around the world with him?'

'Why not? Experiencing the world is not a bad thing.'

'You have no attachment to your home country? Your home city?'

'Of course I do. It's always good to go back there. It's where my parents live. But Brian was my partner and wherever he went, I would have gone with him.'

Her vehemence on that point apparently gave Zageo pause for some reconsideration.

His eyes narrowed and when he eventually made comment, it was laced with cynicism.

'Such devotion is remarkable. From my own experience of women in western society, I gathered that the old biblical attitude of—*whither thou goest, there goest I*—was no longer in play.'

'Then I'd say your experience was askew. I think it's still the natural thing for most women to go with the man they love. Certainly my sister did. When she married Malcolm, there was no question about her going to live with him on his farm in Zimbabwe. She just went.'

'Where exactly in Zimbabwe is this farm?'

'On what's called The High Veld,' Emily answered quickly, relieved to be moving onto a less sensitive subject. 'Malcolm is the third generation working this family owned land and although so much has changed in Zimbabwe he wants to hang onto it.'

Zageo shook his head. 'I doubt he will be able to. The process of reclaiming their country from foreign settlement is a priority with that government.'

Emily heaved a fretful sigh. 'Hannah is worried about the future. Especially for the children.'

'The two daughters.'

'Yes. Jenny is getting to school age and the local school has been closed down. Sally is only three.'

'Will both these young children be accompanying your sister to Zanzibar?'

Emily nodded. 'That was the plan.'

'How was this plan communicated to you?'

'Through a contact address I'd set up on the Internet.' The cloud of confusion that had made any clear path of action impossible suddenly lifted. 'That's what I have to do in Stone Town! Find an Internet Café!'

Zageo frowned at her. 'If you had told me this last night, Emily, there are Internet facilities at the palace. All you had to do—'

'I didn't think of it,' she cut in, throwing her hands out in helpless appeal. 'It was quite a shock being hauled into a place that conjured up thoughts of fairytale Arabian Nights, not to mention being confronted and cross-examined by a…a sheikh.'

A tide of heat rushed up her neck, telegraphing her acute embarrassment at being so fixated on him she couldn't even think sensibly, let alone logically. Horribly conscious of the scarlet flags burning in her cheeks, she swivelled in her chair to look out the saloon windows, ostensibly intent on watching their approach to Stone Town. The public harbour was coming into view and her whole body twitched with eagerness to get off the boat.

'Excuse me while I arrange for a car to meet us at the dock,' Zageo said.

'A car?' The pained protest burst from her lips and her gaze swung back to his, pleading for more freedom of movement. 'Couldn't we walk through the town to the inn? I've heard that the markets here are amazing. Besides, unless you know where an Internet café is…'

'There is no need to find a café. I offer you the Internet facilities at The Salamander Inn. We can go directly there so you can check for some communication from your sister.' He paused to underline the point before adding, 'Is it not your top priority?'

'Oh! Right! Thank you,' she rattled out, knowing she was cornered again and telling herself there was no point in fighting his arrangements.

Nevertheless, having to get into the black Mercedes which was waiting for them at the dock made her feel even more like a prisoner, trapped in an enclosed space with her captor and being forcibly taken to the place of his choice. Never mind that she did want to check out The Salamander Inn and she did want to get onto the Internet, doing both of them under Zageo's watchful eyes automatically held constraints she didn't like.

Common sense argued to simply accept being *his guest*—just sit back and enjoy being driven around in a luxury car. Except *he* was sitting beside her, dominating her every thought and feeling, making her intensely aware that he was sharing this journey and was intent on sharing a much longer and more intimate one with her. Apparently she had no choice about that, either.

Emily's nerves were so twitchy about the overwhelming nature of his current presence in her life, she evaded even glancing his way, staring fixedly out the tinted side-window, forcing her brain to register the images she saw in a desperate bid to wipe out the tormenting image of Sheikh Zageo bin Sultan Al Farrahn.

The problem was in its being far too attractive for any peace of mind; ridiculously attractive because he no more belonged in her world than she did in his; dangerously attractive because just the mental image of him was powerful enough to make her forget things she should be remembering.

'Pyramids,' she muttered, focusing fiercely

on the market stalls lining both sides of the street on which they were travelling.

'I beg your pardon?'

She heaved a sigh at having broken a silence that probably should have been kept if she was to succeed in keeping Zageo at a distance. 'The stall keepers have stacked their fruit and vegetables into pyramids. I've never seen that before. I guess it must be some Egyptian influence. The people here seem to be such a melting pot of races,' she babbled, not looking at him, keeping her attention fastened *outside* the car. 'So far I've seen a Hindu temple, a mosque minaret and a Christian church spire, all in the space of a few hundred metres.'

'Egyptians, Phoenicians, Persians, Indians, even Chinese visited Zanzibar and settled here, along with the East Africans and traders from South Arabia,' Zageo informed her in a perfectly relaxed manner. 'Then, of course, the Portuguese took control of the island for two centuries. They've all left their influence on the native life and culture, including religion.'

Emily's mind seized on the Portuguese bit. She had thought Zageo looked Spanish but maybe his bloodline came from a neighbouring Latin country. 'Are you part Portuguese?' she asked, curiosity trapping her into looking directly at him.

He smiled, blitzing at least half her mind into registering that and nothing else, making her heart flip into a faster beat, causing her stomach to contract as though she had received a body-blow.

'My great-grandfather on my mother's side was Portuguese,' he finally replied, having done maximum damage with his smile. 'My great-grandmother was half-Indian, half-British. It makes for an interesting mix of races, does it not?'

'Your father is an Arab?' The half of her mind that was still working insisted that a sheikh couldn't get to be a sheikh without having a father who was pure Arab.

He nodded. 'Mostly. His grandmother was French. We are a very international family.'

'A very *wealthy* international family,' Emily said, deciding sheikhdom probably had more to do with who owned the oil wells.

He shrugged. 'Wealth that has benefited our people. And we keep investing to consolidate the wealth we have, ensuring that the future will have no backward steps. There is nothing wrong with wealth, Emily.'

'I didn't say there was. It just happens to form a huge gap between your circumstances and mine. And while you take all this for granted—' she waved wildly at their uniformed chauffeur and the plush interior of the Mercedes '—I hate not being able to pay my own way.' A passionate need for independence from him fired up other resentments. 'I hate not having my own money, my own credit card, my own…'

'Freedom to do whatever you want?'

'Yes!'

'Then why not feel free to be with me,

Emily? It *is* what you want,' he claimed in that insidiously silky voice that slid straight under her skin and made all her nerve ends tingle.

His eyes mocked any attempt at denial. She struggled to come up with one that sounded sensible enough to refute his certainty. 'What we want is not always right for us, Zageo. Even you, with all the freedom your wealth gives you, must have been hit with that truth somewhere down the line.'

'Ah, but not at least to try it…to satisfy the wanting…how is one to make an informed judgment without embracing the experience?'

'I don't have to put my hand in a fire to know it will get burnt,' she slung at him and tore her gaze from the sizzling desire in his.

'You prefer to stay cold than hold out your hand to it, Emily? What of the warmth it promises? The sense of physical well-being, the pleasure…'

Her stomach contracted at the thought of

the sexual pleasure he might give her. Panicked by how much she did want to try it, Emily seized the first distraction her gaze hit as the Mercedes started through a narrow alley.

'The doors…' Even on these poorer houses in the old part of Stone Town, they were elaborately carved and studded with very nasty looking iron or brass protrusions. 'Why are they made to look so intimidating?'

'The studs were designed to stop elephants from barging inside.'

'Elephants!' Emily was startled into looking incredulously at him. 'Are you telling me there are elephants rampaging around Zanzibar, even in the town?'

'No.' He grinned at having drawn her interest again. 'There have never been elephants on Zanzibar. The doors were originally made by Indian craftsmen who brought the design from their home country centuries ago. The style of them apparently appealed and has endured to the present day.'

She frowned, not liking them despite their elaborate craftsmanship. 'They give the sense of a heavily guarded fortress.'

'Very popular with tourists,' he drily informed her. 'They form one of Zanzibar's main exports.'

'What about spice? Isn't this island famous for its spice trade?'

'Unfortunately Zanzibar no longer has the monopoly on growing and selling cloves. Indonesia, Brazil, even China are now major producers. The island still has its plantations, of course, but they are not the economic force they once were.'

'That's rather sad, losing what made it unique,' Emily commented.

'The golden years of Zanzibar were not only based on the trade in cloves, but also in ivory and slaves, neither of which you would wish to revive,' he said, his eyes boring intently into hers. 'The past is the past, Emily. One has to move on.'

The words thudded into her heart—words

she had recited to herself many times since being widowed. Zageo was making a pointedly personal message of them. But any journey with him would have to reach a dead end, forcing her *to move on* again. On the other hand, she certainly didn't regret her marriage. She might not regret a sexual dalliance with this sheikh, either.

She stared down at her hands which were tightly clasped in her lap, the fingers of her right hand automatically dragging at the ringless state of her left. What did she fear? The world famous model, Veronique, had taken Zageo as a lover. Why couldn't she? It wasn't a betrayal of her love for Brian. It was just something else. A different life experience.

Except she couldn't forget how out of control she'd been when he'd kissed her. To hand him that kind of power required an enormous amount of trust, and how could she give that trust to a man she hadn't even met before yesterday? To blithely act upon sheer attraction did not feel right, regardless of how strong the attraction was and no matter what Zageo argued.

She sucked in a deep breath, lifted her gaze and once more focused on the outside world. 'How much further is it to The Salamander Inn?' she asked, looking out at a veritable jumble of buildings, many of which were crumbling from sheer age.

'Not far. Perhaps another five minutes.'

'Why build an expensive hotel in this location?'

'It's the most historic part of Stone Town and tourists like local colour. They come to Zanzibar because of its exotic past and because its very name conjures up a romantic sense of the east, just like Mandalay and Kathmandu.' He smiled, his eyes wickedly teasing as he added, 'Sultans and slaves and spice…it's a potent combination.'

'For attracting the tourist dollar.'

'Yes,' he conceded, amused by her sidestep away from anything personal. 'And thereby boosting the economy of the island, generating more employment.'

'So this hotel is a benevolent enterprise on your part?' she half-mocked, wanting to get under *his* skin.

'I am, by nature, benevolent, Emily. Have I not kept you out of the local lock-up, giving you the benefit of the doubt, sympathising with your concern over your sister's whereabouts, offering you a free means of communication with her?' His eyes simmered with provocative promises as he purred, 'I wish you only what is good. And what will be good.'

It was futile trying to get the better of him. He was the kind of man who'd always be on top of any game he cared to play.

The car pulled up outside *his* hotel.

No doubt he could claim any suite he liked for his personal use.

Emily desperately tried telling herself she was only here to use a computer, but a wild sense of walking into the lion's den gripped her as Zageo escorted her into the foyer.

And came to a dead halt.

Right in front of them, impatiently directing a bellboy on how to handle her luggage, was the stunningly beautiful and uniquely glamorous French-Moroccan model—Veronique!

CHAPTER TEN

EMILY could not help staring at the woman; the long glossy mane of black hair, flawless milk-coffee coloured skin, exotically tilted and thickly lashed chocolate-velvet eyes, a perfectly straight aristocratic nose, full pouty lips, and a cleanly sculptured chin that lifted haughtily at the sight of Zageo holding another woman's arm.

As well it might, Emily thought, suddenly feeling like a very common overcurvy peasant in her cotton skirt, casual little top, and very plain walking sandals. Apart from which, her own long hair was not exactly beautifully groomed after an underwater swim and her make-up was nonexistent.

Veronique's entire appearance was superbly put together. Her model-thin figure was wrapped in a fabulously elegant and sexy dark brown and cream polka-dot silk dress which screamed designer wear, and the high-heeled strappy sandals on her feet were so brilliantly stylish, anyone with a shoe fetish would have lusted for them. Her magnificent facial structure was highlighted with subtly toning make-up, her nails varnished a pearly cream, and just looking at the glossy black hair made Emily's feel like rats' tails.

'Veronique…this is a surprise,' Zageo said in his silky dangerous voice. Clearly it was not a surprise that pleased him.

'Your call last night felt like a call to arms, *cheri*,' she lilted, her tone warmly inviting him to take pleasure in her presence.

He'd called her last night?

Emily shot him a sharply inquiring look. Had he lied about having ended his relationship with Veronique?

'Then you were not listening to me,' he stated coldly.

Anger flashed from the supermodel's gorgeous dark eyes, flicked to Emily, then back to Zageo, having gathered a fierce determination to fight. 'You were mistaken in thinking I didn't want to be with you. I came to correct that misunderstanding.'

They were drawing attention from other people in the foyer. 'A private conversation should remain private,' Zageo cautioned sternly, signalling to the man behind the reception desk.

Instant action. A key was grabbed. The man ushered them to a door on the other side of the foyer. It opened to what was obviously the manager's domain, an office combined with a sitting area for conversations with guests.

Veronique stalked ahead, using the arrogant catwalk style of motion that automatically drew everyone's gaze after her. She was a star, intent on playing the star to the hilt, perhaps reminding Zageo of *who* she was, the kind of status she commanded.

'I can wait out here,' Emily suggested, pulling back from being witness to a lovers' quarrel and grasping what felt like the opportune moment to slip away entirely, extracting herself from a very sticky situation.

'Oui,' Veronique snapped over her shoulder.

'Non!' came Zageo's emphatic retort, forcibly steering Emily inside. 'Miss Ross is my guest and I will not do her the discourtesy of abandoning her for you, Veronique.'

It wasn't a discourtesy, Emily thought wildly, but again she was given no choice. *His* decision was punctuated by the door closing behind them.

Veronique wheeled to face them, jealous fury spitting from her eyes. 'You prefer *this woman* to me?'

On the surface of it, the preference seemed utter madness even to Emily's mind, so she didn't take offence, although a strong streak of female pride whispered that for a relationship to last—as her own with Brian had—there had to be more than surface stuff driving it. Two years, she reflected, was the usual time-frame for passion to wear thin.

Zageo ignored the question, blandly inquiring, 'How did you get from Paris to Zanzibar so quickly?'

The mane of hair was expertly tossed. 'You are not the only man I know who owns a private jet.'

If it was an attempt to make him jealous, it was a miserable failure, evoking only a curt, disdainful reply. '*Bien!* Then you'll have no problem with flying back tomorrow.'

Veronique scissored her hands in exasperated dismissal. 'This is absurd!'

'Yes, it is,' he agreed. 'I informed you of my position in no uncertain terms. Your coming will not change it.'

'But you misread my choice not to accompany you, Zageo.' She gestured an eloquent appeal. 'I wanted you to miss me. I wanted you to realise how good we are together. I wanted you to think about marrying me.'

'What?' Sharp incredulity in his voice.

'There was never any suggestion of a marriage being possible between us,' he thundered, hands lifting in such angry exasperation, Emily was able to slide out of his hold, quickly stepping over to the sofa against the wall, out of the firing line between the two antagonists.

'That doesn't mean it couldn't be,' Veronique argued.

'At no time did I lead you to think it. What we had was an arrangement, Veronique, an arrangement that suited both of us. You know it was so. Perhaps it does not suit you to have it ended, but I assure you, this attempt to push it further is futile.'

'Because of *her*?' A contemptuous wave and a venomous look were directed at Emily.

It was a good question, Emily thought, curious to know the answer herself since the ruction between Veronique and the sheikh had only occurred last night. She tore her gaze from the glittering double fangs of Veronique's eyes to look at Zageo, and was instantly shafted by two laser beams burning into her brain.

'Because its time was over,' he answered, speaking directly to Emily, his eyes hotly impressing the point. 'I had decided that before Miss Ross walked into my life.'

Curiously enough, it was a relief to hear this. Being the source of breaking up a long-standing relationship would not have sat easily with her, although she had done absolutely nothing to effect such an outcome.

'But you've let her sweeten the decision, haven't you?' came the furious accusation. '*She* is why you won't take me back. So what has *she* got that I have not, Zageo? What does *she* give you that I did not?'

Emily's cheeks burned.

Nothing, she thought, hating being dragged into what was definitely not her business.

But Zageo was still looking at her and the heat in his eyes simmered with needs and desires that were focused on her, making her heart catapult around her chest, flipping her stomach, shooting her mind into chaos as it tried to deal with responses that were scattering her wits.

'How does one compare a hothouse carnation to a wild water-lily?' he rolled out in a softer tone that somehow caused goosebumps to erupt all over Emily's skin. 'It is foolish to try to measure the differences. Each has its own unique appeal.'

A wild water-lily?

Emily wasn't used to hearing such flowery language from a man, though her heart was thumping its own wanton appreciation of it even as she tried to force her mind into reasoning that this was definitely Arabian Nights stuff, totally surreal, and she *must not* let herself get caught up in it.

Zageo's riveting gaze finally released hers, turning back to the woman who had so recently been his intimate companion. 'Please...do not lower yourself with these indignities,' he urged, appealing for a cessation of personal hostilities. 'Our time together is over. Yesterday is yesterday, Veronique. Tomorrow is tomorrow.'

'You see how it is?' she shot at Emily, highly incensed by the comparison she had forced by her own angry diatribe. 'No doubt you have been as swept away by him as I was. But it will only last for as long as the arrangement suits his convenience. He might not look like an Arab but he is one at heart.'

'An Arab whose generosity is being severely tested.' The warning was delivered with a hard look of ruthless intent. 'Do you want to continue this spiteful scene or do you want the Paris apartment?'

Veronique delivered another expert toss of her hair as she disdainfully returned her attention to him. 'I was doing Miss Ross a kindness, Zageo, informing her of the bottom line so she's not completely blinded by your beauty.'

'You are intent on poisoning something you do not understand,' he whipped at her. 'Make your decision now, Veronique.'

The threat whirling in the air forced the supermodel to take stock. She was not winning. And regardless of her star status, Sheikh Zageo bin Sultan Al Farrahn was by far the more influential person here in Zanzibar, with the power to make her visit very unpleasant. The bottom line was she hadn't been welcomed and had worn out his patience with making herself even less welcome.

She inhaled a deep breath, calming herself, pulling a mask of pride over her more volatile emotions. 'I could not bring myself to believe what you said last night,' she offered in a more considered appeal. 'I came to mend fences.'

It made no difference. He simply replied, 'I'm sorry you put yourself to that trouble.'

She tried a rueful sigh. Her hands fluttered an apologetic appeal. 'Okay, I took our relationship for granted. I won't do it again.'

He gave no sign of softening, implacably

stating, 'If you had truly valued it, you would have made different decisions.'

'I do have modelling assignments lined up throughout the next three months,' she quickly excused.

'I offered you my private jet to get to them.'

He was giving her no room to manoeuvre, not so much as a millimetre. Veronique had no choice but to accept their affair was over. Emily felt a stab of sympathy for her, having been subjected to no choice herself at this man's hands.

'I will take the apartment, *cheri*,' came the final decision, bitter irony lacing her voice as she added, 'I've grown fond of it.'

He nodded. 'Consider it settled. I shall inform the manager here that you are my guest at the inn until you return to Paris. Tomorrow?'

'*Oui*. Tomorrow I shall put all this behind me.'

'*Bien!*' Zageo strode to the desk, proceeding to call the manager on the in-house telephone system.

Veronique subjected Emily to a glare that seethed with malevolence, belying the resigned acceptance of the kiss-off apartment and suggesting that if the model could do her supposed replacement an injury on the sly, she would not hesitate to uproot the wild water-lily and take huge satisfaction in tearing it to pieces.

Emily was glad the supermodel would be flying away from Zanzibar tomorrow. She had enough trouble on her hands without having to deal with the fury of a scorned woman. Besides, the fault behind this situation did not lie at her door. Zageo had made that very clear. On the other hand, it would have been much clearer if he hadn't made the break-up call last night.

The manager of the inn knocked and entered the tension-packed room, warily closing the door behind him as he awaited more instructions from the sheikh. Zageo waved to the computer on the desk, requesting the password for Internet access to be written down for his use. This jolted Emily into remembering the purpose which had brought them here. It amazed her that Zageo had not been distracted from it. She certainly had.

The manager quickly complied. He was then asked to escort Veronique to a guest suite and ensure her needs were met. The main current of tension in the room swept out with the supermodel's exit, leaving Emily feeling like a very limp water-lily, trapped into waiting for the strong flow that would inevitably come from Zageo.

He beckoned her to the desk where he was already tapping away on the computer keyboard. Emily took a deep breath and pushed her feet forward, trying desperately to put the thought of contact with her sister in a more important slot than contact with Zageo. Hannah was her reason for being here. She could not let a totally unsuitable attraction to this man cloud that issue.

She took the chair he invited her to take in front of the computer. Her fingers automatically performed the functions necessary to access her e-mail. The tightness in her chest eased slightly as Zageo moved away, choosing not to intrude on her private correspondence.

Whether this meant he did finally believe her story or whether it was simply ingrained courtesy on his part, Emily didn't know and didn't let it concern her. A message from Hannah was on the screen. It was dated the same day Emily had woken up from a drugged sleep on Jacques's yacht to find he didn't have a wife onboard and she was the only member of his crew and they were already at sea.

Emily—I hope this reaches you before you set sail for Zanzibar. I won't make it there. Can't. We didn't get very far before running into an army patrol and it didn't matter what I pleaded, the men confiscated everything and called

Malcolm to come and get me and the girls. We're all under house arrest now. Not allowed to leave the farm to go anywhere. I'm half expecting the phone lines to be cut, as well, so if you don't receive another message from me, they will have stopped all outside communication.

I'm scared, Emily. I've never been so scared. I don't mind standing by Malcolm but I wish I'd managed to get the girls out. You could have taken them home to Mum and Dad in Australia. There is so much unrest in this country and I just don't know if these troubles will pass or get worse.

Anyhow, I'm sorry we won't be meeting up. And please don't think you can come here and do something because you can't. So stay away. It won't help. Understand? I'll let you know what's happening if I can. Lots of love, Emily. I couldn't have had a better little sister. Bye for now. Hannah.

Emily didn't realise she'd stopped breathing as she took in the words on the screen. Shock and fear chased around her mind. This was the last message from her sister. The last one. It was a week old. Seven days of silence.

'Emily? Is something wrong?'

She looked up to find Zageo watching her, his brow lowered in concern. The trapped air in her lungs whooshed out as she mentally grappled with Hannah's situation. Her mouth was too dry to speak. She had to work some moisture into it.

'Hannah is a prisoner in her own home,' she finally managed to blurt out, silently but savagely mocking herself for railing against being Zageo's prisoner. That was a joke compared to what her sister was going through—her sister and nieces and brother-in-law.

'They might be dead now, for all I know,' she muttered despairingly.

'Dead?'

'Read it for yourself!' she hurled at him as she erupted from the chair, driven by a frantic energy to pace around the room, to find some action that might help Hannah. 'You wanted proof of my story?' Her arm swept out in a derisive dismissal of his disbelief. 'There it is on the screen!'

He moved over to the desk, accepting the invitation to inform himself.

Emily kept pacing, her mind travelling in wild circles around the pivotal point of somehow getting Hannah and her family to safety, right out of Zimbabwe if possible. She did not have the power or the resources to achieve such an outcome herself, but what of the Australian Embassy? Would someone there help or would diplomatic channels choke any direct action?

She needed someone strong who could act…would act…

'This is not good news,' Zageo muttered.

Understatement of the year, Emily thought caustically, but the comment drew her attention to the man who arranged his world precisely how he wanted it, wielding power over her without regard to any authority but his own. She stopped pacing and gave him a long hard look, seeing what had previously been a very negative aspect of him as something that could become a marvellous positive!

Maybe…just maybe…Sheikh Zageo bin Sultan Al Farrahn could achieve what she couldn't.

Veronique had said he owned a private jet. Almost certainly a helicopter, too, Emily reasoned. With pilots on standby to fly them.

Building his hotel chain throughout Africa must have given him powerful political contacts in the countries where he'd invested big money. Apart from which, his enormous wealth could probably bribe a way to anywhere. And out of anywhere.

Zageo wanted her in bed with him.

Emily had no doubt about that.

He'd also once wanted Veronique in bed with him—and for the satisfaction of that desire he'd been prepared to give away what was surely a multimillion dollar apartment in Paris.

A hysterical little laugh bubbled across Emily's brain. Jacques had tried to trade her to the sheikh in return for his freedom, and here she was, planning to trade herself to him for her sister's freedom.

Which would turn her into the whore he'd first thought her.

Emily decided she didn't care.

She'd do anything to secure the safety of Hannah and her family.

She'd try the trade.

CHAPTER ELEVEN

ZAGEO parted from Emily as soon as they returned to the palace. He wanted to alleviate her distress, if possible, by finding out if the Coleman family had survived this past week. He had instructed Abdul to pursue inquiries in Zimbabwe, so some useful information might have already been acquired.

Zageo no longer had any doubt that Emily had spoken the truth all along, and everything he'd learnt about her made her a more fascinating and desirable woman, certainly not one he'd want to dismiss from his life at this early juncture.

They would meet for dinner, he'd told her, hoping to give her news that would clear the worry from her eyes. He wanted her to see that having his favour was good. He wanted her to look at him with the same deep and compulsive desire he felt for her. And he wanted her to give into it.

Abdul was in his office, as usual, more at home with his communications centre than anywhere else. He was amazingly efficient at keeping track of all Zageo's business and personal interests. If he didn't have the information required at his fingertips, it was relentlessly pursued until it was acquired.

'The Coleman family…' Zageo prompted once the appropriate courtesies had been exchanged.

Abdul leaned back in the chair behind his desk, steepling his hands over his chest in a prayerful manner, indicating that he'd decided this issue was very much in the diplomatic arena. 'The M written in the register at The Salamander Inn stands for Malcolm. His wife's name is Hannah. They have two young daughters—'

'Yes, yes, I know this,' Zageo cut in,

quickly recounting the e-mail he'd read at the inn to bring Abdul up-to-date on where the situation stood to his knowledge. 'The critical question is…are they still alive?'

'As of today, yes,' Abdul answered, much to Zageo's relief.

He could not have expected Emily to be receptive to him if she was in a state of grief over the deaths of people he had never met. She would want to go home to her parents in Australia, and in all decency, he would have had to let her go.

'However…' Abdul went on ominously, 'I would call their position perilous. Malcolm Coleman has been too active in protesting the policies of the current regime. His name is on a list of public antagonists who should be silenced.'

'Is the danger immediate?'

'If you are concerned for their safety, I think there is time to manoeuvre, should you wish to do so.'

'I wish it,' Zageo answered emphatically.

There was a long pause while Abdul interpreted his sheikh's reply. 'Do I understand that Miss Ross will be staying with us beyond Monday, Your Excellency?'

'Given that her sister's family can be rescued, yes, I have decided Miss Ross's companionship will add immeasurably to my pleasure in this trip around our African properties.'

'Ah!' Abdul nodded a few times and heaved a sigh before bringing himself to address the problem posed by Emily's family. 'Quick action will be needed. The pressure is on for Malcolm Coleman to give up his farm and leave the country but he is persisting in resisting it. Defying it.'

'Intent on fighting for what he considers his,' Zageo interpreted.

Abdul spread his hands in an equitable gesture. 'It is a large and very profitable farm that has been in his family for three generations. It is only natural for a man to wish to hold onto his home.'

'There will be no home with himself and his family dead,' Zageo commented grimly. 'He must be persuaded to accept that reality.'

'Precisely. Even so, to walk away with no recompense…'

'See if we can buy his farm. It will allow him to leave with his pride intact, giving him the financial stake he might need to start over in another country and still be successful in the eyes of his wife and children.'

'You want to acquire property in Zimbabwe?' Abdul queried somewhat incredulously.

'Very briefly. Perhaps it can be used as barter for the Colemans's safe passage out of the country. Find a recipient in the regime who understands favours, Abdul. The idea of acquiring a profitable farm without paying a cent might appeal. Delivery on delivery.'

'Ah! A diplomatic resolution.'

'Behind doors.'

'Of course, Your Excellency.'

Zageo relaxed, reasonably confident that his plan could be effected. Tonight he would tell Emily that not only was her sister's family still amongst the living, he had also set in motion the steps to extract them from their dangerous situation.

She would want to stay with him then.

She would want to know firsthand the outcome of his rescue plan.

It might not be bending to his will but… Zageo decided that winning her favour was the best way to gaining her submission. In fact, it would give him much satisfaction to arrange a meeting between Emily and her sister. This could not be held in Stone Town. He had to move on. Nevertheless, he would give Emily Ross what she had come for.

Delivery…for delivery.

CHAPTER TWELVE

BACK in the women's quarters of the palace, Emily wasted no time in organizing what she wanted done. Zageo had said they would meet for dinner. With the image of Veronique still vividly in her mind, the presentation of herself with the view of becoming his mistress definitely required perfect grooming, artful make-up and sexy clothes. Since her own luggage contained nothing that could be described as seductively tempting…

'The trunk of belly-dancing costumes…do you still have it, Heba?'

'Yes. Will I have it brought to you?' she offered obligingly.

Emily nodded. 'Let's see if we can find something really erotic in it.'

That was certainly what Zageo had expected of her last night so let him have it tonight, Emily reasoned, deciding that an in-your-face statement of her intention was more telling than a thousand words.

She chose a hot-pink costume with beaded bands in black and silver. The bra was designed to show optimum cleavage. The skirt was slinky, clinging to hips, bottom and upper thighs where it was slit for freedom of leg movement. The edges of the slits were beaded as well, making them very eye-catching.

'It is a bold costume,' Heba commented somewhat critically.

'I have to be bold tonight,' Emily muttered, beyond caring what the women who were attending to her needs thought.

Only one thing was important.

Getting the sheikh *to do something* about Hannah and her family.

She had her mind steeled to deliver her part of the trade, yet when the summons to dinner came, a nervous quivering attacked her entire body. What she was setting out to do wasn't *her*. Yet she had to pull it off. If something terrible happened to Hannah and she hadn't done anything to help, she would never forgive herself.

Besides, it wasn't as though she was unattracted to Zageo. It could well be a fantastic experience, having sex with him. She couldn't imagine he'd want a long relationship with her. The stunningly beautiful and glamorous Veronique, who shared his jet set class, had only held his interest for two years. Emily figured on only being a brief novelty, possibly lasting for the duration of his tour of the Al Farrahn hotels. Once he returned to his normal social life, she'd be a fish out of water—one he would undoubtedly release.

So, what were a few months out of her own life compared to the lives of Hannah and her family? She had no commitments. There was nothing to stop her from offering herself as a bed companion to a man who might or might not take up some time which was of no particular use to her anyway.

The costume trunk had also yielded a black silk cloak which Emily employed to cover herself while being escorted to the sheikh's private apartment. She was ushered into the same opulent sitting room where Zageo had commanded her presence last night. He was back in his sheikh clothes, the long white tunic and richly embroidered over-robe in purple and gold, making her feel even more nervous about his foreignness.

However, she was not about to baulk at doing what she had to do. The moment the door closed behind the men on escort duty, she whipped off the cloak, determined on getting straight to business. However, instead of exciting speculative interest in Zageo, her appearance in the provocative belly-dancing costume evoked an angry frown.

'What is this?' he demanded, the harsh tone making her heart skitter in apprehension. His eyes locked onto hers with piercing intensity.

'You claimed the costumes did not belong to you.'

'They don't! I just thought…' She swallowed hard, fighting to prevent her throat from seizing up. 'I thought it would please you to see me dressed like this.'

'Please me…' He spoke the words as though this was a strange concept to be examined for what it meant. His gaze narrowed, then skated down over the bared curves of her body, seemingly suspicious of their sexual promise.

Emily's heart was thundering in her ears, making it difficult to think over its chaotic drumming. She told herself she should be moving forward, swaying her hips like a belly-dancer, showing herself willing to invite him to touch, to kiss, to take whatever gave him pleasure. A sexy woman would slide her arms around his neck, press her body to his, use her eyes flirtatiously. It was stupid, stupid, stupid to stand rooted to the spot, barely able to breathe let alone shift her feet.

'Why would you suddenly set out to please me, Emily?'

She trembled. His voice was laced with *dis*-pleasure. She was hit with such deep confusion she didn't know what to do or say. Her hands lifted in helpless appeal, needing to reach out to him yet frightened now of being rebuffed, spurned, sent away.

'For the past twenty-four hours you have been determined on putting distance between us,' he mockingly reminded her.

The heat of shame scorched her cheeks. What she planned was the act of a whore. There was no denying it. The trade was too blatant. She hadn't thought it would matter to him as long as she gave him the satisfaction of having what he wanted. But as he strolled towards her, the sardonic little smile curling his mouth made her feel she had lost whatever respect she had won with him.

'Now what could have inspired this change of attitude?' he queried, his brilliant dark eyes deriding any attempt at evasion. 'Was it the proof that my relationship with Veronique is over?'

'That…that does help,' she choked out, realising that the break-up arrangement had contributed a great deal to her thinking. Though it didn't excuse it. No, it was desperation driving this deal and Emily was suddenly afraid Zageo would find that offensive.

He moved around behind her, lifting her long hair back over her shoulder to purr in her ear, 'So…you are now ready to take this journey with me. You *want* to take it. You *want* to feel my touch on your skin.' He ran soft fingertips down the curve of her spine. 'You *want* me to taste all of you.' He trailed his mouth down her throat, pressing hot sensual kisses. 'Let me hear you say that, Emily.'

Her hands had fallen to her sides. They were clenching and unclenching as waves of tension rolled through her. She sucked in a quick breath and started pushing out the necessary words. 'You can do…you can do…whatever you like with me—'

'No, no, that sounds far too passive,' he cut in before she could complete spelling out the deal. 'Though now that you have given me permission…'

He unclipped the bra and slid the straps off her shoulders. As the beaded garment started to fall from her breasts, the sheer shock of being so swiftly bared, jolted Emily into defensive action. Her hands whipped up, catching the cups and plastering them back into place.

'Did you mean to tease me, Emily? Have I spoilt your game?' he asked in the silky dangerous tone that shot fearful quivers through her heart. Even as he spoke, his hands glided up from around her waist and covered her own, his fingers extending further than the bra cups to fan the upper swell of her breasts. 'No matter,' he assured her. 'I'm on fire for you anyway.'

'Stop,' she finally found voice enough to gasp out. 'Please…stop.'

'This does not please you?'

'No…yes…no…I mean…'

'What do you mean, Emily?'

His voice was now like a sharp-edged knife, slicing into her. Tears of confusion welled into her eyes. This scene was going—had gone—all wrong. She simply wasn't sophisticated enough to bring off the subtle sexual bartering that went on in his world.

'I'll take this journey with you if you'll help my sister,' she blurted out in wild desperation.

'And you will withhold yourself if I do not agree? You will push me away, refasten your bra, and scorn my desire for you?' The whip-like edge to his voice gathered more intensity as he added, 'Not to mention your desire for me.'

It sounded horrible. Everything decent in Emily recoiled from using sex as a bargaining tool. It eliminated any good feelings that might have eventuated from being intimate with this man. She shook her head in hopeless shame and humiliation.

'I'm sorry…sorry…I didn't know what else to do.'

'Little fool,' he growled. 'Playing a game that is not in your nature.'

His hands dropped to her waist and spun her around to face him. He cupped her face, his fingers gently sweeping the trickle of tears from her cheeks. The tender gesture was in perverse contrast to the glittering anger in his eyes.

'Did you imagine I was not aware of your distress over your sister and her family?'

'They are nothing to you,' she choked out in a ragged plea for his understanding.

'*You* are not nothing to me, Emily.'

'I was counting on that,' she confessed.

'Yet you did not credit me with caring enough to do whatever I could to ease your distress?'

His words seethed with deep offence. Emily frantically seized on what she thought were mitigating circumstances. 'I don't know you,' she pleaded. 'All I know is you've kept me here to…to play with me.'

'Play with you,' he repeated in a scoffing tone that stirred Emily's blood, triggering a flood of volatile feelings that instantly threatened to burst out of control.

She wrenched her head out of his hold, stepping back to let fly at him with her own tirade of deep offence. 'You've had me jumping through hoops ever since I was forced into your company. First, you play the grand inquisitor, deliberately choosing not to believe a word I said. After which, you left me no alternative but to dress up as a belly-dancer for you…'

'Which you have no problem doing tonight,' he sliced at her.

'Because you made it your game, Zageo,' she asserted vehemently. 'I was only trying to fit into it.'

'Fine! Then fit!'

Before Emily could even draw breath to utter another word, he swooped on her, swept her off her feet, and in a dizzying whirl of movement, carried her through the sitting room and beyond it to another lamp-lit room where he tipped her onto a pile of exotic silk and satin cushions spread across a massive, four-poster bed. Her arms flew out to stop herself from rolling. The bra became dislodged again and Zageo whipped it off, leaving her naked from head to hips.

'No backtracking now, Emily,' he fired at her. 'We have a deal. In return for my services in rescuing your family, you've agreed to let me do whatever I like with you. Right?'

The violence of his feelings made her pulse beat faster, increasing the wild agitation racing through her. 'How do I know you'll help?' she cried, alarmed by the thought he would just do what he wanted anyway.

'Because I am a man of honour who always delivers on a deal,' he stated savagely.

He was shedding his robe, hurling it away. She scrambled to sit up, acutely aware of her full breasts swinging as she did so and realising her nipples had tightened in some instinctive response to the raking heat in his eyes.

'Are you a woman of your word, Emily?' he challenged, discarding his tunic and underpants with swift and arrogant carelessness while fiercely warning her, 'Leave that bed and you leave with nothing from me.'

She sat utterly still, staring at him, not because of the threat but because he looked so stunningly magnificent. She had seen many almost naked men, especially guys who excelled in water sports, and they invariably had well-honed physiques—broad shoulders, flat stomachs, lean hips, powerfully muscled thighs. Zageo had all that but somehow his body was far more pleasingly proportioned.

It emanated an aura of indomitable male strength without the overdelineated musculature that came from excessive weight lifting at a gym. And his dark olive skin gleamed with a taut smoothness that incited an almost compelling desire to touch. Emily was not an expert on judging men's sexual equipment, but the sight of Zageo's certainly set up flutters of nervous excitement.

He stepped forward, his hands virtually spanning her waist as he lifted her into standing on the bed. 'Unfasten the skirt,' he commanded. 'Show me how willing you are to do whatever I want.'

Impossible to back down now, she told herself. The challenge blazing from his eyes seared her own sense of honour, forcing her past the point of no return. He'd taken the deal. She had to deliver.

As she reached around to the zipper at the pit of her back, he released her waist and lifted his hands to her naked breasts, rotating his palms over the taut peaks, making them acutely sensitive to his touch, driving arcs of piercing pleasure from her nipples to below her belly and causing Emily to gasp at the intensity of the feeling.

The unfastened skirt slithered down to pool around her feet. Her gasp turned to a moan of yearning as the almost torturous caress of her breasts ceased. Her hands curled urgently around Zageo's shoulders, unconsciously kneading them in a blind desire for continuity. He bent his head, his mouth swiftly ministering the sweetest balm to her need, licking and sucking as he hooked his thumbs into her panties and drew this last piece of clothing down her legs.

She stepped out of the restricting garment without a moment's hesitation, her previous inhibitions erased by the excitement coursing through her. He stroked her inner thighs, making them quiver, making her stomach contract in wild anticipation as he moved a hand into the slickened folds of her sex, fingers sliding over the moist heat that had been building and building from the erotic ministration of his mouth on her breasts.

Every one of her internal muscles tensed, waiting for a more intimately knowing touch, wanting it, craving it. Slowly his fingers slid inside, moving as deeply as they could, undoubtedly feeling the pulsing welcome her body gave instinctively. They withdrew to circle the entrance tantalisingly while his thumb found and caressed her clitoris, increasing an erotic pressure on it as his fingers pushed in again. And again. And again.

Emily's whole body bent like a bow, driven to an exquisite tension, blinding pleasure consuming every cell and needing to burst into some further place, reaching for it… reaching…the momentum escalating, then breaking past a barrier that was almost pain to shatter into a flood of melting sweetness, her knees buckling at the intensity of the waves sweeping through her.

Zageo caught her as her hands lost their purchase on his shoulders, carrying her with him as he plunged onto the bed, lying her flat on her back amongst the cushions and hovering over her, his eyes glittering fierce satisfaction in her helpless response to him.

He lifted her arms above her head, pinning them there with his own. They were simply too limp to resist the action though she knew intuitively this was a deliberate expression of domination over her and at another time and place she would have fought it. He clearly exulted in what he saw as submission to his will.

Emily smiled. Right here and now she didn't care what he thought. Her body was humming its own exultation. His gaze fastened on her smile. His mouth quirked into a cruel little twist and swooped on it, his lips hard and hungry, forcing hers apart, his tongue driving deep, intent on stirring another storm of sensation. *Her* blissful contentment was irrelevant. This was all about him taking his pleasure and he was the one who had to feel satisfied.

Some primitive streak inside her insisted on contesting the ruthless ravishment of his kiss. Her tongue duelled with his, sparking a passionate fight for possession. He might have the use of her body for a while but she hadn't traded any of her spirit. If he'd imagined getting a tame sex-slave, he could think again.

So consumed was Emily with the need to hold her own in this kiss, when Zageo released her arms she grabbed his head, instinctively moving to wrest back some control over what was happening. She was so caught up in trying to match his wildly erotic plunder, the lifting of her lower body took her by surprise. The shock of him entering her caused a total lack of focus on anything other than the sensation of his hard flesh moving past the soft convulsions of her own, tunnelling to her innermost depths, filling what had remained empty for a long, long time.

The jolt of that intensely satisfying fullness took Emily straight to the edge of climax again. Everything within her pulsed to the rhythmic beat of his smooth and powerful thrusts—each withdrawal setting up a drumroll of exquisite anticipation, each plunge sending her hurtling into a tumultuous sea of ecstasy.

She heard herself moaning, crying out—totally involuntary sounds issuing from her throat. She was barely conscious of her hands squeezing his buttocks, instinctively goading, wanting the rocking to be harder, faster, wilder, until the waves turned into one continuously rolling crest, the explosive spasms of his climax driving it, and she floated off into a space where she was only anchored by him, his arms wound securely around her as she lay on his chest—a heaving chest that felt like the gentle swell of calmer waters after riding through a tempest.

Emily didn't move, didn't attempt to say anything. Not only was she in a daze of sensory overload, she had no idea what should or would come next. Besides, her whole experience of this man was that he took the lead in any activity to be shared with him. Moreover, the bargain she'd made put him in charge of her life. There was no point in even stirring until he showed some desire for it.

He stroked her back, making her skin tingle with pleasure. He certainly knew how to touch a woman, Emily thought, silently marvelling at the incredibly fantastic sexual experience he had just given her. If this was a sample of what she'd have to *endure* at his hands to keep her side of the trade, it was absolutely no hardship.

In fact, she understood why Veronique had come flying to Zanzibar to get him back. It was not going to be easy to say goodbye and walk away from what he gave. Not even an apartment in Paris would make up for having lost a lover of his calibre. Emily had a sneaking suspicion that the memory of what Zageo had just done to her would be a pinnacle of pleasure she might never reach with anyone else. Not even with Brian…

She clamped down on that thought. It was wrong to make comparisons. This relationship—if it could be called that—was something very different to her marriage. It was a slice of life she hadn't been looking for, eventuating from circumstances over which she'd had no control.

Anxiety welled up as she thought of Hannah, fraying the langour she had succumbed to in Zageo's soothing embrace. He was playing with her hair, lifting up the long tresses and letting them trail around his fingers, and as though he sensed her change of mood, he suddenly bunched her hair in his hand, slightly tugging to grab her attention.

'They are alive,' he said.

'What?' His statement seemed surreal, as though he had just read her mind.

'Your sister, her husband and daughters…they are alive. Do not be imagining them dead because it is not so,' he gruffly declared.

Adrenaline shot through Emily's sluggish veins. She bolted up to scan his eyes for truth, breaking his embrace and planting her own arms on either side of his head to lean over him in his current supine position. 'How do you know?' she demanded.

One black eyebrow arched in mocking challenge. 'You question my knowledge?'

She huffed with impatience. 'Not your knowledge, Zageo. I'm asking how you came by it.'

'Given that your sister had not arrived at the inn, as you had expected, I left instructions that her whereabouts be traced while we were out today,' he answered matter-of-factly. 'When we returned from Stone Town…'

'Are they under house arrest as Hannah feared?' Emily pressed, filled with an urgency to know what problems her sister was facing.

'Yes. But the point I am making, my dear Emily, is—' he ran a finger over her lips to silence any further intemperate outburst '—they are alive. And I shall now take every step I can to guarantee their future safety.'

Relief poured through her. Trading herself for this outcome had been worthwhile. No matter how big a sacrifice of her own self it might become, she would not regret making it. Some positive action would be taken to help Hannah.

'What do you plan to do?' she queried eagerly.

'Enough!' He surged up, catching her offguard and rolling her onto her back, swiftly reestablishing his domination. The fingers that had been teasing her lips now stroked her jawline as though testing it for defiance. His dark eyes gleamed with a ruthless desire to re-acquaint her with the trade she'd made. 'You will trust me to negotiate your sister's freedom as best I can. How I do it is not your business. It is your business to please me, is it not?'

Had she?

Doubts whirled, attacking her natural self-confidence.

Was he satisfied with what he'd had of her so far?

Before tonight her sexual experience had been limited to one man—a man who'd had no other woman but herself. Her heart stampeded into thumping with panic as she thought of the high-living, sophisticated Veronique. She didn't know how to compete.

'You'll have to tell me what you want me to do,' she pleaded, frightened of being inadequate.

'Oh, I will,' he promised, smiling some deeply sensual and private satisfaction.

And he did.

Emily didn't mind doing any of it.

The happy knowledge that Hannah and her family were alive bubbled at the back of her mind, but in the forefront of it was the amazing truth that being intimately entangled with Sheikh Zageo bin Sultan Al Farrahn was making her feel more vibrantly alive than *she* had ever felt in her life.

CHAPTER THIRTEEN

ON MONDAY they flew to Kenya.

'But it's in the opposite direction to Zimbabwe,' Emily had protested.

An instant flash of anger had answered her. 'Do you doubt that I will deliver on my promise?'

'It just doesn't seem logical to travel there,' she had temporised warily. 'If you'd explain…'

'The negotiations to secure the safety of your sister's family will take time. We must move through diplomatic channels. While this is proceeding, there is little point in my not keeping to my own schedule. And you will accompany me—' his eyes had stabbed a challenge to her commitment '—as agreed.'

Again there was no choice but to go his way.

And as usual, it turned out that *his* way gave Emily an immense amount of amazing pleasure and it wasn't all exclusively connected to the intense sexual passion he could and did repeatedly stir.

The hotel he was checking on in Kenya was unlike any hotel she had ever seen. It was, in fact, a safari resort, and the rooms were designed to look like a series of mud huts nestled cunningly around a hillside overlooking the Serengetti Plain. Inside they provided every luxury a traveller might want while the decor made fascinating use of the brightly colourful beading and fabrics much loved by the Masai tribe.

Best of all was the magnificent vista from every window—great herds of wildebeest grazing their way across the vast rolling plain which was dotted here and there by the highly distinctive acacia trees with their wide flat tops. It was also a surprising delight to see so many species of wild animals just roaming free, totally ignoring the intrusion by mankind.

When she and Zageo were taken out in one of the special safari vans, they might have been in an invisible spaceship for all the notice the animals took of them. A pride of lions, resting in the long grass by one of the tracks, didn't even turn their heads to look at the vehicle. In another place, a cheetah was teaching her three young cubs to hunt with absolutely no distraction from her mission, despite a number of vans circling to give their passengers a view of the action. Real life in Africa, Emily kept thinking, feeling very privileged to see it firsthand.

It had far more impact than viewing a film, though it wasn't always a pleasant one. It gave Emily the shudders seeing a flock of vultures waiting to feed on a fresh kill—horrible birds with their big bloated bodies and vicious looking beaks. On the other side of the spectrum were the giraffes—fascinating to watch a group of them amble along with a slow, stately grace, automatically evoking a smile.

On each of their trips out—different vehicles, different drivers—Emily was seated in the body of the van where a large section of the roof was lifted so passengers could stand up and take photographs. Zageo sat beside the driver, chatting to him about his life and work, observing how the safari session was handled—radio communication between the vans giving information about sightings so the drivers could change course, if necessary, to get to the scene as fast as they could.

Emily came to realise he didn't just check on the top-level management of his hotels. Nothing escaped his attention. He even stopped to talk to the employees who swept the paths to the rooms and it was not done in an autocratic manner. He accorded each person the same respect, none higher than another, and was clearly regarded with respect in return.

There was no shrugging or grimacing or rolling of eyes behind his back. He was liked, all the way down the line, and Emily couldn't help liking him, too, for the way he dealt with *his* people. It forced a revision of opinion on how he'd dealt with her.

In all honesty, she had to concede her story had probably sounded unbelievable. Zageo could well have been justified in not even listening to her, just handing her over to the police as an associate of Jacques Arnault. Instead of which, he'd given her the benefit of the doubt, proceeding to check the facts she'd given him while extending his highly generous and luxurious hospitality. Looked at objectively, this was more than fair treatment.

Except somehow none of it had been objective.

From the first moment of meeting it had been personal. Very, very personal. And it hadn't been all on his side, either. She'd been reacting against an attraction, an unwelcome one in both its strength and unsuitability, although when it came to a point of physical connection, she hadn't stopped him from kissing her. Now it was totally impossible to deny how much she wanted him to keep wanting her.

It even frightened her when he asked if she'd prefer to relax by the resort swimming pool, not accompany him on yet another safari trip. 'I thought you wanted me with you,' she answered anxiously, wondering if she had displeased him in some way.

He frowned, looking both exasperated and frustrated. 'You do not have to be a slave to me for your sister's sake,' he said tersely. 'I am here to carry out my responsibilities. I do not wish you to be bored, to put on a face of interest when you would rather be…'

'Bored?' Emily cried in astonishment. 'I'm not the least bit bored, Zageo.'

His dark intense eyes lasered hers for the

truth. 'You have had day after day of rough travel. Perhaps you would like a long session of relaxing massages…'

'And miss out on seeing what I may never have the chance to see again? No way!' she asserted emphatically. 'I'm with you!'

A smile twitched at his lips. 'So. The adventure appeals.'

'I've always loved the world of nature. There's nothing in the animal kingdom I find boring,' Emily assured him.

One eyebrow arched. 'Including me?'

Him least of all, she thought, but looked askance at him, unwilling to give away too much. 'For me, *you* are an adventure, too, as I'm sure you're perfectly aware.'

Yes, he was, Zageo silently conceded.

And so was she for him—totally unlike any other woman he'd been with. Her lack of sexual sophistication had challenged him into making each new experience in the bedroom not only a titillating surprise for her but a sensual delight to be savoured over and over again. Her response was always intensely gratifying, sometimes quite intoxicating.

She also had a natural joy in life that revived his own. Gone was the jaded feeling with which he had left France to begin this trip. In fact, he was conscious of feeling a deeper pleasure in Emily Ross than any of the women who had preceded her. Which made it all the more vexing that she had come to him on such frustrating terms, denying him the satisfaction of winning her to his side.

She was happy enough to be there.

No doubt about that.

She didn't have enough artifice in her to pretend.

But would she have ever submitted to his will, given there had been no problem with her sister, pushing a choice that might resolve it?

He hated this trade—hated it with a vengeance. He wanted done with it as fast as possible.

But Africa was Africa and very little moved at a fast pace. The days wore on with no progress towards an agreeable settlement between Malcolm Coleman and the hostile elements responsible for holding his family under house arrest.

Abdul was working overtime on pressing acceptable negotiations. The stumbling block was Coleman himself, not trusting anything he was offered and refusing to give up ownership of his farm. Abdul finally advised that direct confrontation would probably be required to gain an effective outcome.

'So a way to Coleman's farm must be cleared,' Zageo decided. 'Best to go in by helicopter.'

'But how not to get shot down?' Abdul muttered worriedly. 'I don't like this, Your Excellency. Why not explain to Miss Ross that her brother-in-law will not co-operate with the rescue plan? Perhaps she…'

'No!' Zageo flicked him a scornful look. 'Failure is unacceptable. The conference scheduled at our hotel in Zambia…find out what officials are coming from Zimbabwe and ensure that one of them has the power to grant me access with immunity. If you can also get some idea of what inducement would be welcome…'

Abdul nodded, looking relieved to be directed back into familiar territory.

Zageo reflected that this mission could end up costing him far more than he had anticipated. Endangering his own life was certainly going too far just to please a woman, yet there was no question in his mind that if it had to be done for Emily Ross, it had to be done. There had been no quarter asked in her giving to him, no excusing herself from anything he'd demanded of her, no protest at his leading her where she had not gone before. It was as though he had bought a slave. Which went against his every grain.

He *needed* this business finished.

Only after the trade had been honoured by him would he know if Emily Ross desired to stay at his side for reasons other than her sister's safety.

Emily couldn't help fretting over not knowing how things were for Hannah. She wished she could ask Zageo but he interpreted her need for information as a lack of trust in him. Having been sternly rebuffed for showing an impatience about getting results from his side of the bargain, she was wary of bringing up the subject again. However, his announcement that they would be flying on to Zambia instantly loosened her tongue.

They were in bed, relaxed after another exhilarating peak of intimacy, and Emily's mind leapt to a very different connection. 'Zambia and Zimbabwe share a border. Does this mean—?'

'It means we are going to Zambia,' he stated tersely, cutting off the spill of words from her.

Emily gritted her teeth as a wave of rebellion surged through her. She had been obedient to his wishes. She had been patient over the time he needed to clinch his side of the deal. But she was not going to be fobbed off as though she had no right to know what was happening with Hannah.

She heaved herself up, planting her hands on either side of his head, positioning herself directly above him for a very determined face-to-face encounter. 'What for?' she demanded.

His eyes glinted a deliberate challenge as he answered, 'One of our hotels is sited on the Zambezi River, just above Victoria Falls. It is on my itinerary.'

'So this move has nothing to do with my sister?'

'I will be meeting with people who may help.'

'May? *May?*' Her uncertainties coalesced into a shaft of anger. '*May* I remind you, Zageo, that you've had a very comprehensive downpayment on my side of our agreed trade and I have yet to receive any solid indication that you are doing anything productive on your side.'

'A downpayment!' he scoffed. 'Is that what you call doing what you want to do? Where's the cost to you, Emily? What have you paid?'

The counterattack was so swift and deadly, it threw her mind into chaos. Had it cost her anything to be with him? Not really. Which meant the trade wasn't equitable. And that left her without a reasonable argument. Panic whirled, wildly prompting action that might set the balance right again. She flung herself away from him, rolling off the bed, landing on her feet and backing away out of easy reach.

'So you think I would have said yes to you anyway. Is that it, Zageo?' she fired at him. 'You think I find you irresistible?'

He propped himself up on his side, observing her with narrowed eyes. 'If there had been any resistance on your part, Emily, I would have been aware of it,' he mocked.

'Well, how about resistance now?'

'Don't be absurd.'

Emily steeled her backbone. Her eyes defied his arrogant confidence. He might be the most beautiful, sexiest man on earth but… 'I can say no to you,' she declared with enough ferocity to warn him she was serious.

His heavy-lidded gaze raked her naked body, reminding her of how intimately he knew it and how deeply he had pleasured it, sending her temperature sky-high in a rush of self-conscious guilt over her ready compliance to whatever pleased him.

'Why would you want to frustrate both of us?' he asked, his mouth curving into a sardonic little smile that derided such obvious foolishness.

Emily struggled to rise above the sexual pull of the man. If she didn't fight him now she would lose any bargaining power she had.

'You withhold information from me,' she swiftly accused. 'Why shouldn't I withhold myself from you until you share what I need to know?'

'So…we are back to bartering, are we?' Anger tightened his face and flashed from his eyes. 'There has been no progression in our relationship?'

'A relationship can only grow from sharing,' she hotly argued.

'Have I not shared much with you?'

'Yes,' she had to concede. 'But I want you to share what you're doing about Hannah and her family.'

Steely pride looked back at her. 'I have said I shall move them from harm's way and I will. That is all you need to know.'

'*Will!* And just how far in the future is that, Zageo?' She was on a roll now and nothing was going to stop her from pinning him down. Her pride was at stake, too. She had given herself to him in good faith and she was not going to be taken for a ride. '*Will* some action be taken from your hotel in Zambia?'

'Enough!'

He swung himself off the bed, rising to his feet with an autocratic hauteur that squeezed her heart and sent flutters through her stomach. His eyes blazed shrivelling scorn at her as he donned a robe, tying the belt with a snappy action—signal enough that the intimacy they had shared earlier was at a decisive end. He waved a dismissive hand over the bed.

'Consider it yours. I will not require any more *payment* from you…'

His tone was so savage it took Emily's breath away.

'…until you have received satisfaction from me,' he concluded bitingly, as though she had dismissed all the sexual satisfaction he'd given her as nothing worth having.

Emily sucked in some air, needing a blast of oxygen to clear the shocked fog in her brain. 'I just want some news of Hannah!'

she cried. 'Is that so unreasonable? Too much to ask when I'm so frightened for my sister?'

He ignored her, striding for the door which he clearly intended to put between them.

'I don't know where you're coming from, Zageo,' she hurled at his back. 'But where I come from we have a saying that every Australian understands and respects. *Fair go!* It's an intrinsic part of our culture—what we live by. And to me it's not fair of you to brush off my concern when I have tried my utmost to please you in every respect.'

He halted, his shoulders squaring with bunched tension. They rose and fell as he drew in and exhaled a very deep breath. His head did not turn. She could feel violence emanating from him as though it was a tangible thing, attacking her nerves and making them leap in a wild frenzy.

'No harm comes to the source of a lucrative deal while the deal is still pending,' he stated coldly. 'At this point in time, you need have no fear for your sister's life. Nor the lives of her husband and children.' He cast one hard glance at her as he added, 'We fly to Zambia in the morning. Be ready.'

Then he was gone.

CHAPTER FOURTEEN

I WILL *be meeting with people who may help.*

This must be it, Emily kept thinking, observing the preparations for a special dinner being set up on the perfectly manicured and very green lawn, which ran smoothly from the long line of white buildings comprising the hotel, right to the edge of the water. It was a fantastic site, overlooking the vast spread of the Zambezi River just before it plunged down a massive chasm, the spume from Victoria Falls sending up clouds of mist.

Government dignitaries from various African nations had been arriving all afternoon and the paths around the numerous units of accommodation were being patrolled by their security guards. A stage had been constructed under one of the large shade trees, facing the carefully arranged tables and chairs. Three African tenors were checking out the sound system, rehearsing some of the same operatic arias Emily had heard sung by the famous three—Pavarotti, Domingo and Carrera.

She had barely seen Zageo since they had arrived at this unbelievably beautiful place. He had appointed a hotel staff member to see to her every need and arrange whatever Emily wished to do. It felt as though he was divorcing himself from her.

Accommodation was designed in four suite units, two up, two down, each with a balcony or verandah with a direct view of the river. Emily was installed in an upstairs suite and she knew Zageo was in the adjoining one but he had made no attempt to visit her.

Everything inside the suite was designed for two people; a king-size bed, two large lounging chairs with matching footstools, a very long vanity bench with two wash bowls in the spacious bathroom, plus a huge shower recess with a shower-head as large as a bread plate spraying out so much volume it gave one the sense of standing under a waterfall. So much luxury for one person felt very lonely.

Maybe after tonight—if he had a fruitful meeting— Zageo might deign to give her some news of what he was doing about Hannah's family. Emily could only hope so. Confronting him again would not elicit anything but another rebuff.

All along she had known there was a chasm of cultural differences between them, yet she had wanted him to deal with her as though he understood and shared her *Australian* attitudes. Big mistake! His way was *his* way and she had no choice but to accept that, especially with helping Hannah because she had no one else to turn to.

It was almost sunset. Drinks and canapés were being served from the bar at the back of the large wooden deck built around a large shade tree and extending over the edge of the river. Emily sat on a cushioned lounger, sipping a tropical fruit drink, listening to other guests commenting on the fantastic scenery.

The sky was streaked with vivid colour. About twenty metres away in the water was a raft of hippos, most of them submerged enough to look like a clump of rounded rocks. Much further away and silhouetted by the setting sun, a string of elephants started crossing the river from one island to another. Emily counted seven of them.

The splendour of Africa…

She fiercely wished Zageo was beside her, sharing it as they'd done in Kenya. She missed his company, his knowledge and experience, the excitement of his presence, the fine sexual tension that was constantly between them, promising more intimate pleasure to come as soon as they were alone together.

After two years of being single, with no inclination to join up with anyone, Emily realised that Zageo had well and truly revived her memory of what it was like to be in a relationship with a man—the physical, mental and emotional links that somehow made life more exhilarating. Even though common sense insisted this relationship could only be a temporary one, Emily had to acknowledge she didn't want it to end here.

It didn't matter how *foreign* Zageo was, in so many respects he was a marvellous person who lived an extraordinary life. She felt privileged to share just some of it with him. If he cast her off once he'd achieved his side of the trade…a sense of wretchedness clutched her heart.

She deeply regretted having reduced the sex they'd had to a form of prostitution, holding out for payment. The frustration of having no news of her sister's situation had driven her stance, not a lack of trust in Zageo's integrity. However, he'd clearly felt a strong sense of insult on two counts—her rejection of a natural outcome for their mutual attraction and her apparent disbelief in the keeping of his word.

Mistakes… Emily brooded over them, making herself more and more miserable as the evening wore on. She ordered a light dinner from room service but had no appetite for it. In her anguish over what was happening at the special outdoors dinner Zageo was attending, she switched off the lights in her suite and sat on the darkened balcony, watching the VIP guests below and trying to gauge if the meetings taking place were convivial or strained.

The three African tenors took turns in entertaining their audience, only coming together for a grand finale after coffee had been served. They were enthusiastically applauded, deservedly so, each one of them in marvellous voice. Once their concert was over, Emily trailed off to bed, having learnt nothing except for the firsthand observation that powerful people were royally entertained and probably expected it as their due.

Bed was the loneliest place of all. Her body yearned to be once more intimately entangled with Zageo's, to feel all the intense and blissful sensual pleasure he had introduced her to. She tossed and turned for what seemed like hours. She didn't know when sleep finally overtook her restlessness, didn't know how long she had slept, didn't know what woke her.

There was no slow arousal from slumber, nothing pricking at her consciousness. It was as though a charge of electricity had thrown a switch to activate her. Her eyes snapped open. Her mind leapt to full alert.

The figure of a man was standing by the bed. The room was too dark to see his face but her heart did not flutter with fear. She knew instantly who it was. A surge of relief, hope and pleasure lilted through her voice.

'Zageo…' She pushed up from the pillow,

propping herself on her elbows. 'I'm so glad you're here.'

Her gladness ran smack into a wall of tension, which seemed to suck it in and become even stronger, keeping him resolutely separate from her. It sparked a swift awareness that he had not meant to wake her, that he had come in the dead of night to look at her for some private reason and did not like being caught doing it.

Did he miss her, too?

Did he still want her as much as she wanted him?

Was pride forbidding him to admit it?

'Glad?' he fired back at her. 'Because you want news of your sister?'

His voice was clipped, angry, *hating* how his involvement with her now turned on the welfare of people he didn't even know.

Emily sat up, *hating* having dealt with him as she had. 'No,' she answered quietly, seriously. 'I'm sorry for…for making it sound as though being with you was only for the help you might give.'

There was a taut silence as he considered her apology. 'So…you admit this is not true?' His tone was more haughty this time, delivering scorn for the lie.

She heaved a rueful sigh. 'You know it's not true, Zageo.'

'Do not think I am deceived by this meek and mild act, Emily. If you imagine it might gain you more to butter me up than to demand…'

'No!' she cried in horror at his interpretation of her apology. 'I have really enjoyed your company and…and you're a fabulous lover, Zageo. I'll remember this time with you for the rest of my life, the pleasure you gave me…'

'Are you saying you no longer wish to withhold yourself from me?'

Emily took a deep breath, anxious to right the wrongs she'd done him and not caring how brazen she was about it. 'Yes,' she declared emphatically. 'I'd like you to come to bed with me right now.'

There! She couldn't be more positive than that! Her heart galloped as she waited for some response from him, frightened by his chilling stillness and frantically hoping for the desire he'd shown her to return in full force.

After an interminable few moments he spoke. 'You want me.'

Emily wasn't sure if it was a question or an ironic comment, but she answered without hesitation, 'Yes, I do.'

'Then show me how much, Emily.' No doubt about his tone now. It was hard and ruthless, challenging her mind, heart and soul. 'Show me that what I do tomorrow will not be done for nothing.'

Tomorrow…Hannah…the link burst through her brain, and on its heels came the red alert warning *not to ask*! If she brought her sister into this moment which was charged with explosive elements relating to only Zageo and herself, it would blow apart everything that could be good between them. Every instinct she had urged her to seize this night and make it theirs.

She swung her legs off the bed. He made no move towards her. His silence screamed of waiting…waiting to see how far *she* would go for *him*. Her eyes had become accustomed to the darkness, allowing her to see he was wearing the light cotton robe supplied by the hotel. No need for him to dress properly when the doors to their suites faced each other across the upstairs porch. Emily had no doubt he was naked underneath the robe.

She'd worn nothing to bed herself, hoping he might come. Any inhibitions about her body were long gone with Zageo. She was only too eager for him to touch it, caress it, pleasure it. But he didn't reach for her as she stepped close. He maintained an aloof stillness. Waiting…

Emily thought of how much he had *shown* her. Without the slightest hesitation she started undoing his tie belt. 'Were you lying in bed, thinking of what you could be doing with me?' she asked huskily, determined to seduce him out of this stand-off.

No reply.

'I was, for hours and hours,' she confessed, drawing his robe apart, sliding her hands up his chest, lightly rubbing her palms over his nipples. 'I wanted to feel you as I'm feeling you now.'

His chest lifted as his nipples hardened under her touch. The swift intake of breath was inaudible but his body revealed the signs of excitement. Emily moved around behind him and slid the robe down his arms, getting rid of the garment. Her hands went to work on the taut muscles of his neck and shoulders—a soft, sensual massage.

'Relax, Zageo,' she murmured. 'I don't want to fight you. I want to make love to you.'

He didn't relax. If anything, his muscles tightened even more.

She ran featherlight fingers down his back in soft whirling patterns, revelling in the satin smoothness of his skin as she gradually worked her way to his waist. Then she moved in, pressing her breasts against his sensitised back, gliding her hands around to the erotic zones on either side of his groin, caressing them, silently rejoicing in the tremors she raised with her touch.

'You've brought me back to life again,' she confided, trailing kisses down the curve of his spine. 'I've just been going through the motions for the past two years. Meeting you, knowing you…it came as a shock. I didn't know how to handle it, Zageo. But I do want you.' She pressed her cheek into the hollow between his shoulder blades, fervently murmuring, 'I do.'

His diaphram lifted with the quick refilling of his lungs with air. Emily moved her fingers lower, reaching for him, hoping she had aroused the desire he'd always *shown* her. Elation zinged through her as she felt his strong erection, the soft velvety skin stretched to contain the surge of his excitement.

Just the most delicate touch on the tip…and Zageo exploded into action, whirling around, seizing her waist, lifting her, carrying her headlong onto the bed with him, pinning her down, his eyes stabbing into hers with fierce intensity.

'Do not play with me, Emily. This has gone beyond games,' he stated harshly. 'Beyond anything civilised.'

'I wasn't playing with you,' she cried breathlessly.

'Then give me the new sense of life I gave you. I need it now. Now…'

He kissed her with a devouring passion that fired a tumultuous response from her. She wasn't trying to prove anything. Her own wild surge of need met his, fiercely demanding expression, craving satisfaction. His arms burrowed under her. She eagerly arched her body, wanting fierce collision, a swift primitive mating, the ecstatic sense of him driving into her.

It came and her body seemed to sing with exultation in his possession of her, her possession of him. It was marvellous, beautiful, glorious. She was hungry for the wonderfully intense feelings it generated, greedy for them. Her arms grasped him tightly. Her legs wound around him, urging him on, goading him on.

Zageo filled her with his power, lifted her onto wings of ecstasy that had her flying high, then swooping into delightful dips before soaring again, higher and higher until she simply floated in a delirium of pleasure, waiting for the ultimate fusion of his climax, the final fulfillment of their becoming one again.

When it came, to Emily it was sweeter than ever before. She hoped he felt as deeply moved by this special intimacy as she did. His forehead pressed briefly against hers, mind to mind, she thought, body to body.

Then he heaved his weight off her, rolling, scooping her along with him, pressing her head over his heart, his fingers thrust into her hair, not stroking as he usually did, but grasping her scalp, holding her possessively against the thud of his life-beat.

He didn't speak.

Neither did she.

Emily was happy to have her head nestled precisely where it was. Her own heart kept time with his, giving her a blissful sense of harmony, the soft drumming gradually soothing her into a deep and peaceful sleep, cocooned securely in his embrace.

When he removed that embrace and left her, she had no idea. It was morning when she woke again and where he had lain in the bed was cold. For a few minutes she fretted over why he would have returned to his own suite instead of staying with her. Perhaps she hadn't answered his need. Perhaps…

Then she remembered.

Hannah!

Zageo had some action planned for tomorrow and now it was tomorrow. Last night she'd been certain it related to the trade they'd made. If that assumption was right, did he feel it was worth doing this morning? Was that why he was missing from her bed? He'd already gone about the business he had prearranged?

Emily rushed to the bathroom, anxious to be showered, dressed and ready for anything.

Today was important.

On how many counts she couldn't begin to guess.

CHAPTER FIFTEEN

EMILY braved knocking on the door to Zageo's suite, arguing to herself that last night's intimacy gave her the right to at least say hello. There was no response—disappointing, but to be expected, since it was almost nine o'clock and he was probably already attending to whatever he had planned for today.

A tense anticipation was jiggling her heart as she took the path to the central complex of the hotel. She wanted news of Hannah's situation but was frightened of what it might be. Something pertinent had transpired at last night's dinner or Zageo would not have come to her. From his attitude—from what he'd said—Emily sensed the news was not good.

The trade was giving him more trouble than he'd bargained for.

Guests were breakfasting on the terrace and in the main restaurant. Neither Zageo nor his aide-de-camp, Abdul Haji, was amongst them. Emily walked on to the grand reception area—built like a pavilion with its splendid columns and open-air sides. She found Leila, the employee Zageo had appointed to look after her needs.

'Have you seen the sheikh this morning, Leila?'

'Yes. He left the hotel very early with Mr Haji.'

'How early?'

'At sunrise.'

'And they haven't returned,' Emily muttered, wondering if Zageo had left a message for her at reception.

'Mr Haji has,' came the helpful reply. 'I saw him walking by the river a little while ago. Would you like me to find him for you, Miss Ross?'

'No. No, thank you,' Emily answered quickly, acutely aware that Zageo's right hand man was not at her beck and call and would be affronted by such a move on her part. However, if she ran into him accidentally…

'Is there anything else I can do for you?' Leila inquired.

Emily flashed her a smile and shook her head. 'I think I'll just idle away this morning. Thanks again, Leila.'

Where would Zageo have gone by himself? The question teased her mind as she left the reception area, passing by the Livingstone Lounge—honouring the explorer, David Livingstone, who'd discovered and named Victoria Falls after the then Queen of England. It was furnished like a British colonial club room with many groups of leather chairs and sofas, card tables, chess tables, mahjong tables, plus a bar at the end—all designed to cater for every recreational taste. A glance at the few occupants assured her the black bearded Abdul Haji was not present.

She stood on the terrace, looking from left to right, hoping to spot the man. To the left, the view along the river was unobscured. Everything from last night's dinner and entertainment had been cleared away, leaving nothing but pristine green lawn and the magnificent shade trees. She saw no one taking a stroll in that direction.

To the right there were more trees, plus the cabana providing service to the swimming pool, and closer to the river bank two white marquees where various types of massages were on offer. If Abdul Haji was still walking, Emily decided it had to be somewhere beyond the marquees.

Five minutes later, Emily spotted him, leaning on the railing of a small jetty, apparently watching the swirl of the water as it rushed towards the fall. He caught sight of her approach and straightened up, focusing his attention on her with what felt like a hostile intensity, which was highly disquieting. She hesitated on the bank beside the jetty, torn between her need to know about Zageo and the sense of being distinctly unwelcome.

Abdul Haji frowned, made an impatient gesture and tersely said, 'There is no news. We must wait.'

It seemed that Abdul thought she knew more than she did. Hoping to elicit some information, she prompted, 'Zageo left at sunrise.'

Hands were thrown up in disgust. 'It is madness, this adventure—' his eyes flashed black resentment at her '—flying directly to the farm over the heads of Zimbabwe officialdom. What if your brother-in-law persists in not seeing reason, even when your passport is shown to him? So much risk for nothing.'

Shock rolled through Emily's mind and gripped her heart. Zageo was putting his own life at hazard to keep his word to her. It was too much. She would never have asked it of him. Never!

Diplomatic connections…bribery…deals under tables…big money talking as it always did…all these things she had imagined happening, but no real personal risk. However, the comment about Malcolm not seeing reason suggested that Hannah's husband hadn't cooperated with what had been initiated to help the family's situation. And Emily realised her own attitude about *payment* had virtually forced Zageo to deliver.

'I'm sorry,' she blurted out, her own anxiety for his safety rising. 'I didn't mean for it to go this far.'

Abdul glared a dismissal of her influence. 'His Excellency, the sheikh, does as he wishes.'

'Yes, of course,' she agreed, not about to argue against male supremacy in this instance. 'It's just that if we hadn't met…'

'It is futile to rail against Fate.'

Emily took a deep breath as she tried to

stop floundering and gather her wits. 'I didn't realise Malcolm would cause problems.'

'A man does not easily give up what is his. This I understand. But Malcolm Coleman must be made to understand that the loss is inevitable. There is no choice,' Abdul said fiercely. 'That was made very clear last night.'

The meeting…Zageo coming to her afterward…deciding what had to be done to honour his side of their trade.

Emily felt sick. 'I shouldn't have asked him to help.'

Abdul frowned at her. 'You made a request?'

'Yes,' she confessed miserably. 'After I'd received the e-mail from my sister…when we met for dinner that evening—'

'The decision was already made,' Abdul cut in, waving a dismissal of her part in promoting this action.

Flutters attacked her stomach. 'What do you mean…*already made*?'

'On his return to the palace from your visit to The Salamander Inn, His Excellency sought me out and ordered a preliminary investigation into ways to secure the safety of your sister and her family,' Abdul curtly informed her.

'Before dinner?' Emily queried incredulously.

'It was late afternoon. His Excellency wished to alleviate your distress, Miss Ross. Surely he told you so when you met that evening.'

She'd rushed straight into the trade!

It hadn't even occurred to her that Zageo might care enough—on such short acquaintance—to initiate action which might give her some peace of mind about her sister. No wonder he'd been angry at her assumption that he'd only do it to have sex with her.

'Yes, he did say he'd help,' she muttered weakly.

'These are difficult times in Zimbabwe. Our negotiations kept breaking down. It has been very frustrating,' Abdul muttered in return.

And on their last night in Kenya she had more or less accused Zageo of doing nothing!

She'd been so wrong. So terribly, terribly wrong. Feeling totally shattered by these revelations, Emily almost staggered over to a nearby bench seat and sank onto it, her legs having become too rubbery to keep standing.

'He took my passport to identify himself as a friend to Hannah and Malcolm?' she asked.

'It is to be hoped it will satisfy.' Abdul frowned at her again. 'You did not know this?'

'Zageo said he had something planned for today but he gave no precise details.'

'All going well, he intends to fly them out.'

'Without…' She swallowed hard. 'Without permission from the authorities?'

'A blind eye may be turned but I have no reason to trust these people.' The signature tune of a mobile telephone alerted him to a call. 'Please excuse me, Miss Ross,' he said, whipping the small communicator out of his shirt pocket and striding to the end of the jetty to ensure a private conversation.

Emily waited in tense silence, hoping—fearing—this was news of Zageo's rescue mission being transmitted. Abdul had his back turned to her so she could neither hear him speak or see his expression. Her heart jumped as he wheeled around, tucking the telephone back in his pocket.

'We go,' he called, waving her to join him as he strode back to the river bank, clearly galvanised into action.

Adrenaline surged through Emily as she leapt to her feet. 'Go where?'

'To the landing pad. Your presence is required there.'

'Landing pad?'

'For the helicopter,' he explained impatiently, probably thinking her dim-witted.

Emily had imagined Zageo was using his private aeroplane, but a helicopter definitely made more sense in the circumstances—a much quicker in and out. *If* Malcolm and Hannah had co-operated in leaving the farm with Zageo.

She half-ran to keep up with Abdul as he headed up to the hotel. 'So Zageo is on his way back?' she asked breathlessly.

'Yes. But not yet out of danger. He is using one of the helicopters that normally flies tourists around and over Victoria Falls. It allows some leeway over Zimbabwe airspace but not as much as this flight has taken.'

Could it be shot down?

Emily couldn't bring herself to raise that question, though she felt compelled to ask, 'Is my sister…?'

'They are all in the helicopter,' came the curt reply. 'It will be reassuring for the Coleman family to see you, Miss Ross.'

'Right!' she muttered, thinking what black irony it was that *they* didn't completely trust Zageo's word, either.

Guilt and shame wormed through her. She

had not credited Zageo with compassionate caring nor with the kind of integrity that went beyond any normal expectation. He was not only a man of great character, but the most generous person she had ever known. Given another chance, she would show him an appreciation that went far beyond the bedroom.

At the hotel entrance a driver and minibus were waiting to transport them to the helicopter base. This was only a fifteen-minute trip from the hotel and neither Abdul nor Emily spoke on the way. Once there, they were met by the base manager and escorted straight through the waiting lounge where groups of tourists were gathered for their sightseeing flights.

As soon as they were outside again and taking the path to the landing pad, their escort pointed to a black dot in the sky. 'That's it coming in now.'

'No problems?' Abdul asked.

The base manager shrugged. 'Not in the air. Our best pilot is at the controls.'

The limited answer worried Emily. 'Are any of the passengers injured?'

'Not to my knowledge. There was no call for medical aid,' came the reassuring reply.

They waited near the end of the path, watching the black dot grow larger and larger. Emily felt a churning mixture of excitement and apprehension. While she desperately wanted to see Hannah and her family safe and sound, would they thank her for interfering in their lives? Zageo had acted on her behalf, probably being very forceful, intent on *showing* her he did deliver on his word. She could only hope this dramatic rescue had been the right action to take.

The wind from the whirling helicopter blades plastered her clothes against her body and blew her hair into wild disarray but Emily maintained her stance, facing the landing so she was immediately recognisable to her sister. She could now see Hannah in the cabin, directly behind Zageo who was seated beside the pilot.

At last the helicopter settled on the ground. The base manager moved forward to open the door and assist the passengers in disembarking. Zageo was out first. He gave Emily a searing look that burnt the message into her brain—*payment made in full*! Then he turned to help Hannah out, delivering the sister who had not made it to Zanzibar—the sister who had inadvertantly brought Emily into his life.

But would he want her to stay in it?

CHAPTER SIXTEEN

EMILY had found it a strangely fraught day. While there had been joy in the reunion with her sister and relief that the rescue had been very timely according to Malcolm, who was immensely grateful to have his family brought to a safe place, she was wracked with uncertainty over where she stood with Zageo.

He had bowed out of any further involvement with her family once they had been brought to the hotel and given accommodation. 'I'm sure you'll want some private time together,' he'd said, making no appointment with Emily for some time alone with him.

Naturally the moment he had excused himself from their presence, Hannah had pounced with a million questions about *the sheikh* and Emily's involvement with such an unlikely person, given her usual circle of acquaintances.

Where had she met him?

How long had she known him?

What was their relationship?

Why would he do so much for her?

The worst one was—You didn't sell yourself to him, did you, Em?—spoken jokingly, though with a wondering look in her eyes.

She had shrugged it off, saying, 'Zageo is just very generous by nature.'

'And drop-dead gorgeous.' Hannah's eyes had rolled knowingly over what she rightfully assumed was a sexual connection. 'Quite a package you've got there. Are you planning on hanging onto him?'

'For as long as I can,' she'd answered, acutely aware that her time with Zageo might well have already ended.

A big grin bestowed approval. 'Good for you! Not, I imagine, a forever thing, but certainly an experience to chalk up—being with a real life sheikh!'

Not a forever thing… Her sister's comment kept jangling in her mind. Having said good-night to Hannah and Malcolm and their beautiful little daughters, Emily walked slowly along the path to her own accommodation, reflecting on how she had believed her marriage to Brian was to be forever. The words—*Till death do us part*—in the marriage service had meant fifty or sixty years down the track, not a fleeting few.

It was impossible to know what the future held. Life happened. Death happened. It seemed to her there were so many random factors involved, it was probably foolish to count on anything staying in place for long. With today's technology, the world had become smaller, its pace much faster, its boundaries less formidable. Even culture gaps were not as wide. Or maybe she just wanted to believe that because the thought of being separated from Zageo hurt.

She wanted more of him.

A lot more.

On every level.

Having arrived on the porch outside the doors to both Zageo's suite and hers, she decided to knock on his, hoping to have some direct communication with him about today's events. Disappointment dragged at her heart when there was no response.

She tried arguing to herself that he had come into her suite last night and would come again if he wanted to. There was no point in chasing after him. It hadn't worked for Veronique and Emily had no doubt it wouldn't work for her, either. When Zageo decided it was time up on a relationship, that was it.

Tomorrow his private jet was to fly Hannah and Malcolm and the girls to Johannesburg, from where they would catch a commercial flight to Australia. For all Emily knew, she might be expected to go with them. With the depressing thought that this could be her last night anywhere near Zageo, she turned to her own door, unlocked it and entered the suite which she knew was bound to feel even more lonely tonight…unless he came.

He didn't come.

He was already there.

As Emily stepped past the small foyer and into the bed-sitting room, Zageo entered it from the balcony where she had sat watching last night's special dinner. She wanted to run to him, fling her arms around his neck and plaster his face with wildly grateful kisses for his extraordinary kindnesses to her family. It would have been the natural thing to do if everything had been natural between them. But it wasn't. Because of the trade *she* had initiated. So she stood with her feet rooted to the floor, waiting to hear her fate from him.

He didn't move towards her, either, standing stiffly proud and tall just inside the room, his brilliant dark eyes watching her with an intensity that played havoc with every nerve in her body. If he still felt desire for her, it was comprehensively guarded.

'Is all well with your sister and her family?' he asked, his tone coolly polite.

'Thanks to you, Zageo, as well as it can be, given such a traumatic upheaval to their lives,' she answered quietly.

'In the end there was no choice but to accept the upheaval,' he stated unequivocally. 'Your brother-in-law was a marked man, Emily.'

'Yes. So I understand. And while I will be eternally grateful you did go in and get them out, when I made the…the deal…with you, I didn't expect you to endanger your own life, Zageo. I thought—' she gestured a sense of helplessness over his decision to act himself '—I thought something more impersonal would be worked.'

His eyes blazed a fierce challenge. 'Was it impersonal…your joining your body to mine?'

'No! I…'

'Then why would you expect me to do less than you?'

'I didn't mean...' She stopped, took a deep breath, and desperately not wanting to argue with him, simply said, 'I was frightened for you.'

His head tilted to one side consideringly. 'You cared for my safety?'

'Of course I did!'

'As, no doubt you would for anyone in danger,' he concluded dismissively.

It wiped out what she'd been trying to get across to him. How could she build bridges if Zageo was intent on smashing them? Before she could come up with some winning approach he spoke with a chilling finality.

'Nevertheless, all is well that ends well. You no longer have anything to fear, Emily.'

Except losing him from her life.

He gestured towards the writing desk. 'There is your passport. Now that our trade is complete, you are free to go wherever you like. Perhaps to Johannesburg with your sister tomorrow.'

Her inner anguish spilled out, needing to hear the truth from him. 'You don't want me with you anymore?'

A blaze of anger answered her. 'Do not turn this onto me. You have said over and over again I give you no choice.' He flung out an arm as though releasing her from all bondage to him. 'Go where you will. I free you of any sense of obligation to me.'

She lifted her own arms in an impassioned plea. 'I want to go with you, Zageo. Wherever you go.'

He gave her a savage look. 'For as long as it suits you, Emily? To see more of Africa and do it in the style I can provide?'

'I wouldn't care if we were doing it on a shoestring budget. I want more of you, Zageo,' she cried recklessly.

'Ah! So it is the sex you want more of,' he mocked. 'The pleasures of the flesh are enticing, are they not?'

'Yes,' she flung back at him, seizing on his mocking statement to fight his stand-off position. 'That was what enticed you into keeping hold of me in the first place, and it didn't seem to me you were tired of what I could provide for you last night.'

His eyes narrowed. 'Most men facing possible death would want to have sex beforehand.'

She burned, hating the humiliating minimalisation of what they'd shared. 'You were just using me? Is that what you're saying, Zageo?'

'You do not care to be used, Emily?'

The message was scorchingly clear.

He'd hated being used by her.

The heat in her cheeks was painful, but she would not drop her gaze from his, determined on resolving the issues between them. 'I'm sorry. Mr Haji told me this morning you had intended to help with Hannah's situation anyway. Believe me, I already feel wretched over misjudging the kind of person you are. My only excuse is…I thought the way you dealt with Veronique meant dealing with me in the same way would not be unusual for you.'

He gave a derisive snort. 'I knew what I was buying into with Veronique. You, my dear Emily, did not fit any mould I was familiar with.'

'Well, if I surprised you, multiply that surprise by about a million and you might approach how big a surprise you've been to me,' she retorted with feeling. 'Talk about being in foreign territory with a foreigner…'

'Yes!' His eyes fiercely raked her up and down. 'Extremely foreign territory with a foreigner!'

'But we have found a lot of mutual ground, haven't we?' she quickly appealed. 'And we might find even more pleasure in everything if we stay together. And I don't mean only in bed, so if you think I want to tag along with you just for the sex…'

She ran out of breath. The tension in the room seemed to have a stranglehold on any free flow of oxygen. In fact, Emily felt hopelessly choked up and couldn't think what else to say anyway.

'Do I understand you now wish to accompany me on this journey without fear or favour?' Zageo asked, cocking an eyebrow as though merely ascertaining her position, certainly not giving away his own.

Emily swallowed hard and managed to produce a reply. 'I'd like to try it.'

'Being companions and lovers.'

'Yes.'

'No more bartering.'

'No. Complete freedom of choice.'

Let this woman go, Zageo fiercely berated himself. *No more talk. No more delay. Let her go now*!

'Emily, freedom of choice is a myth. There is no such thing, not in your culture nor mine. We are bound into attitudes and values by our upbringing and we think and act accordingly.'

Her beautiful blue eyes begged a stay of judgment. 'But we can learn more about each other, try to understand where we're both coming from, be willing to make compromises...'

She was still tugging on him, getting under his skin. 'No,' he said emphatically. Abdul was right. His mind was barely his own around this woman. She drove him into excesses. He had to put a stop to it, regain control, make sensible decisions. 'What we came together for...it is done, Emily.'

Her shoulders slumped. There was a flash of anguish on her face before her head bowed in defeat. 'So this is goodbye,' she said in a desolate little voice.

'Yes,' he said firmly, hating seeing her like this. She was a fighter, strong, resilient, resourceful. She had challenged him to the limit and beyond. Whatever she was feeling right now, she would get over it and move on.

As he must.

Zageo propelled his feet forward, determined on walking out of this suite, walking out of her life. It was better that the power she had exerted over him was brought to a close. Though he couldn't help thinking there was a bitter irony in her surrendering to his will at the end. He didn't like it. He liked it even less when a glance at her in passing showed tears trickling through her lowered lashes and down her cheeks.

Silent tears.

She had dignity.

Dignity that pulled hard on him.

Emily Ross was not just sexually desirable. She was a very special woman, unique in his experience. When she gave of herself, she gave everything.

He reached the door.

There was no sound behind him. No movement.

Did he really want to give up what he'd found in Emily? Did such a decision make him master of his life or did it make him less of a man for not meeting the challenge of keeping her at his side?

He sucked in a deep breath, needing the blast of oxygen to clear the feverish thoughts attacking what had seemed so clear to him all day. His hand was on the doorknob, ready to turn it. A few more seconds and his exit would be effected. No going back.

'I forgot to say thank you,' she jerked out huskily. 'Not for my sister and her family. For me. All you did for me. Thank you, Zageo.'

The emotion in her voice curled around his heart, squeezing it unmercifully. His brain closed down, instinct taking over, driving his legs back to where she still stood with her head bent in hopeless resignation. He grabbed her waist, spun her around, clamped her to him with one arm, cupped her chin with his hand.

'Look at me!' he commanded.

She raised startled, tear-washed eyes.

'I have decided our journey should not end here. We shall continue to be companions and lovers if you find this arrangement agreeable.'

Sparkles of joyful relief shone back at him. Her arms flew up around his neck, hooking it tightly. The soft lushness of her breasts heaved against his chest, reminding him how very delectable they were, as was the rest of her.

'Sounds good to me,' she whispered seductively, no hesitation at all about surrendering to his will, which Zageo liked very much this time. Very much indeed.

It drew his mouth to hers, the desire to taste and savour her giving was totally overwhelming, obliterating any possible second thoughts about having changed his mind.

It was a kiss worth having.

Emily Ross was a woman worth having.

And have her he would, regardless of where it led.

At least until this passion had spent itself and he was free and in control of himself again.

CHAPTER SEVENTEEN

THE last hotel, Emily thought, looking out the tall windows of their suite, taking in the sparkling view of Cape Town's waterfront. Their journey through Africa had been amazing—so many different facets of the country from wonderful wildlife to highly cultivated wineries—but it was coming to an end now. Once Zageo was satisfied that all was well with this perfectly sited boutique hotel, the next stop would be Dubai.

Emily didn't know how their relationship was going to work in Zageo's home territory. Perhaps he would decide to house her in Paris or London, avoiding too big a cultural clash. Emily didn't mind what he arranged as long as they remained lovers. The thought of having no part of his life was unbearable.

'I see Veronique wasted little time in mourning my departure,' Zageo drawled sardonically.

The mention of his former mistress sent a frisson of shock down Emily's spine. She'd just been thinking of Paris and now she was reminded that the model had been with Zageo for two years. Would her own relationship with him last that long?

Behind her came the rustle of the English newspaper he'd been reading over his after breakfast coffee. 'According to this report, she's about to marry the German industrialist, Claus Eisenberg. It will be his third trophy wife but I don't imagine Veronique is looking for lasting love so they will probably suit each other well.'

His mocking tone goaded her into asking, 'Do you believe that love can last, Zageo?'

The impulsive question was driven by her deep sense of vulnerability about her future with him and she hoped for a serious reply, needing some guide to where they were heading together.

'Yes,' he asserted strongly. 'I do believe it can. My mother and father are still devoted to each other.'

While this statement did not relate to her in any way, it lifted Emily's heart and she turned around, smiling at him. 'That's really nice.'

He smiled back. 'We do have that in common since your own parents are content with their marriage. And speaking of them—' he waved towards the computer notepad he'd acquired for her use '—you haven't checked your mail this morning.'

'I'll do it now.'

She crossed to the writing desk where the small slimline computer was set up, ready for her to connect with the Internet. As she switched on and started keying in her password, she was very conscious that this was yet another example of Zageo's generosity and his caring consideration for her needs, ensuring she had electronic access to her family at any time of the day or night.

She hadn't asked for it. She hadn't asked Zageo for any of the things he'd bought for her along the way. He'd taken her shopping for clothes whenever he'd considered her own outfits unsuitable for *his* companion and Emily had argued to herself she was indulging his pleasure in her, not taking him for all she could get. The clothes were unreturnable but this computer could be passed to Abdul Haji if and when Zageo said her time with him was over.

She wasn't like Veronique.

She had come to love Zageo with all her heart.

'There's a message from Hannah,' she said, wanting to share everything with him.

'Any news?'

'Malcolm is happy to get into the sugar industry, managing Dad's cane farm. Jenny and Sally have started at a playschool to get them used to being with other children and they've both found best friends to play with. And Hannah…oh, how wonderful!' She clapped her hands in delight and swung around, beaming a big grin at Zageo. 'Hannah's pregnant!'

'That's good?' he quizzed with a bemused air.

'She wanted to try for a boy, but Malcolm was worried about her going through another pregnancy when the situation in Zimbabwe was so unstable. Besides, he insisted he was perfectly happy with his girls and didn't need a boy.'

'All children are precious,' Zageo commented.

'Yes, but having been just two sisters ourselves, Hannah and I always fancied having mixed families. I do hope it's a boy for her this time.'

'You wouldn't mind having three children yourself?'

'Actually I think four is the perfect number. Two of each.'

'Four has always been a very significant number,' Zageo mused. 'Did you know it resonates through all the religions of mankind?'

'No, I didn't.'

'Even in your Christian religion, it comes up over and over again—forty days and forty nights in the desert, the four horsemen of the apocalypse…'

Emily's interest was captivated as he went on, spelling out the commonality that underpinned so much of what the people of the world believed in. Zageo was far more broadly educated than herself and he often expounded on fascinating pieces of knowledge. She couldn't help thinking he would be a marvellous father and fiercely wished she could be the mother of his children.

He suddenly stopped theorising and smiled at her, bestowing a sense of warm approval that made Emily tingle with pleasure. 'There's a place I'd like to show you today. Let's get ready to go, once you've replied to Hannah. And please send my congratulations to her and Malcolm.'

'Will do.'

She turned back to the computer notepad, happy to write her own congratulations as well as his and eager to go wherever Zageo wanted to take her.

When they emerged from the hotel, a gorgeous yellow Mercedes convertible with blue and black leather upholstery was waiting for them. 'Wow!' Emily cried excitedly as the doorman led the way to it. 'Is this for us?'

Zageo laughed at her burst of pleasure. 'It's a beautiful day, we will be driving down the coast, and I thought we should have a happy sunshine car to make it a more exhilarating trip,' he said.

'What a great idea! I love it!' Emily enthused, having long given up protesting Zageo's extravagance over anything he did with her. Over the past three months of being with him, she'd learnt that what gave him pleasure invariably gave her pleasure so it made no sense to fight it.

It was, indeed, an exhilarating trip, all the way to Cape Point which offered a spectacular view over the Cape of Good Hope, the southernmost point of Africa. The peninsula ended in a high cliff, on top of which stood a lighthouse. It was clearly a popular tourist spot. Numerous flights of steps led up to it and there was a funicular to transport those who didn't want to do the long climb.

'Would you like to ride or walk?' Zageo asked.

'Walk,' Emily decided. 'We can take our time enjoying the view from all the rest stops along the way.'

He took her hand, encasing it firmly with his. Emily loved the physical link with him. Somehow it was more than just companionable. It felt as though he was laying claim to her in a much deeper sense. Or maybe she was reading into it what she wanted to.

Just savour this time with him, she told herself, and make the most of each day as it comes. Hadn't she learnt from losing Brian so young that it was important to live the moment, not spend it counting her tomorrows?

Yet even as she enthused over the spectacular vista of cliffs and ocean, she couldn't help commenting, 'You really should visit Australia, Zageo. It has the most brilliant coastline in the world. Just north of Cairns we have the Forty Mile Beach, all clean white sand. The Great Ocean Road down in Victoria with the fantastic rock formations called the Twelve Apostles rising out of the sea, is just breathtaking. Not to mention…'

She ran off at the mouth, encouraged by the warm pleasure that danced over her from his twinkling eyes. 'If you would be happy to show me, I would be happy to come,' he said when she'd finished her tourist spiel, making her heart swell with joy. It was clear proof that he saw no end for their relationship in the near future.

Emily's delight in the day increased a hundredfold. Having been assured that this last tip of the African continent had no personal relevance as far as she Zageo were concerned, she could barely stop her feet from galloping up the last flight of steps to the top viewing area around the lighthouse.

They moved to the furthermost point and she stood against the stone safety wall, cocooned from the other tourists by Zageo who stood closely behind her, his arms encircling her waist, making her feel they were on top of the world together.

'Here we are at the Cape of Good Hope and you are looking down at where two great oceans meet, Emily,' he murmured, his head lowered to rub his cheek against her hair, his soft breath making her ear tingle.

'There should be some sign of it,' she mused. 'Waves clashing or different water colours mingling.'

'Instead there is a harmonious flow, a union that does not break because of coming from different places. This is how nature ordains it. It is only people who make demarcations.'

Emily sighed at this truth. Why couldn't the stream of humanity recognise its natural commonality instead of dividing itself into hostile camps?

'Are you brave enough to merge your life with mine, Emily?'

Her heart leapt. Her mind frantically quizzed what he meant. Hadn't she already merged her life with his?

'I'm brave enough to do anything with you, Zageo,' she answered, her stomach fluttering nervously over whether this was what he wanted to hear. She had the frightening sense that something critical was coming.

His arms tightened around her, pulling her body back into full contact with his. He kissed the lobe of her ear and whispered, 'Regardless of the differences that have shaped our lives, we have that natural flow, Emily. So I ask…will you marry me and be the mother of my children? Stand with me, no matter what we face in the future? Stand together as we are now.'

The shock of hearing a proposal she had never expected completely robbed Emily of any breath to answer. Her body whipped around in his embrace, her arms lifting to fly around his neck, instinctively grabbing for every linkage to him. Her eyes drank in the blaze of love and desire in his, taking all the fierce courage and determination she needed from it.

'Yes, I can do that, Zageo,' she said with absolute assurance. 'I will do it,' she promised him. 'I love you with all that I am.'

Sheikh Zageo bin Sultan Al Farrahn looked into the shining blue eyes of the woman who had made it impossible for him to choose any other woman to share his life. He remembered arrogantly determining to put her in her place, not realising at the time that her place would be at his side. He had decided to find a *suitable* wife, and he had found in

Emily Ross a true compatibility in everything he really valued.

He lifted a hand to stroke her cheek in a tender caress, wanting to impart how very precious she was to him. 'And I love you with all that I am,' he replied, cherishing her words to him, repeating them because they carried a truth which should be spoken and always acknowledged between them.

A lasting love…

A love that no force could touch because they willed it so…together.

MILLS & BOON® PUBLISH EIGHT LARGE PRINT TITLES A MONTH. THESE ARE THE EIGHT TITLES FOR JUNE 2006

THE HIGH-SOCIETY WIFE
Helen Bianchin

THE VIRGIN'S SEDUCTION
Anne Mather

TRADED TO THE SHEIKH
Emma Darcy

THE ITALIAN'S PREGNANT MISTRESS
Cathy Williams

FATHER BY CHOICE
Rebecca Winters

PRINCESS OF CONVENIENCE
Marion Lennox

A HUSBAND TO BELONG TO
Susan Fox

HAVING THE BOSS'S BABIES
Barbara Hannay

MILLS & BOON®

Live the emotion

0506 Rom LP

MILLS & BOON® PUBLISH EIGHT LARGE PRINT TITLES A MONTH. THESE ARE THE EIGHT TITLES FOR JULY 2006

THE ITALIAN DUKE'S WIFE
Penny Jordan

SHACKLED BY DIAMONDS
Julia James

BOUGHT BY HER HUSBAND
Sharon Kendrick

THE ROYAL MARRIAGE
Fiona Hood-Stewart

THE WEDDING ARRANGEMENT
Lucy Gordon

HIS INHERITED WIFE
Barbara McMahon

MARRIAGE REUNITED
Jessica Hart

O'REILLY'S BRIDE
Trish Wylie

0606 Rom LP

Praise for *Shine*

"If you take Hallowell's extraordinary knowledge and wisdom and combine them with the latest in brain science, you get this unique, fascinating, and highly useful book!"

—Carol Dweck, author,
Mindset: The New Psychology of Success

"This is an inspiring book that every manager should read. Hallowell has made clear just how important connection is to long-term success and laid out a powerful playbook for how to get the best out of people—and yourself."

—Jim Robinson, General Partner, RRE Ventures, and former
Chairman and CEO, American Express; and
Linda Robinson, Partner and Chairman,
Robinson, Lerer and Montgomery

"Hallowell has a great gift as a doctor, as a scholar, and as a consultant to business. His gift is that he teaches us all how to play. It is that same gift that makes *Shine* such a valuable and enjoyable book."

—George E. Vaillant, MD, professor of psychiatry;
author, *Spiritual Evolution*

SHINE

SHINE

Using Brain Science to Get the Best from Your People

Edward M. Hallowell, MD

Harvard Business Review Press
Boston, Massachusetts

Printed in the United States of America

15 14 13 12 11 5 4 3 2 1

Library of Congress Cataloging-in-Publication Data

Hallowell, Edward M.
Shine : using brain science to get the best from your people / Edward M. Hallowell.
p. cm.
ISBN 978-1-59139-923-0 (hbk. : alk. paper)
1. Employee motivation. 2. Job satisfaction. 3. Performance.
4. Management. 5. Interpersonal relations. I. Title.
HF5549.5.M63H345 2011
658.3'14—dc22

2010024950

The paper used in this publication meets the requirements of the American National Standard for Permanence of Paper for Publications and Documents in Libraries and Archives Z39.48-1992.

To Dr. Shine,

who shines shoes and souls

at Boston's Logan Airport

CONTENTS

ACKNOWLEDGMENTS

Many people helped me in the writing of this book. I interviewed scores of leaders in business small and large, medicine, entertainment, sports, religion, academia, and other diverse organizations, all united by their expertise in bringing out the best in people. I quote some of these leaders in this book, so their names will appear. To them and to those whom space would not allow me to quote, let me say once again, thank you.

I also owe a huge debt to Melinda Merino and her great team at Harvard Business Review Press. Melinda's faith in this project and her insistence that I get it right turned what might have been just an ordinary book into the best book it could be. She positively drew the best out of me!

I also thank Genoveva Llosa, the business writer Melinda put me in touch with to help me find the right framework and tone for a business audience.

Each of my now eighteen books has been delivered with the help of my trusty agent, Jill Kneerim. She has been my faithful guide and cheerleader for almost twenty years now. She is the best!

Finally, of course, I thank the stars in my sky: my wife, Sue, the kindest, most skilled woman I know, who puts up with my quirks and moods and loves me still; my daughter, Lucy, whose passion and verve know no match and who turns twenty-one, heading into a glorious adulthood, as this book goes to press; my son, Jack, who, at eighteen, stands tall, strong, smart, and full of all the best in life; and my youngest, Tucker, who, at fifteen, has the spunk and sparkle to set the world on fire. I thank God every day for these four wonderful people. They are truly my stars.

INTRODUCTION

Brain Science, Peak Performance, and Finding the Shine

WHAT MAKES A PERSON SHINE? What separates people who feel fulfilled from those who suffer with regret? Here's a hint: it isn't money in the bank, fame, trophies, or rank, as much as those may matter. Many people don't finish first but nonetheless achieve greatness and long will be remembered, while many who do finish first will never be called great and will soon tumble into oblivion.

It doesn't much matter what you've got in your personal asset bank. Smart is overrated. Talent is overrated. Breeding, Ivy League education, sophistication, wit, eloquence, and good looks—they matter, but they're all overrated. What really matters is what you *do* with what you've got. If you hold nothing back, if you take chances and give your all, if you serve the world well, then you will exult in what you've done and you will shine—in the eyes of the world, in the eyes of those who matter to you, and in your own eyes as well.

The more a manager can help the people who work for him or her to *shine*, the greater that manager will be, and the greater the organization as a whole. Put simply, the best managers bring out the best from their people. This is true of football coaches, orchestra conductors, big-company executives, and small-business owners. They are like alchemists who turn lead into gold. Put more accurately, they find and mine the gold that resides within everyone.

Managing in a way that brings out people's best is a critical task, perhaps second in importance only to parenting in shaping the future of our world. More than any other quality, it takes heart to be such a manager. Rather than define heart, let me tell you about a man who has it.

When I was traveling to interview people as part of my research for this book, I got to Boston's Logan Airport early one day and decided to use the extra time to get my shoes shined. As I walked up to the stand, I noticed an old man seated next to it, a walker by his side. He was sitting with his head in his arms, which he had peacefully folded over the bars of the walker. Assuming he was just an elderly passenger taking a rest before his plane took off, I asked him if he knew where the shoe-shine guy might have gone.

"*I'm* the shoe-shine guy!" he proclaimed, straightening up immediately and showing the kind of smile that draws an instant smile out of you, too. "Set your bags next to my walker here and step on up into my *office*." Propelled by this elderly gentleman's sudden burst of energy, I hustled up onto the stand and settled into an old chair. Its sagging seat of cracked black leather had seen better days, but its proprietor was still going strong. As I put my feet onto the smooth brass footplates, I had no idea how extraordinary he was or how much he was about to influence me and this book.

He slid his chair over and announced in a slight southern accent, "Good mornin', sir, I'm Dr. Shine." He proceeded to inspect my shoes with the careful eye of a physician sizing up a new patient. He then began to spray water on my loafers, taking care not to wet my socks or trousers. "You in the corporate world?" he asked.

"No," I said, "but I work with a lot of people who are. I'm a psychiatrist and a writer. My specialty is helping people get the most out of their abilities."

"Interesting. Would you believe it, that's *my* specialty, too! I get up every morning, and I look forward to helping people get into the right frame of mind so they can shine, no matter where they go or what they do. When I do that, I'm happy."

"You sound like the better managers I consult with in business," I said.

"Do I?" he replied, then added with a chuckle, "Well, I'm sure I don't make their kind of money. But I do love what I do. For me, it's all about the shine I put on the person. You see, *I reach out.* Too many people don't reach out any more. They hold back. They're too worried 'bout something bad might happen, or they're in too much of a hurry. Or they think they have too many answers already and they're not curious anymore, so they miss *their big chance*. Every time you're with a person, you've got a big chance. I say, *don't miss it*. Don't worry about putting out the fire before you strike the match. I *always* strike the match. I want to find that spark in a person, you get what I mean?"

"I sure do. But how do you do it?" I asked, knowing that this was the crux of my book. Maybe Dr. Shine could sum it up for me. And he did.

"Just keep fishin'. I only get a few minutes, you know, so I gotta get right to it. Everybody's got that spark in them, somewhere."

Dr. Shine, you are so right, I said to myself. *Everybody's got it in them somewhere. But far from everybody finds their spark and makes the most of what they've got.* How come? That's what this book is about: helping managers help people find their spark and make the most out of what they've got.

"What about the grumpy people you meet?" I asked. "What about the people who don't even see you as a person? Working here, you must get a lot of those."

"Oh, sure, but I understand them. You gotta remember, *everybody* has their bad days. I never know what somebody who sits up there is up against, what problems they got, what's working on them. So I treat them good, no matter how they treat me. If you don't like people, you better not be shining shoes. I have multiple sclerosis, and my doctor says I better get ready to slow down, but I tell him my work is my best therapy. I love what I do, and my customers need me."

"You have MS? How do you keep doing this?" I asked.

"I talk to you!" Dr. Shine replied. "When someone is sitting up in that chair, all I think about is what *he* needs and that gives me my energy. If I can't forget about me and think about you, then I have no business shining shoes."

"You're pretty amazing. Where does your drive come from?" I asked.

"From people. I love to find that spark. That's it." A little time passed in silence while I watched Dr. Shine tend to my shoes with the sort of devotion you always see in people who care about what they do. "And you know what? People want what I do. They come from different terminals all over this place just to get a shine from me! I'm known all over Logan Airport."

"Do you work for yourself?" I asked.

"I work for *you*!" he immediately replied.

Like Dr. Shine, great managers serve others; they develop the shine in their people. I marveled at Dr. Shine. Here was a man with MS, working at Logan Airport, who embodied what I've discovered are the most critical elements that lead to achievement at the highest levels, no matter what the endeavor. In fact, without knowing it, Dr. Shine implemented a five-step process for managing high performance that I have come to call the Cycle of Excellence. It is a process managers everywhere can use.

Finding the Shine: Five Steps to Igniting Peak Performance

Life has changed radically from a generation ago. A manager's job is getting harder and harder to do. Some experts even say that managers are becoming obsolete, while others say managers are more important than ever.[1] Whatever the truth may be, the fact remains that managers work hard in pressure-packed, confusing, unsettled times.

The central question for all managers is how to draw the most from their talent. What do you do when your most talented people fall short of their full potential, or worse, fall off their game altogether? How do you find the spark that Dr. Shine always looked for?

Finding the shine in someone, helping all your people perform at their highest levels, isn't rocket science. It's actually more complex, mysterious, and important than rocket science. It's *brain science*, but it has yet to be codified into a simple and reliable process that all managers can use. In this book, I formulate such a code, the Cycle of Excellence. It is a process that I have created and honed over the past twenty-five years as a doctor, practicing psychiatrist, author, consultant, and instructor at the Harvard Medical School. Much as Daniel Goleman used brain science over a decade ago to shed light on emotional intelligence and show the business world how critical that is to success, I similarly draw upon brain science to explain peak performance and provide managers with a practical plan to bring the best from the people who work for them.

Rather than touting a single key idea for peak performance, the process I describe here incorporates many ideas while drawing upon the latest research from diverse disciplines. The five steps in the Cycle of Excellence, and what they will teach you, are as follows:

1. **Select:** How to put people into the right jobs so that their brains light up
2. **Connect:** How to overcome the potent forces that disconnect people in the workplace both from each other and from the mission of the organization, and how to restore the force of positive connection which is the most powerful fuel for peak performance
3. **Play:** Why play—imaginative engagement—catalyzes advanced work, and how managers can help people tap into this phenomenally productive yet undervalued activity of the mind
4. **Grapple and grow:** How managers can create conditions where people *want* to work hard, and why making

progress at a task that is challenging and important turns ordinary performers into superstars

5. **Shine:** Why doing well—shining—feels so good, why giving recognition and noticing when a person shines is so critical, and why a culture that helps people shine inevitably becomes a culture of self-perpetuating excellence

Each step is critical in its own right and translates into actions a manager or worker can *do and do now*. Each step builds upon the other. *The most common mistake managers make is to jump in at step 4 and ask people to work harder, without first having created the conditions that will lead workers to want to work harder*. There is no point in challenging employees to exceed their personal best if they haven't first been placed in the right job, found a safe and connected atmosphere within which to work, and been given a chance to imaginatively engage and contribute to the design of the task. But if you follow the steps you can create the conditions that will lead to hard work and peak performance.

This plan works because it brings together the empirical evidence on peak performance into one integrated series of steps—that create the ideal conditions, the perfect tension in the violin string, for managers to propel their people to excellence.

The Evolution of This Plan

While the Cycle of Excellence is based on the latest neuroscience, it has deep roots. It has evolved in my mind over 30 years during my practice as a psychiatrist. I developed the bare bones of the plan when I was a resident in training three decades ago to help my patients who were underachieving. I knew these individuals were talented, but they were unable to work at their full potentials. Some had the trait we now call attention deficit hyperactivity disorder (ADHD), while others struggled for different reasons. But they all shared the problem of not making the most of their talents.

Their managers assumed that they simply were not trying hard enough. But I could see sometimes they simply were in the wrong job. That's when I began to understand the practical importance of *selection* in achieving peak performance. In other cases, I could see they were shutting down because of a toxic culture in the workplace. That's when I grasped the importance of positive *connection* as a key to peak performance. In still other cases, my patients' talents were being wasted because managers were not challenging them or asking them to use their creative talents. Time after time, I saw that what *appeared* to be a failure to work hard enough actually grew from a frustrated desire *to* work hard. That's when I concluded that almost everyone wants to work hard, if they see they can succeed and grow.

I learned that all people want to work hard and will work hard, given the right job and the right conditions, because it feels supremely good to excel. Deep within all of us beats a primal desire to contribute something of value to this world and to stand out as a positive person in the eyes of others. Great managers make this happen.

But how? That's the riddle I have worked on over several decades. In this book I share the answers, represented by the Cycle of Excellence. Its roots go back to ideas that I offered first in my books about ADHD, *Driven to Distraction* and *Delivered from Distraction* (books that have sold well over a million copies), and later in a book for parents called *The Childhood Roots of Adult Happiness.*[2] But I knew that the method could help organizations as well, especially given how dramatically business conditions have changed in recent years. In 1999 I wrote an article for *Harvard Business Review* (HBR) called "The Human Moment at Work."[3] By the human moment, I mean face-to-face, in-person communication, as opposed to the electronic moment—communication via e-mail, cell phone, smartphone, Facebook, Twitter, text messaging, and instant messaging. From a biological standpoint, people deprived of the human moment in their day-to-day business dealings are losing brain cells—literally—while those who cultivate the human moment are growing them. Simply put, connecting genuinely with other people makes you smarter, healthier, and more productive.[4] Being alone for extended periods reduces your mental acuity.[5] Those are medical facts, but facts many managers don't appreciate or use.

The human moment is the chief supplier of what I call "the other vitamin C," vitamin Connect. Just as you will get sick and die if you are deprived of the original vitamin C, ascorbic acid, so can you get sick and in fact die if you are deprived of face-to-face, human connections (more on the research that proved this later). This led me to identify what I called the *first modern paradox: while we have grown electronically superconnected, we have simultaneously grown emotionally disconnected from each other*. Books like Robert Putnam's *Bowling Alone* and Thomas Friedman's *The World Is Flat* describe and document our new world and some of the obstacles it poses, not the least of which is loneliness.[6] But it is a new kind of loneliness. Modern loneliness is an extraverted loneliness, in which the person is surrounded by many people and partakes of much communication but feels unrecognized and more alone than she'd like to.

In a follow-up HBR article, "Overloaded Circuits: Why Smart People Underperform," I showed how modern life, due to its speed and a volume of data unprecedented in human history, can gradually overwhelm and suffocate the human brain, extinguishing not only human moments but also *neurons* in an individual's cerebral cortex.[7] Using my training as a medical doctor to inform the discussion, I described overload and excessive busy-ness as unique, unforeseen traps modern life sets that sabotage people's best efforts. How strange and ironic it was to see all the supposed "labor-saving devices" actually creating more labor.

The phenomenon of overloaded circuits leads to a *second modern paradox: people's best efforts often fail not because they aren't working hard enough, but because they are working too hard*. The brain has its limits. The tsunami of data comprising modern life can easily flood the brain and rot it. Working hard now becomes like bailing out a sinking boat (or brain) with a can, instead of plugging the leak. Many people try to keep up by frantically processing more and more data, bailing faster and faster even as data pours in, instead of erecting boundaries to prevent the data from gaining entrance without permission.

Both HBR articles provoked a spirited response. I began to hear from businesspeople every week, telling me that I was describing their situations *exactly*. They were struggling to figure out how to cope with this new electronic world of information overload while in a state of high anxiety amid the pressures of economic decline and globalization. I could also see that as managers contended with speed and overload and the loss of the human connection, they were feeling increasingly powerless. They felt they had no choice but to be crazy busy. They were feeling the pressures of "accountability" and other management techniques, they were facing frequent performance reviews and various kinds of electronic supervision, but they were also feeling unguided and underappreciated. They spoke of feeling left out on various limbs—not in a whining or complaining way, but in a stark and dispirited way. Meanwhile, in some business sectors their unscrupulous bosses were reaping huge profits, making out like bandits.

The day of Dilbert had dawned. Cynicism and loss of faith in organizations grew rampant. Disconnection—from fellow workers, from organizational missions and ideals—was gumming up the Cycle of Excellence. The disconnected, overwhelmed employee was too stressed out to imaginatively engage, and therefore he or she underachieved, unable to reach goals, unable to shine. The cycle was breaking down.

I was not the only person describing the problem, but as a specialist on the mind I was offering a perspective and ideas that businesspeople were increasingly asking me to share, which I did in my book *CrazyBusy: Overstretched, Overbooked, and About to Snap!*[8] "The title alone describes me," read many of the e-mails I received from businesspeople not just in the United States, but around the world. Businesspeople had always been busy—but in this new world, busy had gone ballistic. Thus I went on to write the book in your hands as a guide to achieving peak performance amid the pressures of today's crazy-busy, fear-filled, often amoral, insecure world. A key message: if managers can begin helping their people to use new technologies properly and to regulate their lives rather than becoming crazy busy, then they can become positively and usefully connected. The unique tools of modern life can lead people to phenomenal success. As Eddie Lampert, chair of Sears Holdings, told me, "Small can be big."

Fortunately, as management theory has moved away from hierarchical models over the last decades, many businesses have crafted cultures that are low on fear and high on cooperation, and that value innovation over conformity. Agile, matrix-like organizations found at such successes as Google, Wegmans, DreamWorks Studios, and SAS are modeling a new norm. It should come as no surprise that people perform better when they are happy. While we must be prepared to suffer necessary pain in order to achieve our best ("no pain, no gain"), it is hugely counterproductive to suffer unnecessary pain.

Yet even the best, most enlightened modern workplace continues to set traps that create unnecessary pain. Examples: the trap of social isolation, the trap of free-floating fear and insecurity, the trap of information overload, and the trap of a boundary-less, interruption-infested work environment. Managers need a plan to tap into what's best in their people while minimizing the damage from these common traps.

All of this is to say that what I conceived as a plan to help individuals with ADD or other problematic issues blossomed into a plan to help all people who work in organizations sidestep the damage done by the distractions, interruptions, and pressures of modern life. It became a plan that could help managers help their people achieve at their highest levels.

Adapting the Cycle of Excellence for businesses led me to test my ideas with leaders from various fields. I have interspersed some of their comments throughout the book, set off from the rest of the text, but what I learned from them has informed every page. Here is a partial list of people I interviewed.

- Clay Mathile, who built Iams from a small pet food company into a giant business he sold to Procter & Gamble for $2.3 billion

- Woody Morcott, who was CEO of Dana Corporation, a huge auto parts manufacturer, during its glory years in the 1990s

- David Neeleman, founder of JetBlue Airways and inventor of the electronic ticket
- Eddie Lampert, chair of Sears Holdings Corporation
- Heather Reisman, CEO of Indigo Books, Canada's largest chain of bookstores
- Marshall Herskovitz, Hollywood writer, director, and producer of such films as *Shakespeare in Love* and *Legends of the Fall*
- Joseph Loscalzo, Hersey Professor of the Theory and Practice of Medicine at Harvard Medical School and chair of the Department of Medicine at Brigham and Women's Hospital in Boston
- Anna Fels, New York psychiatrist and psychotherapist who specializes in treating high-level executives
- Thomas Shaw, Episcopal bishop in Massachusetts
- General Tom Draude, U.S. Marine Corps (ret.), recipient of the Purple Heart and two Silver Stars, and former executive with USAA
- Michael Pope, an assistant coach to the New York Giants, who has spent twenty-eight years coaching in the National Football League
- Jasper White, chef, author, and owner of several successful New England restaurants
- Nicholas Thacher, a veteran headmaster of various independent schools

- Leon de Magistris, hair stylist and owner of Leon & Company, the oldest business in the town of Belmont, Massachusetts

These people all agreed that the great trick in management today is to get the best out of people's brains. You cannot do it with a stick, no matter how big a stick you wield. Nor can you do it with just a carrot, no matter how juicy the carrot. Rather than a simple carrot-and-stick method, bringing the best out of people today requires that you create harmony. You must match the right people with the right jobs and environments. Craft the right setting, the proper culture, and the prime conditions under which people will *naturally* deliver their best, as naturally as a flower turns toward the sun and grows.

The Latest Research

In transferring my plan from the world of children, families, and schools to the world of businesses and organizations, I got lucky in my timing. As I was developing my ideas, the world burst with new research in several critically relevant fields.

First, neuroscience exploded in the 1990s, the "decade of the brain." The explosion has continued since then, with surprising discoveries that inform and bolster my plan, such as neuroplasticity (the fact that the brain can change throughout life) and the ability to promote brain growth through certain actions and activities.

Second, not only did the world of brain science change, but the world of psychology took a radical positive turn as well. Spearheaded by Martin Seligman, positive psychology emerged as the brightest, most useful new paradigm in psychology since the days of B. F. Skinner and his behaviorist theories. Instead of dissecting what's wrong with a person, positive psychology focuses on how to help people live and achieve at their highest and happiest levels. For example, thanks to the research of Mihaly Csikszentmihalyi, another leader in the positive psychology movement, we know the conditions under which a person's brain is most likely to "light up" and surpass its previous best.

And third, researchers started to take the oddly neglected psychological state called *happiness* seriously. They deepened its definition beyond mere sensate pleasure, and they learned how critical a positive state of mind—a happy state of mind, dare we say it?—truly is to achieving at your best. The old saw that excellence occurs in direct proportion to suffering is dead wrong. Excellence occurs in direct proportion to necessary suffering, but in inverse proportion to unnecessary suffering. We know this now because researchers finally looked scientifically at the roots of happiness and well-being, and how such factors contribute to performance.

These major breakout developments in three different areas provided me with a bonanza as I synthesized my theory of the Cycle of Excellence.

In addition to Seligman's work, I drew upon the research of a wide range of other experts, including Daniel Gilbert, a Harvard professor whose book *Stumbling on Happiness* is full of counter-intuitive insights; Don Clifton, Tom Rath, Marcus Buckingham, and others from the Gallup organization and the strength-based movement; Mihaly Csikszentmihalyi, originator of the concept of "flow"; George Vaillant, the Harvard psychiatrist who did the famous Grant study, a longitudinal study that followed one class of Harvard graduates for decades while identifying the variables that correlated most closely with success, health, happiness, and well-being; David Myers, another great researcher into the field of what makes for a satisfying life; Carol Dweck, the Stanford psychologist who gave us the powerful concept of the "growth mind-set"; Nicholas Christakis and James Fowler, whose work on social networks and connections sparkles with insights relevant to organizations; Stuart Brown, whose research into play shows how profoundly powerful play is for innovative thinking and even life itself; Marco Iacoboni, neurologist and neuroscientist whose work on "mirror neurons" gives insight at the cellular level into how and why people connect; Angela Duckworth, the University of Pennsylvania psychologist whose research into what she calls "grit" is showing that determination trumps IQ in predicting performance; my close friend, John Ratey, whose book *Spark: The Revolutionary New Science of Exercise and the Brain* shows how useful—yet undervalued—physical exercise is in promoting mental acuity; Kathy Kolbe, whose explication of "conation," the most important word/concept you've never heard of, gives managers an amazing new framework for understanding how to get the best out of people; and many others in the fast-advancing interdisciplinary world of peak performance research.

While, as an MD, my own knowledge of human physiology and brain function helped me synthesize the Cycle of Excellence, all of this new research served as important guides, dispelling some of the myths that have misled people about high achievement. These myths include "IQ predicts success" (it doesn't), "hard work conquers all" (paradoxically, hard work can sabotage success by leading you to try to overpower a problem rather than figure it out), and "the brain is hard-wired and unable to change once a person reaches adulthood" (wrong!).

Why These Ideas Matter Now

A while ago our world exploded. The environment and the world of towns and cities and families and communities blew apart, along with the world of ideas and information, of entertainment and communication, of politics and diplomacy, and of course the world of businesses and organizations. It's hard to date when the explosion started, but it was after JFK's assassination and before 9/11. Somewhere in there the modern big bang began. And it's still banging.

Living well in the midst of an ongoing explosion takes work, patience, skill, and luck. Managing well in the midst of an explosion may seem to require superhuman powers. Managers today may feel like the prophets in the Old Testament who asked, "Why me, Lord?"

You have your own answers to that question, such as: the challenge, the mission, the paycheck, the adventure, the calling, the necessity, or just the feeling that if you don't do it, nobody else will. So each day, you jump into the explosion. You do all you can to make sense out of chaos and keep your organization, your mission, and your people moving forward. You draw upon values and lessons you learned growing up, like "never say die," "give it your all," and "look for the best in people." When all else fails you fall back upon your core self—who you are, what you do when no one else is looking.

You can lose your bearings easily. As a manager, you can feel like the blind leading the blind. How are you supposed to know what to do when no one has a clue what will happen tomorrow? How do you reassure and lead people when you are scared as hell, at least in those rare moments when you have time to stop and think about what's really going on? What do you do about it? Shoot from the hip and hope for the best? Learn to love the smell of napalm in the morning?

Of course not. But the explosion that surrounds us makes managing people extremely dicey, to put it mildly. That's why I feel an urgency in offering the plan in this book. I want to give you a mooring you can hold on to and use as the storm gets wild. I want to give you a connection you can use.

A key to working my Cycle of Excellence is making the critical step of connection. When that is threatened, all the other steps go awry. Unless managers realize how crucial it is to create an emotionally stable, connected environment in the midst of the maelstrom of modern business life, they will—and do—sacrifice performance in the name of speed, cost cutting, efficiency, and what they perceive to be necessity. In such a context, deep thought disappears, only to be replaced by decisions based on fear. Frazzled becomes the order of the day.

As global competition and economic stress create problems for businesses of all kinds everywhere, managers who don't have a plan to stabilize operations will be compelled to revert to crisis mode, putting out fires all day, just hoping to survive. The managers who do best develop a method that enables their people to do their work without toxic stress. Most of the time, such plans and methods languish in a book on the shelf, and never get put into action. The method that actually gets used is some simple version of the carrot-and-stick approach: do this and you'll get that. Work hard—or else.

The "or else" seems to grow more ominous every day. Week after week, we read about one corporate calamity or another; one dire economic prediction after another; one reason after another to be afraid, *very afraid*. As the pinch grows tighter, the methods managers use grow more primitive. Fear rules. Management by fear, if not panic, becomes the mainstay of all but the most enlightened managers. And what do those enlightened managers know that others overlook? They know that fear disables the mind just as surely as lack of oxygen.

My plan offers an alternative to panic or serial crisis management. You will learn a method you can set in motion anywhere to bring out the best in any person, no matter what is going on in the wider world. I will also point out what to do when things break down. When a person is not performing at his or her best, it usually stems from a problem in one of the five steps in the Cycle of Excellence, most often steps 1, 2, or 3: select, connect, or play. I will show you how to identify those problems and how to correct them.

Once you understand the Cycle of Excellence as well as the ways it can break down, you will have a more effective plan for bringing out the best in your people than simply wielding the fear of job loss or exhorting them to try harder. You will be able to creatively manage for growth, rather than manage for mere survival. You will know how to capture the positive energy in the explosion surrounding us today and not let it blow you and your organization away.

KEY IDEAS

- People's best efforts often fail not because they aren't working hard enough, but because they are working too hard.
- What matters most is what you do with what you've got.

- Managers help people find and mine the gold that lies within them.
- In the words of Dr. Shine, "Everyone's got that spark in them, somewhere."
- Use the five steps in the Cycle of Excellence to bring out people's best. The five steps are select, connect, play, grapple and grow, and shine.
- Vitamin Connect—the other vitamin C—is a manager's most powerful tool.
- A person's brain can grow and change for the better with the help of a skilled manager.
- Optimism actually improves a person's performance.
- Smart people underperform when their circuits get overloaded.
- As people have connected electronically more than any other time in history, they have simultaneously disconnected interpersonally. This is bad for business—and for life in general. But it is eminently correctable.

CHAPTER ONE

Five Steps to Peak Performance

Greg, an ambitious, talented man in his mid-thirties, knew something was seriously wrong. He wasn't working anywhere near his best, and, despite his efforts to stay positive, he was feeling more and more cynical about his job. He knew he wasn't his usual smart, on-top-of-things self, but he couldn't figure out what was wrong or what to do about it. It was as if he had contracted some strange virus.

Greg was disengaged and underperforming. He felt like a walking cliché, stuck in his marketing position for a large footwear manufacturer, going nowhere. While his performance reviews were passable, he knew he could do far better, as did his superiors. He felt a mounting pressure, sensing that he couldn't keep underachieving like this much longer and still have a job.

He completed his assigned tasks reasonably well and on time, but he no longer offered his customary "extra." And as the company was cutting back, it was clear they wanted extra from everybody. But Greg didn't speak up much in meetings; he rarely volunteered fresh ideas, even though he had lots of them; and he waited to be told what to do rather than proactively taking on initiatives. This was not the usual Greg, the real Greg, but he didn't know where his old self had gone or how to get it back.

He began feeling increasingly desperate, sure that it was only a matter of time before his superiors became dissatisfied with him. The economy being what it was, he didn't want to lose his job, but he also hated stagnating. He wanted to be a good soldier and a team player, but it practically took a crane to haul him out of bed each day to go to the office. Not knowing what else to do, he came to see me, wondering if depression or some other treatable mental disability might be his problem.

I asked him questions about his job, starting with his boss and his colleagues.

"They're good people," he said without much enthusiasm, "but they don't know me. I don't know them, either. We don't have time to socialize or make small talk. It's a very driven, bottom-line kind of place. We always feel extreme pressure to make our quarterly numbers. That's the subtext in every meeting, every conversation—how are we doing with our numbers? Are we on target? Will we survive?"

"Do you like your boss?" I asked.

Greg laughed. "I can see you're a shrink. You want to know about my feelings. I don't mean to dismiss your question, but where I work, whether I like Peter or not is the last thing that matters. All that matters is, Is the work getting done?

"What's worse is that what it takes to *do* the work keeps changing, because the demands keep increasing while all the supports keep decreasing—like assistants and expense budgets," he continued. "Peter doesn't know me, and I don't know Peter. We don't have time to know each other. Oh, I know he plays golf and goes to Red Sox games, but what does that tell me? What we *both* know is that what's expected of us keeps increasing. It's brutal."

"Is that why you don't volunteer your ideas, because the work is wearing you out?" I asked.

"No, I don't speak up because I don't want to be shot down. I'm in survival mode there. But it's more than that. When I'm in survival mode, the ideas that come to me so easily when I'm away from work or even driving into work don't come. It's like I get stupid."

"But other people speak up, right? Why do they speak up, but not you?" I asked.

"I don't know," Greg said, looking at the floor, pushing his fingers through his hair. "That's why I'm here."

"Does Peter ever make suggestions to you? Or do any of your colleagues?"

Greg took a deep breath, and slowly blew it out. "Sure." Pause. "Peter makes suggestions. When he's supposed to. Like at performance reviews. But I could easily write the suggestions down before he makes them, they're so predictable and pretty much useless. Do my colleagues make suggestions? I suppose, but nothing that really sticks. You have to understand, we're all working in a scarcity economy there. Nobody has much of anything to give to anybody."

"How did you end up in this job in the first place?" I asked.

"I like marketing. Normally, I'm a dynamic, imaginative, self-starting kind of guy. I had a great interview there. I loved the culture of the company, or at least I thought I did. That was four years ago."

"What's keeping you there now?" I asked.

"I don't know," Greg said. "It's a job, a place where I go every day. What else would I do?" He paused. "I'm afraid, I guess. God, I can't believe how I've changed. I used to be a bring-it-on, fear-less cowboy type. Now look at me. It's all this uncertainty that's undoing me. How do I know the next job will be better? Assuming, that is, I could find a next job."

The more questions I asked, the more I sensed that Greg liked the substance of his job more than he let on. He liked the product he was marketing. He gave me a fascinating account of what made his company's sneakers so good. And he spoke respectfully, even fondly, about the people he worked with and for, despite his saying he didn't really know them.

Still, he checked some important parts of himself at the door when he walked into the office. He'd lost his swagger and his zest. Once the bold innovator, now he worked hard never to make a mistake, which kept him from taking the chances that would have led him to love his work and do his best. As brutal as the realities of his job indeed were, he let them brutalize him more than his coworkers did. He held back where they did not. The pressures led him to fear, and fear is one of the most formidable obstacles to peak performance.

I explained to him what I thought was going on, that he was in the right job but the circumstances of the workplace were paralyzing him. He was wrestling with the problem of disconnection.

"You're right," he said after some thought, "but what can I do about it?"

Julie was an executive in a large corporation. She was climbing the ladder, impressing her superiors. She was also making friends, even as she leapfrogged over others. She had the great gift of being able to excel without inducing envy. She was also married and the mother of two children under the age of ten. Many of her peers didn't know how she did it.

Increasingly, *Julie* didn't know how she did it, either. She felt as if she might collapse under the burden someday soon. She had an image of herself carrying a load of laundry up the stairs, her BlackBerry cupped under her chin as she talked to the office, one of her kids yelling up to her from downstairs. She envisioned suddenly splintering into a million pieces, laundry spilling down the steps and the BlackBerry landing atop the towels in a slow-motion fade-out.

Julie came to see me because she had heard from a consultant that I could help people who felt overwhelmed. "That's me," she said. "I can keep up, but no one has any idea how stressed I am. How long can I do that? I'm tough, but this is getting out of hand. Being a mom is the greatest thing in the world. Being an executive at Bingham is incredible, too. I'm unbelievably lucky. I never thought I'd climb this far this fast. I'm not even thirty-five yet and I'm higher up than I thought I'd be when I was forty-five. They love me there, and I love them."

"And the problem is?" I asked.

"That I'm going crazy," Julie replied. "Every day I come closer to meltdowns than anyone realizes. There are just so many demands on my time from so many people. I don't care how much women may have advanced in the last fifty years, we still do most of the child care, home care, pet care . . . "

"You're pretty full up," I said.

"That's right, I am. I've been told you specialize in people like me. What do you say to help us?"

"First of all, I say congratulations. You are succeeding in hard times both at work and at home. You deserve a ton of credit."

"Thanks," Julie said. I could see she warmed to that, as if no one said it to her often.

"If you're like most people in your boat, there are, in fact, specific steps you can take to make your life less crazy, without giving up what matters most to you."

The people in each of these stories brought problems to me that I commonly hear about in today's workforce. While Greg was wrestling with disconnection, Julie was wrestling with the equally common problem of overload. Disconnection and overload pose particularly modern obstacles to peak performance. I'll say more on each later in this chapter.

The Game Has Changed: Brain Science and Peak Performance in a Modern Context

As a manager, how many Gregs or Julies do you have on your team? Probably more than you think. As their manager, what is your plan to get them back on track (keeping in mind that "hope" is not a plan!)?

Thousands of workers today, like Greg, underperform and do not feel positively connected with their workplace or, like Julie, feel overwhelmed, teetering on the brink of meltdown. They are not "problem" employees—people with disciplinary issues, for example, or drinking problems—nor are they untalented.

Rather, feeling unable to do one's best while also feeling overwhelmed have become all-too-common problems even for top employees. Like Greg, thousands of underperforming employees incorrectly conclude that they must be in the wrong job, suffer from a mental disorder, or have some "big problem" they can't name that's holding them back. They think they might need some treatment, a medication, or a radical change in their lives. Or, like Julie, they suffer, in dire need of some labor-saving tricks or novel strategies that will enable them to do all they have to do in the limited time allotted.

Meanwhile, their (often also overwhelmed) bosses can't be bothered with the intricacies of such problems. They believe that for the money these people are being paid, underperforming or overwhelmed employees should *get over it* and figure out a way to do more with less. Over the years, these managers have heard from management gurus that the "secret" to turning underachieving employees around is to "empower" them or reward them with financial bonuses or other benefits. Some managers have even come to believe that the only way to deal with underperforming employees is to show them out the door—and then replace them with more "talented" or "motivated" ones, forgetting about the huge expense involved with replacing an employee—or that new hires soon come to resemble the people they replaced.

Drawing peak performance from employees like Greg is not about getting a person to work harder or staffing every position with highly motivated geniuses. And the answer to dilemmas like Julie's is not simply to offer praise. Instead, you need a plan—based on the evidence we have that tells us what works and what does not—to draw the best out of the Gregs and Julies. Of all mandates in management, this may be the most important: find constructive ways to get the best out of yourself and the people who work for and with you.

Plastic Makes Perfect

It is especially helpful for managers to know about one of the most dramatic of all recent findings from neuroscience, namely, that the brain is remarkably *plastic*. "Plastic" denotes *the brain's ability to grow and change throughout life*. Common wisdom has it that people don't change. Science has proven that to be false.

We have learned that not only is the brain plastic, it is also *competitively plastic.* You get better at what you practice, but you get worse at what you neglect. As the saying goes, "Use it or lose it." This is how Norman Doidge puts it in his book *The Brain That Changes Itself*:

> If we stop exercising our mental skills, we do not just forget them: the brain map space for those skills is turned over to the skills we practice instead. If you ever ask yourself, "How often must I practice French, or guitar, or math to keep on top of it?" you are asking a question about competitive plasticity . . . Competitive plasticity also explains why our bad habits are so difficult to break or "unlearn." Most of us think of the brain as a container and learning as putting something in it. When we try to break a bad habit, we think the solution is to put something

> new into the container. But when we learn a bad habit, it takes over a brain map and that prevents the use of that space for "good" habits. That is why "unlearning" is often a lot harder than learning.[1]

For managers—indeed, for all of us—*the discovery of plasticity is really, really good news*. It means you're never stuck with who you are, or who your employees are. We used to think only young brains could change and develop. We now know that the adult brain can do it, too! The adult brain can and does develop, adapt, and change. We can all get smarter and wiser and happier the longer we live. The conventional, dreary wisdom that people can't change is scientifically incorrect.

So, with proper care, the brain of the guy down the hall who keeps failing can learn to perform better, to perform at high levels and for years on end. He can continue to learn and grow for decades.

However, the fact of brain plasticity also means that brain function can go belly-up. It can fail. Without the right care, brain cells die. Put bluntly, without the right care, brains get stupid. Good news, though: such stupidity is preventable and reversible.

As a manager, using brain science simply means you're making sensible use of the relevant knowledge we've gained over the past two decades or so. You don't have to be a scientist to do so.

Not only do we now know that the brain can change and grow throughout life—or deteriorate—we also know many of the forces that make it change for the better or worse. For example, challenging a person in an area where she is skilled is good for her brain and makes it grow, much like a muscle. But overwhelming her with more than she can cope with is bad for her brain. Instilling optimism and hope into your work environment is good for everyone's brain, not just their emotional health. But promoting or allowing a culture of cynicism and pessimism leads to chronic negativity and lassitude, which makes for low-performing brains. Instilling confidence in someone leads to improved performance due to greater involvement of the cerebral cortex. On the other hand, an atmosphere of chronic fear disables the brain, causing a person's neurons to be hijacked from the cortex to deeper sites in the brain that deal with the negative emotion. People cannot perform at their best when they are excessively afraid.

A manager can use this basic knowledge to great advantage. She can encourage positive feelings and positive behavior within her organization, which in turn leads to brain growth. Conventional wisdom holds that human nature is basically selfish, that people don't fundamentally change past a certain age, and that management must protect the organization from the ravages of people's greed, envy, anger, contempt, guile, and deceit.

However, like the notion that brains can't change, the conventional wisdom of human selfishness is also under scientific review. As Harvard's George Vaillant points out, humans are in fact evolving in the direction of increased altruism:

> Over the past 200 million years, the genetic evolution of the human hypothalamus, with its capacity for the four F's—fight, flight, feeding, and fornication—has rendered our selfish "drives" only modestly more sophisticated than an alligator's. Human capacity for negative emotions like fear, disgust, and rage has probably not evolved much beyond that of a cornered rat. In contrast, our capacity for future-oriented positive emotions, like altruistic responses

> to the suffering of strangers and compassion, continues to evolve. Human beings . . . remain a work in progress.[2]

If a manager takes them seriously, these facts can help in the daily grind of running an organization. Many enlightened companies, like Google, SAS, Whole Foods Market, the Cleveland Clinic, and Cisco Systems, now take the care of their employees' brains seriously. They do it in various ways. Some encourage time off or have elaborate work/life-balance programs. Some, like SAS, have gyms and encourage physical exercise on-site. (Physical exercise promotes a protein called BDNF, or brain-derived neurotrophic factor, which stimulates the growth of new brain cells, leading exercise expert John Ratey to call it "Miracle-Gro for the brain."[3]) Some encourage naps and good nutrition. (Did you know that a daily 1,000–2,000 IU vitamin D supplement is good for you in general and your brain in particular?[4]) Above all, these organizations encourage positive emotional energy in the workplace to promote intellectual vigor and enhance productivity.

Evidence continues to mount proving that these "perks" are not mere pleasantries but bottom-line boosters. A 2009 article in *Harvard Business Review* pointed out that time off and downtime can enhance mental acuity, thus boosting productivity.[5] And Robert Stickgold, a sleep expert at Harvard, calls a nap at work, "the simplest way to reboot your brain." Indeed, Stickgold reports that "a nap with REM (or 'dream') sleep improves people's ability to integrate unassociated information for creative problem solving, and study after study has shown that sleep boosts memory . . . Even micronaps of six minutes—not including the time it takes to fall asleep, which is about five minutes if you're really tired—make a difference."[6]

What's All You Can Be?

The five-step Cycle of Excellence I outline incorporates an understanding of neuroplasticity and such "brain refreshers." The plan is practical and concrete, because plans for peak performance are often vague. Let me clarify what I mean by *peak performance*. The U.S. Army coined the slogan, "Be all that you can be." Who wouldn't want that? But we need to get more specific. If you're not careful, as you jump in and try to "be all that you can be," you'll find you're trying to be way too much, taking on more than you can possibly handle, and falling short all over the place. In order for a person to be all that he can be, he must take care not to set himself up to fail repeatedly. While the sky may be the limit, and while it is good to think big, it is also good to think smart.

So, by reaching peak performance, I don't mean taking on every task, embracing every opportunity, and going wild. I also don't mean achieving your personal best, your lowest score on the golf course, or your record-setting day in sales. What I mean by peak performance—and what most of us seek in our own lives and what managers wish to help their people achieve—is *consistent excellence with improvement over time at a specific task or set of tasks*. Those three factors—excellence, consistency, and ongoing improvement—define peak performance for my purposes. *Everyone* has it in them to deliver peak performance defined in that way (while *no one* has ever achieved the goal of "being all they can be").

To achieve peak performance as I define it each person just has to find the right place, the right job, the right conditions, the right fit. Here's where the role of manager becomes so critical.

It's easy to identify peak performance when it happens. Employees working at their peak typically lose themselves in a project or in a discussion with a colleague, client, or customer.

They may lose track of where they are, what time it is, even what day it is or whether or not they are hungry. Mihaly Csikszentmihalyi showed that people do their absolute best when they are in a state of mind he famously named *flow*, a state in which they become riveted and at one with what they're doing (should you ever want to refer to this man in conversation, his name is pronounced ME-hi CHICK-SENT-me-hi).[7] This is one of the most significant discoveries ever made in the science of peak performance.

You may not be able to stay in a state of flow all day, but you can stay in the Cycle of Excellence all day. People who love what they do spend most of their days in that cycle. Once you develop the habit of working in the cycle, you perform well not because you are driven, but because you are inspired.

You can't sprint to peak performance. While a computer can work all day and all night, a brain cannot. It needs rest, food, human engagement, and stimulation. It must be managed with care. If you sprint—work flat-out—for too long, your brain will deplete the neurotransmitters and other neurochemicals required to sustain top performance. We often forget that *thinking is work*. It requires energy, which is in finite supply and must be replenished regularly. To think well, the brain requires oxygen, glucose, and a host of nutrients and other factors, all of which get depleted over time. Without the right diet, sleep, exercise, and physical supports (good lighting, air supply, chair and desk, and so forth), the brain will underperform.

Other ingredients matter, too, such as a feeling of hope, personal control, optimism, and gratitude, to name a few. These emotional factors all contribute to optimal brain/mind function. Sucking it up and running until you drop won't deliver the best results.

Applying the Cycle of Excellence

The Cycle of Excellence works by exploiting the power of the *interaction* between what is within a person and what lies outside. *Neither the individual nor the job holds the magic. But the right person doing the right job creates the magical interaction that leads to peak performance.*

Every manager has the marvelous opportunity to make this magic happen by guiding employees in the five steps I outlined in the introduction. These five steps, when taken as a whole, will lead to peak performance for anyone. I describe each step a bit more here, and in the next five chapters I discuss them in further detail.

Step 1: Select

Step 1, select, starts the cycle in motion. Before a person does anything, he should figure out what he *should* do. Managers can help employees achieve peak performance by making sure they select a job or task that meets the following three criteria: (1) it is something *he is good at*; (2) it is something *he likes to do*; and (3) it is something that *adds value to the project or organization*. The intersection of those three elements creates the magical field in which consistent excellence can happen.

This step is pivotal since it influences everything that follows. Yet it is often overlooked. Millions of employees underachieve simply because they stumbled into the wrong job and never got out of it. It is critical that a manager know her people well enough to help them get into the right slots in the organization. In chapter 2 I provide a structured interview that managers can use to help deploy each person accurately and to his or her best advantage.

Step 2: Connect

Step 2, connect, fuels the cycle. Connection follows on the heels of wise job or task selection. People who are doing things that suit them feel connected to others and to a mission, and they achieve at the highest levels. They are inspired and inspire others. A positively connected work environment in which people feel understood and safe to be authentic is critical for employees to do their best. Fear disables people. Managers who take seriously the task of creating a positive emotional environment inspire their workers and help them to do far more than they thought they could. A positive work atmosphere is not a frill. It leads to a fire-in-the-belly commitment, which can become contagious. It's a workplace imperative that drives the bottom line.

The modern workplace tends to leave people *disconnected*—emotionally alone, isolated, exhausted, anxious, and afraid—with no idea how they got that way or what to do about it. Employees are too mentally overloaded or too stressed to converse and connect, and sometimes they are not even physically in the same location as their coworkers. Restoring their connectedness creates positive emotions that catalyze superior performance. Sometimes people who manage organizations forget about emotion, dismissing how a person feels inside as irrelevant, a soft or touchy-feely concept, or at best a by-product of good management, not a goal. That's a big mistake. Positive emotion can be a manager's greatest ally, his leg up on the competition, his hidden advantage—if he recognizes its power. In chapter 3 I will show you how you can create the kind of positive emotional environment for your employees that leads to sustained performance.

Step 3: Play

All managers recognize the importance of work. Not enough recognize the importance of *play* in catalyzing peak performance. First, let me define play. By play, I mean much more than what most people mean by play, namely, what kids do at recess. By play, I mean *any activity in which the imagination gets involved*. So defined, it constitutes the most advanced, productive activity the human brain can engage in. When workers seem dull or apathetic, it is usually not because they are *innately* dull or apathetic. It is usually because play is missing from their work and they are not engaged in creative problem solving.

Play is sometimes dismissed as trivial in the workplace, but it is not. *If you value play and promote it, it can transform your organization.* People at play produce creative results and leap from the humdrum to the exceptional. In chapter 4, I'll show you how to activate the imagination of your employees and *encourage* them to play. I'll also explain why scientific evidence points to the effectiveness of imagination and play as performance boosters.

Step 4: Grapple and Grow

Step 4, grapple and grow, naturally follows from play. Play leads a person to "get into" a task and, fueled by that feeling, to work harder and harder. It's important to remember that drudgery comes with every job: going over spreadsheet numbers if you are an accountant, updating schedules if you are a project manager, correcting legal briefs if you are an attorney, or grading papers if you are a teacher. No job is free of such tasks and no one enjoys them, which is why enthusiasm for one's work can wane over time. When that happens, managers mistakenly tend to think their employees don't have enough commitment (so they simply drive them to work harder and harder, creating burnout).

But the problem is not employee commitment. Rather, it is being made to work on a task they can't do well, or on one that is going nowhere and over which they have little or no control. In fact, *most people love to work, given the right conditions*. This means that if employees have *selected, connected,* and *played* well, *grappling and growing* in the job will be far easier. When managers ensure that employees work on tasks that suit their skill levels but still challenge them, that they work in an environment where they feel trusted, and that they feel open to play and think creatively, the drudgery of any project becomes bearable. In chapter 5, I'll show you how to maximize steps 1, 2, and 3. Doing so will increase the chances that *your employees will want to work hard.*

As a person continues to grapple and work hard, she makes progress and advances. She gains what I call mastery. *Mastery means making progress at a task that matters to you and is challenging.* It does not necessarily mean that you become the best or an expert. It does mean that you feel a sense of well-being and accomplishment. And it is good for business!

Managers are important because they can help almost any employee to make progress and achieve the feeling of mastery. When that happens, the spectacular lies around the next bend.

Managers often ask me, "Once I've set up my employees to produce great results, how do I motivate them to sustain their peak performance?" The answer is: help them achieve mastery. Nothing matches the feeling you get from making progress at a task that is challenging and matters to you in terms of building confidence and motivation.

Therefore, one of the most helpful skills a manager can develop is the ability to challenge the right person at the right time to contribute something that is important to the life of the organization. It can involve challenging the employee with something small, like drafting more influential presentations, or motivating him to take on something big, like developing a new system design for producing the company's major product. As the employee achieves mastery of the task or project, not only does the business grow, but the employee becomes a more valuable member of the organization.

Keep in mind that although achieving mastery can build confidence and instill motivation in employees, failing to make progress can disrupt their confidence and self-esteem, and serve to *de*motivate them. Great managers make sure everyone in their group is making progress. In the chapter called "Grapple and Grow," I'll explain further why the confidence and self-esteem that stem from mastery are powerful motivators and critical for sustained performance. I'll also show you how to help employees pursue mastery at their jobs.

Step 5: Shine

Step 5, shine, is what happens as employees work hard and advance. As they gain recognition, which affirms what they have done is valuable, they experience one of the greatest feelings a person can have. As a manager, you can help people to shine by providing them with praise, rewards, and awards for a job well executed. People who shine want to keep shining. They are motivated. They feel connected to the team, the group, and the organization. They become extremely loyal and want to help others in the organization advance. This completes the Cycle of Excellence and keeps it in motion.

By helping your employees implement these five steps consistently, you will lead any person to peak performance.

Too good to be true? It would be, if I were claiming that my method is the only one that works. I'm not. But I am promising that I will, in the pages that follow, describe *a* method, an effective, practical plan that an individual can use in his or her own life or that a manager can use in any organization, from a business to a football team to a Hollywood production crew.

What's new here is not just the specific bits of advice. We've all heard that doing what you love leads to success, that creativity begets engagement and growth, that alienation and disconnection are bad for business, and that recognition is a good motivator.

What is unique in this book is the *synthesis* of these seemingly unrelated ideas into a plan any manager can enact. The value of the Cycle of Excellence lies in its melding a wealth of diverse, proven knowledge and wisdom into *a logical succession of steps*—each step growing from the previous one. Taken by themselves, none of the recommendations about helping employees find the best fit, establish connections and trust, and engage them creatively in work is likely to result in lasting excellence. But taken together, these steps will galvanize the untapped energy, creativity, loyalty, and commitment most employees leave at the front door on their way in to work.

With this plan, managers can do consistently what they usually only do sporadically: help people achieve peak performance (as I have defined it). This is hugely satisfying and productive for both manager and employee. Most people never tap the full power of their own minds. Creating the conditions under which employees can thrive and exceed their own expectations is the exciting opportunity every manager can embrace today.

The next five chapters examine each step in the Cycle of Excellence in detail. Each step unearths buried treasure. What may seem obvious—like the need to select a job with care—isn't obvious at all when you think about it. For proof, just look at how many people get it wrong! Managers and workers alike make critical, avoidable mistakes that lead them both to underperform and to lose heart. But as you come to understand each of the five steps, you will see clearly how to reach the ultimate goal, helping all your people to shine.

KEY IDEAS

- You can't sprint to peak performance.
- The brain is competitively plastic: you get better at what you practice and worse at what you neglect.
- Physical exercise builds up your brain as much as it does your muscles and heart.
- Managers can encourage people to try a brief nap around 2 or 3 p.m. to refresh the brain and improve performance.
- Use the unique synthesis of the Cycle of Excellence to bring out the best in all people: Select; Connect; Play; Grapple and Grow; Shine.
- Positive emotion sets the stage for peak performance.

CHAPTER TWO

Select

IN THIS AND THE SUBSEQUENT four chapters, I describe a step in the Cycle of Excellence in more detail. Each chapter begins with an organizational example that demonstrates the importance of the step and shows how its mismanagement can lead to problems. I follow with a definition of the step, and then explain why and how it influences peak performance. After that, I provide specific advice on how to implement the step.

Mary Ann, a customer service associate at a large financial services firm, has hit a performance plateau. She has been answering customer calls for five years, and there isn't a customer problem that she hasn't heard before or solved. Even so, after all these years, she has never felt 100 percent comfortable dealing with customers. She still gets flustered easily when customers become aggravated and, though she has figured out how to respond well to these situations, she dreads the actual calls. As a result, she takes a bit longer than she should answering calls in the queue, which means fewer calls get answered. Customer reviews are OK, but not great. In general, Mary Ann seems to lack enthusiasm for answering any more calls each day than she absolutely has to; she seems to merely go through the motions. Her manager assumes that she is just not a superstar like some of the newer employees, who are a little green but enthusiastic and can be counted on to make their quota.

One night, while talking with Mary Ann at a company-sponsored happy hour, the manager discovers that she donates her time every weekend to a local nonprofit organization by training new volunteers. She loves the work and looks forward to it. What she enjoys most is helping the young volunteers develop their skills.

The next day, the manager reassigns Mary Ann. Rather than taking calls, she becomes responsible for training new customer service associates. Suddenly she begins to thrive. She's excited to come to work and brims with new ideas for training associates and for improving customer service. Younger associates look up to her. The number of calls answered by the department increases and overall customer reviews improve. What happened?

Select: Put the Person in the Right Job

What happened was that Mary Ann found the right match for herself in the organization. With the help of her manager, she made the best selection.

Put simply, *select* refers to matching a person with the right job. As Jack Welch put it, "Getting the right people in the right jobs is a lot more important than developing a strategy."[1]

The best selection results from paying attention to the following three particulars:

What a person likes to do most

What a person does best

What adds greatest value to the project or organization

As a manager, if you can see to it that (a) your people are mostly doing what they like most to do; (b) they are using the skills they have honed most sharply and the abilities that set them apart from others (what Strategic Coach founder Dan Sullivan calls a person's "unique ability"); and (c) what they are doing is adding the greatest possible value to the organization, then you know the match between employees and their tasks is excellent.[2] Step 1, *select*, is solid.

Felicity Follows Fit; Misfit Makes Misery

When the match between employee and task is wrong, everything that follows, no matter how diligently pursued or fervently desired, suffers. Working the wrong job is like marrying the wrong person: it will involve lots of hard work but few happy days.

While selecting well is crucial, many people get it wrong. According to a 2005 Harris Interactive survey, 33 percent of the 7,718 employees surveyed believed they had reached a dead end in their jobs and 21 percent were eager to change careers, while only 20 percent felt passionate about their work.[3] Why do so many skilled and motivated people spend decades going from one job or career to the next? A chief reason is they never select the right outlet into which to plug their brains so that they will light up and glow.

Instead, they fall into common traps, seduced by fool's gold. They pick jobs they think are the most prestigious, the highest-paying, or the most secure. Managers and companies participate, unwittingly, in "bad selection" when they glorify certain jobs over others or provide perks for some jobs and not for others. For example, in publishing, acquisition editors are clearly given perks (such as better offices) and more recognition than are publicists, marketers, and production employees. Thus, English majors out of college yearning to work in the world of books join the editorial department even if sometimes they lack the social skills for networking, the business instincts that are essential for the acquisition process, or the drive to achieve acquisition quotas.

In other professions, perks, salaries, and access to decision makers—not their skills and interests—often influence employees' desire for certain jobs. Certain realities about the economies of supply and demand may be inescapable when it comes to employee compensation, but managers should be conscious that differences in money and status associated with certain positions often attract the wrong employees to the wrong jobs.

Another common mistake is selecting a job based on what parents, friends, or partners think is best. Or a person may follow the path of least resistance and never actually make an active choice at all; instead, just go with the flow.

First, match what a person is good at and likes to do with what adds value to the organization—and then encourage hard work. A person can't will himself to want to work hard, and a manager can't cheerlead employees who are in the wrong spot in the organization.

> *The better the fit, the better the performance. First, you are putting a person in a job you know they are capable of. A person needs to be in a role that's clear, where they can do the job but there's room to challenge and stretch them too. But you don't want the stretch to be too big.*
>
> —HEATHER REISMAN,
> *CEO of Indigo Books*

Another trap that can lead to a poor selection is blind adherence to the adage "Follow your dream." Taken by itself, "Follow your dream" could be the most dangerous advice ever given. Americans are particularly susceptible to it because we built our country on the American dream. "Follow your dream" *is* good advice, but, unexamined, *it can destroy lives.*

While we're all encouraged to dream, we get little guidance on which dream to pick, or how to make that dream come true, other than—you guessed it—*work hard.* Equipped only with the sentimental advice to pursue a dream and the Calvinist command to work hard, it is no wonder so many people never fulfill anywhere near their potential nor gain the satisfactions that come with doing that.

How many people do you know who dreamed of greatness, wished upon a star, worked hard, failed to achieve the dream, and now see themselves as failures or, at best, wistful wannabes? How many people think to themselves, "I coulda been a contender!"?

There is a better way. Pick the right dream, examine it, and make sure it is a dream that suits you well enough that you will *want* to work hard, very hard, to make it come true, and also make sure that *even if it doesn't come true, you will feel glad and proud that you pursued it anyway*. You will feel satisfied to have done what you have done, even if you didn't achieve the dream. If you select wisely, the pursuit of the dream becomes the great reward, the love of your working life. The final outcome matters far less than spending a life doing what you love. As Kipling wrote, words that are now inscribed on the tunnel leading to center court at Wimbledon, one must "meet with Triumph and Disaster and treat those two impostors just the same."[4]

Wise selection of your dream turns work into a lifelong game you love to play, win or lose—and everyone does plenty of both!

Right selection not only protects a person from lifelong disappointment, it also lets us see that there is really no such thing as a stupid, untalented, or lazy person. *All* people look bad when they have chosen the wrong dream. I would look untalented playing center field for the Red Sox, for example, even though that was my childhood fantasy. But when people focus on what they can do well, they look good.

Working hard is of course good, but peak performance requires much more than that. If a person has selected a job poorly, he will never reach his potential, no matter how much effort he puts into it. Sooner or later he will feel defeated and forlorn.

Today, many exciting jobs beckon. Opportunities abound—now more than ever in human history. But so many viable choices means that people can end up blundering from one bad choice to the next. Within the organizational context, at least, managers help employees make better choices by taking time to investigate their skills and interests so as to match each person's brain with the right task for that person. This is one of the best ways to advance the organization.

How to Recognize the Wrong Match

As a manager, be on the lookout for telltale signs of a wrong fit. For example, you can tell if a person is not in the right role if he feels no enthusiasm for what he's doing, if his mind never lights up, if he never gets excited about his job, if he chronically complains. This doesn't mean he's a dull person or that the line of work he has chosen is intrinsically dull, just that he's not assigned to the right task.

One way you can tell if your employees are in alignment with the Cycle of Excellence is to see if they are having fun. Working hard and playing hard go hand in hand when the fit is right. Of course, a manager's primary goal is not to promote fun; it is to promote productivity. But discerning the level of shared enjoyment in the workplace is an excellent test of the quality of fit between employees and the jobs they're assigned to do.

If you don't believe that fun and production go hand in hand, just watch a close football game. The players are working hard, but they're having fun. Or watch a surgeon. Surgery is painstaking, high-pressure work, but surgeons have a blast doing it. Or watch a great conductor, or a member of the symphony. When I go to the symphony I try to sit close to the stage because I get inspired just by *watching* the sublime intensity of the musicians at work. It is magnificent to watch what people can do when they are plugged into the right task in life.

> *You have to find where your passion is. You've got to figure out what it is that makes you hyperfocus. Even if it is something that is not going to earn you the most amount of money, you should go do that because if you don't, you're going to be miserable. You have to find out what it is and then do it. Maybe it's a hobby, and maybe you grit your teeth and make it through work during the day but then reserve some time that you can go fly your model airplanes or whatever. Find something that's your passion, that you become the expert on, and no one in the world knows more about it than you. Find what it is and stick with it. Mine was JetBlue.*
>
> —DAVID NEELEMAN,
> *Founder of JetBlue Airways*

The wrong fit makes the person feel dead in her work, unable to sink the teeth of her imagination into a task. Everybody does better work when they are able to use their brains fully and activate their creative side.

If your employees feel that they are not using their whole selves in their work, or if you see that they are underperforming, realize that this may not entirely be their fault. Find out what their true talents are and figure out what they might do instead to make the most of their talents.

How to Make the Right Match: The Three Frameworks

Selection starts the Cycle of Excellence. It will not guarantee peak performance without the other four steps, but it is crucial. Get it wrong, and years, even entire careers, get wasted. A manager can prevent such waste by intervening in practical and effective ways. In this chapter I offer three frameworks to help. The first framework is an interview template I have developed over my years in consulting and teaching.

The Structured Interview

To promote best selection, you, as a manager, need to begin by gathering key data. It astonishes me how often managers do not take a few minutes to ask basic, obvious questions that will assure the best use of an employee's skills. Clients in my office often tell me, "No one has ever asked me what I like to do or what I do best." When I ask them why they don't volunteer that information, they say they don't want to complain or make waves. While I always encourage them to volunteer the information anyway—it is in everyone's best interest—it would be simpler if managers would take the initiative.

The goal is for employees to spend as much time as possible at the intersection of three spheres: what they like to do, what they are most skilled at doing, and what adds value to the project or organization.

How do you find that out? There are many tests, tools, and instruments available, some quite elaborate and expensive. While these can be valuable, they should not be the first step. The first step is much simpler. As one who has been working in the field of psychological assessment for more than twenty-five years, has performed thousands of such assessments, and has taught medical students and residents at Harvard the ins and outs of such assessments, it amazes me that most people, even the supposed experts, tout tests and technology while routinely neglecting the most powerful "assessment tool" ever invented: the one-on-one conversation.

How do you find out what your employees' strengths and interests are? *You ask.*

"The Hallowell Self-Report Job-Fit Scale" (see box) is a structured interview you can give to your direct reports. Ask the employee to take a few days or a week to think carefully about his replies to each question and then write down his answers. Then it is a good idea to have a conversation to review the answers in person. Much more comes across in a personal interview than can ever come through in written form. In addition, spontaneous information can come out in a face-to-face interaction, understanding and trust can develop, and the conversation can deepen. This allows you, the manager, to ask additional questions or get clarification, and it gives the employee the wonderful and, in some organizations, rare experience of feeling heard and understood at work. That alone will add to his motivation and performance.

I preface the questions in the interview with some written explanation. When an employee—or anyone—fills out a form asking for personal information or takes a "psychological test," there is usually some suspicion. The lead-in to the questions should dispel whatever fears the person responding might have. If, after reading it, the person still does not want to fill out the interview, I would not force the issue, but let it go. Perhaps after building more trust with the employee, he or she may be willing to do this at a later time.

THE HALLOWELL SELF-REPORT JOB-FIT SCALE

The following is a questionnaire that managers can give to their direct reports. The comments in parentheses after each question can provide discussion points and help you as a manager turn the employee's answers into some useful action. It is critical that you create a safe climate in which the employee can respond honestly and fully to each question. Ideally, the answers will provide a starting point for you to help your people enjoy a more successful and fulfilling career.

It's useful to take a fresh look at yourself—as if you were getting to know a new person—as a way of helping you and your employer make the best use of the skills and attitudes you bring to work. The answers you provide to the questions here will give you a chance to organize a wealth of valuable information about yourself and give your employer important information he or she might not have.

Organizations can choose from literally thousands of psychological tests that purport to unravel the secret of who you are. People both love them and fear them for this reason. Fear not. There is no test that will tell you exactly who you are. Even the best are part science, part tea leaves. Ultimately human nature remains elusive, and that's probably good. The best tests allow *you* to formulate the conclusions. When you generate the answer, you will both understand it and feel confident about acting upon it.

So, the "test" offered here is not like most that are out there, whose answers are supposed to carry hidden implications about "who you are." Rather, it's simply a framework and a prod to get you to put what you already know about yourself into words and gather the information into a coherent whole that you can use as a guide.

It's best not to answer these questions only in your mind as you read; instead, write your answers on a separate sheet of paper. You might find it useful to complete this questionnaire with another person, each of you responding to the questions and giving feedback to the other about your responses. This can make the exercise more fun, more accurate, and more useful.

As you answer these questions, you will be generating what amounts to a neuropsychological assessment—not the kind that a professional would conduct, but one that is a lot quicker to generate and is, in many ways, more useful. The questions will help your manager to help you—and will ultimately lead you to conclusions as to how to manage your kind of mind most effectively.

Once you have answered these questions, you and your manager will be better able to find the right fit for you at work because you will have a clearer idea of what your skills and preferences are, where you fit best in the organization, and under what conditions you feel most comfortable and motivated.

1. What are you best at doing? (You ought to do most what you do best. It's amazing how many people spend years trying to get good at what they're bad at instead of getting better at what they're good at.)
2. What do you like to do the most? (This is not always the same as the answer to question 1. Unless it is illegal or bad

for you, you ought to preserve sizable chunks of time for what you like to do the most. If the activity is also productive and useful, it ought to be your career.)

3. What do you wish you were better at? (Your answer here may guide you to a course you should take or a mentor you should work with. On the other hand, it could be an indication of a task you ought to delegate or hire someone to do.)
4. What talents do you have that you haven't developed? (Don't say "none." Everyone has bundles of them. Pick a few. Don't hold back. Just because you name them doesn't mean you have to develop them. But you might want to develop one or two. Or you might not.)
5. What skills do you have that you are most proud of? (This often reflects what obstacles you have had to overcome, as we tend to feel proudest of what came hard.)
6. What do others comment on most often as being your greatest strengths? (This question is designed to help you identify skills you have but may not value because they seem easy to you.)
7. What have you gotten better at that you used to be bad at? (This gives you an idea of where putting in additional effort can pay off.)
8. What are you just not getting better at, no matter how hard you try? (This tells you where not to waste any more time.)

9. What do you dislike doing the most? (Your answer here suggests what tasks you might want to delegate or hire out.)
10. The lack of which skills most gets in your way? (If you lack a skill required in your current job and you can't delegate it, then that is getting in your way. Your answer to this question might lead you to take a course, read a book, or work with a mentor or coach.)
11. What sort of people do you work best/worst with? (Do you hate to work with highly organized analytic types, or do you love it? Do creative types drive you crazy, or do you work well with them? Make up your own categories.)
12. What sort of organizational culture brings out the best in you? (It's amazing how many people won't leave a culture they are hideously unsuited to work in.)
13. What were you doing when you were happiest in your work life? (Could you possibly find a way to be doing that now?)
14. What regrets do you have about how you have run your career? (Could you make any changes based on those regrets?)
15. What are your most cherished hopes for the future, workwise? (Knowing that fear is the only true learning disability, what stands in your way of realizing those hopes?)

16. What are you most proud of in your work life? (Your answer here is another tip-off as to what you should be doing.)
17. What one lesson would you want to pass along to your children about how to manage their careers? (This question is another way of getting at your most important views on what you have done, what's worked, what hasn't.)
18. What was the most important lesson that you learned from your mother and your father (one from each) relating to work? (As you reflect on this, you will get an idea of how attitudes are passed along from generation to generation and shape how your mind works.)
19. What one lesson did the best boss you ever had teach you about yourself? (Tapping into the insight others have about us is extremely helpful. Others often know us better than we do.)
20. In what way(s) do you think your time could be better used in your current job to add value to the organization? (Your answer here provides a guide to your manager and gives him valuable input he may never have asked for.)

Armed with information from such a questionnaire, a manager becomes far more effective in matching people with the tasks they will do best than if he simply relied on performance reviews, chance conversations, or instinct. Employees often don't volunteer the information this instrument elicits simply because they are not asked. Even though you can see that the information is basic, such information often lies buried within each employee.

You might worry that your employees could feel suspicious or even paranoid at the prospect of answering these questions. Don't use this instrument until your people are comfortable with it. You will need to do some preparation. The basic message is that you as a manager can be far more helpful to your people if you know the answers to the questions this instrument contains.

If, for example, you know what a person is good at and likes to do, you can place her properly within the organization. Everybody wins. Instead of relying on guesswork or chance conversations, getting this information systematically through the questionnaire benefits everyone, from employees to you as manager to the organization itself.

But you will need to lay out the ground rules and let everyone know exactly how the information will be used, who will have access to it, and where it will be stored. Only after you've dispelled people's fears will they be able to be honest and give you the most useful information.

I have presented this questionnaire to numerous audiences of executives from around the country. A typical response is, "This is so useful. Much more practical than the elaborate tests we normally give. I'm going to start using this right away."

And once your employees understand that the information is truly being gathered for their benefit as well as for the benefit of the organization, they are usually very pleased to offer the data.

Find the Flow

The second framework, shown in figure 2-1, outlines how to match a person and a task in order to promote *flow*, a term I mentioned

FIGURE 2-1

Matching challenge and skills to promote flow

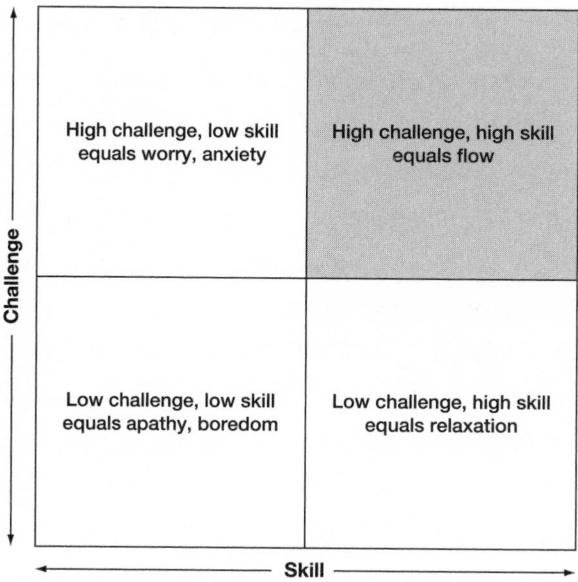

earlier. Csikszentmihalyi, who has studied the concept of flow extensively, has shown that a person most often enters flow when he engages in a task that is both challenging and within his skill set.[5]

In contrast, when a person engages in activities that are challenging but for which he lacks skill, he experiences worry or anxiety. When he engages in activities that are not challenging for which he also lacks skill, he experiences apathy or boredom. When he engages in activities that are not challenging but for which he has skill, he experiences relaxation.

But when he engages in activities that are both challenging and at which he is highly skilled, then he is likely to become one with the task, do his best work, and feel joy as he does it. A manager should do all he can to create that confluence of challenge and skill, and encourage his people to work mostly there.

Know Your Employees' Conative Style

The third framework I offer in this chapter is called *conation* and is the brainchild of a brilliant woman named Kathy Kolbe. In all my years of practice, this is the most powerful concept I've ever come across that most people have never heard of. I summarize her work in the next few pages, but I urge you to explore her books or her Web site (kolbe.com) to learn more.

Conation refers to a person's *natural, inborn style of solving a problem.* Think about this for a moment. What is your characteristic style of tackling a problem? You probably never knew there was a word for how you solve problems as opposed to how someone else does, but there is. Your conative style reflects your characteristic way of addressing any new task.

Before I explain more, consider how useful it would be for a manager to know all her employees' conative strengths so she could help them work with those strengths and not require them to solve problems against the grain of their natural proclivities. Just as a manager ought to help her people achieve flow, so she ought to help her people work with their conative style.

Your conative style is fixed and unchangeable. It has nothing to do with your IQ. Conative strengths are not good or bad, high or low, strong or weak—any more than hair color or being left or right handed is positive or negative. They also have nothing to do with your emotional makeup or style. They occupy their own, unique realm in the mind and combine to create what Kolbe calls your natural MO, or modus operandi—your natural way of interacting with the world, solving problems, and initiating actions.

You can see the MO in action even in toddlers, when one toddler picks up a clock and looks at it while another picks it up and throws it, another walks past the clock and ignores it, and yet another stares at it and bursts out laughing. Your conative strengths drive what you naturally and spontaneously do, as opposed to what you are told to do or feel you ought to do. People do their best when allowed to use their natural conative strengths. They get frustrated and do poorly when told they can't. Many workplaces force people to work against the grain of their natural MO, which leads to frustration and inferior performance.

The word *conation* derives from the Latin *conari*, to try. Literally, conation refers to *how you try*. I bet that as a manager you could describe the conative style of *all* your employees now that you understand the term. "Oh, yeah," you'll say, "this one goes online and researches the topic for an hour, while this one asks for more explanation, that one immediately teams up with someone else, that one pulls out a pad and starts writing a plan, and that one goes into a thoughtful silence."

Kolbe's extensive research, based on tests of more than seven hundred thousand individuals of all ages, shows that once a person is allowed to work within his MO, a major obstacle to peak performance is lifted.

One brief way to get a look at a person's conative strengths and their MO is to give that person a pile of junk and ask her to make something out of it. *Her natural conative style, her MO, will dictate what she does next*, assuming no one gets in her way. One person will ask endless questions before even looking at the pile of junk. She will get annoyed and even angry if her questions are not answered. Another will dive right into the junk, putting this and that together before the instructions have even been completed. If you ask her to wait while you give more instructions, she will simply tune you out. Another will listen to the instructions, then carefully sort the pile, separating the overall junk into categories. Metal here, cloth there, broken items here, organic matter there. Another will spend considerable time pondering the pile before taking any kind of action. She will put her chin in her palm, cock her head, and stare. You will wonder what she is thinking, but rest assured, she is thinking. And someone else will pick up every single piece of junk, as if she has to feel each piece before she can make something out of the various pieces.

Each of these approaches is "right" for the given person involved. The different approaches all have merit. Which method you decide to use is not determined by how intelligent you are (whatever that elusive word means) or how you were raised or what your emotional makeup might be. It is determined by your conative strengths, an element long overlooked in psychology.

Often managers (and schoolteachers, parents, and coaches) fall into the trap of believing that there is a right way to solve problems and a wrong way. This leads them to rigidly insist upon a certain approach, which may be right for the manager or whoever "wrote the book," but may lie totally outside the MO of the employee. This sets the employee up to fail. If only the manager understood the concept of conation and of a person's MO, he could avoid many failures and create many successes.

A bit more about conation, since it is likely that this is all new to you. Think of the mind as comprising three domains. One is emotion, or affect. Another is thought, or cognition. The third is conation, the action-oriented part of the mind that leads you to respond in a certain way when confronted with a problem or task. All three functions are important. Emotion is the on/off switch. It starts the engine, generates ambition, motivation, and zeal, and triggers conation. Given the pile of junk, you might feel anxious, confused, excited, or even angry at being given such a task. Your conative selector decides how you will act and interact with the emotional energy you feel. It will naturally stimulate the actions that help you perform at your best—without prior instruction or training. It generates the pattern of your behaviors and a sense of purpose. Cognition and thought then ponder and edit what you are doing, leading to a finished product, whatever that might be.

Kolbe's Four Major Conative Traits

Based on extensive testing of subjects on her Kolbe A (Adult) Index and Kolbe Y (Youth) Index, Kathy Kolbe has discerned four major conative traits, or Action Modes, as she calls them. Her tests locate you on a scale from 1 to 10 in these four Action Modes.

The scoring vocabulary runs counter to most tests we take, where scores are either "good" or "bad." Avoid the temptation to read a score of 1 as bad because it is a low number and 10 as good because it is a high number. The numbers describe you; they do not rate you.

Each conative score does, however, relate to a human instinct. If you score 1, 2, or 3 in a certain trait, you are called *resistant* in that mode. If you score in the middle—4, 5, or 6—you are called *accommodating* in that mode, which is to say you can operate one way or not, depending on the situation. And if you score 7, 8, 9, or 10 in a mode, you are called *insistent* in that mode, which is to say you insist on acting in a certain way and get frustrated when not allowed to. The best managers, you may be interested to know, tend to fall in the accommodating zone.

Kolbe has identified four conative styles: Fact Finder, Follow Thru, Quick Start, and Implementor. Once you understand this framework you will be able to explain why people do things differently from one another, and this will allow you to get rid of the stigmatizing notions of ineptitude, stupidity, or stubbornness. What's more, by being able to understand and identify an individual's conative strengths, you will become a far more effective manager.

Since you can be resistant, accommodating, or insistent in each mode, and since there are four modes, that means there are twelve conative styles or strengths, as follows:

1. Fact Finder, Resistant
2. Fact Finder, Accommodating
3. Fact Finder, Insistent
4. Follow Thru, Resistant
5. Follow Thru, Accommodating
6. Follow Thru, Insistent
7. Quick Start, Resistant
8. Quick Start, Accommodating
9. Quick Start, Insistent
10. Implementor, Resistant
11. Implementor, Accommodating
12. Implementor, Insistent

Every person must have four, and only four, of the twelve strengths named above, one in each of the four modes (Fact Finder, Follow Thru, Quick Start, and Implementor). Remember, the "resistant" label describes a strength just as much as "accommodating" and "insistent" do. "Resistant" isn't bad, any more than "insistent" is good. Each simply describes different tendencies, different conative strengths.

Being resistant, accommodating, or insistent in each zone of an Action Mode drives you to act through a natural strength. Scoring low in one mode does not mean you are weak in that mode; it means you resist doing things the way people who score high in that mode like to do things. No mode is better, stronger, or more effective than any other—any more than red hair is better than black, mathematical ability is better than artistic, or loving baseball is better than loving basketball.

The "Fact Finder" Trait

An insistent Fact Finder (score of 7–10) has a need to be specific and gather lots of data before making a plan. This is the person who will ask a thousand questions before doing anything with the pile of junk. He will need to check sources, double-check data, and seek more information when others would stop short. His strength lies in gathering information, and if he is frustrated in doing this, he will not perform at his best.

A resistant Fact Finder (score of 1–3), on the other hand, has the strength or ability to simplify things, and will grow impatient with too much searching after facts. He needs to get on with the show. If he is forced to listen to too many instructions or recite too many facts, he will get frustrated and not do his best.

The accommodating Fact Finder (score of 4–6) will go either way, depending upon resources and pressures. Such a person has the gift of being able to explain things accurately. Those who can accommodate help the resistant and insistent ones work together. That's why they make good managers.

The "Follow Thru" Trait

A person long on Follow Thru (insistent) has a natural drive to make sure that matters are properly scheduled, that plans turn into actions, and that all systems are well coordinated and integrated. An insistent Follow Thru person (score of 7–10) would be the one who arranges the pile of junk into subpiles and sub-subpiles.

A resistant Follow Thru (score of 1–3) is a natural multitasker who easily adapts. This person can change sets quickly, reverse direction, juggle a complicated schedule without losing track of what's going on, and orchestrate the needs of many others without losing focus. He does not need to see one task completed before starting another, while the insistent Follow Thru usually does.

The strength of an accommodating Follow Thru is to maintain order. He can help the resistant and insistent work together without getting angry at one another. Again, you can see why this is a strength of good managers.

Before explaining the next two modes, let me emphasize how useful it is to examine how people naturally solve problems, and how helpful it can be in step 1 of the Cycle of Excellence, *select*. Usually, from school days onward, people are taught one "right" to solve a problem that becomes *the* right way. If a person is not naturally inclined to do it the prescribed way, he is deemed deficient.

In the Kolbe framework, however, strength rules. There is no deficiency. Everyone is perfectly capable of creatively solving problems if they are given permission to work within their MO. The key is for them to discover and use the strengths that come naturally to them.

The "Quick Start" Trait

The insistent Quick Start (score 7–10) drives toward innovation, improvises and takes risks, thrives on being novel, and avoids the standard and conventional with a visceral dislike. Entrepreneurs tend to be insistent Quick Start types. These folks will take the pile of junk and start putting together the most unlikely combinations, trying to create the most surprising of all possible junk jewels.

On the other hand, the resistant Quick Start might grow angry, even indignant, at being asked to perform a task with so little instruction, guidance, or explanation. COOs tend to be resistant Quick Start types. Their strength is to stabilize. As a manager, it is particularly good to know if an employee is this type of person. Before you conclude she is stubborn or difficult, understand that she *needs* more explanation before going ahead. It is no more a failing on her part to require this than it is a virtue for the insistent Quick Start to jump right in. Both styles come with advantages and disadvantages, depending on the context.

The accommodating Quick Start, as with all accommodators, can bring peace to the conflict. While the insistent Quick Start is screaming, "I'm bored with all these instructions, let's just jump in and get started!" and the resistant Quick Start is sternly responding, "Now just slow down here and act responsibly for once in your life," the accommodating Quick Start can intervene with, "If we just wait a second or two, then everybody will feel comfortable, and we can all jump in together, so let's hold on and do this as a team."

As I have pointed out, the most natural managers tend to fall in the accommodating range.

The "Implementor" Trait

A person high on the Implementor scale needs to use her hands and naturally builds, shapes, crafts, and constructs. A resistant Implementor is someone like me, a bit of a klutz when it comes to being handy at home. I may see the shower head needs to be changed, but when I try to do it myself, I twist the pipe too hard and break it off. I turn to my son, an insistent Implementor, for help! The accommodating Implementor could go either way. He could see that the shower head needs to be replaced, and he could stand a pretty good chance of being able to do it himself, but he might also ask for help from someone more skilled if that person were available.

My own Kolbe Index score is 5-3-9-2:

Fact Finder: 5 (accommodating)

Follow Thru: 3 (resistant)

Quick Start: 9 (insistent)

Implementor: 2 (resistant)

You can see that with a 2 in Implementor I come by being a klutz naturally; my strength is in envisioning, not in building. And you can see with a 9 in Quick Start, I am about as insistent as a person can be in that mode, which is often the case for a person who starts many projects and is creative, like me. Combined with my resistance to Follow Thru, I of course go nuts when I am told to wait, listen, follow directions, or do what I'm told. I practically jump out of my skin. This doesn't mean I am "difficult" or "undisciplined," the message many employees with my MO get in workplaces, but it does mean I'd better have a plan for setting my ideas in motion or risk getting into trouble with various people in authority.

Rather than throw a fit, which is the primitive "strategy" I'd employ if I didn't have better strategies, I have learned to wait simply by drumming my fingers, running my tongue around my mouth, anticipating a great meal, or recalling a great football game. Such seemingly trivial ways of passing the time give me an outlet for my frustration. If the waiting goes on longer, I have a little puzzle game that I play. All I need is a piece of paper and a pencil and I can draw the puzzle. It's an initials game. I randomly write down a column of five letters and across from it write five more random letters, thus creating five pairs of initials. The game is then to think of a famous person with each pair of initials. It can amuse me through the most boring of waits, the most boring of speeches, the most boring of explanations.

On the other hand, the 5 score indicates that I am an accommodating Fact Finder. While my Quick Start score drives me to jump in immediately, whatever the project might be, my Fact Finder trait acts as a buffer. For example, in writing this book it was important that I do research first. As absurd as it might sound, my natural inclination is to write the book first! But my Fact Finder protects me from doing that and writing what would be a very bad book. My Fact Finder edits, or puts on the brakes, so I accommodate and do my research. Of course, my MO turns the research into an active adventure so it becomes interesting in itself. I travel to meet people; I seek out unusual facts and interesting ideas. I discover new experts and concepts—such as Kathy Kolbe and the idea of conative strengths. I ask direct and provocative questions. I do what it takes to make fact finding interesting to me, and use my

Follow Thru strength of varying my schedule to keep it from being rote and dull.

This is the kind of strategizing I urge you to do with your employees, especially when it comes to creative problem solving or conflict resolution. Once you know a person's conative strengths, you can help her adapt her MO to the workplace.

The Kolbe model is one innovative way by which you can identify your employees' strengths and help your people to use them. I invite you to go to kolbe.com, take the short test, and ask your employees to do it as well. When you understand the concepts, you will be amazed at how helpful they can be.

Once you have the right person doing the right job, then step 2, connect, follows naturally. It is difficult to connect comfortably if you are in the wrong job. But if you are in the right position, doing the right things, then you can easily connect with the task, the mission, and the people around you.

In the next chapter I take you into the world of this critical second step. Connecting means feeling a part of some larger force that you feel proud of and good about—be it an organization, group, team, or project. The feeling of being positively, passionately connected drives superior achievement more powerfully than any other single force.

KEY IDEAS

- The best job incorporates (1) what a person likes to do; (2) what she is best at doing; (3) what adds value to the team, task, or organization.
- Poor selection often lies behind such misleading labels as "stupid," "lazy," or "untalented."
- Good selection draws on an idea from Mihaly Csikszentmihalyi: high challenge plus high skill equals *flow*.
- Peak performance occurs in a state of flow. This usually occurs when a person is engaged in a task that he is skilled at, that is challenging, and that is important to him.
- The Hallowell Self-Report Job-Fit Scale is one simple tool managers can use to assess and guide selection.
- The Kolbe assessment determines conative style. See kolbe.com for a test and explanation.
- The best managers are usually accommodators, scoring in the middle of each scale.
- Entrepreneurs and "idea people" are usually long on Quick Start on the Kolbe scale and short on Fact Finder and Follow Thru. Managers can help these people excel rather than disappoint.

CHAPTER THREE

Connect

Maggie worked as a columnist for a large metropolitan newspaper. She'd been at the *Courier* for more than twenty years and felt great loyalty, even affection, toward the paper and its staff. Over the past decade, however, the paper had suffered an annual drop in revenue and circulation. Everyone talked about the death of newspapers due to the rise of the Internet. The paper itself was available online, which made Maggie wonder why anyone would buy it on the newsstand or have home delivery. But she left these marketing and business decisions to the people who ran the organization. She devoted her energy to doing what she loved, which was researching and writing her columns.

Her column was ideally suited to her, because she could write about whatever she wanted. It ran twice a week, so she had to generate two stories every seven days. She put her heart and soul into every piece, which meant those two columns took a lot of work. She wrote what could be called "human interest" stories of love, tragedy, forgiveness, bizarre happenings, births, deaths, divorces—the human tapestry in all its textures and colors.

As the paper struggled to survive, Maggie had twice been offered a buyout, and she had twice declined because of her love for the job. Her husband made a good income as a doctor, so they could survive without her salary, but the money she earned was certainly nice to have. She had no intention of leaving.

Then something happened. It was one of the most unusual incidents Maggie had ever experienced personally at work. A young guy in his thirties, Jim, had taken over the editorial department. Although Maggie was in her fifties, she thought the age gap would make no difference. But it did gall her to be ordered around by this *kid*, and it bothered many of the other "experienced" reporters, too.

Jim came in talking a good game, saying he was there to support everyone and help the paper survive through the hard times. But then he started cutting support staff, offering no explanation other than to say the word had come down from above. He had told everyone he had an "open-door" policy, but whenever the staff tried to talk to him he was always brusque, dismissive, and preoccupied. People yearned for the days of Jim's predecessor, Hank.

Maggie's own problems with Jim culminated in a conversation in his office late on a Friday afternoon. She went in to ask his opinion on a column she wanted to write about a homeless shelter.

"It's a tired topic," Jim said in a way that, to Maggie, felt disrespectful of her idea.

"But I will breathe new life into it," Maggie said. "I always do!"

"Not always, Maggie. If you want my honest opinion, that last column about death row was nothing but morose. And now a homeless shelter? Who wants to read that kind of stuff these days?"

"Are you kidding? We got a ton of mail on the death row piece. That column started a whole debate. In fact, I want to write a follow-up."

"Please don't. You gotta give people what they need these days—hope, optimism, positive energy. Not depressing columns about death and homelessness."

"So now we're supposed to be cheerleaders, not journalists?" Maggie challenged.

"We're trying to survive as a newspaper," Jim said. "I don't think death row is the way to survive, that's all. Call me stupid, but that's what I think."

Something inside Maggie snapped. "OK, Jim, you're stupid. I've been a reporter longer than you've been alive. I know more about this business than you'll ever know. For you to traipse in here and start making these kinds of pronouncements is insulting and ignorant. You've never even taken two minutes to try to get to know me, to find out what value I really bring to readers. You just come in here with your agenda and start firing people and ruining morale. I've had it with you." At that, Maggie stormed out of Jim's office.

When she got home she wondered if she'd still have a job Monday. She talked it over with her husband and they both agreed that if she got fired, she could work as a freelance writer for magazines and start the novel she'd always wanted to write. So they had a Plan B.

On Monday, Jim sent Maggie an e-mail. It floored her. She expected it to read, "See me" or even, "Clean out your desk." Instead it read, "Maggie, in the middle of your tirade in my office Friday, you said something that I thought about all weekend. You told me I'd never taken even two minutes to get to know you and to find out how you can best add value to this paper. And you know, you were right. I could fire you for the way you insulted me and tried to buck my orders, but I really don't want to do that. So, if you've calmed down, why don't you make an appointment to see me, and we can get to know each other. Best, Jim."

Maggie reread the e-mail a couple of times. She was stunned—and, to be honest, a bit guilty. After all, had she taken two minutes to get to know Jim? Looking back, she could see how she had jumped on his age as an immediate reason to resent him, and then of course, he wasn't her beloved Hank, which she also had held against him. She had joined in the mob mentality of blaming him for the downsizing when, in fact, much larger forces over which Jim had no control were at work.

When she went in to meet with Jim, she was in a very different frame of mind. Jim, as well, had set aside enough time to talk through the tough issues. They spent time trying to understand what each of them was up against, what the paper was up against, and how best to handle the pressures each of them faced.

Once they'd done that, it wasn't difficult to reach a compromise on the death row column. They both ended up laughing at the symbolism of their coming to blows over death row, as if that were the plight of the paper in general. They agreed to work together toward a stay of execution.

Connect: The Most Powerful Step

In the Cycle of Excellence, *connection* refers to the bond an individual feels with another person, group, task, place, idea, mission, piece of art, pet, or anything else that stirs feelings of attachment, loyalty, excitement, inspiration, comfort, or a willingness to make sacrifices for the sake of the connection. The more intense the connection, the more effective the employee will be. Intense connection generates positive energy, and the more positive energy a person brings to work, the better work he will do.

By contrast, disconnection refers to disengagement and distance from a person, group, task, idea, or mission. It short-circuits the Cycle of Excellence more quickly than anything else. Disconnection is one of the chief causes of substandard work in the modern workplace. But it is also one of the most easily corrected.

Therefore, promoting positive connections of all kinds within the workplace should be a top priority for managers. Identifying disconnection, and intervening to create connection where disconnection is found, can quickly lead to improved productivity.

> *What is the biggest mistake that management makes? They treat people like commodities. They treat people like numbers, not like people. It is just that simple.*
>
> —CLAY MATHILE,
>
> *Former owner, Iams*

Why Connection Matters

Connection, which Dr. Shine so instinctively attempted to initiate the instant a customer climbed into his "office," is one of the most powerful tools we can use to bring out the best in others and in ourselves. In contrast, disconnection in the workplace may be the single most preventable detrimental force that leads to underachievement, depression, disloyalty, and job loss.

To help a person achieve peak performance, once the correct selection has been made, let connection drive the process. The feeling of connection stabilizes and propels a person. It promotes growth. It is often trivialized or ignored in today's high-tech, fast-paced world. But, as John Naisbitt observed in his prescient 1982 book *Megatrends*, high tech requires high touch.[1] Without the invigoration of connection, the brain shrivels and life sags.

> *The shortest appointments I have with people are a half-hour. Once in a while fifteen minutes, but almost always a half-hour at least. People just assume that if you have a job like mine that you are too busy to talk to them. I think that a lot of people in jobs like this take advantage of that perception and keep people away. I don't think that is the best way to operate. This job could be very easy if you let everyone else assume you're too busy to see them . . . There are people in positions like this who have cut back from almost everything. They hardly see patients, they don't teach, don't do research, and they wind up being full-time*

administrators. A person can do that. It is an easy trap to fall into. The pay is the same.

—JOSEPH LOSCALZO,

Professor, Harvard Medical School, and chair, Department of Medicine at Brigham and Women's Hospital

I have made a point of interviewing as many happy people as I can find. Happy people know the most about how to live life right—and thus give us a sense of how people can make the most out of their work and perform at the highest level. When I sense I am in the presence of a happy person—and I can always sense it quickly, as I bet you can too—I get curious and ask a few questions.

I might say, "You seem quite upbeat. Are you usually like this?"

"Why not?" he will say. "I'm alive." Or, "I'm lucky," she will reply. The first response is usually humble. Happy people tend not to brag about their happiness. By contrast, many high achievers who are in fact secretly not very happy at all often go out of their way to tell you about all the wonderful things they have been doing and how gloriously happy they are with their work and life. People who truly do get the most out of life don't need to impress it upon you.

I want to know more, and so I ask, "How did you get to be like this?"

Now the secret gets revealed. "My dad." "My mom." "My twelfth-grade English teacher." "My high school football coach." "Grandma." "My uncle Jim." Almost always the answer involves a connection with a person. Sometimes a group of people, like a team or a club or a class. But almost always the shaping force is connection with a person or people.

But such connection is never simple. The human connection is endlessly complex, as the world's literature attests. The example of Jim and Maggie at the outset of this chapter points out a few of the complexities (traps? dangers? frustrations? surprises? rewards?) of connecting. Connecting as a manager is never as simple as "being nice" or keeping an "open door." The realities and pressures of the workplace conspire to make being nice all but impossible at times, and the open door a downright impossibility if it is taken to mean unlimited availability.

It also points up how easily employees, even (perhaps especially) sophisticated, intelligent employees like Maggie, can jump to conclusions, be biased against a trait a person can't help (in this case, age), and fail to appreciate the obstacles a manager faces.

Psychiatrists call this kind of blind thinking "transference," and it is one of Freud's greatest discoveries. Transference arises from the unconscious, so it is not planned or deliberate. It derives from relationships in our past, feelings we had toward significant people we depended upon, like our parents, teachers, bosses in previous jobs, romantic partners, and anyone else we had deep feelings for.

We all bring transference, this simmering kettle of old relationships, with us wherever we go, and it shoots up out of us suddenly, without warning. Typically, we transfer feelings onto our current boss and others who have any kind of authority over us, from the president of the United States, to a police officer directing traffic, to our parish priest, to the clerk behind the counter at the airport. Feelings that derive from transference account for many of our most troubling and unexamined responses.

When the feelings are positive, which results in what is called an *idealizing transference*, those feelings can lead us to believe the boss is someone far more beneficent and powerful than she really is. That's just fine. If you are a manager, never correct an idealizing transference. Such feelings bring out the best in the people who work for you. The idealizing transference turns you into someone for whom people will run through brick walls, work day and night, and sacrifice, sweat, and toil far beyond what is asked.

If you are a manager, don't protest, saying, "I'm really not that good." It is fine to be humble, but allow your people to make you into someone better than you think you are. This is what the greatest managers—and coaches, generals, CEOs, teachers, leaders all over—rely on. None of them is that good! They are all human, after all. But what all of the greatest leaders share is an ability to mobilize the idealizing transference, an ability to be seen by the people they lead as far more smart, effective, reliable, and possessed of magical powers than they really are. When people believe the leader is that powerful, in a sense the leader really becomes that powerful. His people make him so.

On the other hand, when, as a manager, you run into a *negative transference*, beware. This is, in part, what was happening with Maggie and Jim. Of course, there were many real issues involved, but the irrational, intense part came from the kettle of transference. Maggie blamed Jim for actions over which he had no control. A naturally understanding person, she uncharacteristically made no attempt to see things from Jim's point of view; an independent thinker, she joined the mob mentality of running Jim down; and a woman who normally could tolerate the tension of not getting what she wanted, she snapped when Jim told her not to write morose articles. As a psychiatrist, I would speculate that maybe she had a younger brother with whom she had a conflicted relationship.

But what matters most here is that Jim managed to rise above the heat of emotion and reflect upon the conversation. Jim did what great managers do. He didn't take Maggie's outburst personally. He put his own feelings aside long enough to look at both sides of the discussion, while looking out for what was in the best interest of the organization. This takes enormous discipline. It would have been easy to fire Maggie on the spot, or on Monday. In fact, Jim's superiors likely would have been pleased: one less check to write.

But Jim took the weekend to reflect. He had listened to what Maggie said and detected an important truth in the midst of her tirade. So, before letting her go, wouldn't it be in the best interests of the organization to find out if Maggie could be part of the solution to the problems the paper faced?

Jim then took steps to forge a genuine connection with Maggie. He helped her get past her negative transference (neither of them, of course, would ever have called it that) and opened the door, so to speak, to a new relationship based on mutual understanding.

Many of the thorniest issues managers handle turn on situations like this one. Of all the elements in the Cycle of Excellence, this step, connection, requires the most skill and patience from managers. It is therefore where the cycle most often goes wrong, but it also packs the greatest power to drive the cycle to excellence.

The all-powerful propeller of connection begins with a link to a particular person, then grows. It becomes sustaining and ever-present, a feeling of being a part of something positive that is larger than yourself, a feeling that life is workable no matter what bad things come up. This is the one force that, above all others, brings out the best in people.

George Vaillant is a psychiatrist who has empirically studied what goes into health, happiness, and success by following a cohort of men who entered Harvard in the late 1930s. Not a random sample of America's population, to be sure, but still, the data gathered over seventy-plus years from the lives of the 268 men who entered what is called the Grant study stands as one of the most useful (and unusual) sets of longitudinal information we have on what predicts a full and successful life. The bottom line? Says Vaillant, "The only thing that really matters in life are your relationships with other people."[2]

Just ask people who regularly achieve peak performance what the key to their success is. Like happy people, most often they will tell you about a person—a parent, a coach, a teacher, a partner, a spouse, a manager early in their careers—who believed in them and drew out of them more than they knew they had. That's the magical power in connection.

The Power of Social Networks

The force of connection spreads much farther than you might think. Just as individuals came to Dr. Shine from "all over Logan Airport," we may assume that, being in an airport, they also came from all over the world. Dr. Shine was creating a much larger network of connection than even he imagined.

He was creating and participating in a social network. The past decades have spawned revolutionary research into the power of connection and social networks, research that was so surprising many at first doubted it (but then, that is usually the way with new and important truths). In the 1970s, Lisa Berkman, now a professor at Harvard, led a pioneering study that proved social isolation leads to early death.[3] A link between social isolation and mortality? Hogwash, the skeptics in the scientific community snorted. But that study now has been replicated over a dozen times, both in this country and abroad, such that we now know that social isolation ranks up there with cigarette smoking, high blood pressure, elevated cholesterol, and obesity as a correctable cause of early death. *Connecting with others is really good for you. And it's really good for business.*

Recent research shows that if an employee feels disconnected from her manager and believes that she is unskilled or lacks the ability to do the job well, that worker is more likely to get sick, miss work, and even suffer a heart attack than those who feel connected. The study that brought us this information was based on data from some twenty thousand employees in Sweden, Finland, Germany, Poland, and Italy who worked in a wide range of jobs.[4]

Furthermore, simply feeling insecure in one's job can make a person sick. The impact of feeling insecure at work in fact can be more severe than losing a job. A study done by Sarah Burgard of the University of Michigan looked at over 1,700 adults over periods ranging from three to ten years. The study controlled for such factors as temperament, innate pessimism, or depression and so was able to isolate job insecurity as the pivotal variable in increased sickness and absence from work. Burgard found in one of the groups that job insecurity was a better predictor of poor health than either high blood pressure or cigarette smoking.[5]

While a manager can't remove all feelings of job insecurity, of course, she can make it a priority to reduce such feelings. This is not hand holding; it's proactive management. Regardless of the realities in the outside world, employees feel more secure in a positively connected environment. The manager doesn't need to pretend the outside world is secure. But she can do everything in her power to create a connected atmosphere in the organization. This will lead people to feel more optimistic, upbeat, and secure while at work and in turn lead to less absenteeism and improved performance.

Further documentation of the power of connection comes from Nicholas A. Christakis' and James H. Fowler's captivating research. Their 2009 book, *Connected: The Surprising Power of Our Social Networks and How They Shape Our Lives*, shows how social networks can bring out far more than each individual in a group possesses. As they point out, social networks can work for good or ill. From spreading happiness to spreading obesity, such networks work wonders, some desirable, some not. As Christakis and Fowler put it:

> The surprising power of social networks is not just the effect others have on us. It is also the effect we have on others. You do not have to be a superstar to have this power. All you need to do is connect. The ubiquity of human connection means that each of us has a much bigger impact on others than we can see.[6]

This is good news for managers, and important to use to their advantage. Social networks can become one of a manager's most powerful tools, if he understands them. Many of Christakis' and Fowler's most important findings are not at all intuitively obvious, but they can be especially useful for managers. The authors investigated not only the dyadic spread of happiness (the spread between one person and his friends) but also the hyperdyadic spread (the spread between one person and his friends' friends, and *their* friends, which is what takes place in offices and organizations of all kinds). You might think that it is not possible for happiness to spread among second and third parties, but you would be wrong.

Believe it or not, if a friend of a friend of a friend of yours becomes happier, this can directly impact you in a positive way.

These innovative researchers found, through mathematical analyses of social networks, that, "a person is about 15 percent more likely to be happy if a directly connected person . . . is happy." But it doesn't stop there. The happiness effect for a friend of a friend is 10 percent, and for a friend of a friend of a friend is 6 percent.[7]

They also found that the spread of happiness did not depend on deep, personal connections. Equally powerful in spreading happiness were frequent, superficial face-to-face interactions.[8] This is also good news for managers, as you can't be running group therapies, but you can encourage simple interactions, like saying hello while waiting for the elevator or talking about last night's ball game at the water cooler. Believe it: these interactions can boost your bottom line.

This research confirms what I advocated in my 1999 article in which I touted the value of the "human moment"—face-to-face interaction—over the electronic moment—e-mail, voice mail, teleconference, and so forth.[9] Christakis and Fowler made further surprising findings when they studied the effect of geographical proximity on happiness. They found that when a person's friend who lives less than a mile away becomes happy, the probability that the original person will be happy goes up 25 percent. Amazingly enough, if the friend lives more than a mile away, an increase in his happiness has no effect on the original person. Along the same lines, if your spouse becomes happy, the chances of your being happy go up (but the happiness of separated spouses has no effect).[10]

It is as if social networks—which certainly include workplaces—exert a kind of gravitylike effect on the people within them. Perhaps Johannes Kepler could come back from the grave and devise some mathematical equation to describe *these* orbitals. The force of the attraction does seem inversely proportional to the square of the distance between the elements.

In any case, research is edging in on discovering exactly what this attractive force between people is all about. But managers can already take advantage of what we know now. Managers typically get so caught up in the crises of everyday business that they look past the power of connection. Everyone—not just people consulting a psychiatrist—can tap into the power of connecting and use it as a turbo-charge. But it isn't easy. In my conversations with managers I hear time and again that their greatest obstacles are the "people problems." What may seem easy—helping people to connect and work together toward a shared goal—turns out to be devilishly difficult and at times maddening, but also of critical importance.

Consider this from *New York Times* columnist Thomas Friedman, speaking about war:

> Early in both Iraq and Afghanistan our troops did body counts, à la Vietnam. But the big change came when the officers running these wars understood that R.B.'s ("relationships built") actually matter more than K.I.A.'s. One relationship built with an Iraqi or Afghan mayor or imam or insurgent was worth so much more than one K.I.A. Relationships bring intelligence; they bring cooperation. One good relationship can save the lives of dozens of soldiers and civilians. One reason torture and Abu Ghraib got out of control was because our soldiers had built so few relationships that they tried to beat information out of people instead. But relationship-building is painstaking.[11]

Painstaking, indeed. But well worth the pain. It would make a good mantra for managers: R.B.'s before K.I.A.'s. Although it is difficult, every manager *can* learn to connect, even with prickly people, and can help all his employees learn as well.

The Power of Positive Connections

If you are managing others, *they will perform better if you yourself are happy and show your joy. They will also perform better if you help them to connect with others.* They will also do better if you help them connect with their work with single-minded intensity. As Robert Sternberg, a lead authority on intelligence and creativity, has written, the major determinant to success "is not some fixed prior ability but purposeful engagement."[12] "Purposeful engagement" is synonymous with connection. Connection, both to a person and to an endeavor, is crucial because when a person connects with another person or a task, his mind changes for the better. As Dr. Shine said, when you get that spark, *everything changes.*

But be careful. You have to be genuine in your efforts to connect. Otherwise you roam into *Dilbert* territory. A manager who reads these words and says, "I get it, I should wear a smiley button at work," will get the opposite result of what he hopes for. Fake smiles and forced connections backfire. But if you try to put your most positive self forward, if you notice and appreciate others in simple and honest ways, if you promote others before you promote yourself, you will go a long way toward creating the all-important positively connected atmosphere in your workplace.

In such an atmosphere people will naturally make friends. Research by Tom Rath and the Gallup organization published in 2007 showed that having a best friend at work is a major predictor of superior performance. According to Rath, people who have a best friend at work are seven times more likely to be positively engaged with that work.[13] So friendship—positive connection—enhances the bottom line.

Additional evidence comes from the field of positive psychology and the pioneering research done by Martin Seligman at the University of Pennsylvania. He urges organizations to promote feelings of well-being (positive connection) in the workplace because "increases in well-being are likely to produce increases in learning . . . Positive mood produces broader attention . . . more creative thinking . . . and more holistic thinking . . . in contrast to negative mood which produces narrower attention."[14] Seligman cites the work of numerous other researchers to support his thesis, which by now can be taken as fact.[15]

In a state of connection (as opposed to isolation), all the ideas, impulses, energies, and bits of information that might otherwise swirl around within a person's mind line up naturally and in proper order. Pulled by the magnetic focus connection creates, they organize themselves into a logical chain without the individual having to interrupt or even consciously monitor the process. In peak performance, a person loses self-conscious thought and becomes one with the action at hand, entering into flow. This is not to say that thinking ceases; on the contrary, it intensifies. But it is unencumbered by self-consciousness, fear, or worry. It is also in flow that a person is happiest and feelings of well-being are greatest.

You can see how the ideas from the previous chapter on selection have an impact on connection. When you select wisely, flow can follow and the connection intensifies. But when you select poorly, or when you are forced to work outside the zone of your conative strengths, feelings of competence and well-being are replaced by feelings of frustration, anger, or despair.

Let me summarize the ideas put forth so far. I've pointed out that wise selection facilitates enthusiastic connection, and that such connection promotes peak performance. Friendship, a manifestation of positive connections at work, promotes peak performance, as do feelings of well-being. And social networks can bring out much more in a group than the group imagines possible.

This leads me back to the work of Christakis and Fowler, one a doctor, the other a social scientist. Their work on social networks shows how contagious positive feelings truly are. They write:

> A nice demonstration involved outfitting thirty-three professional male cricket players with pocket computers that recorded their moods four times a day during a match (which can have the insane duration of five days). There was a strong association between a player's own happiness and the happiness of his teammates, independent of the state of the game; further, when a player's teammates were happier, the team's performance improved.[16]

This is powerful news for managers, providing yet more evidence that happiness is not trivial. Happiness and peak performance go hand in hand.

Since organizations certainly constitute social networks, managers ought to do all they can to promote—dare I say it—happiness! No, I am not suggesting you convene a camp sing-along, I am just pointing out that the leading-edge scientific research confirms what many wise people, like Dr. Shine, have intuitively known all along. Happiness is no frill. It is critical to the bottom line.

> *You like to think that at the higher levels of management you have awareness about how to impart the important skills to the people who are getting closest to the customer.*

> *The lowest-paid person actually has the biggest impact on the entire company, both positive and negative. So having a culture where they feel that they're contributing and they feel valued is very important. As a consumer I go into Toys 'R Us and nobody talks to me. I go into Home Depot and they're all coming up and saying, How can I help you?*
>
> —EDDIE LAMPERT,
> *Chair, Sears Holdings Corporation*

The Danger of Fear When Connection Is Weak

In the absence of connection, fear usually rules. Fear is the great disconnector. It is rampant in modern organizations. We've grown so accustomed to fear that we hardly notice it, be it fear provoked by an announcement at the airport that we're on "orange alert," a report in the newspaper that another company has closed down, or a rumor that our own jobs may be heading to India soon. Fear is the great disabler, more dangerous today because it is so widespread.

Not managed correctly, fear can hold you or your employees back more than any other single force. Tens of millions of people do not achieve as much as they could simply because they are hampered by fear—unable to speak up at a meeting, unable to submit the proposal for the plan they have worked so hard to formulate, unable to be who they otherwise could be at work. There is no greater cause of underachievement than fear.

> *If you can provide a culture and a climate in an organization where people can feel that they are OK*

just the way they are, and feel understood and valued because of who they really are, if you can get to that point, you can do anything.

—CLAY MATHILE

Many employees are afraid to make a mistake. Some of their fear may be due to their genetic makeup—research has shown that toxic worrying can be carried in one's genes. But some of their fear may also be due to their manager's style. Worrying that their job is in jeopardy, these workers play it safe. They play not to lose, rather than to win, which leads them to fall far short of what they could do.

What they fear varies. It may be disapproval, a poor result, criticism, looking stupid, going beyond their comfort zone, making others look bad—they may even fear making themselves look good! Oddly enough, some people feel that to stand out even by excelling is to court rejection, so they consciously or unconsciously perform below their abilities. A mob mentality can preserve mediocrity by punishing those who achieve excellence.

The process can work in the other direction as well. People can want so passionately to excel that they put too much pressure on themselves. This is one of the great paradoxes of peak performance: wanting too much to win can keep a person from winning. If employees believe everything is riding on the outcome of their performance, fear can freeze them up and lead them to perform poorly. Or, as a golf pro friend of mine put it, "The key to putting is not caring too much if the ball goes in the hole."[17]

Fear also can drive an employee to take on more than he can handle. He may feel *obliged* to do more than he *can* do. Feeling that his job, the success of the project, the making of the quarterly number, or his self-esteem is at stake, an employee may try to carry much more than he possibly can—leading to less-than-excellent, if not disastrous, performance.

Employees may fear that stating their limits will lead their manager to fire them, downgrade them, or, at best, think less of them. In my consulting work, this is one of the most common fears I address. "How can I tell my boss that he is making my job impossible? If I do, he'll think I'm complaining or not gutting it out and doing what's required. I can't afford to lose my job or lose his respect." This is why it makes sense for the manager to inquire, rather than wait to hear from the employee.

Not all fear, however, is detrimental. Some underlying anxiety can in fact sharpen performance. One of the best validated of all relationships in the behavioral sciences is the so-called performance-anxiety curve. It shows that as anxiety increases, performance improves, *up to a certain point*. Beyond that point, the curve starts a rapid decline, as performance deteriorates while anxiety continues to rise. Managers should try to keep employees off the descending slope of this curve. A bit of reassurance, some coaching, or, if possible, giving additional resources or education all can serve to reduce anxiety and pull a person back from that downward slope. If nothing else, simply joining the person in their worry can, interestingly enough, reduce the worry. One of my favorite and most useful maxims is: "Never worry alone."

Among all the sources of fear discussed today in the business literature, perhaps the most common is simply change. The person who can't manage a fear of change can't win in today's world. We all fear change at some level. It ties into our basic desire for security, even immortality. At an unconscious level, change represents the ultimate cause of human insecurity—the prospect of death. So it makes sense that all of us fear change, to some extent.

At a conscious level, change triggers our fear of the unknown. Because we don't know what change will bring and can't control it, we tend to fear it. Anything that threatens our feeling of being in control triggers fear—or anger—or both.

Much of a manager's work is helping the people who work for him or her manage their fears of change and of the unknown, their feelings of insecurity and powerlessness. If a manager can turn that fear on its head so that it becomes excitement at the prospect of change, he will get enormously more out of his people. The great manager helps his people make this emotional flip, thus regaining the mental energy they would otherwise have lost to fear.

But how do you do this? One way to transform fear into confident action is by reframing the situation. Let's say some people have been laid off, leaving those who remain fearful that they might be next. As you reframe the situation you have to be careful, because you don't want to sound phony. However, you could honestly say, "The good news is that the people upstairs are going to look elsewhere for the next cuts, so we have some time to pull together and come up with some new ideas." Or, "With fewer people, we need each other now more than ever. Let's take this as a chance to create some super teamwork with one another." You don't deny the reality of the situation, but you work to see its realistically bright side. You work to instill rugged optimism in the culture of your place.

A word about optimism. It can jump-start peak performance. Often dismissed as Pollyanna-ish or unrealistic, the best kind of optimism looks disaster straight in the eye and says, "We'll find a way to deal with you." Such optimism is muscular and brave. And, it can be learned.[18] As a manager, if you model an optimistic attitude, it becomes contagious. It fosters what Stanford psychologist Carol

Dweck calls a "growth mind-set," one that welcomes challenges because the person believes he can learn whatever is needed to overcome whatever obstacles arise. The person who has what Dweck calls a "fixed mind-set" believes that talent, or lack thereof, limits outcome, and so shies away from what he doesn't know how to do. Dweck's copious and groundbreaking research shows that the most successful people are not necessarily the most talented but rather those who develop a growth mind-set. And the really good news is that, like optimism, a growth mind-set can be taught and can be learned—at any age.

How? Here is how Dweck put it:

> I believe that managers can best communicate a growth mind-set to their people by conveying that the skills of the job are learned skills and that they, the managers, are there to teach and support employees in the learning of those skills.
>
> In that context, managers can also emphasize that they value passion and dedication (not just "natural talent"), that they value employees' challenging and stretching themselves to tackle new things (rather than just remaining in their comfort zones), and that they value teamwork (over individual stardom).
>
> My research has taught me one thing more than any other: People are tuned into what those around them value. If managers convey these growth mind-set values, their people will adopt them and live/grow by them.[19]

The manager who rules by pressure and fear (who usually is ruled from above by superiors who also use pressure and fear) lobotomizes his people. Believing he is doing what must be done to bring out their best, he in fact renders them ineffective over time. Fear is a short-term motivator but a long-term disabler.

Here again brain science shows us why. As fear mounts, the brain's deeper centers take over. High-level thinking—which requires imagination, mental flexibility, focus, memory and anticipation, the ability to listen and to change one's mind, the ability to take in new information quickly and synthesize it into something useful—takes place in the higher parts of the brain, the cerebral cortex.

The deeper centers of the brain regulate our more primitive, survival-related activities, like breathing, body temperature and heartbeat, and reflexive behaviors. When a person feels fear beyond a certain level, the brain shifts to red alert. Deep centers of the brain, like the amygdala, the hypothalamus, and the locus coeruleus, light up. Higher cortical thinking—appreciating irony, laughing at a joke, concocting a new idea, seeing shades of gray—ceases, as the brain must now devote its full attention to the perceived threat. If there were a saber-toothed tiger about to jump out at you, this would be good. You would not want to be appreciating irony, laughing at a joke, concocting a new idea. You'd want to be either fleeing or killing the tiger. A saber-toothed manager can elicit the same response. Excessive fear renders peak performance neurologically impossible, and even just halfway decent performance difficult.

More insidious than the saber-toothed manager is a paranoid, fear-filled culture in the workplace. Much of the method I offer in this book is aimed at keeping fear at manageable, desirable levels. Remember, some fear is good. If you feel no fear, we have a term for that as well. It's called denial. The business world is full of danger, and, as Andrew Grove said in the title of his book, "Only the paranoid survive."[20]

Useful fear or worry can be distinguished from harmful fear or toxic worry by what each does. Useful fear and worry lead to problem solving. Toxic fear and worry freeze people up, drive them into isolation, reduce their intelligence, and render them far less effective than they otherwise could be.

Because toxic fear usurps the higher regions of your brain, redirecting their neurons to the perceived danger, you lose your sophisticated brain and enter into a primitive state. You become curt, peremptory, aggressive, dogmatic, deaf, unempathic—in short, stupid. Or, at best, you become a poor imitation of your highest functioning self. This is because your brain has directed its resources to supporting your panic system.

Primitive, low-level thinking is the great danger of fear-filled work environments. People lose the very tools that they need the most: their ability to hear and listen to others, their creativity, their flexibility, their empathy—even their memory.

A study done on medical students at the University of Virginia provides a good example of how toxic stress and fear are not required for top performance. In this study, conducted by a biology professor, researchers looked at two groups of medical students. One group was graded traditionally: A, B, C, D, F. The other group was graded on a pass/fail basis. The two groups performed equally well, but the pass/fail group reported much less toxic stress.[21] The old notion that excellence occurs in direct proportion to suffering is incorrect.

I would suggest that excellence occurs in direct proportion to necessary suffering, but in inverse proportion to unnecessary suffering or toxic stress. Connection is the best antidote to unnecessary suffering.

A Real-Life Look at Connection and Disconnection

Let me give two quick examples of connection and disconnection. The first involves SAS, the high-tech company in North Carolina, and the second, the Harvard chemistry department.

SAS commits many resources to creating a positively connected culture. One of its mottos is, "If you treat employees as if they make a difference to the company, they will make a difference to the company." People live the motto. In 2009, it was ranked number twenty in *Fortune* magazine's "100 Best Companies to Work for in America," a list it has made for the past twelve consecutive years.[22]

At SAS, employees are actively discouraged from working more than seven or eight hours per day. The Cary, North Carolina, headquarters boasts four on-site child care centers, and the central cafeteria is stocked with high chairs, as employees are encouraged to invite their families to join them for lunch. There is also a large fitness and recreation center on-site, and the company will launder employees' gym clothes for them, returning them in time for the next day's workout. Snack stations full of healthy foods abound in all buildings across the campus, and bowls of M&M's (not so healthy but oh-so appealing) appear on tables everywhere. The company refills them every Wednesday, going through some *twenty tons* of M&M's per year.

How do M&M's and a legendary benefit program affect the bottom line? Very well indeed. By some estimates, SAS saves about $70 million each year by retaining employees. That number derives from comparing the retention rate at SAS to the industry standard. Since SAS retains a much higher percentage of its employees, it saves millions that would otherwise be spent on headhunters and training new hires.

Beyond that is the less measurable, but likely more valuable "brain benefit" such a connected environment provides. Particularly for a knowledge-based company like SAS, it makes sense to keep the brains producing the knowledge in top working condition. As CEO Jim Goodnight says, tongue-in-cheek, "It's a no-brainer."

At the other end of the spectrum lay the Harvard chemistry department a decade ago. Harvard chemistry is like a small, high-powered corporation with about three hundred graduate students and postdocs, a hundred research associates, thirty-four faculty, five of them Nobel laureates, and an annual operating and research budget of approximately $35 million. But for many years it harbored a toxically disconnected culture.

The problem came to a tragic head in August 1998 when one of the department's most gifted graduate students committed suicide, leaving behind a note that explicitly blamed the department for his lethal despair. The chair of the department, Professor James (Jim) Anderson, called me in as a consultant, and along with Dr. Paul Nghiem, one of the postdocs, we examined the problem.

It turned out this most recent suicide was just one in a long string of suicides going back for years in the department. The culture of the department left students desperate and isolated. Harvard proved to me that as much as a connected culture can promote growth, a disconnected culture can literally kill people.

Jim Anderson courageously put his own research on hold and resolved to fix the problem. Over the ensuing several years he made changes in the department that did indeed transform the culture. He brought students together for biweekly buffets in the department library. The shy, socially awkward chemistry grad students and postdocs who would never come out for a mixer could be enticed to come out for food! Jim changed the advising system, so that students had more than one professor to turn to in case a relationship soured. He even changed the architecture of the building, replacing heavy oak doors with glass, and adding a piano and espresso bar where canisters of chemicals used to be stored. He convened a quality-of-life committee that he actually listened to, and he enacted many of their suggestions.

Gradually, the culture of cynicism, pessimism, and disconnection gave way to a culture of connection. While the department did not achieve bliss, there have been no suicides—a statistically significant fact—since Jim Anderson stood up to the problem of disconnection some ten years ago.

SAS and Harvard chemistry offer just two examples of thousands that testify to the power of connection and disconnection, and the power managers have to effect change, particularly when they are armed with the knowledge of how to cultivate social networks.

How to Build a Positively Connected Workplace

Start simply by intending to connect. Make it a priority. Instead of relying on metaphorically beating people up, build relationships. Become curious and interested in others. When you take an interest in someone, you just might be setting up step 1 on the way to excellence for that person. Using the tool you know best—yourself—to connect with others and help others also connect, you can bring out the best in the people you lead.

> *We also want to improve the intake, the history and physical. We want to train our doctors in such a way*

that they have time to make a relationship with the patient, talk to the patient, not just spend the time typing, cutting, and pasting an electronic record.

That's one piece of the process we want to change. Another is the physical exam. Some people think all you need is a head-to-toe scan and lab tests, and the physical exam becomes superfluous. Training in doing a physical exam is suffering extraordinarily because some doctors think it doesn't matter anymore and that an echocardiogram, for example, will tell you what the heart looks like.

But there are important reasons to do the physical exam. The most important reason is to make physical contact with the patient. That is key to forming the relationship and increases the possibility that you can make the patient better.

—JOSEPH LOSCALZO

The work of connecting can be done by almost anyone because we humans are biologically wired to connect. We can't help it. Recent research has identified, at least in part, the neurological basis for this.

It turns out we all have a set of neurons called "mirror neurons" that fire in imitative fashion to what we see another person doing. When we see someone kick a ball, some of our own ball-kicking neurons fire, even though we do not move a muscle. When we see another person in distress, our mirror neurons create an imagined version of that distress within us. This is the biological basis for empathy, and it is common to us all. Just as we have noses, we have empathy.

The neurologist and neuroscientist Marco Iacoboni writes about this notable discovery, in which he played a part. "We achieve our very subtle understanding of other people thanks to certain collections of special cells in the brain called mirror neurons," he writes. "These are the tiny miracles that get us through the day. They are at the heart of how we navigate through our lives. They bind us with each other, mentally and emotionally." He goes on:

> Our neurobiology . . . commits us to others . . . We are deeply interconnected at a basic, prereflective level. This we now know, and this *fact* seems to me a fundamental starting point for social behavior that has been largely neglected by an analytical tradition that emphasizes reflective behavior and differences among people.[23]

If we all can connect, why do so many organizations falter at it? Again, the answer is that we are too busy. We are overloaded and hurried. We do not spend enough time in each other's presence, face to face. We over-rely on electronic connections and find ourselves not developing the trust required to be candid. But all these forces can be overcome if, as a manager, you make it a priority to do so.

How? As I've suggested, start simply by noticing the other person. Then mention to her what you notice. See, then speak. *Notice and react.* We live in a world in which people feel more and more unknown. Noticing and saying what you notice lets a person feel known, and can unleash her untapped energy.

> *These are the four magic words of management: "What do you think?" It is unbelievable the ideas that you can*

get from a machine operator or anybody on the floor, the janitor, about how they are going to lay out a set of machines or whatever. I'm telling you, the power of that question is just unbelievable.

—WOODY MORCOTT,
Former CEO, Dana Corporation

The power of noticing was demonstrated decades ago in a study done by Elton Mayo of Harvard Business School from 1927 to 1932. The researchers set out to study what the ideal *physical* setting would be to promote peak performance in the workplace, in this case, the Hawthorne plant of Western Electric in Cicero, Illinois. They ended up discovering that the physical variables were not the crucial determinant.

They looked at variables like humidity, lighting, and temperature in the hope of finding the ideal conditions to promote the best work. To their surprise, they found that the workers' performance improved when lighting was increased—but it improved even more when the light was subsequently decreased. It wasn't the lighting that mattered most, it was the fact that the workers felt noticed (through this effort to improve their lighting) that made the difference. The phenomenon has since become famous as the Hawthorne effect.[24] While experts still debate the validity of the Hawthorne effect, almost all agree that performance improves when a person feels recognized and valued. Indeed, this is so obvious that it wouldn't be worth mentioning were the fact not ignored in many workplaces.

Millions of workers (and all others who strive toward some goal) fail to do their best work simply because no one ever *really* notices them, systematically and persistently. Noticing is such a simple task that it is unfortunate how much human potential goes to waste for lack of it.

What about you? What can you do if you work in a disconnected place or manage such an organization?

In chapter 1, I gave the example of Greg, who was ready to quit his job because he was underachieving and unhappy. I suggested he begin simply by trying to make a friend or two at work and build a community there where he could be real. That is the starting point for everyone, manager and employee alike. Try to be real. Make a friend, just one. Create something at work that you and your workers can look forward to every day.

If you as a manager don't look forward to going to work in the morning, it is likely that your employees don't either. It's probably because your work environment is disconnected. Take steps to change that. It's not all that hard to do, once you face up to what's really going on. You might try a mini-retreat and use exercises that promote connection. One of my favorites, one that I have used with hundreds of executives over the years, involves pairing people up. I learned it from Hollywood writer, director, and producer, Marshall Herskovitz. Here is how he described to me in a conversation we had in 2008 how he learned it when he was in film school:

> *We had an actress who taught directing the actor. Her name was Nina Foch who was quite a brilliant teacher. She had us do an exercise in the first week where you brought in an object that she called a "hot object," which meant it had some meaning to you. It evoked feelings to you and she wanted you to talk about the object. And the reason for this exercise was to observe what happens when an actor is reminiscing about something that is*

> *connecting to something. It was meant to teach us something about acting. But it taught us more about who everybody was in the class. And that was what she also knew. We would reveal ourselves that way. I brought in something that was owned by my grandfather, which was a ruler. My grandfather was a cabinet maker and he had a ruler that had my dad's woodworking company logo stamped on it which I kept, and so I brought it in and talked about my grandfather. And Ed brought in his grandfather's pocket watch, and talked about his grandfather . . . He came up to me that day at lunch. He said, "I couldn't help but notice we both were talking about our grandfathers," and that's how we became friends.*
>
> —MARSHALL HERSKOVITZ,
> *Hollywood writer, director, and producer*

The "Ed" Marshall is referring to is Ed Zwick, who has been Marshall's writing, directing, and producing partner ever since their days in film school some thirty years ago. From films like *Shakespeare in Love* to *Legends of the Fall* and such TV series as *Thirtysomething* and *My So-Called Life*, their work has won many awards. They share one of the most solid partnerships in Hollywood, a place not know for successful sharing. It all began with this simple exercise in connecting.

Be innovative. Make up your own exercises, your own strategies, your own plans. Ask your people what they think will work. You can adapt the steps we used in the Harvard chemistry department and apply them in your own workplace, from creating gatherings centered around food, to making changes in the physical environment, to altering the culture such that asking for help and acknowledging vulnerability come to be seen as strengths, not weaknesses.

Whatever you do, your goal as a manager should be to minimize feelings of alienation and falseness within your organization, while increasing feelings of openness and honesty. You want to make sure people feel permission to be real.

If you intend to connect and want to create a connected environment, you can. It's a matter of making it a priority.

> *I always made creating a connected environment a priority, when we were small and when we got big. We always found various ways to do it. We had quality work teams, we had quarterly meetings, and we had monthly plant meetings. We found all kinds of ways to create dialogue. I spent a lot of time with people in the plants. I would go into the plants myself, I would have quarterly meetings and after the meetings I would have lunches with eight to twelve people. We would sit around the room and talk. Not just the top people, I am talking about the hourly people: the janitors, production workers, maintenance workers, and so forth.*
>
> *The key to it all is just be honest, do your best, and treat others with dignity and respect. That's it.*
>
> —CLAY MATHILE

Here are some simple, concrete steps that you, as a manager, can take to get the sand out of the gears of the Cycle of Excellence and to promote the feeling of connectedness that lubricates those gears so well:

1. Notice and acknowledge people. Everyone is so busy these days that the simple niceties often get overlooked. Bad idea! People feel good when they are acknowledged—and they feel bad when they're not. All you have to do is say hi, or even just smile. But to walk past someone as if that person were not there—which happens *all the time*—is a surefire disconnector! You do not need to have deep conversations to promote connection. A simple high-five can work wonders.

2. Allow for people's idiosyncrasies and peccadilloes. Encourage people to be who they are—and we are all a little strange. When you are relaxed about yourself as a manager, you give others permission to be the same.

3. Develop an organization-wide e-mail policy, such as: (a) agree that everyone checks e-mail no more than x times a day; (b) never send an e-mail without first considering if the time it will take the recipient(s) to open and read the message is worth it; (c) before sending an e-mail consider whether delivering the message in person or via phone might be better; (d) never try to work out emotionally-laden issues via e-mail. These simple changes will reset people's attentional system in a way that will surprise you. They will become less ravenous for distraction and less likely to look to e-mails or text messages for a "fix." Instead, people will train their brains to wait, while they do more important work. And they will be more likely to communicate with others in person, which fosters connection.

4. Encourage everyone to have human moments—that is, face-to-face human contact—at least once every few hours. It's good for people, mentally as well as physically, to connect in person.

5. Encourage people to recognize stress within themselves. When they start to feel it, urge them to stop what they're doing and take a short break. Many of the most disconnecting episodes—flare-ups, arguments, and the like—occur as a direct result of stress.

6. Praise others freely and genuinely. Just about everyone needs and appreciates authentic praise, even over trivial matters such as how they dress or what they said at the last meeting. People who can give praise freely are like cultivators of a great garden.

7. As a manager, try *not* to think in judgmental, moralistic terms—a person is good or bad, a deed is good or bad—but in psychological terms—why did this person do this? Thinking in moralistic terms, which we were all raised to do, seduces you into thinking in terms of black and white, right or wrong, while the truth usually lies in the gray zone. Moralistic thinking also seduces people into blaming others or blaming themselves, which is usually counterproductive. I am certainly not saying that morality is bad; it is the compass we live by. I am merely saying that asking why a person did something, rather than whether the action was bad or good, actually stimulates people to act with more integrity.

8. Light up the world of your workplace. Sunlight is best, electric light is good, candles are great if the fire code

allows them, moonlight is exotic. Good lighting or mood lighting is a connector.

9. Keep food and drink around. Food is a symbolic form of nurturing. Fruits, nuts, bottles of sparkling water are the healthiest. And remember the great results SAS gets with M&M's!

10. Foster impromptu get-togethers. Planned parties are fine, but they are often command performances and can feel stilted. Impromptu get-togethers—going out for a beer, catching the Red Sox, grabbing lunch—all promote connectedness.

11. Encourage people to reach out. Remember Dr. Shine. Don't stand on ceremony. Bring in the people who are on the outs. Whatever your environment may be, everyone in it suffers if even just a few people are left out and feel it. Do whatever you can do to make sure everyone has at least one friend. That's really all it takes for your employees to look forward to coming to work.

KEY IDEAS

- Connecting is not just about being nice or being available—but that can help!
- Connecting begins with a desire to find the spark in other people.
- Connected organizations thrive; disconnected ones perish.

- Watch out for and understand transference—people's tendency to turn you into someone you're not.
- Disconnection has been correlated with early death.
- Your people will perform better if you, as a manager, are happy *and show it*.
- Research shows that having a best friend at work predicts superior performance.
- Christakis' and Fowler's research demonstrates that positive feelings in the workplace are contagious.
- Technology can disconnect us. As John Naisbitt said years ago, "High tech requires high touch."

CHAPTER FOUR

Play

"Dirk dreaded work." That was the phrase Dirk would sometimes write on the yellow legal pad he kept on his desk, as if it were the first line of a novel. But this wasn't fiction; it was his life.

Sometimes more lines would follow. "If only Dirk could shirk work . . . but Dirk was stuck. And no one cared about the plight of poor Dirk." He rarely could get farther than that before some signal brought him back to the "job at hand," as Louis, his manager, liked to call whatever it was Dirk was supposed to be doing.

"You must attend to the job at hand, Dirk," Louis would intone. "You have time for amusements before and after work, on your time, not ours."

He is such a joke, Dirk would think. And then: *We're both out of a* Dilbert *cartoon.*

Dirk worked as an accounts manager for a large insurance company. He felt anesthetized at work, going through his duties mechanically. He had his yellow pad for his musings, which he would scribble now and then, but otherwise he was more robot than human. In college, he had wanted to be a cartoonist. Now, he felt as if he were living the cartoon, not writing it.

Once, in a rare moment of spontaneity, he had asked Louis why the job he did had to be so repetitive, and why there couldn't be at least a little room for innovation. Louis had replied, "Would you want the surgeon operating on you to innovate? I think not. You'd want him to do the job at hand, and not think about anything else. You'd want him to be a professional."

That was another word Louis used all the time that Dirk detested. Professional. It seemed synonymous with dull, predictable, mechanical, emotionless, dry.

"Then why don't you leave the place?" Myra, Dirk's wife, would ask him in exasperation when he discussed work. Dirk rarely brought up the topic with Myra precisely because he didn't want to get into this discussion. But on the rare occasions when he complained, Myra always challenged him.

"Because I'm not the kind of person who quits," Dirk would reply. Of course, that was not the real reason. The real reason he didn't leave his job was that he was afraid to give up the security. Fifteen years in one job was nothing to let go of easily. There was certainly no guarantee he'd find anything better, especially at his age.

But what about the young turk he once was, fresh out of MIT with a degree in math, and destined to become an entrepreneur? What about the clever quipster who once wanted to write cartoons? Dirk tried never to think that far back. When he did, he reasoned, *I'm not the only one in my class who didn't fulfill his promise. MIT spawns more broken dreams than dreams that come true. I should count my blessings. I have a great wife, great kids, and a job that pays me well enough. I should shut up and give thanks for what I have.*

Dirk's dad had died a year after he graduated from MIT. That sudden death shook Dirk harder than he realized at the time. It changed him altogether. He lost his edge, and he lost his nerve. He grew cautious, looking for a sure thing. He started looking over his shoulder, wondering what accident or tragedy fate might offer up next.

His life likely would have continued in its drab way had Louis not been promoted, astonishingly in Dirk's opinion, to a different division in the company. Ellie became his new manager. The day after she came on board, she called him into her office. Ever on guard, he was ready for the worst.

After they exchanged niceties, Ellie asked, "What do you actually do here?"

"I do the job at hand," Dirk replied automatically.

Ellie took off her red-rimmed glasses and asked in her slight southern accent, "Do you actually like your job?"

Dirk paused. Louis had never asked him that question. Only Myra had asked him that question. "Do I like my job?" he repeated back.

"Yes, that's what I'm wondering. Do you like your job?"

"No, I can't say that I do. But I am not complaining. I'm a professional."

Ellie burst out laughing. "Dirk, stop it, please! I'm not Big Brother. You can tell me the truth. You're a genius, and unless you truly like the monotonous job you've got, I want to see if we can't use your talents in some more interesting ways."

Dirk looked at her as if he were dreaming. "No one has called me a genius in a long, long time," he said.

"Well," Ellie responded, "your IQ is right here in your file. I don't put much stock in IQ, but when it's 162, it's hard to ignore. On the other hand, I know some geniuses want to fly under the radar. Are you one of them?"

Dirk actually felt a lump in his throat, as if he were going to cry, something he hadn't done in years. Instead, he cleared his throat and swallowed. He took a deep breath, looked out the window, and took in the clouds floating by behind Ellie's red hair. She waited, saying nothing.

"No," Dirk said, feelings rising up within him. "I am *not* like that. That's not who I am."

"I am so glad to hear that," Ellie said.

"Well, I'm actually quite glad to say it," Dirk said. "Thanks for asking."

"So, who are you, really?" Ellie asked.

"I'm a hot-shot mathematician and a wannabe cartoonist, that's who I am. And I'm a damn good writer. And I'll work my ass off for you if you let me sink my teeth into something interesting. Otherwise, I'm someone who probably ought to get the hell out of here instead of just taking up space. You'd do me a favor to fire me."

Ellie clapped. "Bravo, Dirk. I am so glad you still know who you are. Why did you go into hiding for so long?"

Dirk laughed. "They say it's unprofessional for managers to ask personal questions."

"That's BS," Ellie said. "It's bad management for them not to."

"Well, let me put my answer on hold until we get to know each other better, would that be all right?"

"Of course," Ellie said with a smile.

Play Unearths Talent and Ideas

There are millions of Dirks working in America and around the world, talented people who for one reason or another are not using their talents and are overlooked by managers. As workers like Dirk get plugged into the wrong slot, step 1, select, goes wrong. If they work for a manager who fails to make a true connection, they gradually withdraw into the limbo of disconnection, so step 2 fails. After that, step 3, what I call "play," becomes impossible.

And yet, without play, peak performance is impossible. By play, I mean any activity that engages the imagination. Hence, imaginative engagement and play are synonymous.

Play is what humans can do and computers can't. Play is the activity of the mind that allows you to dream up novel approaches, fresh plans. Columbus was at play when it dawned on him that the world was round. Newton was at play in his mind when he saw the apple tree and suddenly conceived of the force of gravity. Watson and Crick were playing with possible shapes of the DNA molecule when they stumbled upon the double helix. Shakespeare played with iambic pentameter his whole life. Mozart barely lived a waking moment when he was not at play. Einstein's thought experiments are brilliant examples of the mind invited to play.

Play leads to all great discoveries. Of course, more goes into great discoveries than that. Edison, whose imagination seemed always to be engaged, had that "more" in mind when he said,

"Genius is one percent inspiration and ninety-nine percent perspiration."[1] The next chapter—on grapple and grow—will tell more of that aspect of the tale, but here I focus on play, which drives creativity. And it is creativity that drives profits.

The opposite of play is doing exactly what one is told to do. It leads to robotic behavior, slavish adherence to the rules, and an inability to deviate from standard operating procedure no matter what.

Let me give you an example of an adult whose play function failed him. I was driving with an executive one day when we got lost. As we came to a dead end in the middle of nowhere, I began to maneuver into an empty parking lot to turn around. The executive suddenly barked, "Stop!" so I stopped.

"Can't you see the sign?" the man asked me, as if in disbelief. "It says, 'Do Not Enter.' "

I laughed. "John, are you serious?"

"Of course I'm serious. Laws are laws, whether a cop is watching or not."

"John, the only reason that sign is there is to control the flow of traffic when this lot is full. Do you really want me to back up and enter the lot where the sign says, 'Enter'?"

"I'd feel better about it if you did," John said.

John had somehow lost his capacity to imagine a circumstance where a rule did not need to be obeyed. Rather than make him feel uncomfortable, I backed up and drove in the legal way. But I felt sad for John and how restricted he'd become because of his inability to imagine acting in any way except blind obedience to rules.

Sometimes bucking the tide, going against the grain, leads to massive gain. A culture of play and imaginative engagement encourages people to speak their most off-the-wall ideas, to go in the opposite direction from everyone else, if that's where their intuition leads them. Even if they may go astray, it's well worth it to establish permission to be different, to play, in all organizations.

> *One of the beauties about the market is you can be right about something and if everyone else disagrees, you can still end up with a good outcome. In most fields of endeavor if people disagree with you, enough people disagree with you, you're sort of out of luck. That was I think one of the attractions for me, for somebody who in many ways is an individualist.*
>
> —EDDIE LAMPERT,
> *Chair, Sears Holdings*

Play, as I define it, is not restricted to the "creatives" in your organization. That's a common misconception. If you're reading this page, you can play! Everyone has it in them to imagine and to question. The best organizations create a culture that fosters play in everyone, especially those to whom it does not come naturally, because in play those people will discover talents and ideas they didn't know they had. An expectation of rigid conformity, of political correctness and robotic obedience to procedure and rules, may prevent lawsuits, but it deadens people and sooner or later kills organizations. No one ever got great by doing only what they were told.

Play Promotes Connection and Creativity

Daniel Pink divides the past 150 years into three phases. First was the industrial age, dominated by factory workers, whose most important assets were physical strength and character. Next came the information age, dominated by knowledge workers, whose most important asset was left-brain, linear, logical thinking. Now, Pink asserts, we have entered the conceptual age, dominated by what he calls creators and empathizers (in my terms, people who can play and people who can connect). Their key assets are right-brain qualities like intuition, vision, ability to switch contexts easily, ability to quickly get the gist, and the like.[2] While it may have created a distraction in the heyday of the information age, the ability to play is an essential tool in the conceptual age.

Furthermore, in our current world of information overload, speed, and mandates to increase productivity, people tend to drill down and get into a negative mood. As Martin Seligman states, citing abundant research, "Positive mood produces broader attention . . . more creative thinking . . . and more holistic thinking . . . in contrast to negative mood which produces narrower attention . . . more critical thinking, and more analytic thinking."[3]

> *It used to be if you were a big company you could count on being a big company fifty years later. Today, that's no longer true. You have to re-earn the customer's commitment each year. The chances that you can sustain leadership long-term without being incredibly innovative are really slight. That's why when you look at companies like Microsoft, Walmart, or General Electric, it's hugely impressive.*
>
> —HEATHER REISMAN,
> *CEO, Indigo Books*

It is useful now to promote the more positive state of mind that allows for free play of the mind, rather than demand answers quickly. The hurried, focused, pressured thinker is prone to stifle new ideas or misinterpret what he sees.

Let me give a couple of examples of how your first or even second thought can lead you astray.

In logic there is a famous example called the "Monty Hall problem," named after the host of the old TV game show *Let's Make a Deal*. The problem goes as follows: let's say Monty shows you three curtains and tells you that behind one curtain there sits a new car, but behind the other two curtains lurk booby prizes—a donkey and a rubber boot. He asks you to pick a curtain, and you pick curtain #1. Then Monty opens curtain #3, which reveals the donkey. Now he gives you the opportunity to switch your choice from curtain #1 to #2. Assuming you want the car, what do you decide to do?

Think about it before you read on.

Most people see no reason to switch. But, in fact, you double your odds of getting the car if you switch to curtain #2. At the outset, when you picked curtain #1, the odds were 1 in 3 that the car was behind that curtain, and 2 in 3 that it wasn't. After Monty opens curtain #3, those odds do not change. There is still a 1 in 3 chance that the car is behind curtain #1. That means there must be a 2 in 3 chance the car is behind curtain #2. So you double your chance by switching. Knowing what's behind curtain #3 has helped you. But you have to be adept enough with logic and statistics to take advantage of what that knowledge has given you.[4]

Here are two other examples.

The price of a ball and a bat is $1.10. The bat is priced one dollar higher than the ball. What is the price of the ball?

Think about it before you read on.

Most people quickly conclude that the bat costs $1.00, and the ball costs 10 cents. But that would mean the bat costs only 90 cents more than the ball, not the required $1.00. For the total to be $1.10, the ball must cost 5 cents and the bat $1.05. Getting the right answer does not depend on having a high IQ; it depends on other factors that, as psychologist Keith Stanovich points out, IQ tests don't measure but matter a great deal nonetheless.[5]

Stanovich also cites the following problem developed by his colleague, Hector Levesque, a computer scientist at the University of Toronto:

Jack is looking at Anne, but Anne is looking at George. Jack is married, but George is not. Is a married person looking at an unmarried person?

(A) Yes (B) No (C) Cannot be determined

Most people choose C. But that is the wrong answer. The right answer is A. Think about it. We know whether or not Jack and George are married, but not if Anne is married. If Anne is unmarried, then a married person is looking at an unmarried person because Jack is married and he is looking at her. If Anne is married, then a married person is looking at an unmarried person because George is unmarried and Anne is looking at him. Either way, a married person is looking at an unmarried person, so the answer is A.

Once again, getting the correct answer does not depend on having a high IQ, but rather on not settling too soon for what at first glance seems to be the correct answer.[6]

In offering the preceding three examples, not only was I demonstrating a point about what the quick, goal-directed mind can miss, I was also providing you, the reader, with a chance to play. If you're like most people, you found the problems fun. Even though you likely came up with incorrect answers (unless you peeked), it was fun to be fooled, get surprised, and learn from what you missed.

Instead of my simply telling you the point I wanted to make, I allowed you to interact with the issue and learn from your own mistakes. This is the great beauty of play: it *engages* people in a way that straight didactic lecture or linear explanation can't. You remember far better what you discover experientially than what you are told. That's why Confucius said experience is the greatest teacher and why Socrates asked questions.

I have stated that play drives creativity. Stuart Brown, founder of the National Institute for Play, takes its importance much further than that. He writes:

> Of all animal species, humans are the biggest players of all. We are built to play and built through play. When we play, we are engaged in the purest expression of our humanity, the truest expression of our individuality. Is it any wonder that often the times we feel most alive, those that make up our best memories, are moments of play?[7]

As a manager, you may say, "That's fine, but my people are here to work, not have peak experiences or enjoy the best moments of their lives. They're here to produce results. That's why they get paid. The *last* thing I want them to do is improvise and play. What a terrifying idea!"

And there's a good point in that response. When I interviewed Jasper White, a highly creative chef, restaurant owner, and entrepreneur, he said to me, "A customer who had the pan-roasted lobster one week expects it to be the same the next week, so the last thing I want is for someone in my kitchen to get 'creative' on me and produce a pan-roasted clump of glue."[8]

To be sure, it is essential for workers of all kinds not to jeopardize a project by going off on wild tangents. As Louis, Dirk's supervisor, said, you wouldn't want your surgeon to start improvising in the middle of the operation, just as Jasper White would fire anyone who altered his pan-roasted lobster.

But you *would* want your surgeon to improvise if he encountered some problem that the standard procedure didn't account for and had no means to fix. You *would* want him to be able to think up some new approach, rather than let you die on the table. This is where play becomes critical—not to undermine standard operations, but to save the day when the standard approach fails or blows up.

Let me give you an example from my own professional life. This is not a situation managers reading this book will likely encounter, but it does demonstrate why the ability to play—to imagine new approaches—matters.

After I graduated from medical school, I did a residency in psychiatry at a Harvard teaching hospital in Boston called the Massachusetts Mental Health Center. It was both an academic teaching hospital and a state hospital, which means it took in the indigent mentally ill, the most rejected and often despised of all people in our society.

One night when I was on call, a man walked into the hospital and asked to see a doctor. When the security guard paged me, I came down and greeted the gentleman who wanted to see me. He was scruffy, in his early twenties, and was wearing a U.S. Navy pea jacket, jeans, and worn-out boots. I shook his hand, found out he was called Buddy, and invited him into the small office where we interviewed the people who came in at night.

"I need help," Buddy said.

"What kind of help do you need?" I asked.

"*You know*," Buddy replied, narrowing his eyes.

"Gee, Buddy, we just met. How could I know what you need?"

"*You know*," he growled.

By now, I knew he was crazy. It doesn't take long to know that. But there are many kinds of crazy, and I did not know which kind of craziness Buddy was struggling with. "If you know I know what you need, why do I feel like I don't know?" I didn't want to argue with Buddy, but I did want him to elaborate.

"You're nothing but a lying bastard," he snarled.

"Well, of course, you know more than I do," I replied, as low key as I could.

"You got *that* right," Buddy replied. He looked at the floor and spit. Spitting indoors on the floor is another sign of being crazy, unless you're drunk, primitive, or angry. Then he did something no one had ever done to me before. He pulled a gun on me.

There was a little button on my side of the desk that doctors were supposed to push if they needed Security. I had never pushed that button before, but I figured this was a good time to do it. Now, remember, this was a state facility. It should therefore not have surprised me that when I tried to push the button, I found no button. There was just a hole where the button used to be. The security guard was in another part of the hospital, well out of earshot, had I been foolish enough to yell or scream. I had no training for what I was supposed to do next. Our only training had been, "If you find yourself in danger, push the panic button." The training had omitted what to do if the panic button didn't exist.

So, I was on my own. It came down to Buddy, me, and Buddy's gun.

I surprised myself by how I reacted. Looking back, I would have thought I'd be terrified, but, maybe because of the intensity of the situation, I simply focused entirely on the scene itself. I focused only on Buddy and his gun. There wasn't room for fear. I knew I had to do something. So I did what I do best. I improvised, which is to say, I played.

"Buddy, I can't help you if you use that gun. You're right, I do know you need help. And you have needed it for a long time." Buddy was listening, so I kept talking, just making it up as I went along. "You have really tried. Man, oh man, have you tried. You've tried *everything.* You've asked everyone who will listen. But nobody listens. Just like me, when you came in here, I didn't listen. Geez, you had to pull a gun on me to get me to listen. I know you didn't want to do that, but you had to. That was one smart move, Buddy. But then, you're a smart dude. That's part of your problem, you're so much smarter than almost everyone else you deal with. You're definitely smarter than I am. But that's my problem. I want to help you, but I'm not sure I'm smart enough to help you. I need you to teach me."

As I talked, I watched Buddy. I knew I was making progress when, after I said, "You've tried *everything*," Buddy nodded. That was huge. He was buying what I was selling. He believed that I understood him. He didn't care that we'd never met. Because, in a sense, we had. I'd met many others like Buddy. Knowing what people like Buddy have in common was what I was drawing on.

Buddy put up his hand, as if stopping traffic. "You're smart enough to help me," he said. "That's why I came here tonight. I knew *you'd* be here. I know you know how to help me."

"Yes, I do know how to help you," I said, even though I had no clue.

"Let's get started, then," Buddy said.

"OK, good idea, we really ought to get started. You've been waiting long enough."

"Yes, I have," Buddy said. "I've been waiting a real long time. Do you know how long a long time is? It's longer than anyone should ever have to wait."

"You're a smart man, Buddy," I said. I could tell he actually was a very smart man, by his ability to abstract and create the concept of how long a long time is.

"How do *you* know I'm smart?" Buddy asked, for the moment angry, as if he had been BS'd many times in the past.

"Your vocabulary, your talent with ideas, stuff like that. It's my job to be able to tell."

Buddy smiled, satisfied. "I knew I came in on the right night."

"Shall we get started then?" I asked.

"Yes. It is time to get started."

"There's one problem, though, Buddy. I honestly can't help you if you are holding a gun on me. I'm just too focused on that gun to give you my full attention. The gun's a distraction."

"No, of course you can't help me if I'm pointing this gun at you," Buddy said and put the gun down on my desk. "But it did get your attention, didn't it?" he asked with a smile.

"Yes, it surely did," I said, and picked up the gun. I didn't know what to do with it, so I just looked at it for a second or two, then put it in the desk drawer. I said to myself as I did it, *Be sure to remember you put a gun in the desk drawer.* I even laughed to myself at the image of some of my colleagues' reactions should they happen to open the drawer and discover a gun. Then I stood up and asked Buddy if he'd like to check into the hospital.

"Yes, I would," Buddy replied. "And give me a nice room. Do you have private baths?"

So ended one of my more memorable episodes during a night on call and so began one of my more interesting cases as a resident.

When Buddy pulled the gun on me and the panic button failed, I was on my own. That's when I started to *play*, to make up my own dialogue, to improvise.

Such crises arise all the time in most work settings. They don't usually involve guns, of course, but they do involve the possibility of disaster. The superior employee is the one who can handle it, who can improvise, who can work outside the "book" and contrive new plans for new contingencies. I was simply relying on my imagination and my gut to guide me, and they saved the day.

The point of that story is to demonstrate what I mean by play—how serious play can be, how crucial, and in this case, perhaps lifesaving. Stuart Brown, in fact, makes that precise claim for play. He writes:

> I don't think it is too much to say that play can save your life. It certainly has salvaged mine. Life without play is a grinding, mechanical existence organized around doing the things necessary for survival. Play is the stick that stirs the drink. It is the basis of all art, games, books, sports, movies, fashion, fun, and wonder—in short, the basis of what we think of as civilization. Play is the vital essence of life. It is what makes life lively.[9]

I would add that play is what makes work lively as well. If you can't play at work, as Dirk couldn't, you lose your most valuable ability to contribute at work. Play builds your brain. Play stimulates the secretion of brain-derived neurotrophic factor, or BDNF, which I mentioned in chapter 1, a recently discovered molecule that triggers the growth of nerves in the brain. Play also stimulates the amygdala, which is a clump of neurons deep within the brain that helps regulate emotions and exerts a beneficial effect on the prefrontal cortex in the brain.

The prefrontal cortex is especially important at work because that's where executive functions are regulated. *Executive function* is actually a neurological term, not just a business term. The brain's executive functions include planning, prioritizing, scheduling, anticipating, delegating, deciding, analyzing—in short, most of the skills any executive must master in order to excel in business. So, play is good for business, and not being able to play hurts business. I learned this firsthand during my years consulting to the Harvard chemistry department, an organization that transformed itself, as I recounted in chapter 3, from a pathologically disconnected environment to a more positively connected culture. Another lesson I learned during my six years of working with that department pertains to the importance of play.

Organic chemistry, Harvard's forte, is famous for its demands of twenty-hour days and persistence in the face of negative results. Few people would associate the word *play* with the work grad students and postdocs do in organic chemistry, especially in high-powered academic settings like Harvard. However, the ability to play is actually critical in organic chemistry. I learned this in the following way.

Each year Harvard accepts a new group of grad students and postdocs from elite applicants the world over. Since Harvard is ranked among the very top departments, the very best students (on paper) apply. When they arrive in Cambridge and go to the lab they are assigned to, they are asked to get to work discovering new knowledge.

One group of students rushes into the lab, excited at the prospect of being able to play with molecules, test hypotheses, and discover new facts. This is what they've always wanted to do as scientists. Now they can fulfill their dream.

But another group of students freezes up. They say, "I'll do anything you want, I'll wash test tubes, I'll run experiments all night, I'll grade undergraduate exams, but please don't ask me to discover anything new on my own." These are the students who long ago lost the ability to play. Around fifth grade or so, they decided the best thing to do was exactly what they were told, and they did that extremely well. They scored high on all tests, they received excellent recommendations for being so diligent and disciplined, and they believed they were on track to winning a Nobel Prize.

How wrong they were. They continue at Harvard, or wherever, and get the degree they seek, but they never make much of a difference in the field, and worse, they rarely take much joy in what they do.

The manager who can encourage play, who can model imaginative engagement and encourage others to do so, is the manager who brings out the best in the people who work for her. This is the manager who develops peak performance. Or, as Southwest Airlines puts it in their mission statement on their Web site, "People rarely succeed at anything unless they are having fun doing it."

I have a friend, Richard Rossi, who is a successful entrepreneur and now CEO of a company named EnvisionEMI, an organization that brings thousands of teens to Washington, D.C., for life-changing experiences that involve them with government in various hands-on ways. Richard calls himself a "creator." He is very much a participant in the conceptual age, but he is also very much a money-making, practical businessman. The two go hand in hand, as do work and play in Richard's life. In fact, Richard puts the following quote from a Buddhist text at the end of all his e-mails:

> The Master in the art of living makes little distinction between his work and his play, his labor and his leisure, his mind and his body, his education and his recreation, his love and his religion.
>
> He hardly knows which is which. He simply pursues his vision of excellence in whatever he does, leaving others to decide whether he is working or playing. To him, he is always doing both.[10]

Don't worry. I know life's not all fun and games. I will address suffering in the next chapter (betcha can't wait!). Yes, hard work and some degree of pain are prerequisites for peak performance. But to induce people to work hard and endure pain, it is best for them to imaginatively engage *first*. Play numbs pain.

How to Encourage Play

As a manager (or a teacher, a coach, a parent, or anyone who wants to help people imaginatively engage), there are many steps you can take to encourage the deep and exciting state I call by the deceptively simple term *play*.

Here are ten practical suggestions, in no particular order:

1. Ask open-ended questions, those without a yes/no or other specific answer. For example, "What day is it today?" is not open-ended, but "What shall we do today?" is.

Open-ended questions engage the imagination. Socrates was the greatest master of this technique, which now bears his name. The Socratic method remains one of the best ways to teach. Instead of giving answers, ask questions. People will give you answers you never expected, and often answers they never knew they had.

How can that be? you ask. It is the power of the unconscious. I learn much of what I want to write *while writing.* Similarly, people can learn what they think and discover ideas they didn't know they had by responding to a question. As a manager, don't feel you are putting someone "on the spot" by asking a question. Instead, you are helping that person discover what he knows or imagines.

So ask questions like these:

- What can we learn from what just happened?
- Where did we go wrong?
- What do you think?
- What are we doing right?
- What else could we do to bring out the best in everyone?
- What changes could we make to the prototype?
- Why are we spending so much time on this topic?
- What are we avoiding?

These kinds of questions invite people to brainstorm, reflect, come up with ideas, and play.

2. Model a questioning attitude. As a manager, you have to show people that it is safe to disagree with the party line

and with the boss—that it is in fact *good* to bring up opposing points of view. If you don't model this, your employees likely will not initiate such behavior on their own.

3. Consider having a goofy day of some sort now and then. It must conform to the basic rules and values of your organization's culture, of course. But make it fun. For example, one manager I know at a company that makes presentation videos for businesses instituted a "Bad Dress Day." The idea was to come to work dressed as unattractively as you could (or dared). Come as if you were competing for a place on the Ten Worst-Dressed People of the Year. The idea became such a success that it is now a yearly practice.

4. Decorate your work space imaginatively, but also with an eye toward practical ways you can facilitate play with architecture and setup. For example, a high-tech company might put whiteboards with markers next to elevators so people could diagram or draw their ideas as they waited. Or, you might choose color schemes that are lively and engaging, rather than subdued. Or, you might rearrange work areas to promote increased staff interaction, as the Atlanta Housing Authority did when it revamped its cubicle system. It lowered the heights of the cubicle wall to improve sight lines between employees, and it set up "teaming tables" at intersections where employees could conveniently share ideas and show work.[11]

5. Help people think in ways they normally don't by having an "opposite meeting." At one of your regularly scheduled

meetings, you might lead off by saying, "We've got a big problem here. Everyone is way too productive. What can we do to reduce productivity?" You'd be surprised how productive people can become exploring ways in which they could be less productive.

Or, invite everyone to describe all the mistakes they'd love to make. Or, you might simply begin by saying, "What could we do to make this meeting the biggest waste of time possible?" You don't have time for such nonsense? Try it. You might just find it one of the more ice-breaking, valuable meetings you've ever convened.

6. Try automatic writing. If you or one of your employees has hit a bottleneck or is frustrated in making progress, try communicating directly with your unconscious through the process of automatic writing. Use a keyboard or pen and paper, whichever medium allows you to write fluently without thinking. Just start typing, or writing, without thinking at all about what you are writing or pausing even for a second to reflect. Just keep the words coming, even if they seem like nonsense, and they probably will. Do this for at least five minutes, up to ten if you can. Then read what you've written.

   Most likely you'll find the germ of a helpful idea. Or, you may simply feel as if you've broken the logjam. Automatic writing is an extremely simple but practical way to tap into your unconscious, a rich reservoir of ideas.

7. Read a book on creative-thinking techniques. *Thinkertoys* by Michael Michalko offers many simple, practical exercises to stimulate imaginative engagement.[12] Michalko

divides the book into sections, such as "Intuitive Thinkertoys" and "Group Thinkertoys." The book is both fun and rich in instruction for anyone who feels stuck.

8. Give your people some time to go somewhere away from work and think. This will stimulate their imaginations. It is amazing how few people, when asked where they do their best thinking, reply, "At work." The most common answer I get is, "In the shower." So, do the next best thing. Send them anywhere but work.

   Of course, you have to have some flexibility to do this. My friend Dirk Ziff runs a large investment fund, and he sends his traders for long weekends in the Caribbean, all expenses paid. The only requirement is that they not use e-mail and that they report on what they thought about—while getting a massage, say.

   And Bill Gates is famous for taking seven days twice a year in a secluded cabin where he reads, drinks diet Orange Crush, and thinks. You don't have to be Bill Gates to do this.

9. Play with a child. If you don't have kids of your own, borrow a niece or nephew, or even the child of a friend or neighbor. Let the child lead you. It may be awkward at first, but if you allow for some self-consciousness on your part, the child will soon help you open up long-dormant parts of yourself. Children are our greatest experts on play. And we were all children once, remember?

10. Try what organic chemists call "retrograde synthesis." In chemistry, you work backwards from the molecule you are

trying to synthesize. But you can also use the idea to jump-start play and creativity. Simply envision your goal, then start working backwards, step by step, until you get to where you are now. Presto! Project done.

KEY IDEAS

- Play is any activity that engages the imagination. You can play while solving a geometry problem or giving a speech. You can play doing anything.
- Play is the most creative activity of the human brain. In play the brain totally lights up.
- No one ever got great by doing only what they were told.
- Play stimulates BDNF, which promotes brain growth.
- As a manager, promote play by encouraging disagreement and asking open-ended questions.

CHAPTER FIVE

Grapple and Grow

Lorraine is a trader in a large brokerage firm. She ranks high in productivity, but her record of late has been less than her usual level of excellence. She doesn't want to talk about it, but she knows Anne, her manager, is aware of the issue because Anne has already made a couple of veiled comments couched as questions, like, "Is everything going well?"

As Lorraine looks back at the months of lowered productivity, she tries to figure out what changed. Same job, same manager, same clients, same coworkers, same support staff. She arrives for work at the same early hour and stays until the same late hour.

Unable to figure out what her problem has been, she decides she will be proactive and discuss the matter with Anne. She begins their meeting by stating the issue. "As I'm sure you've noticed, my numbers have been down a bit for the past three months."

Anne nods. "Yes, I've noticed, but I'm not worried. I know you'll bounce back."

"I appreciate your confidence. That's really nice. But I am puzzled. That's why I'm coming to you."

"And I appreciate your confidence in me. I just assumed your focus was off a bit. Is there anything going on in your life that may be distracting you?"

"No. At least not that I can put my finger on. I'm doing everything the same way I always have. Same hours, same routines, same personal life."

Anne paused. "All right, how about your health?"

"I'm fit as a fiddle. I work out all the time. I get good sleep. I eat well, and I drink only now and then. Boring, huh? So it's not my health."

"What would Sherlock Holmes do?" Anne said. "The case of the mysterious decline. What clues do we have?"

"None. At least none that I can find. That's why I'm talking to you. It's like I just became stupid all of a sudden."

"Really? Are you making bad decisions?"

"Sort of. It's more a matter of my not digging as deep and doing as much research."

Anne then volunteered an idea. "I spoke to a consultant about my own work a month or so ago and it really helped. The first thing he zeroed in on was how much time I spent on e-mail and the Internet. He said that's the biggest sinkhole of wasted time in the modern workplace. He said lots of people waste more time than they're aware of, doing what he calls 'screensucking.'"

Lorraine stopped and looked away, thinking. "Hmm," she said. "You might be onto something. Come to think of it, this all started about the same time we upgraded the computer system and Jerry gave me a tutorial. He showed me a ton of stuff I could do online that I'd never heard of."

"And?" Anne asked.

Lorraine clapped her hands. "And, I think you are a total genius! I think you just figured it out, Sherlock. What was the term your consultant used?"

"Screensucking," Anne said with a laugh. "He said people waste hours without even knowing they're doing it because they go into a kind of mindless trance while they screensuck."

"Did this consultant give you any ideas on how to stop screensucking?"

"He said it can be difficult. In fact, he said screens are the new addiction. Involves the same brain chemistry as any addiction. But he suggested I move my computer from front-and-center on my desk to a table behind me, so to use it I have to swivel my chair around. And that millisecond of reflection gives me the chance to resist the temptation to go to e-mail. When the computer was right in front of me, it was like a jar of M&M's. I'd reach for it reflexively. Now I don't spend nearly as much time online."

As simple as it sounds, this solution worked for Lorraine as well. It caused a bit of an inconvenience, because so much of her work involved the computer, but it did add the element of intention to her screen time, and cut way back on the screensucking. Once she got the habit under control she was able to move her computer back onto her desk.

Step 4 in the Cycle of Excellence, grapple and grow, often bogs down in the modern workplace because of various distractions and interruptions, the most common being e-mail and the Internet.

The Pain of Gain

By grapple and grow, I mean the *combination* of work and progress. A person may work a hundred-hour week, but make little progress, while someone else may leap ahead working a fifty-hour week. The key move for the manager in handling this step is to make sure that the hard work is also smart work, that effort is leading to growth. Too many employees do the equivalent of driving on square wheels. All that effort to go 10 feet!

How do you, as a manager, round out the wheels? I suggested one technique in the example of Lorraine, above. You want to look for hidden time sinkholes, hidden inefficiencies, places where effort goes wasted.

You also want to make sure the first three steps in the cycle have been successfully negotiated. Before you ask a person to work harder, ask:

1. **Select:** Is she operating at the intersection of what she likes, what she's good at, and what adds value to the organization?

2. **Connect:** Does she feel safe at work, comfortable enough to be candid and open, connected enough to look forward to coming in?

3. **Play:** Is she imaginatively engaged with her work? Is she able to feel control and ownership of what she's doing?

Only when "yes" is the answer to those questions will the grappling in step 4 lead to growth. Otherwise you get what happens all too often: hard work leading to stress, frustration, mistakes, depression, absenteeism, or, at best, inferior performance.

When hard work leads to growth, then you know you've successfully negotiated step 4. The beauty of this is that it leads a person to want to work even harder. When a worker makes progress, when he gets good results, he naturally wants to work even harder. All people—well, almost all people—want to succeed. When they taste success, they redouble their efforts. As the saying goes, success breeds success. The great manager sets each employee up to make progress, regardless of skill level or intelligence.

The most common mistake managers make when work isn't going well—when the desired growth isn't happening—is simply to demand more work. Often, more work is not at all what's needed. Usually, the problem lies upstream, in steps 1, 2, or 3. Poor selection, lack of connection, or the absence of imaginative engagement are the most common reasons that work fails to lead to growth or progress.

But when the problem truly resides in step 4, as it did for Lorraine, when a person's best efforts do not lead to the desired results, then a manager should look specifically at what is getting in the way.

Making Work Pay Off

Grapple and grow is where you meet success or failure. This step puts the numbers up on the board, where everyone is watching. This is the game, it's showtime. Preparation is over. When it goes smoothly, everyone is happy. But, as all managers know, it often doesn't go smoothly.

> *It's the constant reminder to strive, never getting into a comfort zone of thinking we've finally arrived. You should never get to that state. We never finish painting the Golden Gate Bridge. It always needs work. At some point in time maybe we're going to finish. We can climb up on the top of one of those hills on the Sausalito side and look down and say that's a beautiful bridge. But when we think we've finished painting that bridge, it needs painting on the other side, so we need to go back and start all over again. It never stops . . . Striving. Always . . .It's never perfect. If someone only makes a magnificent play, I say, that's a 99 or that's a 98. What would have made that a 100 would have been just a little of this or that. So you never want to reach that level of athletic repose where you just stand back and relax and take a deep breath. It doesn't go with the job.*
>
> —MICHAEL POPE,
> *Assistant coach, New York Giants*

When work—grappling—doesn't lead to growth today, it is often due to the chaos of modern life, the constant interruptions, the myriad distractions, and the pressure to do more in less time with fewer resources. Workers get so frazzled that they overheat and become inefficient. The manager's job now is not to deliver inspirational talks that will generate harder work, but to deliver practical strategies that will help workers work smarter.

As the consultant who helped "Anne" in the opening example (you might have guessed, that consultant was me) pointed out, and as many other experts have noted, electronics constitute the newest addiction, or at least a dangerously habit-forming activity.[1]

And even if a person is not addicted to e-mail or surfing the Internet, he likely gets distracted by both. Electronics can also provide a convenient dodge, a respectable dodge around more difficult projects that require thinking, organizing, creating, and dealing with frustration.

Ironically, the most difficult work can be avoided in today's crazy-busy world simply by staying busy. After all, what manager would criticize an employee for being busy? But managers need to catch on. They need to see how much time gets wasted in being busy. *People avoid thinking by being too busy to think.* They dodge the hard work of developing something new by responding to a thousand e-mails or text messages a day instead. They deceive themselves into believing they are working productively, when in fact, they are merely processing messages.

Instead, they should protect time to do what matters most: to think. To think in depth. To grapple. To feel the pain of frustration when the solution isn't clear or when the problem is so complex it hurts your brain. This is good pain. This is the pain that leads to gain.

It is the most difficult part of the step I call grapple and grow, and it is the most crucial. Let's say you are trying to roll out a new advertising campaign, or you're planning a difficult piece of surgery, or you are trying to sell more toasters than your competitor or develop a better investment policy. What's going to be the most difficult but most important part about doing it successfully? Answering all the e-mails you get every day? Making sure you keep yourself booked in meetings? Keeping one finger always poised above your BlackBerry? Thinking and grappling with a problem is an especially endangered activity today because modern life affords so many plausible excuses to avoid it. Our marvelous electronic devices can seduce us into believing we are hard at work, but we are merely sending and receiving insignificant messages, while the real work goes undone, day after day, week after week, year after year. Real thinking and grappling hurt like hell. That's why so many people avoid it like a root canal.

As Ernest Hemingway said when asked how to write a novel, "Well, first of all you clean out the refrigerator."

> *The doctors in training don't have time to think about the patients' problems in as much detail as they should. That thinking is the best part of what we do. It is how we learn. But now everything is so abbreviated, captured in space and time in very short bits. Snapshots. Trainees look for a quick paragraph on how to manage TTP [thrombotic thromcytopenic purpura, a disorder of the blood coagulation system], but the quick paragraph causes it to lose many of the layers of understanding and enjoyment that I think most of us got from our training.*
>
> —JOSEPH LOSCALZO,
> *Professor, Harvard Medical School, and chair, Department of Medicine at Brigham and Women's Hospital*

Grapple and grow is the step where people should spend most of their time. If it is not done right, work becomes miserable and life sags under the weight of a disliked job. This step is the most dramatically misunderstood of all aspects of the Cycle of Excellence. But if you tend to the first three steps—select what to focus on, create a positively connected atmosphere, and engage imaginatively with what you're doing—you will find that work becomes what it ought to be: fun. Your people will want to spend most of their time in step 4, working.

People say that practice makes perfect, but they usually overlook that the best way to get a person to practice is to ensure that practice emerges *from play*. It's exciting to work toward a difficult goal with people you like and respect using ideas and techniques you have had a hand in creating and implementing.

From a strictly neurological perspective, grappling will lead to growth. Let's say you're trying to memorize a telephone number. At first, you need to write it down. The nerve cells involved in learning that number fire a neurotransmitter, glutamate, to get the process started. If you never dial the number again, nothing changes. But, if you use the number, if you grapple with memorizing it, the synapses enlarge and the connections between the nerve cells involved become more securely established. Eric Kandel shared the Nobel Prize in Physiology of Medicine in 2000 with two other scientists for discovering this phenomenon, which is called synaptic plasticity.

For our purposes, this is excellent news. Grappling is good. Work works! And if they follow the steps in the Cycle of Excellence, your people will *want* to work hard.

Don't misunderstand me. I do not mean to say great managers can obviate all suffering, or that there will never be drudgery. Some suffering is both good and necessary. If you're an athlete, you have to put in tough hours in the weight room. If you're a doctor, you have to do your paperwork, and medical paperwork is among the most diabolical. If you're a writer, you have to rework passages many times. If you're a research chemist, you have to put up with negative results from experiments. It is true: you must suffer to grow and achieve excellence. Most of the pain is embedded in the grapple-and-grow step.

Grappling with Stress

People associate hard work and overload with stress. But, like suffering, stress is complex. Overload—of information or obligations—is always, by definition, bad. That's why it's called *over*load. When you try to keep track of more information than you can, or meet more obligations than you are able to, your performance declines. Hence, the title of my article for *Harvard Business Review*: "Overloaded Circuits: Why Smart People Underperform."[2]

Stress, on the other hand, can be good or bad. What's the difference between good and bad stress? Bad stress is stress that a system can't endure without suffering damage. It is unplanned, uncontrolled, allows no time for rest and recovery, and exceeds the capacity of the system to adjust to it. Bad stress usually is applied from without—for example, in nature by the weather, in human physiology by disease, and in business by the economy or by a boss or manager. Sometimes even the employee, in an effort to excel or just to meet a deadline, actually drives herself into the realm of toxic stress.

Such ambition or sense of responsibility usually backfires, because bad stress ultimately kills. It kills projects and good work. It kills brain cells, heart cells, and people. To manage yourself properly, and to manage others, it is important to court good stress but avoid the bad. Let me illustrate what I mean when I say that bad stress is unplanned, unpredictable, and uncontrolled.

Let's say an employee, Holly, is working in her office trying to meet a deadline. Suddenly her manager interrupts her with an emergency that can't wait. Reflexively, she agrees to turn her attention to the emergency, not feeling permission to ask if the emergency is more important than her deadline. But, as she works on the emergency, she seethes inside due to the unplanned demand. Her seething detracts from both her performance and her sense of well-being. Now she can barely focus on the emergency at all. Without meaning to, Holly and her manager have just colluded to create toxic stress. Holly's part in it was not speaking up; the manager's in not asking what else Holly had going on. The interruption was *unpredictable*, Holly felt that she had *no control* over the situation but instead had to agree to do what was asked, and she was *not able to effectively perform what she was being asked to do.*

In addition, bad stress allows no time for a person to recover and readjust. As James Loehr, one of the leading practitioners in the field of teaching peak performance, puts it, "Stress is not the enemy in our lives. Paradoxically, it is the key to growth."[3] But you have to get the right balance between stress and rest. Without time for recovery, good stress becomes bad. Because Holly was forced to immediately shift from one stressful situation to another with no break, the toxicity of the new stress intensified. With no control, no planning, and no chance to recover, her performance precipitously declined.

Effective management limits bad stress as much as possible, while promoting good stress in the form of surmountable challenges. For example, if a manager asks an employee to take on a new task but gives him time to prepare for it, allows him to discuss what else he has on his plate that might get in the way, and then makes adjustments accordingly, the new project can be the kind of stress that person welcomes: a challenge he can rise to, grow from, and use to hone new skills. In this kind of stressful undertaking, new brain cells can grow and new neural pathways get paved because the person is stretching to tackle a difficult task under conditions that he can control.

> *A player must have a calm mind and a racing heart, or he's not going to succeed. The racing heart is energy. It's a violent physical game and there's huge enormous bodies flying out there in all different directions at all times. In order for you to perform at your highest level, your blood pressure has to go up. Your heart rate has to go up. The adrenaline has to be flowing and yet somewhere in this quandary of all these things that are going on inside your body, your head has to be able to still handle that playbook and handle the decisions that have to be made in that short period of time. You achieve that with practice. You rehearse situations over and over and over again. The motivation of that player so that his heart is racing is my responsibility. A lot of what the player has to do is retain what's in that playbook and that requires his own study. He can't just come to work thinking everything that he's going to need to play in this next game is going to be done in a six- or seven-hour day. It's going to take two or three and in some cases four hours after he leaves here. No different than if they were working in a Wall Street job or going to medical school or whatever. It's not just a daytime job. That's where his calm mind has to come from, the feeling of confidence.*
>
> —MICHAEL POPE

In the brain, this constructive process of "good stress" involves what's called long-term potentiation, or LTP.[4] As you stress your brain by asking it to absorb new and unfamiliar information, what at first was difficult becomes easier (that is, less stressful) because the longer the neurons associate with one another in a given activity, the stronger the pathways become. This is why practice—which in neurological terms means the repeated firing of a neuron or group of neurons—leads to improved performance. Or, as the neuroscientists say, neurons that fire together wire together. Practice not only makes perfect, it makes new neural connections.

At first the process may hurt, because growth usually does hurt. It may lead employees to complain or even to hate their manager for an afternoon, but it still can lead to growth. And, after it is over, employees are glad to have endured it. In other words, good stress is good.

Bad stress evokes the opposite response. After it is over, people tell horror stories about it. They may be permanently scarred by it, even traumatized. They may be disabled by it. In any case, they suffer, you suffer, and the bottom line suffers.

A good manager makes it a priority to preserve employees' feeling of control over their work. Overload, the demand to be available 24/7, being subjected to frequent unplanned interruptions, never being asked for an opinion, having a support service discontinued with no warning or explanation—these all contribute to a diminished sense of control at work. Such a feeling detracts from both work quality and quantity.

This is because feelings of low control reduce brainpower. New research from Adam Galinsky of the Kellogg School of Management as well as researchers from the Netherlands show that when a person feels a diminished sense of power and control, that person's executive functioning is *significantly impaired*.[5] A diminished feeling of power impairs a person's ability to make decisions, prioritize, plan, organize, implement new ideas, communicate effectively with others, shift between tasks fluidly, delegate effectively, complete tasks in a timely fashion, and many other high-level mental skills. All these functions, absolutely critical in peak performance, plummet the more a person is denied control and power over his work.

Growing Through Hard Work

Although the work ethic lies at the heart of the American formula for success, managers should consider it critically. Hard work—extra effort—is the antidote to poor performance, fear, mental overload, and stress that most managers reflexively reach for. In fact, "Work hard!" is *the* most common, time-honored advice on how to achieve peak performance. It would be fine, except for one pesky problem. *Hard work alone is not enough.* Our most-trusted advice is dangerously misleading. It can lead a person to spend his or her entire life trying to run through a brick wall—instead of looking for a way around or over the wall.

Don't misunderstand. I am not recommending sloth. Working hard is of course good and necessary. As Malcolm Gladwell points out in *Outliers*, becoming a master of any task or craft requires at least ten thousand hours of practice.[6]

What the skilled manager does is find the talent in each person in the group, match that person up with a task that draws upon that talent, help remove obstacles to the application of that talent (layers of bureaucracy and the like), and then watch and relish the magic that always ensues when the individual works and makes progress at this task. As step 4 picks up the pace, as people work and make progress, enthusiasm builds, buy-in becomes a lock, and you get what I call liftoff. You, an individual, or your group take off, now able to fly much higher than before and do more than you or they knew they could.

The crucial strategic move for managers using step 4 is to make sure your people are making progress at whatever they're doing. Make sure they are engaged in an activity that matters to them, draws upon their best abilities, and challenges them without being beyond their reach. This opens the door to flow, that wonderful state in which focus becomes total and peak performance ensues.

But what if one of your people is stuck and not making progress? One good ploy is to play with the problem. No matter what the issue is, ask the worker to explain the difficulty, and then make a suggestion—anything, just to get the process started. It might go like this:

Manager: So what's the obstacle you're facing?

Employee: It's the cerebrex plan. I can't figure out how to incorporate it into the software.

M: Have you talked to Sharon about it?

E: That won't help. She's not up on this system.

M: What about using the Dixter paradigm?

E: Oh, that would never work here. Wrong module.

M: How about if you reversed the process?

E: I can't do that. But wait a minute, maybe if instead of reversing it, I took down the lattice that's already there and inserted cerebrex above it. That might work!

M: You think so?

E: Let me try it.

Of course, that was a nonsense conversation, since cerebrex and the Dixter paradigm don't exist. But it does demonstrate how to get brainstorming started so that people can come up with new approaches. Here the manager acts not as an answer-man but as a catalyst, throwing out any suggestion to put the problem into a new light. Then the other person becomes better able to get unstuck.

Harvey Towvim, who specializes in helping people develop ideas, calls this a Ping-Pong discussion. He told me, "It doesn't matter what the problem is and it doesn't matter if I know anything about it. Using Ping-Pong I can help anybody get past whatever is getting in the way and holding them back."[7]

Once a person starts to make progress again, confidence grows, which leads to more progress. There is a big difference between *feeling* confident and *acting* confident; the first is real, the second an act. Various experts can advise you on how to *act* with confidence—make eye contact, give a firm handshake, act enthusiastically, and so on. But until you feel confident, your behavior will only be an act. A cynic once quipped, "Sincerity is the key to success. Once you can fake that, you've got it made." In spite of the cynic's remark, if you rely on faking confidence, the minute you have to confront major, unexpected adversity, you will wilt.

As a manager, you can most effectively help people build confidence—and motivation—simply by setting them up to make progress, and intervening when they fail to do so.

But this powerful step cuts two ways. If, try as a person might, she fails to make progress, that is a sure-fire confidence buster, a self-esteem breaker, and a potent demotivator. Who wants to try and fail over and over again? Much of what looks like laziness is simply avoidance. People start to avoid what they have found they can't do well. Rather than exhort them to try harder, it makes more sense to sit down with them and figure out where their efforts went wrong. And don't conclude too quickly that a task is too much for the person. Most people work their hardest when the challenge is great. As a manager, you simply want to offer support and suggestions to help the person make progress.

Perhaps the best example of our willingness, indeed eagerness, to work hard takes place outside of work. It is the example of being a parent. As Steven Johnson comments in his book *Mind Wide Open*:

> The evolutionary biologist Donald Symons has an elegant explanation for how our emotions evolved: we have powerful feelings precisely because the goals our emotions are propelling us toward are difficult ones to achieve. *The more difficult the objective, the more powerful the feeling.* [emphasis mine] In the environments where our brains evolved, finding food and tending to children were extremely challenging tasks, yet vital to reproductive success. So evolution hit upon a way to encourage us, by creating reward circuits in the brain that made us relish both our offspring and our meals.[8]

So emotion intensifies the desire to take on challenges. The development of positive emotion begins in the first three steps of the Cycle of Excellence, then blossoms in step 4 and becomes indispensable when difficulties and challenges arise.

Angela Duckworth, a psychologist at the University of Pennsylvania who works with Martin Seligman, has done fascinating research with her team to prove this very point:

> We suggest that one personal quality is shared by the most prominent leaders in every field: grit. We define grit as perseverance and passion for long-term goals. Grit entails working strenuously toward challenges, maintaining effort and interest

> over years despite failure, adversity, and plateaus in progress. The gritty individual approaches achievement as a marathon; his or her advantage is stamina. Whereas disappointment or boredom signals to others that it is time to change trajectory and cut losses, the gritty individual stays the course.
>
> Our hypothesis that grit is essential to high achievement evolved during interviews with professionals in investment banking, painting, journalism, academia, medicine, and law. Asked what quality distinguishes star performers in their respective fields, these individuals cited grit or a close synonym as often as talent. In fact, many were awed by the achievements of peers who did not at first seem as gifted as others but whose sustained commitment to their ambitions was exceptional. Likewise, many noted with surprise that prodigiously gifted peers did not end up in the upper echelons of their field.[9]

Duckworth's team developed a "grit scale" by which they could measure grit and see how it correlated with achievement in a number of different settings. For example, her team looked at 1,218 freshman cadets who entered West Point in July of 2004. They filled out questionnaires that included measures of grit and agreed to be followed by the research team. The first summer at West Point is particularly arduous, so much so it is called "Beast Barracks." The "grittier" cadets were the least likely to wash out.

So where does grit come from? That is as yet unanswered definitively, but several things certainly make a difference: how a person is raised, who a person admires and emulates, and the kind of training a person receives.

I spoke to Angela Duckworth when I was researching this book, and in our conversation she made an interesting and useful point for managers. She told me she gives herself biannual days for reflection on the direction she is headed in her life. Twice a year, she takes time off to decide if she wants to continue on her current course or change it. That means for the other 363 days, she does not entertain the notion of quitting what she's doing. Of course, if a major opportunity arose unexpectedly, she would not wait until her next reflection day to decide. But barring such unexpected opportunities, Duckworth's practice reinforces her own grit. She keeps at whatever she's doing.

"I think managers in the workplace ought to encourage a similar attitude," Duckworth told me. "Urge people to keep at it, whatever it is. Don't reevaluate every ten seconds. That opens the door way too wide to the natural human tendency to want to bail out the moment the going gets tough."[10]

Work Hard, but Work Smart

The power of the Cycle of Excellence is such that grit does not have to do the whole job. Once workers have the right tools and see progress in their work, most people will naturally work hard. That's because it feels good to do good work. The next task for the manager is to make sure her people not only work hard, but work smart.

In today's world, working smart means learning how to stay focused, avoid distractions, and preserve a positive mental state. Let's return to the difference between good stress and toxic or bad stress. Good stress, like necessary suffering, is a prerequisite for peak performance. As Jascha Heifetz, the great violinist said, "If I don't practice one day, I know it; two days, the critics know it; three days, the public knows it."

But bad stress, or unnecessary suffering, kills peak performance. The Harvard chemistry department was a hotbed of unnecessary suffering when the student committed suicide. Unnecessary suffering abounds in organizations that are poorly managed. Managers can help reduce such toxic stress by teaching people how to preserve their mental and emotional equilibrium in the face of the maelstrom of their working day.

I urge managers to help people preserve what I call "C-state" and to stave off what I call "F-state." C-state is where we do our best work. It is characterized by adjectives that begin with the letter C: cool, calm, collected, concentrated, convivial, cooperative, curious, creative, careful. F-state, on the other hand, is characterized by adjectives that begin with the letter F: fearful, frantic, frenzied, forgetful, feckless, frustrated, and about to utter another F-word!

These two states are rooted in physiology and chemistry. As interruptions mount and distractions interfere with getting work done, stress hormones pour into the system, negative emotions take over, and the mind begins to lose its focus. It is critical to learn how to nip this process at its outset, because once F-state takes over, it can do tremendous damage to your work, your relationships, and your career.

How to Help People Grapple and Grow

Following are steps you can take to help your employees grapple with the demands of the job and achieve consistent progress.

1. Before you ask someone to work harder, look back to steps 1, 2, and 3. Is she in the right position? Does she feel positively connected at work? Is there room for imaginative engagement

in what she's doing? Often, if you attend to problems in one of those prior steps, better work will naturally ensue.

2. Always be on the lookout for frustration or lack of progress in a person's work. It is critical to promote motivation and confidence that a person is making progress. As a manager, if you can intervene to break the logjam, to redirect the worker or get some mentoring that will help him master the task, then he will be on his way to superior performance. Much of what a manager does is help people overcome obstacles, or find someone who can offer such help.

3. Encourage grit, and model it. Throughout this book I have stressed many factors other than a never-say-die attitude, but if you can combine that outlook with all the other factors I've described, then you'll be a champion.

4. Try not to use fear as a management tool. There is enough fear in any organization—in life, for that matter—without a manager's intensifying it. Fear works as a motivational tool only for a short while. After that, it leads to burnout.

5. Teach people how to cultivate C-state and avoid F-state. Avoiding F-state begins by naming it. Teach people that when they start to feel overwhelmed, confused, or frustrated, they need to *slow down or stop* what they're doing. Persisting in F-state is like spinning your wheels in mud. You just get deeper and deeper in the muck, and you make no progress.

6. Cultivate C-state by emphasizing the first three steps of the Cycle of Excellence. In addition, the following all help promote and preserve C-state:
    - Put photographs in your workplace of people, places, and animals you love. When you feel F-state coming on, sit back for a moment and gaze at them.
    - Keep a joke book in your drawer. Humor is a great antidote to F-state.
    - A quick burst of exercise—three minutes of push-ups, jumping jacks, or running up and down stairs—will push the reset button on your brain. After those three minutes, your brain chemistry will change and you will return to C-state.
    - Have a few minutes of silence. During that time you might meditate—which simply means you close your eyes, focus on your breathing, and watch your thoughts flow by as if they were leaves in a stream, and you do not evaluate them or react to them. Or you might simply sit in silence, but try not to brood. Rather, try to clear your mind. Or you might pray.
    - Speak to a friend. This is best in person, but phone will do. E-mail or texting will *not* do. Speak about something trivial and insubstantial. This also will refresh your brain.
    - Go outside. You don't have to go for a long walk, but just ten minutes outside will put you in a different frame of mind.

- Eat a piece of fruit or an energy bar. You can also have coffee, but try not to drink too much as it has side effects.
- Keep a crossword or other puzzle book in your drawer. Five minutes on a puzzle will reset your brain.
- Ask for help. It is important that managers let people know it is not only OK, but desirable to ask for help when you need it. F-state is a time you need it.
- Build boundaries according to the needs and flexibility of your job. Encourage people to have set times when they sign off e-mail or close their doors for a half hour of concentrated work or thought.

7. As a manager, have conversations with your people about how they are using their time at work. Be flexible enough to help them create optimum conditions under which to work.
8. Try to keep people working at the intersection of three spheres: what they're good at, what they like, and what adds value to the organization. When they get off that spot, brainstorm ways to bring them back.
9. Allow people to be themselves rather than conform to some corporate stereotype (within reason obviously). Many people underperform because they feel they must leave half their brain in the glove compartment when they get out of their car.
10. As a manager, it can help to get a second opinion. If someone continues to make no progress despite all the work he

is putting in, and if you have exhausted your bag of tricks, then before you move him elsewhere ask for another manager's advice.

KEY IDEAS

- Being busy can be a way to dodge the hard work of thinking about complex issues and grappling with problems.
- To grapple and grow you must limit interruptions and distractions.
- Beware of screensucking.
- Promote C-state; limit F-state.
- Grit matters more than talent. Teach grit by modeling it and encouraging it.
- Confidence leads to growth, and growth leads to confidence.
- Set people up to gain confidence by making sure they are making progress at whatever they are doing.
- Instead of exhorting people to work harder when their performance tails off, look at steps 1, 2, and 3.

CHAPTER SIX

Shine

Henry worked quietly but effectively in the marketing department of HealthCo, a large health care conglomerate. He was like a middle child: reliable but often overlooked. At his performance reviews he always got excellent scores, but his supervisors over the years always urged him to speak up.

"You've got to be assertive if you want to get ahead here," one superior told him. "This place moves too fast to notice nice people who hold back. You have it in you, Henry. Come out of your shell a bit and you'll move up for sure. Hell, you could probably have my job by next year."

But Henry wasn't quite sure what it meant to be any more assertive than he already was. He did volunteer ideas, he did argue his point of view, he did communicate with others and make himself available for extra work when needed. If being more assertive meant being a blowhard like some of his colleagues, well, then he felt he did *not* have that in him.

At another performance review, when he was given the same advice, this time to "be more aggressive," he asked for a definition. "I don't mean to be difficult or argumentative, Marion, but I've received this advice before, as I'm sure you can see in my file. I'm just not sure what it means. I know you don't want me punching holes in the wall."

"I don't see that question as argumentative at all, Henry. I see it as you being you, asking good questions, wanting clarification. Let's see if I can give it to you, at least from my point of view. What I mean when I encourage you to be more aggressive has to do more with your *presence*, if you know what I mean. I know that sounds vague, but let me try to pin it down. It has to do with your tone of voice, how much enthusiasm is in it; your body language, how open and receptive you are; how much of a team builder you are; and it has to do with how well you give credit to others. I just believe you could have much more of an impact on the group. Maybe if we work together on this, I can help you make progress."

Henry liked Marion. She had always been fair with him, and he thought she was smart. So he took her advice seriously. But the more he thought about it, the more he felt Marion was advising him to be someone other than who he was. And how was he supposed to do that? Take a course in charisma? Dress in a more impressive way? Color his hair? He knew coworkers who had done each of those things—the results sometimes good, sometimes laughable. (The one who took the charisma course routinely made a fool of himself in meetings until someone mercifully clued him in that the course wasn't working.)

But he really appreciated her taking an interest in him and not just telling him to change and leaving it at that. He wanted to cooperate and not be resistant, so he didn't want to go back to her and say, "I've gotta be me," or words to that effect.

Then one phrase she had used popped into his mind. Marion had mentioned how he needed to give credit to others. She had a point. It's not that he withheld credit, he just didn't offer it. No one had ever mentioned that before to Henry.

His wife had been telling him this for years. She blamed it on Henry's father, who was a classic old-fashioned, close-to-the-vest, approval-withholding dad. "He loves you, but has he ever told you that?" she'd ask. The answer was no.

Henry grew up with the belief that you simply did your job, and that was reward enough. If you were strong, you'd succeed. In the workplace, a paycheck meant "I love you." That was how he'd always seen it. That was how he'd lived his life.

But now, at thirty-nine, he felt at a crossroads. He did want to advance, to do whatever he needed to do to develop his full potential. Until now, he just had lacked the specific advice.

"Marion, I've thought about what you said," Henry said at a meeting he set up a week later. "You may be surprised, but I remember your words exactly. Especially the words about giving others credit. I do need to work on that, don't I? People look up to me, I know that, because I have good ideas and I'm good with numbers—"

"Henry, they look up to you because you're damned smart," Marion interrupted. "They just get the feeling you think they're not smart."

"I get it," Henry said. "I truly do get it. Isn't it amazing? People usually don't get it when it comes to stuff like this, but I get it. And you didn't have to hit me with a two-by-four," he added with a laugh.

He was right. People are usually blind to psychological traits such as being stingy with praise, and, when informed of them, they usually protest rather than try to change. Henry was one of the strong few who could take such feedback and act on it. Of course, life didn't change overnight for Henry. New habits are tough to learn, and old habits rooted in personal psychology die hard. But insight and motivation can move mountains. With Marion's help, Henry gradually learned how to act in such a way that people no longer found him condescending or aloof.

In fact, Henry's true self was neither condescending nor aloof. He was a generous, big-hearted man. He simply had never learned how to show it. He had succeeded by working hard and doing well. But he had not learned how to attend to other people in such a way that they felt recognized. Once he learned how to do this, not only did he become more effective—a much more powerful presence, to use Marion's word—but he also received much more validation and support from his coworkers, who had seen him as standoffish before.

How did he learn how to change? With Marion's tutelage. Recognizing others came naturally to her. Since Henry was a motivated pupil, the learning process moved quickly.

"Here are the basics," Marion said. "Before you speak, listen. Then, when someone else speaks, comment on what they said before you put forth your ideas. This proves that you actually did listen, and people need that proof because they are so accustomed to being unheard. Just watch. You'll start to get a different response from others.

"Then, when someone says something that interests you, surprises you, or impresses you, tell them that, or tell the meeting that. Don't fake it, though. Nothing is worse than false praise. But when you do feel someone has made a good contribution, just say so. Even if the person protests or others make fun of you for being complimentary—you know, like saying, 'Hey, Henry, do you have a man-crush on Bob?' or something like that—don't worry. It will produce good results. We all like to feel noticed."

"This won't feel natural to me," Henry said. "It will feel forced."

"So, force it," Marion said. "Any change at first feels funny. But this is a good change. After a while it will start to feel natural, and good. Because you will be getting better results. Mark my words. You will become more of a leader. Being a leader has much more to do with recognizing others than promoting yourself."

Recognition Picks Everyone Up

Shine, step 5 in the Cycle of Excellence, requires recognition. Recognition—validation and praise of what's positive—is one of the key ingredients in helping people to shine. And when you give recognition, you shine as well. That is the lesson that Henry learned.

Recognition, the acknowledgement of achievement, may come from a coworker, a supervisor, a customer, even a rival (that's especially sweet). It may come in the form of a pay raise, a trophy, or other award, or in the form of a high-five, a handshake, or a pat on the back. It may be planned or spontaneous, raucous or subdued, humorous or serious. It may be as brief as a wink or as drawn out as a speech. However it comes, it packs a potent punch. Unless it is insincere or undeserved, recognition, especially from people you respect, works wonderfully to build motivation, confidence, enthusiasm, and loyalty. On the other hand, lack of recognition, even if it is inadvertent, can destroy morale and lead to disloyalty.

Giving people recognition sounds like a simple idea, but, like all the steps in the cycle, it's deceptively simple. Like the shining of the sun, recognition is powerful, but complex in its specifics. How do you do it? When do you do it? Why do you do it? What happens when people turn against each other because of unequal recognition? What about the people who are forever sucking up? What do you do with people like Henry who feel they just don't have it in them to recognize others? And what do you do about people who need *constant* rewards and recognition?

Books have been written about each of these questions. Performance appraisal and recognition plans are some of the most discussed and debated topics in all business literature.

Recognition is so powerful because it answers a fundamental human need, the need to feel valued for what we do. Managers are in a unique position to offer—or withhold—such recognition, and with it, the feeling of being valued. Actually, everyone in the organization should contribute to the process of recognition. Even though Henry was not a manager, his inability to offer recognition held him back, and held back the progress of his group. In other words, everyone can contribute to everyone else's ability to shine.

My employees responded well to the example of me showing up when they didn't expect me to, not that I was sneaking up on them. They used to say it was an opportunity for me to catch them doing something right and also to be there after hours and on Saturdays. When I first began to do that, the employees would say, "Why are you here?" and I would say, "Because you're here. And if you're here doing the things that are necessary the least that I can do is to dignify your efforts with my presence."

—GENERAL TOM DRAUDE,
U.S. Marine Corps (ret.) and former executive, USAA

Yet many organizations spend more time focusing on errors and shortcomings than on giving recognition. They dissect failures and give "constructive" feedback that actually is often destructive. Steeped in many organizations' collective consciousness is the idea that exposing mistakes leads to improved performance. The need to learn from mistakes is one of our most time-honored principles, drummed into us from early in our lives, through our educational years, and into our careers.

But new research is showing otherwise, as does most people's daily experience. Think about it. Do you usually learn from your mistakes? Or do you just feel embarrassed or upset and try to forget or cover up what happened? Do performance reviews that detail your shortcomings really help you? Or do they bring you down? Does being criticized in public improve your performance, or not?

People do vary on these issues. Some people actually do improve after a public humiliation or a scorching performance review. But I challenge the absolute sanctity of the learn-from-your-mistakes credo. Certainly, when a person errs, and a manager notices it, there is a chance to learn. But there is also an excellent chance *for emotions of shame and fear to short-circuit whatever higher learning process might otherwise develop* in the brain.

Earl Miller, a neuroscientist at MIT, and a group of other researchers have been looking into this issue. In one experiment, they found that when monkeys achieved success in a certain task, it led to greatly enhanced performance in the next, different task. However, if the monkey failed in the first task, not only did he not "learn" from it, his performance on the next task was not influenced at all by the mistake.[1] "Success has a much greater influence on the brain than failure," says Miller.[2]

While of course mistakes need to be acknowledged and, one *hopes*, learned from, it may be more likely, from a purely neurological point of view, that a person will learn more from a success than a failure. All the more reason to promote the Cycle of Excellence.

Recognition Promotes Moral Behavior Through Connection

Giving people the recognition that helps them to shine consolidates all the good that step 4, grapple and grow, creates: achievement, confidence, self-esteem, motivation, loyalty, and excitement. But recognition also serves a second, critical purpose. It leads to moral behavior. It connects the person being recognized to the person or group doing the recognizing, leading the person to feel ownership in the group.

When a person feels recognized and connected to the larger group, she knows viscerally, not just intellectually, that she has made a contribution others value. Not only does this motivate her to do more and try harder, but it instills a desire to look out for the larger group.

Looking out for others can be called moral behavior. It leads a person to do the right thing even when no one is looking. At its most spontaneous and least fearful or guilt driven, moral behavior derives from feelings of being a valued part of a larger group, a feeling that a person belongs, that she is appreciated, in short, that she is *recognized.*

Managers—and people in many other contexts—ponder long and hard how to encourage people to do what's right and not to do what's wrong. It seems that many, if not most, programs to promote moral behavior in organizations these days focus on catching wrong-doers and punishing them, rather than proactively encouraging steps that will lead people to be right-doers.

For example, a Google search on "moral behavior in business" brought up the following near the top of the list:

> LEGAL AFFAIRS: WHITE-HANDED
>
> Prevent and detect white-collar crime with proper corporate compliance programs.[3]

It's an uncomfortable truth. You may be on a first-name basis with the people who pose the greatest threat to your company's security: unethical employees.

"No company is immune from an investigation or prosecution, whether it's public or private, big or small," says Kurt Stitcher, partner in the Litigation Practice Group at Levenfeld Pearlstein, LLC. "Whenever any employee could engage in conduct that might open you up to criminal or civil liability, you're vulnerable, and you should have a compliance program in place."[4]

The article then reported on the interview with Attorney Pearlstein, who provided a by-now standard, thoroughly convincing, altogether frightening collection of reasons why organizations should make copious use of the kinds of services he offers. My quarrel is not with Attorney Pearlstein or his ilk. They have identified a need and are doing their best to meet it. My quarrel, if it can be called that, is with organizational and even national and international cultures that make such *gotcha!* services so plentiful and seemingly necessary. (A Google search of the phrase "liability prevention in business" yielded 7,660,000 hits!) The existence of such a multitude of books, Web sites, lawyers, and other professionals devoted to catching and punishing speaks to the disconnected, even paranoid mentality prevalent in many organizations. This is not to say that programs or courses in "connection and recognition" could wipe out the need for surveillance. I am not that naive. But I do believe that if organizations devoted more attention to connection and recognition, they would need to spend less time and money on surveillance.

There is, of course, a need for suspicion, or what Roderick Kramer of the Stanford Business School calls "prudent paranoia."[5] From the Enron debacle to the financial collapse of 2008, we have seen only too well how leaders we trust, and organizations we thought were beyond reproach, can behave immorally, to put it mildly, when inadequately supervised.

But the purpose of recognition and connection is not to remove supervision. It is simply to make wrongdoing less the natural way, less the default position, and ultimately less tempting. The most reliable motive to do what's right is self-interest; you do what's right because you want to do it. A person who must constantly resist temptation usually slips and gives in. Therefore the most successful efforts to induce people to do what's right result not from surveillance programs but from programs designed to instill in people the *desire* to work within the rules of the group. Recognition is key in creating such desire.

People who feel recognized and valued do not feel nearly as inclined to rip off the system, so to speak, as people who feel unrecognized, exploited, ignored, or devalued. This is as true for adults working in organizations as it is for teens in high school, people in families, doctors in hospitals, golfers on the golf course, or anyone anywhere. Greed is the by-product of insufficiently robust connection to the wider group. Sufficient recognition of each individual strengthens that connection, thereby promoting moral behavior and reducing self-serving guile.

How to Recognize People and Promote Shine

Let me give two examples of public recognition, taken from two quite different sources: Harvard University in the 1990s and into the 2000s, and Dana Corporation in the early 1990s.

Celebrating Harvard Heroes

In the mid-1990s, Sally Zeckhauser, the vice president of central administration at Harvard University, commissioned a program to help Harvard boost the morale of its nonacademic employees. She observed that the academic community was constantly being feted while the support staff was getting increasingly demoralized because no attention was ever paid to them. A kind of two-tiered "town-and-gown" system was developing.

To celebrate those who worked in nonacademic jobs, an outside group helped create an event called "Harvard Heroes." It was a phenomenal success until it was discontinued for budgetary reasons in 2009.

Once a year, exactly one week after Harvard University's commencement ceremonies, the university held a parallel ceremony to honor selected employees who had gone above and beyond everyday achievement in their work. The ceremony always drew an audience of close to a thousand and was held in Memorial Hall—an imposing, prestigious building redolent with Harvard history. It was always presided over by the president of Harvard. Neil Rudenstine did it for years, then Larry Summers, Derek Bok, and Drew Faust, who presided over the final event in 2008. In a ceremony that was nearly as formal as commencement, each of the year's "heroes" stood as the president read a brief personal description of why the person was being honored. Groups of people, "Hero Teams," were honored as well, and a brief video was shown that explained and touted their achievements.

The ceremony ended with an audiovisual presentation, accompanied by an emotional song performed by two live singers, where a beautiful photographic portrait of each hero was projected onto a large screen. The song is an anthem—rousing, stirring, emotional—with lyrics like "You are the Harvard Heroes, the rock on which we stand, the ones behind the scenes, we salute you . . . Veritas."

One hero, Manny Diogenes, was a man of Greek heritage near retirement age. He came to the event with his extended family. Larry Summers asked him to stand, and then he read a few of the comments people had sent in about Manny. Manny was a caretaker for one of the freshman houses, and one of the student residents wrote a particularly moving letter, which I'll paraphrase here: "Coming to Harvard was really the first time I had ever left home and I was terribly afraid that I'd be too homesick to endure. Manny instantly adopted me and seemed to love and care for me as much as my actual family did. He will remain my close friend for life." After a couple more comments like this, Summers then bellowed, "I ask you, assembled ones, how many days has Manny called in sick during his twenty-seven years of service? How many? None. Manny has never missed a single day of work." There was an explosion of applause while Summers turned and pointed directly at Manny and said, "Manny Diogenes, I pronounce *you* to be a Harvard hero!"

By then, tears were streaming down Manny's face, the faces of his proud family, and about half of the audience. I imagine that this day was as important to Manny as the day of his wedding or the birth of each of his children. How much more significant this ceremony of public recognition and praise must have been to Manny than an increase in his paycheck or a bonus. A cynic might say this whole ceremony is Harvard's way of keeping employees happy while keeping their wages low. Even if that were true, which I doubt, so what? It was better to have the ceremony than not.

Not all the heroes had blue-collar jobs like Manny. There were people from the Harvard real estate office, staff from *Harvard Magazine*, and all sorts of high-tech workers as well as many from dining services and facilities maintenance. The audience was a true melting pot of all types of jobs, ages, personalities, and skill levels. This was in fact a secondary goal of the event—for everyone to realize that they all work under the same umbrella and play an important but extremely diverse role in Harvard's family. And yes, to realize that they are all connected.

One more hero who particularly stood out was a woman whose job was to arrive at some ungodly hour like 3:00 a.m. at one of Harvard's parking garages. When her name was called, loud cheers rang out from disparate sections of the audience. As the comments were read, the cheers increased. People had sent in statements like, "Whenever I dread driving into work on a cold day in pitch dark, I know I will be warmly greeted by Angela and her unforgettable smile." Or, "She just starts every day off right!"

How do you imagine this employee felt hearing these kinds of remarks, publicly read by the president of Harvard to an audience of one thousand in historic and majestic Memorial Hall?

Appreciating the Underappreciated at Dana Corporation

A second example of how to promote the kind of recognition that helps people shine comes from Woody Morcott, CEO of Dana Corporation during that company's glory years in the 1990s. He described an annual award at Dana called the Chairman's Award:

> [One year we had] a man named Ralph who had a job that was very underappreciated, not at all glitzy—working on our pension plan. Sounds boring, but for a couple of years in a row we were in the top 10 percent of performance for plans like ours. The year that we were there to celebrate, Ralph had us at the very top. He was shooting the lights out, protecting our future with his pension plan that benefited everybody.
>
> Well, Ralph was a guy who loved Scotland. So, we had a bagpiper come into the meeting and when he starts piping, everybody is wondering what in the world this is all about. Then we asked Ralph to come down and we gave him two first-class tickets to Edinburgh for him and his wife, because in his very quiet, unassuming way, he had made all of our futures more secure.[6]

This kind of recognition is often trivialized or dismissed as hokey, but when used right, it is powerful and effective. The key to using it right is using it the way Dana did: carefully selecting who ought to be recognized so that credit can be spread around and include people who might otherwise be overlooked, personalizing the recognition so that it has special meaning to the recipient, and relating the person recognized to the progress of the organization as a whole.

Make Noticing the Positive a Habit

Large, public recognition, like that described by Woody Morcott or the Harvard Heroes ceremony, is only one of many ways to use this powerful tool. But it doesn't always have to involve a grand gesture. Depending on the situation, sometimes a simple pat on the back can create a decisive moment in a person's life.

> *Just keep reinforcing the good in people, reinforcing the positive things about what they do and what they say and how they are. If you continue to do that, the productivity just keeps going up. When we started in 1984, our productivity was $180,000 per employee. When I sold the company in 1999, it was $550,000 per employee. There wasn't a lot of inflation in that period of time, compared to that 300 percent increase in productivity.*
>
> —CLAY MATHILE,
> *Former owner, Iams*

Most of us can recall a moment when a supervisor made a big impact on us simply by saying, "Good job," or even just by giving a nod of approval. Sure, it's great to get tickets for a trip to Scotland in front of a large gathering of peers, but it can be just as significant to get approval from the boss at a moment of uncertainty or doubt, or to get recognition from a peer after extending yourself in a way you weren't sure would be appreciated.

In the disconnected, crazy-busy cultures that color so many organizations, good work can easily go unacknowledged, coming up only at performance reviews or awards ceremonies.

Instead, as a manager, try doing what Clay Mathile did to build Iams into the giant it became. Just keep recognizing the good in people, day in and day out. Of course, don't do it in a fake or forced fashion. But try to make noticing the positive a managerial habit. Unfortunately, the opposite is the ruling habit in many organizations. No mistake goes unnoticed, but many good works do. It is not coddling to notice and appreciate good work. It is managing for peak performance.

Here are ten tips for promoting shine among your people:

1. Recognize effort, not just results. Of course, you want the results, but if you recognize ongoing effort, results will more likely ensue. Cheerleading works.

2. Notice details. Generic acknowledgment pales next to specific recognition.

3. Try, as much as possible, to provide recognition in person. E-mail packs much less of a punch than human moments.

4. In meetings—and everywhere—try to make others look good, not bad. Scoring points off the backs of others usually backfires.

5. As a manager, you should know that the self-esteem of each employee is perhaps your most important asset. Recognition is a powerful tool to preserve self-esteem.

6. Acknowledge people's existence! Try always to say hello, give a nod of the head, a high five, a smile in passing. It's withering to pass someone and feel as if that person didn't even see you.

7. Tap into the power of positive feedback. Remember that positive feedback often consolidates gains better than learning from mistakes.

8. Monitor progress. Performance improves when a person's progress toward a goal is monitored regularly.

9. Remember, as a manager, the more you recognize others, the more you establish the habit of recognition of hard work and progress as part of the organizational culture.

10. Bring in the marginalized people. In most organizations, about 15 percent of people feel unrecognized, misunderstood, devalued, and generally disconnected. Not only is recognition good for that 15 percent to help them feel valued, it is good for the other 85 percent as well, as it boosts the positive energy across the organization.

KEY IDEAS

- Recognition of achievement leads a person to shine, the culmination of the Cycle of Excellence.
- As a person shines, she naturally connects with the organization and those who recognize her achievement.
- Such connection also drives moral behavior, loyalty, and increased motivation.
- People often learn more from success than from failure.
- Beware of performance appraisals that dwell on the negative.
- Don't be too busy to notice a person's shining moments—unless you never want to see them again.

CHAPTER SEVEN

The Cycle of Excellence

IN DETAILING THE CYCLE OF EXCELLENCE, I've dissected the five components as if they were discrete and separate. But, in life, they link, interweave, and operate simultaneously. The cycle is like a living organism that constantly renews itself when it is running properly.

In practical terms, in your daily management of your people or your own work, you typically don't examine what's happening step-by-step as you proceed. You're acting within a process—traditionally called work—and you are often juggling so much that it's all you can do just to complete your basic tasks.

But in this book, I have stepped back with you to take a wider view. I've presented a way of examining all that juggling to reveal how people can achieve at their highest level in the unique world we have created. I've also suggested ways to intervene by noting problems at different stages of the cycle.

Here is a quick summary of the five steps and some tips on how to intervene as a manager.

Step 1: Select

The goal of this step is to work at the intersection of three elements—helping your people to find:

- What they're good at
- What they like
- What adds value to the organization or world

If there is a problem with selection or fit, managers can refer to the three frameworks suggested in chapter 2 for help:

- The Hallowell Self-Report Job-Fit Scale
- The framework for flow (see figure 2-1)
- The Kolbe conative assessment scale (see kolbe.com)

Step 2: Connect

From either a manager's or employee's standpoint, the goal of this step is the same: create an atmosphere at work that is high on trust, optimism, cohesion, openness, permission to be real, and positive energy. Do all you can to reduce toxic fear and worry, insecurity, backbiting, gossip, and disconnection.

Creating connection requires daily commitment, because modern life conspires to disconnect people. A few simple tools:

- Take Dr. Shine's advice. Look for that spark.
- Model and teach what Carol Dweck calls a growth mind-set, as opposed to a fixed mind-set.
- Model and teach optimism, a belief there's no problem as a team we can't overcome.
- Use the human moment judiciously instead of always relying on electronic communication.
- Get to know a little bit about the outside life of each person you work with.
- Treat everyone with respect, especially the people you dislike.
- Understand, as a manager, the meaning and impact of transference.
- Meet people where they are. Don't expect a person to be someone he is not.
- Encourage people to be real.
- Encourage humor (but not cruel humor).
- Seek out the marginalized people and try to bring them in.

Step 3: Play

The goal of this step is to create a culture that encourages free play of the mind. Play is not just what kids do at recess. Any activity in which the imagination kicks in and lights up is play. Imaginative engagement produces new ideas and creative thoughts. It also boosts morale, reduces anxiety, and makes a heavy load seem lighter.

To encourage imaginative engagement and play:

- Ask open-ended questions.
- Encourage everyone to produce at least three new ideas each month and require management to evaluate and respond to each. (Woody Morcott did this at Dana Corp. when he was CEO, with excellent results.)
- Allow for irreverence or goofiness (but not disrespect), and model these yourself.
- Brainstorm.
- Reward new ideas and innovation.
- Encourage people to question anything and everything.

Step 4: Grapple and Grow

The goal here is to help your people engage imaginatively with a task they like and are good at, and then to work their tails off!

As a manager, you want to make sure each person is making progress at whatever project is at hand. As long as people are making progress all should go well. If they get stuck:

- Don't pound the table and demand they work harder.
  This is ever so tempting, but it rarely helps and often backfires.

- Look instead at steps 1, 2, and 3 and see what might have gone wrong upstream. Then make adjustments there.

- Play what I refer to as "Ping-Pong," borrowing a phrase from a man who specializes in helping people get unstuck. Simply keep offering ideas and suggestions, and even as they get rejected, keep offering more. You're trying to provide a catalyst, not an answer.

Step 5: Shine

The goal here is for *every* person to feel recognized and valued for what they do, not just the stars of the show. Remember, as valuable as it is to learn from mistakes, people grow even more when success is noticed and praised. Empty praise is useless, but true recognition of achievement motivates people and secures loyalty.

If a person is dispirited or underperforming, consider lack of recognition as a cause. Usually, the person won't come right out and tell you, so you have to look a bit and be subtle.

As a manager:

- Always be on the lookout for moments when you can offer a word of recognition. Don't make the mistake of withholding compliments (even if your dad treated you that way!).

- Create a culture that is generous with praise. It becomes far easier to examine and learn from failures when successes are recognized regularly.

- Recognize not only achievement but also attitudes, like optimism and a growth mind-set.

The Synthesis Creates the Song

The synthesis of the five steps—no single element, but the process of the five elements working together—leads to excellence. What's unique in this book and in the Cycle of Excellence is the bringing together of the five steps, each one of which is not new in itself, but taken together create a new and powerful approach to bring out the best in people.

Remember that all elements of the cycle operate simultaneously. Just as the heart keeps beating while the lungs exchange gases, the liver detoxifies the blood, and the brain thinks, so a person selects what to do while connecting with the task, or engages in imaginative play while working.

The steps in the Cycle of Excellence can create the supremely satisfying stimulation you feel when you're in perfect sync with the task, working with profuse positive energy, exulting in doing whatever it is that you were truly meant to do. Along with loving someone, it is one of life's greatest extended joys: performing consistently at your best over a prolonged period of time.

If you look at someone doing this, you can see the cycle at work. As an example, let's go back to where we started. Let's go back to Dr. Shine.

Dr. Shine selected the perfect job *for him*. He loved people, so he chose an airport, where lots of people come and go all day. He chose a task that would allow him to sit, which was important due to his MS. And he chose a job that would allow him to talk to people one-on-one, which was his passion.

Having selected brilliantly, he got right to the heart of the matter. He got to what he loved, connecting with others, inquiring and finding the "spark" that he knew everybody has within them.

Once connected, he engaged imaginatively with his customer. He played with him or her. He had to be quick, as he put it, so he found ways to draw them out and put a shine not only on their shoes, but on their selves.

And he worked at it. Did he ever! Day after day, he drove himself to the airport, got himself and his walker to the stand, set up shop, and practiced his craft, both of shining shoes and connecting with people. He told me he gets better at it all the time, so he is making progress (although I don't see how he could get any better at it).

Being known all over Logan Airport, Dr. Shine receives recognition every day. He knows others value what he does. He takes enormous pride in his work. He is a good and happy man who improves the lives of other people.

Think of yourself. Think of the people you manage. Think even of your children, or other people you care about. Think how much of your and their satisfaction in life derives from the successful implementation of what is essentially the Cycle of Excellence. The opportunity to create a life a person loves to live is open to everyone. *Anyone* can enter into the Cycle of Excellence. Any time. Anywhere. It's *never* too late. Regardless of innate talents or other resources, anyone can select, connect, play, grapple and grow, and shine. Which is to say that not only can anyone achieve peak performance, but they can also find meaning and joy in life and add value to the world.

Many people need help in getting rid of the obstacles in their way. In the workplace, this is the challenge managers face: to help people overcome those obstacles and enter into the cycle.

While I have made many suggestions on how to do this, my concluding suggestion is this: *do it your way*. Ultimately, neither I nor anyone else can tell you what to do more skillfully than you can tell yourself. In the end, after you have gleaned what you can from me and from whatever other sources and people you turn to, you will do best to pull from your own bag of ideas, to work with the confidence you can feel only when being true to yourself.

So don't look over your shoulder or let fear and anxiety rule you. Go for broke. Let passion blaze your trail. Look ahead and pursue the dream that fits who *you* are as a person and a manager. Learn what you can, but don't get bogged down—in today's world, there's so much to know that learning can actually take the place of action and hold you back. Learn *enough*, then trust your gut and act. Be bold—or crazy—enough *not* to hold back. Take advantage of the freedom to be your own person. When the game is over, regardless of the score, you'll revel in what you've done.

NOTES

INTRODUCTION

1. Daniel Pink, *Drive: The Surprising Truth About What Motivates Us* (New York: Riverhead, 2009).
2. Edward Hallowell and John Ratey, *Driven to Distraction* (New York: Pantheon, 1994); Edward Hallowell and John Ratey, *Delivered from Distraction* (New York: Ballantine, 2005); Edward Hallowell, *The Childhood Roots of Adult Happiness* (New York: Ballantine, 2003).
3. Edward Hallowell, "The Human Moment at Work," *Harvard Business Review*, January–February 1999, 58–66.
4. Gilles Gheusi et al., "A Niche for Adult Neurogenesis in Social Behavior," *Behavioural Brain Research* 200 (2009): 315–322.
5. Laura Fratiglioni et al., "Prevention of Alzheimer's Disease and Dementia: Major Findings from the Kungsholmen Project," *Physiology & Behavior* 92 (2007): 98–104.
6. Robert Putnam, *Bowling Alone: The Collapse and Revival of American Community* (New York: Simon & Schuster, 2000); Thomas Friedman, *The World Is Flat: A Brief History of the Twenty-First Century* (New York: Farrar, Straus and Giroux, 2005).
7. Edward Hallowell, "Overloaded Circuits: Why Smart People Underperform," *Harvard Business Review*, January 2005, 54–62.
8. Edward Hallowell, *CrazyBusy: Overstretched, Overbooked, and About to Snap!* (New York, Ballantine, 2006).

CHAPTER ONE

1. Norman Doidge, *The Brain That Changes Itself: Stories of Personal Triumph from the Frontiers of Brain Science* (New York: Penguin Books, 2007), 59–60.

2. George E. Vaillant, *Spiritual Evolution: A Scientific Defense of Faith* (New York: Broadway Books, 2008), 160.
3. John Ratey, *Spark: The Revolutionary New Science of Exercise and the Brain* (New York: Little, Brown, 2008), 40.
4. Robert Przybelski, quoted in Diane Welland, "Does D Make a Difference?," *Scientific American Mind,* November–December 2009, 14.
5. Leslie A. Perlow and Jessica L. Porter, "Making Time Off Predictable—and Required," *Harvard Business Review,* October 2009, 102–109.
6. Robert Stickgold, "The Simplest Way to Reboot Your Brain," *Harvard Business Review,* October 2009, 36.
7. Mihaly Csikszentmihalyi, *Finding Flow: The Psychology of Engagement with Everyday Life* (New York: Basic Books, 1997).

CHAPTER TWO

1. Jack Welch, from numerous lectures, confirmed in private communication with author, 2009.
2. "Unique ability" is a term coined by Dan Sullivan, founder of The Strategic Coach. He uses the term in many of his lectures and books.
3. The New Employee/Employer Equation Survey conducted by Harris Interactive, Inc., 2005, quoted in http://www.management-issues.com/2006/8/24/research/attitude-and-engagement-creates-turbulence-in-corporate-america.asp.
4. Rudyard Kipling, from his poem "If," in *Rewards and Fairies* (New York: Doubleday, Page & Co., 1910).
5. Mihaly Csikszentmihalyi, *Finding Flow: The Psychology of Engagement with Everyday Life* (New York: Basic Books, 1997).

CHAPTER THREE

1. John Naisbitt, *Megatrends* (New York: Warner Books, 1982).
2. George Vaillant, quoted in Joshua Wolf Shenk, "What Makes Us Happy?" *The Atlantic,* June 2009, 46.
3. Lisa F. Berkman and S. Leonard Syme, "Social Networks, Host Resistance, and Mortality: A Nine-Year Follow-Up Study of Alameda County Residents," *American Journal of Epidemiology* 109, no. 2 (1979): 186–204.
4. Karolinska Institutet, "Poor Leadership Poses a Health Risk at Work," press release, November 11, 2009.
5. Sarah A. Burgard, Jennie E. Brand, and James S. House, "Perceived Job Insecurity and Worker Health in the United States," *Social Science and Medicine* 69, no. 5 (2009): 777–785.
6. Nicholas A. Christakis and James H. Fowler, *Connected: The Surprising Power of Our Social Networks and How They Shape Our Lives* (New York: Little, Brown, 2009), 305.

7. Ibid., 51.
8. Ibid., 54.
9. Edward Hallowell, "The Human Moment at Work," *Harvard Business Review,* January–February 1999, 58–66.
10. Christakis and Fowler, *Connected,* 53.
11. Thomas Friedman, "The Class Too Dumb to Quit," *New York Times,* July 21, 2009.
12. Robert Sternberg, "Intelligence, Competence, and Expertise," in *The Handbook of Competence and Motivation,* eds. Andrew Elliot and Carol S. Dweck (New York: Guilford Press, 2005).
13. Tom Rath, *Vital Friends* (Washington, DC : Gallup Press, 2006).
14. Martin E. P. Seligman et al., "Positive Education: Positive Psychology and Classroom Interventions," *Oxford Review of Education* 35, no. 3 (June 2009): 293–311.
15. B. L. Fredrickson, "What Good Are Positive Emotions?" *Review of General Psychiatry* 2 (1998): 300–319; B. L. Fredrickson and M. F. Losada, "Positive Affect and the Complex Dynamics of Human Flourishing," *American Psychologist* 60 (2005): 678–686; A. M. Isen et al., "Positive Affect Facilitates Creative Problem Solving," *Journal of Personality and Social Psychology* 52 (1987): 1122–1131.
16. Christakis and Fowler, *Connected,* 9.
17. Christopher George, golf pro and head of instruction at Kingsmill Resort, Williamsburg, VA, personal communication with author, 2009.
18. Martin E. P. Seligman, *Learned Optimism: How to Change Your Mind and Your Life* (New York: Pocket Books, 1990).
19. Carol Dweck, personal communication with author, October 17, 2009.
20. Andrew S. Grove, *Only the Paranoid Survive: How to Exploit the Crisis Points That Challenge Every Company and Career* (New York: Currency Doubleday, 1996).
21. Robert A. Bloodgood, Jerry G. Short, John M. Jackson, and James R. Martindale, "A Change to Pass/Fail Grading in the First Two Years at One Medical School Results in Improved Psychological Well-Being," *Academic Medicine* 84, no. 5 (2009): 655–662.
22. "100 Best Companies to Work for in America," *Fortune* magazine, February 2, 2009.
23. Marco Iacoboni, *Mirroring People* (New York: Farrar, Straus and Giroux, 2008), 4, 268.
24. For a critical review of Mayo's work and life, see Richard C. S. Trahair, *Elton Mayo: The Humanist Temper* (New Brunswick, NJ: Transaction Publishers, 1984).

CHAPTER FOUR

1. Martin André Rosanoff, "Edison in His Laboratory," *Harper's Monthly,* September 1932.

2. Daniel Pink, *A Whole New Mind: Moving from the Information Age to the Conceptual Age* (New York: Riverhead Books, 2005), 48–49.
3. Martin E. P. Seligman et al., "Positive Education: Positive Psychology and Classroom Interventions," *Oxford Review of Education* 35, no. 3 (June 2009): 293–311.
4. For a discussion of the Monty Hall problem, see Michael Kaplan and Ellen Kaplan, *Chances Are . . . Adventures in Probability* (New York: Viking, 2006), 72–74.
5. Keith E. Stanovich, *What Intelligence Tests Miss: The Psychology of Rational Thought* (New Haven: Yale University Press, 2009).
6. Keith E. Stanovich, "Rational and Irrational Thought: The Thinking That IQ Tests Miss," *Scientific American Mind,* November–December 2009, 35.
7. Stuart Brown, *Play: How It Shapes the Brain, Opens the Imagination, and Invigorates the Soul* (New York: Avery, 2009), 5.
8. Jasper White, interview with author, July 31, 2006.
9. Brown, *Play,* 11, 12.
10. Quoted by Richard Rossi, personal communication with author.
11. Personal communication with Pat Jones of Draper and Associates.
12. Michael Michalko, *Thinkertoys: A Handbook of Creative-Thinking Techniques* (Berkeley, CA: Ten Speed Press, 2006).

CHAPTER FIVE

1. John O'Neill, director of addiction services for the Menninger Clinic in Houston, quoted on LiveScience.com, January 25, 2008.
2. Edward Hallowell, "Overloaded Circuits: Why Smart People Underperform," *Harvard Business Review,* January 2005, 54–62.
3. Jim Loehr and Tony Schwartz, *The Power of Full Engagement* (New York: The Free Press, 2003), 13.
4. John Ratey, *Spark: The Revolutionary New Science of Exercise and the Brain* (New York: Little, Brown, 2008), 39.
5. Pamela K. Smith, Nils B. Jostmann, Adam D. Galinsky, and Wilco W. van Dijk, "Lacking Power Impairs Executive Functions," *Psychological Science* 19, no. 5 (2008): 441–447.
6. Malcolm Gladwell, *Outliers* (New York: Little, Brown, 2008).
7. Harvey Towvim, founder of Ideas Grow, personal conversation with author, 2009.
8. Steven Johnson, *Mind Wide Open: Your Brain and the Neuroscience of Everyday Life* (New York: Scribner, 2004), 115–116.
9. Angela L. Duckworth et al., "Grit: Perseverance and Passion for Long-Term Goals," *Journal of Personality and Social Psychology* 92, no. 6 (2007): 1087–1101.
10. Angela Duckworth, personal conversation with author, December 2, 2009.

CHAPTER SIX

1. M. H. Histed, A. Pasupathy, and E. K. Miller, "Learning Substrates in the Primate Prefrontal Cortex and Striatum: Sustained Activity Related to Successful Actions," *Neuron* 63 (2009): 244–253.
2. Earl Miller, as quoted in Frederik Joelving, "Why Success Breeds Success," *Scientific American Mind,* November–December 2009, 8.
3. Elizabeth Grace Saunders, "Legal Affairs: White-handed," *Smart Business,* December 2007, http://www.sbnonline.com /Local/Article/13551/68/0/White-handed.aspx.
4. Ibid.
5. Roderick Kramer, "When Paranoia Makes Sense," *Harvard Business Review,* July 2002.
6. Woody Morcott, personal interview with author, June 2007.

INDEX

ABOUT THE AUTHOR

Edward (Ned) M. Hallowell is a child and adult psychiatrist with offices in Sudbury, Massachusetts, and New York City. He is the author of seventeen previous books. Dr. Hallowell lives in the Boston area with his wife, Sue, and their three children, Lucy, Jack, and Tucker. He can be reached through his Web site, www.drhallowell.com.